Lily shifted her pos... the door. The seam op... ...ipped to the floor in a tumbling faint as the first alien stepped through. Seeing the girl fall, the alien walked three paces past Lily and the robot, Bach, before realizing they were there. The second alien halted in the arch of the open seam; he held a snub-nosed gun in his right hand.

Lily jumped—dislodged the gun with her first kick, with the second slammed him back against the door frame. Landed with a hammer strike to his temple. His head, flung back by the unexpected force, struck the metal ridge of the seam with a hard thud, and he crumpled to the floor.

Lily spun. The other alien turned back, weapon raised. Too far away for a quick kick. She lunged. Its hand shifted on the gun. And suddenly the alien was falling forward, fumbling in the air. Lily barely avoided its flailing arms, using its momentum to shove away and to one side. It fell flat-faced on the floor, gun knocked to one side. At its feet lay Paisley.

She had tackled it.

THE HIGHROAD TRILOGY

Volume One:

A Passage of Stars

✳✳✳✳✳✳✳

By Alis A. Rasmussen

BANTAM BOOKS

NEW YORK · TORONTO · LONDON · SYDNEY · AUCKLAND

A PASSAGE OF STARS
A Bantam Spectra Book / February 1990

ISBN 0-553-28372-3

Published simultaneously in the United States and Canada

*Bantam Books are published by Bantam Books, a division of Bantam Doubleday
Dell Publishing Group, Inc. Its trademark, consisting of the words "Bantam
Books" and the portrayal of a rooster, is Registered in U.S. Patent and Trademark
Office and in other countries. Marca Registrada. Bantam Books, 666 Fifth Avenue,
New York, New York 10103.*

PRINTED IN THE UNITED STATES OF AMERICA

KRI   0 9 8 7 6 5 4 3 2 1

This book is dedicated first of all to the original Lily,
and second to all the teachers who have helped me along the
   road.

But most of all, this is Jane's book.
Thank you, Jane.

Will ye gang tae the Hielands, my bonnie, bonnie lass?
Will ye gang tae the Hielands wi' Geordie?
And I'll tak' the high road, and ye'll tak' the low,
And I'll be in the Hielands afore ye.

—Traditional

A Passage of Stars

1   The Academy

****

Because she would, inevitably, have hit her, Lily chose not to throw her glass at her mother.

"And furthermore," continued the Saress, "if what Hiro has told me is true, I think it is time we reconsider our decision to let Lilyaka continue attending *that man's* academy."

"What did Hiro tell you?" asked the Sar.

"It's not true." Lily turned to look at her cousin.

"It is too true," said Hiro, undeterred—or perhaps spurred on—by Lily's hand tightening on the glass. "I saw it. Six bounty hunters, with blazers, with license tags on their wrists, and Heredes took them all out. He was unarmed, and he scragged them all. And then he calls Security and has all six arrested for assault. What a push!"

"Nephew." The Saress swept her hand across the tight coils of her head scarf. "You will not use vulgar street terms at this table." She regarded her husband. "Bounty hunters. I always knew *that man* was a criminal. Well? Will Lily be allowed to continue?"

The Sar considered in silence, a silence that spread to the adolescents' table in the far corner of the room. Even Eldest Aunt's whispering to her ancient husband faltered and ceased as everyone else turned to hear the verdict. Lily did not move. The focus of her breathing centered on the tension in her fingers. Finally the Sar sighed. "That is a subject best discussed between Lily and me. In private."

"And I think this nonsense has gone on far too long," said the Saress. "Lily has been indulged to a ridiculous extent by you letting her attend class there, while she meanwhile refuses to show any interest at all in mining."

Lily remained silent.

"You know, Lily," said her eldest sister, "the Kollek Ransomes need a supervisor over in sector five-oh-two. It would only take a two-month course for you to be qualified."

"But I don't care about aluminum ore," said Lily.

"Spessartite," corrected her sister automatically. "That vein's spessartite."

Hiro laughed behind his hand. "They certainly aren't going to offer her the tech opening over in Tanrin's sector."

"You could have had an excellent bond alliance," said the Saress.

"That's true, Lily."

"Yeah."

Lily jerked her head up. "What—the one Shardra Bajii Ransome contracted with, that fat Jai Foxmore merchant, just because his uncle owns some fleet of cargo boats? I think it's disgusting."

The Sar's face remained impassive, but he flicked an impatient finger over the square of buttons on his chair's arm. Strands of light shuddered to life on the wall behind him, tracing mineral veins, tunnels, current and future work, then died, fading back into the flat grey of the wall. "There is other employment available to members of this House, Lily."

"Should I be daring like Phillippa and try for a civil service posting out in the asteroid belts? But she had to have two children before she could even apply."

"I'll never understand why she agreed to be posted all the way out there," said one brother to another.

"Probably to get out of here," retorted Lily. "Does anyone here really have any idea of what I'd like to do? What I might be suited for?"

"What you'd *like* to do?" cried the Saress. "I fail to see

how ten years of training by *that man* can be put to use, except by enlisting in the government troops, which you *also* refused to consider—not even when the Immortals came recruiting—" She broke off, as if this ground had been covered once too often. "It's time you realize that you have to contribute to the enterprises of this House like the rest of the clan. And we will start by forbidding you to enter Heredes's Academy again!"

"No!" With a crack like a sharp exhalation, the glass shattered under Lily's hand. "Never." She stood, a single scarlet drop of blood spreading into the white sheen of the tablecloth. "Beg leave to be excused from the table, Sar-father."

"Surely," began the Saress, "you won't allow her—"

The Sar raised a hand. The Saress stopped speaking. "You may go, Lily. I will expect to speak with you later, however."

In the silence, a last sliver fell from her fingers to land with a subdued chime on the porcelain. She nodded.

At the door she turned back to look at her cousin. "Master Heredes isn't a criminal, Hiro, no matter what you and your friends in that claustrophobic town say—just because he's a foreigner." But even as the door hissed shut behind her she heard voices opening into avidity as Hiro was encouraged to elaborate on his story. And behind that, lower, the Sar discussing the sixth vein workings with his eldest daughter.

Frustration as much as anger impelled her down the hall. She felt enclosed, tiled in, buried within rock. Ransome House might be vast, kilometer after kilometer of tunnel curving away into darkness, forgotten passages ending in abandoned rooms, but it was also utterly contained, sheathed both in metal and in the strictures necessarily imposed on a large conglomeration of people bound together under the surface of as turbulent a planet as Unruli.

She halted at the warehouse lock. The sheen of the walls mirrored her: the slant of her eyes; the pale, graceful line of her neck; her slender, upright figure. There was a set to her shoulders, a cast of her legs in the finely woven trousers, a

turn to her wrists, that betrayed her strength and agility.
The Hae Ransomes were renowned for their beauty, all wil-
lowy height and brown skin and tightly curled hair. Some
other strain had crept in to pollute Lily with straight black
hair, pale skin, and a stature a full head less than her ten
siblings—and, her mother claimed, with irresponsibility. Although less than five years from her majority at thirty, she
had not shown any inclination toward a profession, an ap-
prenticeship, a bond alliance, or the University. Had, in fact,
shown no inclination at all toward anything except recalci-
trance, stubbornness, and Master Heredes's Academy.

The lights on the door panel blinked red. The gauges ran
into the warning zone: storm. How appropriate, she
thought, gazing at these signs with the dispassionate gaze of
a native as she pulled on parka, gloves, goggles, and hard
hat. She smiled wryly, encoding the opening sequence into
the panel. When the door rustled aside she slid a breathing
plug on and went into the warehouse.

Only a few lights burned. Shadows disguised the distant
walls of the cavern and spread, as disease brings decay and
disrepair, over the equipment that littered the expanse of
floor. Darkness hid the roof. Lily walked, her footsteps muffled on the bare rock, past broken-down mine engines and
new machines from the provincial suppliers, to a far corner.
Here lay the relics, machinery from the early days, smaller
and more sophisticated—machinery her father could not
use or repair but would not sell or scrap.

By the time she had graduated First School at fifteen it
was obvious she was no technician: the five mechanical Kollek Ransome cousins had laughed at her because her suit-
ability ranking for tech was impossibly low. So she had crept
out secretly to the warehouse one night, piqued, furious, and
humiliated as well by a failed attempt at running away from
home, and she had made one of those ancient machines
work.

Barely, not understanding it or its function, scarcely
knowing how she had done it, but she *had* done it. It had
taken one year before she could communicate with it in the
most rudimentary fashion and five more before, achieving

reasonable fluency, she had discovered that it could speak and understand Standard but preferred not to use it, because Standard was, after all, primitive compared to the sophistication of its own language. That was the year when, hidden in her room, it had somehow latched onto the University screening "computer programming" examination file and, taking the ten-hour test in fifty-two minutes, had gotten a perfect score—in her name. Five months later, she had received miserable scores on the entrance examination taken at Apron Port, and so ended that sensation.

Reaching the line of dust-ridden machines, she whistled a quick, intricate melody. After a pause, a light blinked in the darkness, steadying to blue, and the reply came, sung, as a recapitulation of that single line in four voices. A spherical shape, perhaps half a meter in diameter, moved toward her, out into the half-light, hovering at her eye level. Two appendages dangled like stunted arms from its equator.

A robot, of course, but when she had carefully asked her tech brother what it was, he had laughed: an ancient line, workings unknown.

In ten years she had learned that its primary language was based on music, that it seemed sentient, and that it was, with a few adjustments, in perfect repair—or so it had once claimed with an exultant full cadence. And because she, Lilyaka Hae Ransome, had saved it from decay and disintegration—the phrases it used translated more closely to power loss and loneliness—she gained its complete devotion and loyalty, and its series name and number: Bach 1689.

It was a felicitous relationship. Bach had infinite patience with her limitations, because, after all, she could only whistle or sing one voice at a time, and assured her she was making excellent progress through the collected works, rewarding her with a variety of pieces from other series, which bore equally strange names: Mozart, Gabrieli, Melep. For his part (she thought of it as a "he"), he loved to play on her computer. She would hook him up whenever she could get him to her room unseen. For she had told no one, not even Master Heredes, about Bach.

Bach sang now a lilting question.

I go to the Academy, she whistled.

A green light blinked on its topmost port and it sang back, seemingly oblivious to the complex formality explicit in all of its statements and absent from all of hers. *Very well. And wilt thou require my assistance or attendance?* A quickening of tempo here, like eagerness.

It is storm weather. I need you to stay here and track me, in case I have an accident.

Bach sang happily back and sank down behind a corroded drilling machine to compose.

At the surface lock she fished a beacon out of a rusting bucket and clipped a beam-light to her hard hat. Her code flashed on the com-panel. Ignoring it, she punched the exit sequence. The door shunted aside, sand scraping under its glide. In the lock, she waited through the long lift to the surface, felt the familiar rush of air, the moment of dense silence. The outside door opened, straining into the wind.

Lily stepped outside.

Turmoil greeted her. Clouds and wind roiled the turgid air. The ground lay unmoved by the furious swell and tear of the wind, but it rested in steep angles of rock, deep plunges, and abrupt thrusts upward, as if in some long-past era the wind had forced the stone into the turbulent dance and then left it, locked into the patterns of its forgotten frenzy. Behind her, the wind generators spun frantically.

She used hands and feet as she went. The wind pulled her one way, pushed her another. Streams of air caught on the rocks and whipped round to strike her face. She steadied herself with her hands, testing each step before she put her full weight down. Only the lull of her breathing through the plug remained constant. In the distance she heard the echoing roar of an avalanche. The early settlers to Unruli had suffered an astonishing number of casualties; later, with the discovery of the stability of the rock below, they built primarily underground, cutting themselves off, except for their generators, from the surface. And now, Lily thought, their descendants could not understand that such containment might seem restrictive to one of their own.

Master Heredes's home, and Academy of Instruction in a

wide variety of martial arts, lay on a brief stretch of unbroken ground. From a distance it appeared to be a swelling of polished stone covered with the dense, flashing swirl of wind generators. Lily trudged across the flat, her head thrust into the wind, shoulders hunched and tight. She felt, pushing against it, as if it were the physical manifestation of all that she was struggling against, and that the sloping door of the Academy was her only refuge.

As she laid her hand on the lock, the door slid open. A blast of wind pushed her in. Sand skittered across the floor in frenzied patterns, freezing suddenly in haphazard lines when the door shut. The ceiling receded into darkness. She took off her goggles and rubbed at her eyes. The floor sank, stopping at last at the inner door, which opened with a low beep. In the anteroom, she changed quickly into the obligatory loose white pants and waist-belted tunic worn by Heredes's many students. Barefoot, she padded down the corridor beyond, her strides keeping time to the frantic melody she whistled, an out-of-series song Bach had taught her. The door to the master's parlor was open; she went in. He was reading, seated cross-legged next to the holograph, but as she entered he laid down his screen and turned to face her.

"Well, Lily," he began, halted abruptly, and frowned. "Finish it," he said.

For a moment she did nothing. Then she remembered what she had been doing. She picked an appropriate measure in the song and whistled to the end of the elongated phrase.

"Can you sing it?" he asked.

She laughed and sat down on the floor next to him. "I haven't got the voice."

"No," he agreed. "Melep is notoriously hard to sing. But you've got the inner melody." He smiled, reaching out with a dark hand to touch the holograph. He looked much younger than her father, but she was sure, without knowing why, that he was much older. "I haven't heard that for years."

"But how could you—" She halted, confused. "How did you know?"

That made him blink. "How did *you* know? I've never heard that Melep was taught in these schools. Well, Lily." He studied her thoughtfully.

"I learned it. But I didn't think anyone else—Melep was a composer?"

"Oh, yes." She had known Heredes ten years and now she watched as a thought developed in his eyes and moved out to adjust the positions of his body. "You're angry," he said.

She stood abruptly and walked to the wall. "My mother means to forbid me from coming here. She's using—" She stopped, unwilling to mention Hiro's bounty hunters. Heredes waited; his eyes were of a clear green cast, set wide apart, his cheeks broad, so that his expression, expectant, appeared almost childish. Lily spun away to face the wall. "I can't entirely blame them. No one's ever accused me of being lazy, not with the hours I study here, but it's true that I don't know what I can use all this training for. And it's true that the Sar has indulged me. It isn't as if I've tried to involve myself in House business like the rest of the clan. But I just don't care about new mines and next week's trading schedule and tax percentage." She let her palms support her on the wall. Behind her, the measured, quiet breathing of the master brushed through the room. "I should. But I can't."

"And there rests the flaw in hereditary systems of class and government," he said. She allowed herself a reluctant smile. "That's better," he continued. "Although you're still tense."

"Maybe I should have joined when the Immortals came recruiting," she said into the wall, then shook her head. "But that would just have exchanged one set of restrictions for a worse set. I've gotten to the point where I would apprentice in anything just to get out of here."

"And I not knowing a single person in this sector."

"Well, I'm not accusing *you*. But there isn't a chance in high weather that mother will let me out before I'm thirty, not now, not without a bond or a sponsorship. Without either of those, I've got no resources to draw on. None, even though Ransome House is one of the richest on Unruli." She paused, thinking over the inequities of this system. "And I *won't* bond."

The monotone hum of the circulation vents hung in the air. "Your father," Heredes began, "once told me that you received the highest score on your computer programming exams ever recorded in this system. The University might have let you in without the pregnancy requirement."

"Damn that," said Lily. "I'm sorry." She turned. "It was a mistake. I didn't really get that score."

He stood, the loose, ankle-length pants and cloth-belted tunic rustling as they unfolded. Under the cloth his posture and his way of moving revealed complete self-possession. "You would have received it at this University." He went to the door. "Come with me."

She had never been in his study before. He coded in to open its door, and a light winked on as the panel hissed aside. The room seemed alien, tinged with an organic scent, dominated by a huge desk made of a material unknown to her, grained, dark as Heredes's skin. But the chair was built for a human frame, the artifacts meant for human, not alien, hands. On one wall a picture protruded from the wall: slung-bellied cars with sails, sitting on a textureless surface that resembled oil, but was blue. A curtain, patterned in a weave so coarse that she could identify the colors of individual threads, screened the opening to a farther room. She stared until, aware of her staring, she jerked her attention back to Heredes.

"You know well enough, Lilyaka," he said in the tone of voice he reserved for use of her full name, "that you are my best pupil. What you don't know is that you are the best pupil I have ever had." His tone was grave, almost alarmingly so. "I should give you what opportunity I can before it is, perhaps, too late."

"Too late for what?"

He walked behind the desk, fussed there a moment, and lifted out a tangle of light chain. "I do know someone, but it depends on how far you are willing to go."

"Since I can remember I've wanted to get as far from here as I can."

A pause. He stared, for a moment, at the picture. "As far away as you can might be farther than you think. Would Central be far enough?"

"Central!"

He smiled. "I know a woman there. She is my—ah—sister. She teaches, and on Central her Academy would be much larger than mine. Give her this, and she will apprentice you." He handed her a necklace, a burnished medallion of five interlinked circles pierced by a spear.

In this room, appointed so strangely, the odd symbol she now held in her hand reminded her forcibly that no one knew where Heredes had come from. He had simply arrived fifteen years ago and opened his Academy. There had, perhaps, been a handful of incidents: a woman who had flown in in a state of terror and shock and yet left ten cycles later in excellent spirits; the heavily robed stranger who came in furtively but was never seen to leave. But memory fades when times remain quiet, and Heredes lived very unobtrusively.

Until Hiro's bounty hunters. Was that what Heredes had meant by "too late"? Here was a man who recognized the Melep song, a song he could not possibly know, because it existed solely in her little robot, a creature removed from her time and her world. What if Hiro were right?

Lily put on the necklace; it slipped like a cool circle of hope under her shirt, snaking down her skin. She looked up at Heredes. "What do I have to do?" she asked.

"Trust me," he said. "She'll refuse to take you, at first, but she will take you. You need only persist. Her name is Wingtuck Honor Jones."

"Jones? That's a strange name."

"In those days, we all got rather strange names." He nodded toward the door, and they left the study and its extraordinary curios behind. "Ask the Sar if he'll agree to let you go to Central."

"And if he won't?"

"Ask him first."

"I'll ask him now." Her eagerness made him smile. For an instant she stood, as if unsure what action to take next, then lowered her hands, palm to thigh, and bowed to him.

In the anteroom she changed with remarkable speed, almost throwing her Academy clothes on a bench, forcing herself to fold them neatly and stow them in her locker. The lift eased upward, annoyingly slow. But she could savor it—Central! Administrative center for the far-flung systems of Reft space—navigable space. Center of everything.

Storm greeted her at the lock, but the trudge across the twenty meters of flat felt exhilarating. A goal, like the first line of heights, seemed reachable, achievable. A third of the way up the slope, she paused in the lee of a cliff of striated rock to look down at the swell of the Academy. Of course Heredes had found something for her. He would never fail her.

Movement to her right. A flash of dull light, of bright blue, and a ship, lit fore and aft, bolted into view. The storm tore at it. Its bow swung up crazily, flung down, yet still the vessel moved along meters above the ground.

An aircar. No one had aircars. Of course they were possible, theoretically; her tech siblings speculated sometimes—

The ship rocked to a halt, hovering tenuously above the telltale rise of the Academy. An appendage snaked down from the hull and touched ground. The ship sank until it hung scarcely half a meter off the windswept flat. An opening appeared in one side, and three forms emerged, stepping down, the wind whipping their short tunics and shoulder-caped cloaks around their thin bodies. Lily knew with the immediacy of instinct that they were aliens.

They went swiftly to the lock and disappeared into the lift. A fourth emerged, stumbling slightly as it touched the ground. It turned, and the wind whipped back its cloak and hood.

So close to human, but excruciatingly thin; delicate, she might have called it, but it remained unbowed in the strength of the wind.

For long moments, the solitary figure remained motionless below. The lift opened.

Four figures emerged, but one was limp, carried by two of the aliens. Heredes. Completely in their power, unconscious —not dead, not that—as if he had been as helpless as an infant against them. The fourth alien clambered up into the ship.

Lily, breaking out of shock, impelled herself forward, sliding and scrambling down the slope. But the aliens were faster; oblivious to her presence, they loaded Heredes like an unwieldy sack of food into their ship. Before she reached the plateau, the last one pulled himself up and the hatch shut behind a final billow of cloak.

Lily stared, as helpless as Heredes, as the alien ship rose into the hard wind, turned and, buffeted constantly, flew away in the direction of Apron Port.

2 In Ransome House

✳✳✳✳✳✳

Clouds boiled up toward the heavens, colored violet near the ground but changing in a dizzying shift up the spectrum until, at heights she could barely make out, they appeared red. It mirrored her, this whirlwind of violence; like the clouds, torn upward, she felt powerless against the forces that had taken Heredes. Without him, there would be no classes, no long discussions about interpretation and tactics, no Academy: the entire focus of her last ten years, gone. She had to find him.

She pulled herself along a ledge, wind pushing her toward the edge, and at last found the escarpment that led to the final stretch of ground before Ransome House. A flash of white startled her. A thin, interwoven lace of white filaments drifted into view; a gust flung it forward. She slipped, staring, and threw out her hands to catch herself. Jagged rock cut into her hand, but for a moment she forgot even Heredes as Unruli's native life swept past her, as intangible as the wraith it was named for. Dream, the settlers had called it: Boo, the spirit, the ghost of loved ones lost in storm—like Heredes.

Three meters from her an updraft caught it and it disappeared into an eddy of violet cloud. The rock slipped beneath her. She scrambled for an outcropping and clung to it as the shale around her spilled down, avalanching, drowning the wind in its roar. She held tight as her footing began to go and clutched higher, until the spill slowed, stopped, and only the echo remained. It shuddered around her as she picked her way up to the top of the defile. The House beacon shone before her.

At the lock, she had to encode high risk clearances in order to cut through the security shutdown on the lift. Her glove, ripped clean from her wrist to the base of her fingers, dangled open, revealing a ragged cut on her hand. Slow drops of red formed and fell, shattering into invisible fragments as the wind caught them. The hum of the lift rising to the surface lay like an ominous undertone to the clatter of the furiously spinning wind generators. The light on the panel blinked and a wailing beep sounded. She hastily tucked the bleeding hand under the opposite arm. The door yawned open.

"Lily!"

She ducked inside to face her eldest brother.

"You fool!" He hit the "close" button with one fist. "Do you want to shut the whole system down?" The door scraped shut behind her, a swirl of sand settling at her feet. "Why you think it's such a lark to go out in high weather I'll never understand. We already have a breakdown in the second vein—can you imagine if we'd gotten a code two in the warehouse just because you had to run outside?"

"This is serious," said Lily. "I have to take the tunnel into Apron Port, right now."

"Of course we'll divert the car from second vein. We don't really need to send anyone out there to prevent the collapse of the entire workings."

Lily reached past him to the com-panel and punched up the "status" codes. The second vein blinked in third, under a broken wind generator and a mine engine in fifth vein. "That's not bad enough that two hours will make any difference."

"Lily, we can't let everyone who gets it into their head go diverting maintenance and schedules for whatever trifles—"

"Heredes was kidnapped! Don't you care?"

The door slid away to reveal the warehouse. The whine of a drill pierced above the rumble of grinder and one engine that sputtered into life, held on tentatively for a drawn-out space, and failed abruptly.

"Lily." Her brother stepped into the warehouse and walked toward three figures who had gathered around the spent engine. "I have work to do."

Cast carelessly back over his shoulder, the words barely reached her. She ran to her room, stripped off her outside gear, and bandaged the cut on her hand. A duffel bag of traveling gear packed, a change of clothes, and she went in search of her father.

The metal walls slid off in bareness around her, linking lab and workshop, kitchen and private rooms. Some led into the blankness, ended without reason, work abandoned or not yet begun. They were so alike, each to each, as to be indistinguishable, but the entire House was laid out so succinctly on a grid that it was impossible to get lost. And what joy, thought Lily, in a world where there is no uncertainty at all?

In the center of the grid lay the offices, grouped around a circular chamber. From the communications center the back talk from the intercom link to the field supervisors whispered in the still air: "Ten–eighty-eight. Let me have a spiker on five-eight. Ten-four. I'll send it with Seke." One of her sisters sat at the com-desk, playing "Vector Storm" on the computer and periodically responding with a terse "Eight-twelve, you're coded in" to a request. Squawks and static punctuated the low exchanges; now and then a high beep sounded from the game.

"Lilyaka!" Her mother's voice penetrated forcefully into the quiet of the foyer. "Come in here."

Lily walked to the entrance of her mother's office.

"Come in, girl. You needn't pretend to avoid me." The Saress rose from her chair, pausing to erase a screen from her computer. Lily stayed in the doorway. "You continually disobey me," the Saress continued, beginning now to pace the large room. Metal-sheathed walls mirrored her stride, her height, the long, tapering fingers that she clasped and unclasped before her. Only her expression was lost, for lack of detail. "I have offered you any number of options for your future, but you refuse to listen to me. The time has come that you simply no longer have a choice—"

"This is an emergency," Lily said, stepping back.

"You will wait, young woman, until given my leave." The Saress swept one hand over her scarf, brushing a stray strand of black hair, tensing as she forced it back into its place under the coiled cloth. "Emergency! I tell you, my girl, when the next offer—"

"You never listen to me!" cried Lily.

Her sister stepped out from the communications room, shrugged, and went back in. Lily whirled and ran to her father's door.

"Lily!" came her mother's voice from behind her. "As of this moment—"

The Sar's door slid open. Lily dodged inside as the door sighed into place behind her. Here, the still, dry air smelled as if it had been touched by some unidentifiable spice.

"Excuse me, Sar-father," Lily said into the silence.

His dark head remained bent over a graph. "If you must argue with your mother, at least do so in private, not where the entire field division can overhear you." He turned in his chair to face her, straightening a sleeve that had slipped askew. "I am aware," he continued, "that we have not been able to provide you with a job that suits your talents. I don't want to force you into a bond that you would despise, but eventually you may leave me no choice. You must have some occupation, Lily." A frown creased his face, a soft break in the copper of his complexion. "I feel constrained to add that you haven't even done us the courtesy of providing children for our House."

The familiar litany faded past her. "You don't understand." Eight strides took her to his chair. "I just came from the Academy. Someone—they weren't even human—someone abducted Master Heredes."

"An alien abduction? Lily, that's ridiculous. In this weather? And what you were doing out I can't—"

"They had an *aircar*. I saw it."

Black eyes met black eyes. "By the Void, did they now." He stood up. "An aircar." He paused suddenly, considering her. She, in her turn, was struck by that unequal balance of years between him and Heredes. The Sar was as young a sixty as anyone Lily knew, since he could afford the occasional dose of rejuv. Yet Heredes, looking thirty years younger, felt as old to her. And picturing him, she experienced so strong a rush of fear that it took all of her years of training not to run out of the room.

"Lilyaka," said the Sar finally, almost a sigh. "Only Central has clearance to grant bounties and to allow intersystem arrests. And only Central would have access to aircars, if there were any. I'm afraid that Hiro's tale must have been correct. If you like, we'll send out a query, follow the usual channels. I'm sure we can get word of him. What happened to your hand?"

She thrust the bandaged hand behind her. "It's nothing to do with Central. I know it."

"Even if it were nothing to do with Central, which I doubt, what possible responsibility do you have toward Heredes?"

"Because—" She faltered, thought of Heredes unconscious in an alien grasp, and went on. "Because he's the only person who understands what I want out of life. The things that matter to me. Not mining."

For an instant she saw a flash of emotion in his face, as if some old pain had returned to haunt him. "Of all my children," he said slowly, "you have been the most disobedient, Lily. And in that way, you have always reminded me of myself at your age—but I did not have the luxury to seek some more—shall we say—spiritual calling. I had to rebuild the Ransome mining operation, and whatever inclination I might have had to an artistic vocation—or to an elite military group like the Immortals—" With a slight grimace he shrugged, as if relieving himself of old dreams long since withered. "My responsibility was—had to be—first of all to Ransome House."

Another time she might have been surprised at this revelation, or perhaps flattered that her stern and single-minded father had shown this side of himself to her. But now she only shook her head. "Then you see why I have to go after Master Heredes."

"No, I don't see. Your obligations are here, Lilyaka."

She bowed her head, but she did not reply.

"Daughter." He looked down at her with forty years of authority over Ransome House in his gaze. "I forbid you to go. Do you understand?"

"I understand," she replied, quite levelly.

She walked, without undue haste, to her room; the undecorated walls, white bedcover, and uncluttered plastic desk revealed nothing of her character. She had left no mark here. Without regret, she grabbed her gear and left.

It was alarmingly easy to get Bach through the warehouse and into the hangar. Bach had played this game before, on furtive trips to her room where lay the wonderful and much-loved computer, his idiot relative. He shielded his outside lights; his two sensors he dulled to a deep orange, like sparks guttering on the ground. Dust puffed out along his track, and Lily walked beside, her parka and duffel hanging from one hand to screen him. Once, when the drill and grinder and the reluctant engine all wailed at once in an excess of high harmonics, Lily heard the little robot sing softly, as on an indrawn breath, his anguish at such dissonance. Workers hurried to help consolidate these hopeful repairs, and Lily and Bach escaped into the hangar lock.

The hangar was empty and cold. A single light hanging over the counter that housed the computer lit the room. Shadows held court here, filling the far limits of the stone hall, covering the little fleet of trucks and remodeled vehicles. Huge dents in their exteriors seemed more a trick of the light than the mark of their world. In the dimmest reaches lay the salvage and the one incredibly flattened vehicle, no longer recognizable as a truck, that her sisters had teased her with when she was young, telling her that it still contained the body of a man, the metal crushed so tightly around him by some fearful combination of rock and wind on Unruli's surface that he could not be recovered. Lily savored the stir in the dry air, the hiss of her breathing plug, and walked over to the computer. Bach rose, singing, behind her.

She coded the computer to turn on at its lowest level and left Bach to monitor it. Checked and fueled a truck, stowing her gear in the well-armored driving compartment. It took three tries before the engine steadied and stayed alive. Its roar echoed in the hanger, drowning out Bach's melodic lines. She eased it forward, coming to rest with only a slight sputtering one foot from the lift doors, and swung down from the seat.

At the computer, the lance of light from her hard hat illuminated the keyboard. Bach was playing chess on half the screen, while the other half still monitored the lift and hangar doors. As Lily passed behind him, he checkmated the computer. Lily covered her eyes. With a few sheepish chords he exited the program and sat ready for her command.

We go, she whistled. Bach typed in an elaborate sequence. Lily jogged back to the truck and climbed in. Three bell-like tones chimed above the swell of the engine, and the lift doors began to slide aside.

The intercom snapped on. "Contact. Contact. Please identify. No clearance has been given."

Lily put the truck into gear. It lurched forward into the lift, sand gritting under the tires.

"Please identify. We have storm warning. Close the lift doors."

Lily whistled a quick half-phrase. Bach detached himself from the computer and floated toward her. They got inside the lock at the same time. The com-panel in the wall of the lift came to furious life before Bach reached it, flashing warnings and prohibitions. Behind, the doors were shutting, but beyond them Lily saw the hangar door panel blinking and the first stirring as the lock into the warehouse began to open.

"Come on," she said under her breath. The lift doors came together with a metallic thud. One of the warning lights on the panel immediately snapped off, but another took its place. Someone behind was keying in the "open door" sequence for the lift. The roar of the engine echoed around her, deafening.

Bach keyed in the lift sequence. Several things happened at once. Someone pounded on the lift doors. A flurry of messages lit up the panel's screen in a pallette of colors. The intercom crackled and a high voice shouted, "What, by All, do you think you're doing?"

And the lift began to move, slow, shuddering at first, then smoothing into the long rise toward the surface.

"Who is this?" shouted the voice over the intercom. An alarm, high-pitched and strident, began to wail, piercing in the closed lift. It shut off abruptly.

"Lilyaka," said her father's voice suddenly over the intercom. "Stop this at once."

Lily shoved her duffel bag a little deeper under the instrument board and adjusted the safety belt for the extra seat so that it would fit over Bach.

"Answer me." For the first time in her life, she knew he was angry. "Very well. We will go into the central computer." The intercom clicked off. The lift shuddered once and stopped.

"Bach," Lily shouted. The lift began to descend. "Override it! Override!" Her hands clenched the steering wheel, white-tipped at the knuckles. Bach had been typing; now he pushed forward a second appendage and plugged directly into the panel. There was a furious riot of color on the screen. The intercom sputtered with voices and failed. The lift shuddered. Bach was not singing at all.

A violent jolt threw Lily into the wheel, winding her. The lift halted. The alarm began to shriek. Yelling came over the intercom, suddenly cut off. The lift began to rise. The screen went black except for a single column of white rising like the level of water in a slim tube. The alarm ceased, as if it too had been cut off. The white column rose, rose, rose, and they were there.

Air rushed past her face as she leaned out. Bach detached himself from the com-panel and sped to her. She felt the air pressure thicken around her, as if the doors and walls were bracing. Bach slid onto the seat beside her and she belted him in and shut the metal cage around them. A loud crash cut above the noise of the engine. The doors creaked and moved and, with the sudden movement of something released from restraint, popped open.

The wind screamed in at them. Lily was blinded by its force. With both hands she pulled the safety goggles down from her hard hat. She could see scarcely ten meters in front of her. But she merely tightened her grip on the wheel and eased the truck forward. As they came out completely from the lock, into the full fury of the storm, a hard gust picked the left side of the vehicle fully a meter off the ground, then let it free to come crashing down. Lily's head struck the metal mesh above her as she was flung up, but the hard hat absorbed most of the shock.

Bach, held hard in place by the cross-strapping of belts, began somewhat shakily to sing.

> *Befiehl du deine Wege*
> *Und was dein Herze kränkt*
> *Der allertreusten Pflege*
> *Des, der den Himmel lenkt.*
> *Der Wolken, Luft und Winden*
> *Gibt Wege, Lauf und Bahn*
> *Der wird auch Wege finden,*
> *Da dein Fuss gehen kann.*

> *"Commend your way,*
> *and whatever troubles your heart,*
> *to the trustiest care of him,*
> *who controls the heavens;*
> *he who gives clouds, air and winds*
> *their paths, course and track,*
> *he will also find ways*
> *where your feet can walk."*

Lily hung grimly on to the wheel, and they went forward.

3　A Bird in the Hand

✷✷✷✷✷✷✷

The hard hat saved her. Her head and the metal mesh ceiling of the cage met more times than she could count, until her back and neck ached with the shock. Bach sang obscure hymns with strange and inexplicable lyrics for almost half the trip. But, coming around a nondescript corner of rock, a sudden blast of wind picked the front end of the truck up until they were vertical, then slammed it down so hard that the engine died, and Bach's singing ceased. A lower, ominous tone rumbled down from above: avalanche. Lily fought the engine, but it coughed and started only to die again as a massive fall of rock thundered down directly on top of them. A huge boulder hit square on top of the cage, shattering into pebbles and debris that, showering down through the mesh, scored a tear through the right sleeve of Lily's coat and scratched a long, ugly line into the impeccable surface of Bach's exterior. With her reflexive jerk, ducking, she jolted the engine into a strong surge, and the truck lurched forward over the new heap of sliding, unstable debris. When Bach began to sing again—for the third time—the one beginning "A mighty fortress is my truck," Lily told him to shut up.

　　He remained silent, except for the occasional dissonant chord surprised from him by some close encounter with imminent destruction, until Lily brought the battered vehicle to a halt in the wind shadow of Apron Rock, the huge, stable monolith of rock that demarcated the western edge of Apron Port. Here he ventured a brief thanksgiving chorus, very softly.

Lily had to uncurl each finger separately to get her hands ungripped from the steering wheel. Massaging each hand in turn, she gazed down at the scattered lights below.

Apron Port lay in a gorge. Broad enough that competent pilots could land between the high walls, the gorge sheltered the town from the worst of the winds. A foundation of stable rock prevented avalanches, so much of the port was built above ground, better to serve the ships, which came in great numbers to carry away the products of the three House mines of the region: Chan, Ooalata, and, of course, Ransome.

Red and blue warning lights blinked in wild patterns across the landing fields to the south of the town. In the town itself, the streetlights glowed amber. The sighing clatter of the wind generators hummed in the air, almost drowned out by the swelling tear of the wind. The flash of their whirling faces lit most of the heights around the gorge. Here and there orange lights marked maintenance shafts.

Lily rubbed the screen of dirt off her face with the palm of one glove. The buckles of the safety belts around her and Bach took several moments to unfasten because they were clogged with debris. Bach, listing slightly to one side, followed her as she climbed down. They stood in a shallow cave. On three sides the rock rose over them; on the fourth the wind whipped past. Lily stamped her feet, and a faint shower of dust drifted from her to the ground.

"Hoy," she said. Bach, his shine dulled by dust, was still rolling slightly to one side as he rose two meters. All his lights came on, blinking in a maze of colors, and he sang an unfamiliar phrase and righted himself.

"Right ho," said Lily, watching him, and she whistled, *Let us go.*

They hiked against a rising wind to the nearest lift shaft. Inside it was blissfully silent except for the low hum of the machinery. Lily leaned back against the cold smoothness of the metal walls and shut her eyes. Bach hovered a hands-breadth above the floor as if he was examining himself in its brilliant sheen and was not, perhaps, entirely happy with what he saw. A sound like an indrawn sigh signaled their halt, and the doors opened into an underground tunnel.

"Hoy," she repeated, picking up her duffel bag. "What a ride that was."

Bach's repy was very brief.

Stairs led to Mineral Avenue; there they turned up Gourmet Street. Shielded boutiques lit in gaudy colors as the light faded. Beside her, Bach hugged the ground like an oversized soccer ball, but the dusk protected them from stares.

At Handfast Boulevard they turned right toward the Harbormaster's offices. It was closed, but not locked.

"Please the Void let him be on duty," breathed Lily as she and Bach coded in to enter. The door swept aside to admit them to the outer offices, plastic desks and dark terminals and the long "permits counter" lying in dim stillness under the glow of two auxiliary light tubes. A short hallway in back, barred by a waist-high gate, which Lily hopped and Bach floated over, led to three doors. Lily punched into the central door's panel, heard a click, a beep, and finally a voice.

"Who is it?"

"Finch," she said, "let me in."

"How'd you get here?" asked the voice, but the door slid open. Lily and Bach went through, and it huffed shut behind them. "And what by the Seven Hells is that?" finished the voice, thoroughly startled now.

Lily had to pause while her eyes adjusted. The only light in the room came from ten lit screens on the curved console. A dark figure rose, hands moving on the console, and all the room lights flashed on. Lily covered her eyes with one palm, slowly lowered it.

Heneage Finch Caenna stared first at her, then his eyes slid to gaze astonished at her spherical companion.

"Never mind," said Lily firmly, recollecting herself and starting forward. "I need your help." She walked around the console to stand beside him, examining each screen in turn. Besides the console and its three chairs, the room was empty. Three walls had a blank, metallic cast; the fourth was sprayed with the telltale pinprick of lights that marked it as a wall screen. A low rumble of music came from one of the console's speakers.

"How did you get here?" He extended one hand to touch Lily's coat. "There's no Ransome cargo runs due for eight revs."

Lily leaned forward to peer intently at the screen marked "Departures." "I drove."

He laughed. "No."

"I need a listing of ships that have just left or have just gotten clearance to leave."

Finch sat down. "You did. Lily! You could have killed yourself! You may not care, but some of us still cherish ideas about you—"

"Finch," she interrupted, almost harsh, "not now. I need those listings."

He looked again to the door, where Bach hovered patiently, lights blinking. An appendage snaked out from his interior and began to polish his surface. "Hoy," said the young man. His eyes, deep-set and brown in an olive-toned face, shifted back to Lily. "Don't tell me *I* can't care," he finished, "not after everything we've done together," but he reached past her to bring up a series of numbers and a log on one of the screens. "Station window is not at optimum. There's a code two storm. You're not going to get any lifts for the next two revs."

"Come *on,* Finch. Just check."

"Okay. Okay. Move back." She stepped back, trailing a mist of dust. "You're as filthy as a tattoo. Maybe you should go take a shower while I check." He brushed dirt off one sleeve of her tunic, let one hand settle there.

She pulled away from him and set down her bag. "I'll wait."

He made a face at her, but began typing. A few screens scrolled past, two tones sounded, and new numbers flashed on the screen. "By the Void. Unauthorized lift at dock seven, thirty-two minutes ago. That hasn't happened for years."

"Good watch you keep." She moved forward to inspect the figures on the screen.

"Don't be a push, Lil," he said, angry now. "Why monitor that close when no one ever lifts without going through us?"

"Don't call me that. And what about bootleggers?"

"Much you know about booters," he retorted. "What do you know about this ship?"

"What classification?"

He checked, came up only with "no match." The ship had no name or home port listing, just an ID number, and gave only a Station clearance and a captain's name, Cha. "Never seen them before," Finch said. "Never heard of them. I wasn't on shift when they landed and Mom didn't say anything to me, to watch them close or anything. Berth tax is paid up."

Lily whistled.

"What?" Finch turned. "Hey!"

Bach was moving, singing a brief answer.

"Move aside a blink, Finch," said Lily. "This is Bach."

Finch merely stared, mouth slightly open, at the approach of the robot. Bach settled in beside him and reached out to plug into the console.

"Hey!" cried Finch, starting up.

Lily put out a hand and pushed him back into his chair. "It's safe."

A few more figures flashed on the screen, winked off, and Bach began to sing. Finch ran one hand through his dark hair, pulling it back behind his ears. When Bach finished, the screen reverting to what Finch had originally brought up, the young man turned his eyes up to look at Lily, his hand still in his hair as if caught there.

"That doesn't make sense," said Lily.

Bach sang a short phrase.

"I'll say." Finch lowered his hand. "Lily! What is that thing?"

"He's a very old, very smart robot," replied Lily, "and he just told me that that ship is, and I quote, 'a Kapellan class oh-one-oh-oh-one-oh schooner, late Imperial ID vested class with special powers clearance,' and 'Cha' is not a name but a title. Does that make any sense to you?"

"None of this makes any sense to me."

"Damn. Damn. Damn." Lily walked to the door and back. "It's got to be." She turned abruptly on Finch, who slowly lowered his hand to the console. "When's the soonest jump window out of system from Station?"

"Absolutely none for six revs," he said straightaway.

"Then I've still got a chance."

"Although—" He tapped out a command and watched the reply flash onto a screen. "They could be hanging out at Tagalong. They've got a window at two point five revs."

"No one's got *that* much energy to waste—" She stopped, remembering the aircar. "Maybe they do." She whirled away again, pacing.

"Likely chance, Lil."

She spun back, reached to grab his tunic, and pulled him to his feet. "If you call me that again I'll smash your face in."

Finch grinned in his lazy, half-sensual way. "You have such a way with words, Saressa. I remember the first time you propositioned me—"

"Heneage!" She let him go like he was fire and flushed as if the heat had caught her.

He threw up his hands, palms up. "You win. What a horrible name. I'll never forgive my mother for giving it to me."

"And anyway," continued Lily with a smug grin, "my first proposition to you was to climb Apron Rock."

"Then it must have been the second one."

"Finch." She laid her hands on his shoulders. "Master Heredes was kidnapped this afternoon."

He put his hands on hers. "I'd heard he had some trouble in town. I heard it was bounties."

"No." She drew back from him, explained about the aircar and the aliens. When she finished he sat down and stared morosely at Bach for some time. Bach had resumed polishing, hovering about a meter above the floor. Part of his exterior now gleamed with a brilliant sheen, in stark contrast to those areas that still had a pall of dust on them.

"What can I do?" asked Finch finally. "After all, I used to take classes from him, too."

Lily sat in the chair beside him. All her energy and purpose seemed suddenly dissipated. If Heredes was taken out of system, she would lose him completely. She sighed, resting her chin on one hand. The hard hat shadowed her eyes. "*No* one is lifting off in the next rev?"

There was a slight pause, pregnant with unspoken information.

Lily lifted her head to look at Finch. He cleared his throat, rubbed one ear, and drummed his fingers on the console. The muted music swelled infinitesimally in volume, a melancholy voice singing about being trapped in a chain gang of tattoos sent to mine in the asteroids.

"Finch?"

"Not officially."

"Finch."

This office is not allowed to—"

She threw herself at him, landing mostly in his lap, her hands on either side of his face. "Finch!"

"You *are* filthy." He put his arms around her and settled her firmly into his embrace. "Now listen here, my unclean one, this is serious. Harbormaster is a position appointed by Central, and it's a good one."

"Then how do you know about unofficial lifts?"

He regarded her thoughtfully, but seemed to be thinking of something else. "I don't mind the berth taxes," he said. "Or the old cargo taxes, based on percentage of profits and so on and so forth. But it's the new cargo taxes and the destination taxes, not to mention the clearances, that are pushing the independents out of the good contracts. And the forced routes. And now Central is assigning what cargoes people can carry. It's just not fair."

"So you help the booters."

"Never so noble," he said with a slight grimace. "Bootleggers go up in the nonoptimum times. It's more expensive for them, but they can't be traced by Station or by Elly Port tracers, and for the same reason, we're in no danger of being caught looking the other way, since at those times we're their only monitor. But there's never an authorized lift from Apron Port. Only unofficial ones. Even the booters go through us."

"Do your parents know?"

He grinned again, that engaging blend of indolence and sensuality. "Mom and Grandmam Caenna set the whole system up. Dad doesn't know—he'd feel duty-bound to turn them in."

Lily looked at him intently for some moments. He basked in the force of her appraisal. "I never took you for a revolutionary," she said finally.

He tightened his embrace to pull her closer. "Do you love me for it?" he asked softly.

"No." She pushed away from him. "I won't lie to you. There isn't a man I've met here who—I don't know—I just feel like they're all so—"

"So predictable," he said glumly. "I know. You've said it often enough. Even that hot-tempered asteroid miner you left me for last year?"

She winced. "Don't throw it in my face. You're worth ten of him."

"You didn't think so then."

She shrugged, embarrassed. "He had his—good qualities. But even a short temper becomes predictable after a while."

The admission brought a faint smile to his lips. "At least I'm not alone. The only man I've never heard you condemn with that quality is Master Heredes."

"Of course not. But Master Heredes isn't—"

He gave a short, ironic laugh. "Master Heredes isn't the kind of person who propositions, or gets propositioned. Even if one was tempted."

"*Are* people tempted?" Lily asked, abruptly curious. "I guess after all these years as his student, it had never occurred to me. I'm not sure why."

"Perhaps his unpredictability isn't unpredictable enough for your tastes."

"Oh, Finch! Maybe he's just too important to me as my

sensei. Hoy. And I *do* like you better for it, for what you're doing. I mean that."

He sighed and let her stand up. "I'm going to regret this," he said, turning to the console. "Go shower yourself and your clothes. I'll see if the booter who's going up in half a rev will take you. But only to Station, mind." He caught her movement toward him in his peripheral vision. "Don't say it," he said hastily, "because you won't mean it." She stopped. "Just go clean up."

Almost half a rev later she and Finch stood, Bach at her feet, by the ramp that led on to the in-system shuttle run by a pair of elderly and extremely well-dressed brothers. Finch handed over her duffel bag, which he had insisted on carrying, and stood somewhat awkwardly in front of her. The wind tugged at their clothes and hair, incessant and strong.

"These two are safe," he said finally. "They'll get you to Station, no problems—you won't be idented or anything. You shouldn't have any problem finding that Captain Cha."

There was a pause.

Lily smiled slightly. "I suppose you mean the problem will be cutting Master Heredes loose. You're sure you don't want to come?"

"Frankly, Lily, I doubt if I would be any use. And Swann said she'd only cover for me for as long as it took me to get you here and back." He shrugged, smiling with a trace of self-mockery.

"Don't underestimate yourself," said Lily softly. "It's your worst fault."

One of the brothers stuck his head out of the hatch and called for her.

She put out a hand to grasp Finch's shoulder, pulled him toward her. He put his arms around her and they embraced, then kissed.

"Is it really my worst fault?" he said into her ear.

"Oh, yes." Lily thrust him gently away from her and picked up her duffel bag. Bach rose, rocked to one side by a gust of wind, and righted to his correct axis. "You do more things well than you think you do."

He smiled, a bit wanly. She stepped onto the ramp. "When will you be back?" he asked quickly.

Lily paused. "I don't know." She felt the medallion lying smooth against her skin under her shirt. The wind whipped her black hair up across one cheek, shifted to strike directly into her face, bringing tears to her eyes. "I don't know," she repeated, gazing out at the high rock walls that sheltered Apron Port, at the distant huddle of buildings that marked the town, the scatter of ships lying still and windswept in their berths, and at Finch, his hair and clothes seeming alive in the air. "Maybe I'll never be back," she said, too softly for him to hear, and she took an abrupt step toward him and hugged him fiercely. He held her, let her go as soon as she relaxed her hold, and she went quickly up the ramp, Bach beside her.

Inside, she turned to watch the ramp retract into the ship, the slow rising of the hatch. Beyond, Finch stood alone, a solitary figure buffeted by the wild air on the field, the distant howl of the wind generators and the shriek of the wind around rocks and buildings accompanying his wave. The hatch shut with a solid click, and she stood sealed in the silence of the shuttle.

One of the brothers appeared. "This way, luv." He led her and Bach to launch chairs behind the pilot seat. "We're lucky to still be running, sure enough," he went on. "The current laws are killing decent commerce, just so Central can run its own monopoly. Do you realize that three small independents I know personally have been forced to booting —ourselves included—not 'cause we like this line of work. But it's better'n the five others who lost their ships and had to turn to Station-hopping, or go to ground, or—worst—to Government Assistance just as if they were no better'n tattoos, all because the greedy elites pretend to govern in the name of all of us"—he strapped himself in and his more taciturn brother began lift-off proceedings—"so indeed we're happy to do the Caennas a favor, them having done so much for us independents, all things considered." He ceased talking because his attention was needed for the launch.

A surge of power, and they were up. Breaking past the

walls of the gorge, the storm hit them like the blow of a trained fighter. They were thrown and wrenched until Lily thought she would lose the quick meal Finch had insisted she eat. But the voluble brother made a few jokes, dispelling her fear, and they passed the cloud layer and arrived in the calm of the high atmosphere.

"Nice 'bot," observed the taciturn brother, glancing back at Bach, whose lights had all gone off during the turmoil. A single orange light winked on. Lily agreed mildly.

" 'So appear the blessed children, prisoners, and guardians of the Void,' " said the voluble brother. The screens that covered the shuttle's windshield rolled back.

Lily gasped.

Stars. A million. A myriad. Astonishing. The sky, which was never anything but clouds on Unruli, was black, strewn with an infinity of brilliant points of light.

"This must be your first time up," said the voluble one.

"Ten years ago I came up to Station," said Lily softly, still transfixed. "I was fifteen. I ran away from home."

"Didn't get far," remarked the taciturn one.

"I got as far as Remote," she said. "But I never forgot this."

Bach began to sing, softly,

Wie wunderbarlich ist doch diese Strafe!—

"How miraculous indeed is this punishment!"

Static on the radio, and a disembodied voice cut in with numbers.

"Ah, there's Station on," said the voluble brother. "We'll be there faster'n you can say your periodic table."

"Hoy," Lily said in a breath, staring at the stars.

4   Station

❋❋❋❋❋❋❋

The radio traffic, Lily soon discovered, had nothing to do with them, except as a guide to avoid Security as they approached Station.

Of the three small moons that orbited Unruli, one had been found to be large enough and stable enough to house the interlacing spread of Station. Here cargoes came up from Unruli or, routed through Tagalong, from the asteroid belt on in-system ships and were transferred to the highroad merchanters or the unmanned lowroad freighters for the haul between systems. Here news and information, personal communications, and government edicts were, for Security reasons or for astonishingly high prices, loaded into the occasional military cruiser and sent through windows at vectors only highly trained personnel on the best ships could risk, so the news could arrive at the next systems before the fastest merchanter would dare to. Here lived folk who by biology or prejudice could not exist on the world below. Here, on the fringes, the old areas long since left to decay, the poor and the unemployed and the desperate eked out a life separated from vacuum by the thinnest of patched walls. Here, beyond the reach of Security mostly because Security could not be bothered by an organism that would, if driven to ground, only spring up somewhere else, the booters landed, using their wits rather than the Portmaster's controllers.

The elderly brothers landed swiftly and, despite the pronounced jar at impact, efficiently. Lily offered to help offload their cargo; they refused. They did, however, request Bach's assistance in clearing up a small matter—not illegal, they assured her—on Station's mainline computer, and in return detailed for her a variety of shortcuts that would make her trip through Station quicker and more unobtrusive. She left alone to find the Portmaster's office.

As she waited in the port lock, it occurred to her that if the Sar hadn't sent her to Heredes's Academy after that attempt at running away, she might have been back here long ago. She smiled ruefully. The lock coughed and jerked open onto a scene quite unlike that brief glimpse of Station she remembered from ten years ago. But, of course, she had come nowhere near *this* area then.

Each elongated finger of Station consisted of a public corridor allowing access to shops, offices, housing, docking facilities, and warehouses. Lily remembered the constant hum of machines and a quiet background of humans and pygmies and the occasional sta moving with purpose and order from dock to shop to office.

Now, stepping over the bulkhead into the corridor, Lily smelled first: the odor of rotting food kept for too long in a closed area. Heard the pandemonium of life occasionally broken by the shrilling of a machine or the hiccuping jolts of an ill-repaired motor.

Directly across from her, plastine two-by-fours boarded up the entrance to a shop; faded letters peeled off from the wall. Nearby, a lean-to of scrap metal jutted out into the corridor. Children, their faces colored in wild patterns with tattoos, gawked at her. A woman sat in a stain of wetness, singing in a loud, tuneless voice. Blue-and-orange checks patterned her hands and arms. A disfiguring burn that covered her left eye and cheek and ear marred the broader pattern on her face. Two men and a woman, dressed in identical cheap synthetics, spat on the woman as they passed her and paused to eye Lily with curiosity. Tattooed children cowered as the three walked on down the corridor. A tattooed shopkeeper, arms and legs a riot of purple swirls, bobbed up and down in a frenzy of bowing as the trio halted by him. One of the men spoke; something changed hands; they went on.

"Hoy." Lily turned to go in the same direction. "They could have warned me." She stepped carefully over a pile of filthy rags, shifted to avoid the weaving path of a man whose face was mottled with blue dots and a suppurating rash, and made her way down the corridor. Litter lay strewn across the street. Children picked through it. Under a ripped and dirty awning, scrawny adolescents, dressed in clothing that revealed the elaboration of tattooed decoration on their bodies, beckoned to Lily as she passed.

The lock into the next section was closed. She shifted from one foot to the other. Two dark alleys, shortcuts, branched off on either side of the seal. The lock blinked green; she stepped in and waited in the five-meter-square dead zone as it shut, repressurized—a moment of lightness as the gravity field switched placement—and opened into the next section.

Like the other, this section curved away, alleys, shabby storefronts, and docking entrances breaking the dull sheen of wall. The untattooed trio she had seen before stood ahead at the curve, surrounding a tattooed woman who seemed to be pleading with them. As Lily approached she saw the woman give a handful of beads to one of the men. Again they paused to glance at Lily before they went on. The tattooed woman, weeping, ran into her shop.

Lily came to the lock. A tattooed man in poor but neat clothing bowed to her from his storefront. Behind him, a clean child swept under the awning, careful with the orderly display of homewares. Lily smiled at the man, and he smiled back, bobbing again, as the lock opened and she stepped in with two other people.

Immediately she saw a difference. The storefronts onto the next corridor were lit and in good repair, and each establishment name was suffixed by the official section number, F1. And at least half these people were not tattooed. For the first time, she saw the occasional black-and-gray uniform of Security personnel.

In section F2, a few of the businesses had signs: "No tattoos allowed." "Ridani *not* spoken here." Machines droned in the background. One front advertised a school, another a medical clinic.

In the next lock, a good dozen people passed through with Lily to the main sections. Five brightly dressed pygmies, their two-fingered, two-clawed hands waving frantically in the air as they talked, hurried into a well-lit alley that would lead, Lily knew, to one of the low-gravity sections where they lived. Two women sat conversing at a street-side café, a thin tattooed girl standing behind them holding their packages. A cargo robot motored carefully down the corridor. With her neat tunic and trousers and clear skin, Lily rated scarcely a passing glance. The one tattooed girl who walked alone up the street, not carrying anything, was stared at. Even the pygmies, barely a meter tall, with their half-human, half-birdlike features, were considered commonplace.

In the next section at least four corridors thrust out from a main square. A small computer gazebo in the center displayed, after several transactions, a map of Station. Lily cast a quick eye over the berth arrangements, laid out numerically by sections; the zones she had first come through were labeled as "abandoned" and not referenced for docking at all. A distinctive sign marked Portmaster's office.

Section A3, like all sections that housed government sections, had a high incidence of the black-and-gray Security uniforms. Portmaster's office adjoined the central square and by itself took up an area as wide as a street. All manner of folk stood in line at the Permits counter. Others sat, patient but noisy, on plastine benches. Along one wall, the arrival and departure and assignment lists scrolled past on huge screens. Lily unclipped her com-screen from her belt and found an open plug-in on the wall. Next to her a long-limbed sta, dressed in expensive silks whose color complemented the rust sheen of her scalelike skin, cursed in a fluid undertone as unwanted information came up on her screen. Her clipped and tied mane shook with suppressed emotion.

Lily queried for the berth and departure time of the ship

that had left with Heredes. The screen went blank while
memory was searched. For all she knew, they had gone on
to Tagalong, skipping Station entirely. She would never be
able to pick up their trail. But numbers rolled up on the
screen, and there it was. The right ident, listed on the Apron
Port log, with—and she smiled—a complaint of unauthorized launch duly logged against them by Caenna Harbormaster (H. F. Caenna, controller on duty). Perhaps the
complaint had forced them to land at Station to receive
clearance directly for a jump window out of system. Whatever the reason, they were there, berthed at M2–11, no
departure time listed. And at Station, where ships in the
official sections were manacled into place as a safety measure—so regulations stated—it was impossible to leave without authorization.

Lily logged off. Beside her, the sta still punched numbers
in, her double-thumbed, four-fingered hand fluent on the
keys, and received unacceptable replies.

The M2 berths lay in a stretch of corridor that housed
docks and warehouses. The double doors of one warehouse
stood open, revealing a hive of silent activity within, pygmies sorting with almost telepathic cooperation through a
cargo. At berth 5 two copper-skinned sta towered above a
woman dressed in the tunic and belt of a mercenary. They
acknowledged Lily as she passed and returned to their lighthearted conversation. The rest of the odd-numbered berths
were vacant; green "free" lights advertised space. Two people passed Lily. A cleaning unit backed out of a berth several doors farther along. But at berth 11, Lily saw just the
orange "occupied" light, the smooth blankness of the closed
lock doors, and the com-panel empty of message or request.

Had she really thought it would be so easy? That she had
only to present herself at their door and they would hand
Heredes over to her, recognizing her superior claims? Or
that, finding an open, unguarded lock, she could walk onto
the ship and free him? She realized now that she had never
considered what she would do if she found the ship.

The orange light glowed a steady negative at her. She
smiled. She would just have to storm them—sometimes

speed and surprise was the only tactic when the enemy had the better defensive position. If she was lucky, some of them might be stuck in line at the Portmaster's office. But they wouldn't be there forever. She needed Bach. She had to act now.

She took the shortcuts back, narrow alleyways that snaked between the outstretched arms of Station. She had to backtrack to the K5 section before she found the first short-cut; damp and smelling of mold, it led her in a low, dark arc to section B7. A handful of makeshift seals branched off it into unimaginable dwellings, so close to vacuum that each movement must seem an invitation to disaster.

Another alley led from B6 to G2, a short run from there from G4 to F4. In F4, three alleys branched out into dim-ness. She took the central one, found herself touching moist walls that gave beneath her hands. The floor was rough and broken. Here, where the corridors widened or where some hastily patched break had left space off the main path, peo-ple huddled, whispering, trading, watching. In the low light, Lily saw the telltale dapplings of tattoos.

The corridor she entered was unnumbered and unnamed. But from here just one last alley would bring her to the section where she had landed.

The alley was old, broad, and inhabited. Once she stum-bled over a child, lying in a shadowed patch of the path. After that she went more slowly. A low, cracked voice begged for a drink. Far ahead, someone screamed. A family had gathered in an open seal that led into a patchworked hovel of one room, plastine ribbing covering old leaks. Bunks crowded two walls; at the third stood a low altar. When they saw Lily, they slid the seal shut. The green phos-phorous torches that usually lit, however poorly, the alleys gave way to the inconstant flickering of red. Lily could scarcely see her hands. The screaming, half-sobs now, sounded from just beyond the corner. She paused.

Sounds of a struggle, but an unequal one. Someone strik-ing someone else. A determined but useless resistance. Threats: prison, rape, death.

Lily came around the corner. In the first instant she saw

three thugs beating and kicking and ripping the clothes off a child. In the second instant she saw that it was a girl, profusely tattooed, and that the child was fighting with all the frenzy of hopeless panic.

"—think you're too good for this kind of work," said the man nearest Lily as he struck the girl across the face. "Getting above yourself, I'd say." He saw Lily.

She took him out cleanly, before he could react, doubling him over with a kick, striking to the head. He fell heavily to the floor. The tattooed girl shrieked and bit the arm of the woman who was holding her. The other man, jumping back, drew a short blade.

"Let her go," said Lily.

The woman kicked the girl in the ribs, jerking her arm away, and launched herself at Lily. Lily sidestepped and pushed her into the wall, on the same beat spun backward and kicked the knife out of the other man's hand. He hesitated. Lily snapped a kick hard into his groin. As he doubled up, grunting, she drove a final kick up into his chin— "Let the momentum go through your target," Heredes would say—and felt the impact, the shattering of bone. With a high scream of pain, the man fell in a heap clutching his jaw.

The girl had grabbed the knife; now she shouted a warning. Lily felt a hand grip her shoulder; she spun into it with an elbow straight to the woman's face, and with her hips still turning, a punch solid to the belly. The woman fell, retching.

Lily grabbed the girl's arm, pulling her to her feet. "Come on," she said.

"Shouldna we—" The girl gestured with the knife. The first man shifted on the ground; the woman caught her breath.

"Run," said Lily, and she ran, tugging the girl along behind her.

They had to push through a group of onlookers. None hindered them, but Lily did not stop until they came out of the alley into the wild disorder of the corridor. She let go of the girl's arm and strolled as if undisturbed toward the berth

the brothers had put into. The girl followed two steps behind her. When they came to an awning that sheltered three
children and a rack of knee-length tunics, Lily paused, un-
clipping her com-screen.

"Now," she said. "I'll buy you something to replace that
—" She halted, staring.

The girl stood in the corner of the shop's portico, shielding herself as well as she could from the street. She had
stuck the knife under her belt and with both hands held
together her torn shift to cover her abdomen and breasts.
The three children had run into the shop, so the girl stood
alone under the incandescence of a lighting tube.

She was beautiful, despite, or perhaps because of, the
branching intricacy of the tattoos on her face and body. She
had that peculiar transparent loveliness that can settle on
the most unlikely adolescents, giving them an uncanny quality of perfection. An edge of cloth slipped to reveal the budding swell of a breast, swirled with the yellow and rose and
soft green pattern that marked her throat and face.

"That were fast," said the girl in a matter-of-fact voice
that held no self-consciousness.

"What was?"

"That fight were. Whoosh, and gone."

"It seemed slow to me." Lily looked pointedly at the rack
of clothing. "We'd better get you some new clothes."

"Why?" said the girl.

"You can't go around in something that's ripped to
pieces—"

"Why'd you help me?" The girl's voice had a husky quality much older than her years.

"I couldn't let them—" Lily faltered. "Whatever they
meant to do."

"They meant to sell me to ya man from B run, as a bed
girl. But I wouldna have it."

"*Sell* you? That's against the law."

The girl regarded Lily with disbelief. "Sure, it be against
ya law. Be you supposing that ya Security bothers to protect
us tattoos?" She shook her head, a wise old soul marking the
illusions of the innocent.

Lily, abashed, and knowing that it was perfectly true that prejudice against the Ridanis extended to a double standard in protecting them from such abuses, looked away.

"Anyways," Paisley continued defiantly, "I got my pride. I mean to be ya technician."

This choice of vocation surprised Lily enough that she glanced up, appraising the girl. "Better you than me."

Now the girl looked surprised. "You don't think it be loony?"

"No, I don't. Though I don't suppose it will be easy. Now would you choose one of these tunics?"

"Sure," said the girl cheerfully, stepping forward to thumb through the rack, drawing out immediately the most expensive sleeveless tunic. "You can call me Paisley. I like ya one."

"Fine," said Lily. The shopkeeper came out, the transfer of credits quickly accomplished. Paisley, meanwhile, had changed garments by the simple expedient of putting the new one on over the old and ripping the old one off until it lay in tatters around her feet. The knife had disappeared.

"Sure." She smoothed the fabric down with one hand. "I do like this."

"I have to go," said Lily. "Can you get back to your family all right?"

Instantly the stubborn expression settled in the girl's face. "Don't have none," she declared. "Turned me out. See, I got as much time in ya eddication networks as I could sneak, and I tested and got ya good enough marks to get me into ya school, but ya school said it be not fitting for ya tattoo to set in ya same room with ya unmarked students. Sure, and supposing thems parents were to find out—wouldna none of thems be coming back to ya school after it be known ya tattoo were allowed in."

Lily winced. "I'm sorry. I really am. It's wrong. But I have to go. Will you be all right?"

"Sure." Paisley pulled at one of the crop of bead-encrusted braids that surrounded her face. "I be going with you."

"You can't go with me."

"You in trouble? I know every way around here."

Lily raised her hands, lowered them. "I'm sorry, Paisley. Good-bye." She turned and walked away down the corridor.

Paisley followed her, padding along three meters behind, not at all chastened. By pretending to be going on and breaking suddenly into the lock, Lily managed to get the door shut before Paisley could react. She saw, briefly, a look so close to desolation on the girl's face as the door slid to that she almost reopened the lock then and there, feeling that she had somehow succumbed to the same prejudice that oppressed the Ridanis throughout the Reft.

But she needn't have worried. When she reappeared with Bach and her duffel bag, Paisley had not moved. The girl's face brightened when she saw Lily, shifting to astonishment as Bach floated out behind.

"Sure," she breathed, staring at the robot. "And glory."

"Hoy," said Lily. "Okay. Get me to M2 as fast as you can. I'll pay you for it."

The girl stiffened. "It ain't payment. It ain't right to offer me credit. It be poor of you." Then, seeing that she had caught Lily off-guard, she smiled. "So come on. I can get you there in three alleys. Quick as ya vacuum through ya leak."

"Pleasant thought," muttered Lily.

"But you got to introduce me."

"Introduce you?"

"To ya 'bot."

"His name is Bach. Can we go?"

Paisley made a solemn movement halfway between a bow and a curtsey. "Much pleased, min Bach. I be Paisley." Bach winked lights and made a muted response. "And you?" She looked at Lily.

"My name's Ransome. Now are you going to show us or not?"

"Sure," replied Paisley, cheerful again. "Just got to get all squared between us, min Ransome. Seeing as you saved my kinnas and now got my service. Till it be returned, a'course."

"Your kinnas?"

But Paisley was already off.

She traveled at a run. For one so slender, she had remarkable stamina. Bach had trouble keeping up, and in the locks, he invariably lost his equilibrium and rolled upside down. It did indeed take only three alleys—the longest of which was completely empty, barely lit, and resonant with low hisses and echoing footsteps—one inconvenience with four Security personnel, and two importunate drug dealers to reach M2 section and berth 11. The entire corridor was deserted.

"Night cycle," said Paisley succinctly as she stared at berth 11's com-panel. "Why you want in here?"

A muffled beep sounded, and the light on the panel changed to yellow.

"Hoy," breathed Lily. She whistled a brief command to Bach. He skimmed out to the far wall, opposite the lock. Lily edged out along the wall. When Paisley began to follow, she halted, turning her head.

"Get to the other side," Lily hissed. "I'm going in."

The tattooed girl nodded. "What for?"

"A man."

"Sure," said the girl, her eyes wide with excitement and understanding. She pushed away from the wall and darted down the corridor.

Another beep; the lock door began to open. Lily stepped out away from the wall and moved closer to the opening lock as if she were simply a passerby. The quick, low exchange of two people conversing sifted out on the air, and one stepped out.

At such close quarters, it—he?—was incontrovertibly alien, as tall as a sta but much thinner, pallid with the suggestion of colors under the skin. Scant yellow hair, not quite like hair, crowned him. He was nothing she had ever seen before.

His glance, sweeping the corridor, seized up abruptly and obviously on Bach. He spoke words to someone unseen behind him and fell into a crouch. From his side he drew some weapon. Aimed it at Bach.

Lily threw herself on him, knocking him down; as they both fell, she flung herself onto one shoulder and rolled in a somersault up to her feet. He lay sprawled, reaching for his gun. Paisley darted forward, grabbed the weapon, and ran on. Lily turned, to face the doorway, turned—

A force like a solid wall of wind struck her. It spun her around as if an arm had shoved her back and sideways. She saw a tall, painfully thin figure in the lock door, weapon in hand. There was a piercing brilliance and a cry from Paisley. Bach began to sing. A hammer came down on her like a fall of rocks and she knew nothing more.

5 Paisley's Story

****

Lily woke to the sound of her own voice, a faint, peculiar counterpoint to the dull ache in her head.

". . . nevertheless this matter of gathering firewood for the school remained unresolved," she heard herself say.

"What be firewood?" asked a new voice.

Lily sat up, immediately regretted it. "Ah," she said—felt herself say this time—bringing a hand to her forehead.

"Min Ransome!" The second voice raised considerably, a lance aggravating the pain. "Want ya water?"

"Quiet," said Lily. Reconsidered the phrase. "I want quiet." About four meters away, leaning against the opposite wall, sat Paisley. She held a metal flask in one hand as if frozen in the act of handing it over. Next to her hovered Bach. He rotated a quarter-turn and sang a muted question.

"My head hurts," replied Lily. "But I think I'm all here."

"I got ya food and water," whispered Paisley. "Might help."

"Hoy," said Lily, but she reached and took containers from the girl and drank and ate. Bach and Paisley waited, patient as only robots, those long used to poverty, and true hunters can be.

Lily rose gently to her feet and paced out their cell. About four meters by four meters of grey wall, so high ceilinged that it seemed out of proportion. A door-shaped seam was in one wall, with a recessed control panel next to it, encased behind plastine. She sat down finally and looked at Bach.

"I didn't know you could do that," she said.

A rising second from Bach.

"Do what?" asked Paisley.

Lily took another drink from the flask. "My voice."

Bach sang, *Thy voice know I best.*

"What'd he say?" asked Paisley.

"Sure," said Bach, the girl's voice now, "and glory."

Paisley shrieked and started away from him, then giggled.

Lily whistled a long phrase.

"What'd that mean?" demanded Paisley. "If he kin talk, why's he make ya music? Why don't you just talk to him?"

Bach sang back to Lily and she smiled faintly, looking at Paisley. Against the grey monotony, the girl's tattoos seemed muted. "At first, when I found Bach, it was the only way we had to communicate. By the music. Later of course I discovered he knew Standard, and he got into the computers, and it would have been easier, sure it would have, but less of a challenge. And much less efficient for Bach."

"Oke," said Paisley, trying to look wise. "Maybe, I guess."

"Consider this," continued Lily, "it keeps me sharp, staying in that kind of practice. And the two of us can communicate and no one else can understand us."

"Sure." The girl found firm ground here. "Like ya hand talk. No one else knows."

"Right." Paisley beamed like a student just given the day's gold star. "After all," Lily finished, "the extra effort gives you the advantage."

Paisley nodded sagely, surveying Bach with a more calculating eye. "Once we scam here, we could haul ya fast imperial."

Bach sang, *If thou pleasest, couldst thou translate?*

"Does that mean theft?" asked Lily.

"Oke much!" said Paisley, growing enthusiastic. "With min Bach we could run ya real—" She faltered. Bach was singing in a dissonant key to Lily, who frowned. "I didn't mean it!" cried Paisley. "I just—" She caught her breath. "I really do want to be ya tech. Honest lock. Not nothing else. Glory hang me if it ain't true."

Lily blinked. "I believe you. It just occurred to me that to —ah—scam this place we might have to burglarize our way out. Out of wherever we are. Both of you"—her gaze fixed them together—"I need a complete description of everything that happened. Everything you saw, or think you saw, or heard."

"We be gone," said Paisley. "You went down, min Bach went all bright, so I couldna see. One of ya boyos grabbed me and I couldna shake loose and he dragged me in." She appeared, for an instant, forlorn, but her face brightened. "But I lit fussy, sure," she concluded.

The young lady did most commendably bite, kick, scratch, and scream. God in Heaven alone knoweth what alarms her commotion raised down the section. As thou wast interred within the vessel, it seemed most prudent to me to follow. At this time seven Kapellan crew members arrived at the lock.

Lily whistled for an interruption, and Bach closed his phrase elegantly. "What did you call them?"

They register to the description of Kapellans, an alien sentient bipedal species native to a star system near the one which humans once referred to in the common Terran usage as Kapella. However, according to all current information in my data banks, their presence in this sector of space is anomalous, therefore—He halted abruptly midphrase.

The ship shifted like a great animal beneath them. Bach rolled slightly in the air. Paisley lunged out with a hand to steady herself. The watch call echoed above them, three short chimes, one long one, and a brief spoken phrase.

Vectoring to window, sang Bach. *Thou desirest estimate?*

"Yes."

I transpose. Window transition will occur in twelve minutes.

"What's for eating?" Paisley's attempt at a calm voice failed. She had shrunk against the wall, one hand tugging her shift in an unconscious gesture down over her wildly patterned knees.

"We're going over," said Lily grimly. "I can't have been out that long. They must have got to Tagalong. Hoy. They must have power."

"We on ya road?" Paisley's eyes widened. "I never thought."

Bach sank down to the grey floor next to Lily.

You mentioned them before. She put a hand on his cold metal surface. "Kapellans." She tried the word slowly in speech.

"What?" Paisley pushed herself upright and walked across the cell to sit beside Lily.

"Imperial class ship," Lily muttered. "Anomalous. This sector—sector?—of space. Therefore what, Bach?"

Therefore data doth not compute. Thou wilst find nevertheless that it alone fits the required specifications.

There was a silence. Paisley pulled a comb out from her mass of braids and, unraveling a slender plait near one ear, combed the hair out, a cupped hand holding loosed beads, and began braiding it again.

"What happened after we were all in the lock?" asked Lily.

"See," said Paisley, her deft fingers unslacking in their task, "we was all on, so I stopped fussing and started looking. Ya boyos didna like me much. They let me go and herded me, much as they could. Just corridors, smaller'n Station. Closed doors. I counted, though. I could scam us out easy as frilled back, honest lock. Didna hear naught. Saw three of ya boyos in different clothes off to one place. None more. They tossed us here. Bit later we hooked off from Station. Noisy, that. And here we be."

Bach's description was more detailed, if about as succinct. He had monitored color changes, heat patterns, sound referents. He had found one clue: using his internal lights he shone a map of the ship on the grey floor. Paisley oohed gratifyingly and traced their route for Lily. Bach, diverted, complimented her on her sense of direction.

And? prompted Lily.

Here. (A green light.) *Through one closed hatchway not*

immune to heat sense awareness—he began to digress on Kapellan optical sensory evolution; Lily cut off this variation—*was a human pattern.*

Then these Kapellans aren't human?

Negative.

And this pattern?

Definitely human. Enclosed in such a cell, seemingly, as thou and I and the child.

You can sense through this seal? She looked to the seam in the grey wall.

Certainly. I am, as thou seest, equipped to mimic most sentient sensing patterns, in this case infrared heat patterning.

Is anyone out there? Lily stood abruptly, walked over to the seam.

Negative.

She turned and walked to the other side of the cell, walked back.

"What you be talking about?" Paisley demanded.

"We're being held by aliens, who are evidently called Kapellans. And I believe the man I'm seeking is on board this ship, too."

The ship jolted; chimes echoed above. Paisley fell forward. Bach rolled almost half over, and he began to sing an incomprehensible melody. Lily kept her feet.

They went through.

She saw the kata whole. The moves branched out in a lattice into infinity, but simultaneously came to rest at their beginning—finite circle of endlessness. The finger bent just so, the wrist, the angle of the knee here, the window made by the hands: "to look at the sky."

Die Kunst der Fuge. Countersubject. B-A-C-H. Ah. So it is finished.

The universe patterns. Energy without end. We dance, each from birth. Each dance patterns uniquely. Each pattern so marks its subject/owner/object/worshipper. The colors move on the body as the body moves. The pattern defies stillness. Such do we pattern you, child, so you may understand. Learn your pattern. Wear it proudly.

And came out.

First, the silence of reorientation. Lily still stood, centered, and her hands began to move, rising together. She sighed and dropped them. Paisley, flung onto the floor, gasped and pushed herself up to sit again. Bach had righted himself; now he sang quietly, *Vom Himmel hoch da komm' ich her!*

"Where are we?" said Paisley in a very small voice.

Lily crouched beside the girl, laying a hand on her shoulder. "If we go over again, we'll be coming into Remote. But if we're coming into system now, it's Dairy. I don't care how much power these spooks have, it's got to be one or the other."

"Spooks?" ventured Paisley.

Lily sat back on her heels. "You've never been downside, on planet?"

"Never."

"Hoy." Lily stood and paced back to the seal.

"See," said Paisley, "we can't go much of anywhere."

"We?"

Paisley lifted her arms. The tattoos twined in their vivid pattern down flesh, lost themselves under her tunic.

Lily sighed and turned her head toward the opposite wall. "Spooks? Funny word." Paisley waited.

"It's a thing, a creature; we also call it Boo, the ghost. It lived down there on Unruli before ever we came. So we call anything funny or weird that, people sometimes, but mostly just—well, those things, they're nothing like us. Folk say they capture the souls of dead people. Who knows if they have any awareness at all."

Paisley sighed, an unconscious mimic, and dropped her chin to rest on one fist. Lily walked to the door.

When they came out of the berth, it was you they recognized. She turned to gaze at Bach. *You they stopped for. They knew you. But no one* here *knows you.* With one hand she drew her hair back, let it fall forward. *What did you mean, another sector of space?*

Bach sang a gentle end to his piece, paused. His lights winked, and a spray of bright points of light scattered around him, spreading on the floor as he rose higher above it. *Thou, my patroness, didst commission me in this district.* A light blinked red. Paisley slipped back as the pattern spread, staring at it in awe. *My calculations indicate we have appeared here.* (A blue light.) *Or here.* (A second blue light.)

Where is Central?

"It be ya star map!" cried Paisley.

Data incomplete. My investigations indicate thy sphere of trade encompasseth limited regional boundaries. Navigation links nonexistent beyond such sphere.

"You been telling me," said Paisley, " 'bout growing up. Where be you born?"

At first neither Lily nor Paisley saw the two green lights flash. But when the section of stars they were looking at made no change, their eyes roved further afield.

"Impossible," said Lily.

"Sure," said Paisley in a breath, "and glory."

Where do you think this ship came from? asked Lily. *You said before, the common*—she hesitated over the unusual pattern of notes—Terran *usage.*

A new light, yellow, winked on closer to the green ones than the blues and red, but still far—almost the cell's width —from either. Bach had risen high enough now that the scattered points filled the floor, dappling Lily and Paisley.

"Paradise," breathed Paisley.

"Who?" Lily turned to the girl.

Paisley began to sing in a high, slightly nasal voice:

> *Ya Dancer hae, he come, he come,*
> *Tae lead us far, tae home, tae home.*
> *Lost we are, belly down day,*
> *Through ya mountains winds ya way.*

She paused, regarded for a long, silent moment some aspect
of the tattoos on her right arm. "But no one knows ya way
no more. Ya way back."

"No one knows ya way," echoed Lily.

Paisley's expression cleared. "You know ya story, too?"

Lily shook her head. "I don't know it. Is it a Ridani
story?"

"Sure. It be ya story about how ya people, us *tattoos*"—
she spoke the word like it was a curse—"come to be here.
Long ago, there be ya place where many o' ya people lived
in sore poverty. Not so much different, really. And ya govinment wanted to be rid o' them—allays has, here or there,
cause they never understood ya patterning." She lifted a
colorful hand as if in illumination. "But there be no way, as
ya people be too poor to go elsewheres, despite wishing for
ya better home. Until Dancer come. He were one o' us, you
see, but graced with ya power to see farther into ya pattern.
Ya story starts with him."

"Tell us," said Lily.

Paisley's voice changed, took on a deeper, even huskier
tone.

> *Dancer come took his folk out*
> *Morning bright-o day,*
> *Said, "Follow my pattern," hey come ho*
> *Sun shine bright-o morning.*
>
> *Folk they had not one day's bread*
> *Morning bright-o day*
> *Nor job nor rooftop hey come ho*
> *Sun shine bright-o morning.*
>
> *Dancer say, "We go on ya road"*
> *Morning bright-o day*
> *"Tae green grass land come" hey come ho*
> *Sun shine bright-o morning.*

She smiled, pausing. "It be ya long tale."

"Go on," urged Lily.

Paisley took a deep breath. "Ya folk certain wanted ya green grass land, but they be scared o' ya lowroad. *'Cold as night's breath,'* it be. *'Still as death's hand.'* Dancer, he fell wrath and sore, cause they said they never go on ya ships. So he curse them with ya old grey flat. It be ya worst place o' all to live. Death and sickness and ya babes crying all day for milk."

"And what happened?"

Paisley began again in her husky singsong, punctuating her words with stylized hand movements.

> *Now up then spoke min Bonny's child*
> *Morning dim-dark way*
> *Jehanna said, "No danger here"*
> *"Sun is up, come morning."*

> *Folk they heartened to her voice*
> *Morning bright-o day*
> *Come they back to ya lowroad ships*
> *Sun shine bright-o morning.*

> *Jehanna she caught Dancer's eye*
> *Morning bright-o day*
> *He promise green grass land once more*
> *Sun shine bright-o morning.*

"So they go there," said Lily.

"Sure," said Paisley. "Dancer, he led them on ya lowroad. He be caught by Jehanna, lift her up and now he wish her to pattern with him. Bless be. But Jehanna turn round her bright head, speak out proud. Refuse him. See, she never wanted ya man. She wanted ya green grass land."

"What did Dancer do?"

"Sure, now *there* be ya story." The pinpoint lights speckled them, slipping in and out of Paisley's tattoos as if they had always been part of her pattern.

> *Now grew he fierce now grew he cold*
> *Morning dim-dark way*

Never she wavered hey come ho
Sunlight dims, dark morning.

Now cast he folk out on lowroad
Morning dim-dark way
And lost they wandered hey come ho
Sunlight dims, dark morning.

Jehanna led them far and cold
Morning dim-dark way
Till came they here come hey come ho
Sunlight dimmed, dark morning.

"And never shall you come back," he cried
Morning dim-dark way
"Never in green grass land abide"
Sunlight dimmed, dark morning.

"Not till Jehanna gets child by me"
Morning dim-dark way
"And our son grows tae lead you back"
Sun shine dim-dark morning.

Now live we far from green grass land
Morning dim-dark way
But Jehanna's proud come hey come ho
Sun it brings the morning.

Jehanna she'll get Dancer's child
Morning bright-o day
Jehane she'll call him hey come ho
Sun shine bright-o morning.

We'll come one day tae green grass land
Morning bright-o day
When Jehane he dance us down ya way
Sun shine bright-o morning.

The girl lowered her hands first, like the settling of waves, then let her breath out in a long sigh that filled the room. She looked up at Lily. "So ya people be waiting," she said in her normal voice. "Till Jehane come to dance us down to ya place where we can live without being hated and poor."

Lily raised a hand to brush at her eyes. "It's a very sad story, Paisley."

"Sad?" Paisley looked confused, glancing at Bach, who still hovered silently above, as if for corroboration. "It ain't sad. You only grow patience by waiting for ya ship what may only come for ya great-grandchildren. That be ya way it be."

"I suppose it made me think of my parent's House, in a way," Lily said, almost to herself. "I never belonged there. Maybe some people can't ever find their true homes. Or don't recognize them when they find them." She studied the winking spread of lights across the floor.

"Sometimes you got to lose it first," said Paisley. "To know what it were."

But Lily was now staring at the lights. "It fits!" she exclaimed. She whistled to Bach. The robot flashed a series of lights on his surface, singing, and the projection vanished.

"What'd you say?"

"I said I knew he was old, but I didn't know he was as old as all that."

"As all what?"

"Well." Bach drifted down to the level of Lily's head, a soft melody accompanying her explanation. "You know yourself from your story that we all came here—except the sta, of course—from a place a long ways away, a long time ago."

"Tirra-li," said Paisley. "But no one knows ya way back no more."

"That's right. Terra. And no one does know, any more, how to get back." Lily frowned. "Could you get back there, Bach, given a ship?"

Negative. Data incomplete.

"No one kin get back," repeated Paisley stubbornly. "Ya first highroaders, they tried. But ya way be haunted now, with ya old ghost ship, lost forever. And it be sure horrible torment if ya ghost ship find you looking on ya old way."

Lily smiled. "I don't know if I think it's haunted, but it's sure lost. At least to us."

"And who not to? Central'd be happy as if kin to be rid of us." Paisley paused and with a mutinous expression lifted one patterned hand to touch a patterned face. "Us tattoos."

"Then where did these aliens come from? If what Bach says is true."

Paisley, much struck by this point, lowered her hand and said nothing.

Lily resumed her pacing. "Hoy. Bach must have been sitting in that garage for ages."

"Don't min Bach know?"

"He was deactivated. It's all a—ah—blank. It was pure chance I activated him at all, anyway."

Paisley rose and went over to where Bach hovered, laying a hand on his cool, hard surface. "Sure," she said. "You tingle." She looked at Lily. "Min Bach, he ain't like other 'bots. He be smart. I mean, real smart, not fake smart."

Several of Bach's lights winked. "Thank you, Miss Paisley," he replied in Lily's voice. Paisley giggled and patted him.

Stop that, Bach, Lily whistled. *Use a different voice, please.*

Forgive me, patroness. Thy voice and the child's are the only voices I have had leisure to study at enough length to reproduce.

Forgiven, whistled Lily, and she came over and touched him. He began, softly, a sweet hymn. "We'll have to find him someone else's voice to study," Lily said to Paisley.

"Ah," said Paisley wisely. "What about ya spooks?"

"Ya spooks," said Lily. She began pacing out the circumference of the cell, as if she were a moving wall around the girl and the robot. "I've never heard or seen anything like them before. They have enough energy to waste on non-premium windows. They have—by the Void—aircars. And Bach says they shouldn't be here. If that map—" She halted. "If they came over the highroad, to here—maybe, back there, the navigation routes weren't lost. Maybe them, or our old people, from the places we must have come from, maybe they just didn't care, to come here. Too far and too unimportant. Or maybe they couldn't. Or—" Her speculations failed her. "But it explains why they recognized Bach, if he's from back over the long road."

Bach sang, in corroboration, that he was.

"But what kind of threat are you to them?"

It appeareth to me that since I have never met any of their kind before, I must therefore be no threat at all.

"Never?" She frowned. "Then why did they try to shoot you? And in Station, when everyone knows that to shoot in Station—"

"Five terms," Paisley supplied, and at Lily's inquiring look, "It be ya sentence, for lockup, for using ya guns." There was a pause. "Min Ransome," Paisley began again, hesitant now, "be you thinking they mean to kill us?"

"I don't know. Though if they'd meant to you'd think they would have done it by now."

"Reckon they be curious why we be here?" asked Paisley. "Sure, and you did say before that—" She faltered. Lily had suddenly gone very still. Her body mirrored her thoughts, poised, alert, ready to spring. She stared at the opposite wall, as if looking through it to something veiled beyond.

"Heredes," Lily said. "They must know we're after Heredes."

"Who be Heredes?" said Paisley promptly.

"My teacher," Lily replied mechanically. "My sensei. The man we came for."

The watch rang out above them, four short chimes, two long, the alien voice.

Docking procedure. Shall I transpose? sang Bach. *Docking procedures shall commence in twenty-nine minutes. Therefore, according to thine information, we have achieved Dairy system.*

"They came in fast," Lily said. "From window to docking."

Affirmative. What plans dost thou have for our removal from this vessel?

"Sure," said Paisley, "and glory. I never been nowhere but Station. And I told them I'd go over ya highroad some-day. They all laughed."

Lily was still staring at the wall, an unrevealing expanse of grey. "If they're from over the way, why do they want Heredes?" she repeated.

6 Chance on Remote

✳✳✳✳✳✳

Paisley had not exaggerated in calling the docking noisy. For some reason known only to the aliens, the entire sequence of grappling and coming to, in-ship bells and commands, and ship-station communications went on over the intercom. Loudly. When the noise ceased, as abruptly as if a knife had cut it off, the silence felt like a muffling cloth had been thrown down around them.

"I be hungry," said Paisley softly.

"I'm thirsty," said Lily. She dropped into a crouch beside Bach. *Can we see that plan of the ship again?* It appeared on the floor. "Show me again," she said to Paisley, "how we got here. By what route."

The girl traced it out, and again, until Lily had memorized it.

"No doors or locks to go through? Except this one and the station lock? No lifts? This one here, Bach—it had the other human?" Lily settled on to the floor, legs crossed. "We either have to break for it and hope we're not seen, or grab one for hostage for a safe conduct. Hoy." She whistled, *Bach. Can you get into their com system? Open the door that way?*

Negative. I have not the relevant information on Kapellan computation networks. However, I am in their spoken tongue forty-seven percent fluent according to the specifications of the

Habir-Xu xenographic language index. Dost thou desire its compilation figures?

"I believe you," said Lily.

"How we going to run ya scam?"

"I don't know." Lily inspected the thin seam of the door. "Dairy downside is supposed to be a great place to take the holidays, but Dairy Station—I don't know. It's an orbiter, I guess. Like Remote's. But at least I've been on Remote Station before. I have an idea of the layout, where we can run for."

"You bin on Remote?"

"Just Remote Station. About ten years ago."

"And this couldna be ya Remote?"

Lily smiled slightly. "Not unless they have much more energy *and* the best pilot in Reft space. Far the best. No." She paused, considering. "Paisley, do you still have that knife?"

Paisley seemed, suddenly, to become a statue. Her head froze in the act of turning, the angles of her face shadowless in the diffuse light, her hands still. Then, as if she were stop action thrown into forward, she completed the movement without any obvious self-consciousness and directed a wide-eyed smile at Lily. "What knife?" she said.

"The one," Lily replied, looking straight at her, "that you grabbed off the man I knocked out."

"Sure," said Paisley without hesitation. She reached down the front of her tunic and brought up the knife. "It be ya sharp," she finished, offering it hilt first to Lily.

Lily tossed it in the air a couple of times, held it lightly, testing the balance. "It'll do," she said. Paisley, watching her handle the knife, came to a decision.

"I got ya gun, too," she said, standing up. This time she produced the weapon the first alien had used to shoot at Bach.

"Hoy," breathed Lily, stepping forward to take it from the girl. She held it gingerly. It was a dull grey with unlit controls and a standard structural design. "That must be the trigger," she muttered. "Paisley." The girl started, took a step back. "Didn't they search you?"

Paisley shrugged. "I fussed. Lit in good. Maybe ya spooks didna see me grab it up. They just threw us in here, nip and tuck. Min Bach, he were bright as ya kinnas wheel. They left you ya belt screen. Maybe they didna notice."

"Maybe." Lily held the gun out. "Here." Paisley stayed put. "Take it."

"You want me to—" The girl broke off, reached slowly forward, and took the weapon from Lily. "Sure," she said under her breath.

"Don't try to make it work," Lily warned. "But if we're running, you can use it to bluff them. But carefully, Paisley. If your bluff doesn't work, they'll use their guns on you, shoot you. Do you see what I mean?"

"Sure," said Paisley a little unsteadily. She thrust the weapon between her belt and her tunic. "What will you use?"

Lily tossed the knife up again, caught it. "I'm best in close. We'll have to trust to that."

Bach sang a few chords.

"If we get the chance," Lily added. She sat down, slipping her knife next to her com-screen on her belt. "So let's conserve our strength. *Bach, watch the door. Warn us if anyone approaches.*

Paisley settled down beside Lily "What we going to do?" she asked.

Lily sighed and put a hand on the girl's shoulder. "Remember, Paisley. They're better armed, better prepared, and on their own ground. We have one chance. It's got to be fast and hard, or we won't incapacitate them. Then we go for Heredes and go for the lock, and out."

"But what do we *do?* I mean, how? And when?"

"What my sensei always told me to do," she answered. "Set patterns never work. You have to make it up as you go along."

"Hoy," said Paisley, and smiled.

Bach had sung most of the way through *Meine Seufzer, meine Tränen*—"My Sighs, My Tears"—when he cut off midphrase. Paisley, curled up half-asleep, started awake, hands slapping to the floor as she steadied herself. Lily was already standing. She whistled two notes. Bach replied with four.

"Paisley, up. Two."

Paisley pushed herself up, one hand on the weapon at her belt. "Coming in?" Her voice was barely audible.

"Can't tell." Lily shifted her position to the other side of the door, paused, and with a move of her head signaled to Paisley to move to the end of the cell opposite the door. "They can see where we are," she added in an undertone. "If they come in, you—"

A low bell. The seam opened. Paisley dropped to the floor in a tumbling faint as the first alien stepped through. Seeing the girl fall, he walked three paces past Lily and Bach before realizing they were there. The second alien halted in the arch of the open seam; he held a snub-nosed gun just like Paisley's in his right hand.

Lily jumped—dislodged the gun with her first kick, with the second slammed him back against the door frame. Landed with a hammer strike to his temple. His head, flung back by the unexpected force, struck the metal ridge of the seam with a hard thud, and he crumpled to the floor.

Lily spun. The other alien turned back, weapon raised. Too far away for a quick kick. She lunged. Its hand shifted on the gun. And suddenly the alien was falling forward, fumbling in the air. Lily barely avoided its flailing arms, using its momentum to shove away and to one side. It fell flat-faced on the floor, gun knocked to one side. At its feet lay Paisley.

She had tackled it.

Lily grabbed both guns, thrust one into Paisley's hands as the girl extricated herself. Bach floated forward, coming to rest above the alien. It began to push itself up. An append-age snaked out of the robot.

"Paisley, back," hissed Lily. The girl wriggled away.

The alien reached for its waist. The appendage touched its neck. Bach flashed, an instant of brilliance, and the alien went limp.

"You didna kill him?" whispered Paisley, eyes riveted to Bach.

Negative. Rendered unconscious. Bach sang.

"He didn't," said Lily. "Let's grab the other one. We'll need him to open doors."

Paisley got to her feet. "It be all ya real, ain't it?" she said. Her mouth tightened into a straight line. "Bless me, Mother of all," she muttered under her breath, making a furtive series of signs with one hand.

"Paisley." Lily was at the door, lifting the alien. "By the Void, he's light." Bach drifted out into the corridor. "Can you support him?"

Paisley came forward. She looked at that moment even thinner than the alien. "A'course." She adjusted herself to take the creature's weight. The body hung all over her. "I done ya dock work, ain't I?"

Lily stationed herself at the alien's head, knife out. It had not yet stirred. As they moved out of the seam, the door to the cell shut soundlessly behind them, concealing the other body. The corridor curved away, as grey as the cell, touched here and there by the tracery of a door seam.

Bach led them. Right at the first branching. Voices at the next, disappearing into some sealed-off area. Left, straight, right again. Bach halted before a seam.

"Here?" Lily stepped forward.

Bach sang.

"No!"

"What be wrong?" Paisley's voice had taken on an even huskier tone. Under the tattoos, her face seemed pale. The alien shifted on her shoulder, a tentative movement.

"Bach says no one is in there. It can't be." Lily slapped the alien. Its eyes blinked open. Paisley caught in her breath. First the eyelid opened, then, beneath it, another skin, thin as membrane, flicked up. Lily lifted the knife; the point rested at the inner corner of the alien's eye, blade along the high curve of nostril. She whistled to Bach.

Bach spoke. The alien shuddered and replied. Bach replied. Lily held the knife.

"Move him," she said to Paisley. The girl dragged it, Lily

still with the knife pressed against its face, to the small panel outside the door. The alien fingered it. The seam opened to reveal an empty room.

The intercom came alive. Bells, a whistle, and a long command. Voices raised behind them, echoing.

"Bach, put him out."

Bach, touching him from behind, sang a warning. Lily and Paisley jumped back. Brightness. The alien fell.

"Paisley, grab one arm." Lily stooped and began pulling. She whistled.

Paisley grabbed. "Leave him. It'd be faster."

"And how do we get out of the ship? Can you pull faster? Stop. Lift him."

They got him rigged between them, set off at a trot. Bach floated behind.

"Right here," said Paisley. They turned. A door opened behind them. Someone shouted. Light, a loud, shrill noise, and a scream, cut off. "Where be Bach?"

"Catching up. Left here?"

Paisley's breaths came ragged. "Right. Big room. Then ya lock. I saw what sequence it touched, back there. I kin open ya lock."

"Can't chance it."

All grey. The corridor opened into a large room. Equipment hung along the walls. Outworld equipment. A low bell rang nearby. The door into the room slid shut behind them.

"Min Bach!" cried Paisley, dropping her hold on the alien and whirling back. She flung herself at the door.

Lily staggered, pitched sideways by the sudden shift of weight. The alien slipped out of her grasp onto the floor.

"Paisley!"

The girl had found the com-panel. She fingered it, gasping back sobs. "But I saw him! It were this pattern. It were!" The door remained shut.

"Paisley!"

Paisley turned. "But we can't leave him. Him and you be ya only friends I got."

"Help me," ordered Lily. "Where's the lock?"

"Through there." Paisley pointed at a dim recess, lifted a hand to wipe at her cheeks. She sniffed.

"Come on." Lily dragged the alien by his arms. "Grab his feet, something."

Paisley ran after, and they hauled the limp body into the recess.

"There," said Paisley through her tears, and she flung the alien down at the end of the niche, by the lock door. The com-panel blinked orange. Muted bells sounded over the intercom. A shrill whine rose from the room behind them. Paisley turned toward it.

"Paisley, help me get him awake." Lily slapped the alien. "Do that."

Paisley slapped it full on the cheek, a second time, with, perhaps, a shade too much enthusiasm. A word escaped it. Its eyes flickered. A voice came over the intercom. The shrill whine behind them increased in pitch, and it was that perhaps more than Paisley's final, hardest slap that brought the alien bolt upright, eyes open. Lily stuck the knife along its face and pointed at the panel.

"You know what I want." She eased the point of the knife a little closer to its eye. Its eyelids flickered again, as if it were about to pass out, but it stood, very slowly, and lifted a hand to the panel. It touched the panel once, again, again. A sign, a sudden command over the intercom, five high bells. The lock opened.

"But it be still—" Paisley's words cut off as the second seal, five steps on, eased open. Beyond, they saw the familiar bands and symbols of a station docking sector.

"By the Void," said Lily. "I could swear that logo is Remote Station ident." The alien shifted. Lily slugged him abruptly in the stomach. As he doubled over, she cupped his neck in one hand, and with the hilt of the knife hit it directly at the base of the neck. The alien went limp in her hands. She laid him over the doorway.

"Now get past me, to the other door," she said to Paisley. "Stand *in* the doorway."

"We ain't leaving min Bach!"

"No, we ain't. Go. Don't move from that doorway." Lily
ran back into the big room.

The whine had reached an excruciating pitch. Lily could
no longer hear the intercom above it. But the seal opposite
was beginning to glow. Approaching it, she had to stop.
Heat rose off it, spread toward her. She backed away, lifted
one hand to shield her face, the other to cover one of her
ears. A flurry of sound came from the intercom. The whine
pierced through the chamber. Lily backed into the recess.
Glancing over her shoulder, she saw Paisley poised in the
lock opening; beyond the girl, a figure in purple halted, curious, in the station corridor.

With a shriek like a ghost caught in a drill, the door into
the room ruptured outward, and Bach sailed through. Behind him, pale, scrawny figures merged and parted but did
not move forward. Lily jumped backward over the unconscious alien.

"Throw your gun down," she said, backing up next to
Paisley and tossing her own down. The knife she thrust back
into her belt. Paisley let the weapon in her hand fall onto the
floor of the lock, but her eyes focused on the interior of the
alien ship, her mouth open. The recess lighted. Bach appeared, his surface glowing. Heat shimmered off him.

"Step back," said Lily, pushing the girl with one hand,
and Paisley moved backward into the station. Bach came
into the lock. Behind him, Lily could see tall shapes approaching. A sharp whistle, and she and the robot were both
out of the doorway. The lock slid to. Bach sang a quick,
dissonant chord. His metal casing glowed a strange copper-
ish tone in the harsh glow of station lighting. Lily turned.

They had attracted a crowd. Paisley stood stock-still, her
tattoos showing up florid against the unmarked faces gawk-
ing at her. Someone asked a question. The station corridor
curved away, berths and, where the curve bent out of view, a
portside shop district.

Lily forced herself to single out a face, an individual:
there, a silver-toned sta, male by his cresting mane.

"Excuse me, esstavi. Is this Dairy?" She scarcely recognized her own voice. Her gaze shifted once right, once left.

The crowd seemed thinnest to the right, where it would lead on to more berths. Safest, perhaps, to go left, toward the shops.

"Dairy?" The sta's accented reply, half-sibilant, half-unvoiced growl, caught her back.

"Dairy system. What system is this?"

The sta, unable to blink, turned a head to glance pointedly at a companion, a brown-skinned woman in a pale robe.

Behind, a beep sounded from the berth console. Paisley yelped. The orange "occupied" light snapped to yellow.

"Left," Lily said, almost conversationally. She whistled three notes. "Run." And she broke left.

Paisley dove, rolled under a number of moving feet, and emerged on the far side of the crowd. Bach rose straight to the ceiling, trailing above behind Lily. Lily elbowed ruthlessly past the meat of the gathered crowd, took one quick survey to apprise herself of Paisley's position alongside her, and sprinted.

A swelling of sound came from behind them, a rush of voices and a yell. Faint, faint, and far above her, Bach was singing. People dodged out of her way, cursing, laughing, startled. Paisley bumped into a gold-skinned sta, shoved past. The commotion spread before and behind. Shops appeared now on the right-hand side of the station corridor; Lily, trying to keep as near the edge as possible, tripped over an out-flung chair at a café, rolled, and came to her feet. Paisley, ahead, paused to let her catch up. At the tables, diners pointed up at Bach's advance over their heads. Lily glanced back. A milling crowd, confusion—and pale, thin forms pushing purposefully through.

"Go," she shouted at Paisley. But Paisley did not move. The girl's eyes had fixed on something inside one of the shops. Lily, coming up beside her, took hold of a tattooed arm and began to pull—and froze.

Three of them emerged from the shop door, guns in hand.

"Now what's this?" said the woman. She had startlingly light hair, almost white, set off by her black-and-gray Security uniform. Three gold bars, sergeant's rank, tipped her sleeves. "Quite a fuss on com, I must say." She aimed her weapon at Lily. "Let the tattoo go. You own her?"

"No." Lily released Paisley and stepped forward. "And I don't—"

"She your servant?" The woman's voice held steady and cold.

"No," said Lily stiffly. "She happens to be—"

The woman made a motion with her free hand to one of her companions. "Take it down to Block 7. File it in."

"Hold on." Lily stepped back and put an arm around Paisley, who stood as if transfixed, staring in horror at the black-and-gray uniforms. "You can't just take her."

One of the men came up next to Paisley. "Just be happy you ain't going where she is," he said, not unkindly. "Cute, ain't she?" He took one of Paisley's arms and twisted it up behind the girl's back. "Let her go, kid."

"No!"

"Let her go," said the sergeant.

The noise of the crowd rose abruptly, a sudden swell, then ceased. Five gaunt aliens filtered in around Lily; two of them kept their eyes fixed above, on Bach. All were empty-handed. One fastened its gaze on the sergeant. It spoke, a rush of unknown words.

"Say it in Standard," said the woman, lifting her gun slightly, "or don't say it at all."

A hurried consultation. Another stepped forward. "I so claim," it said in a heavy, unfamiliar accent, "these my prisoner." It pointed to Lily, Paisley, and the robot.

"Yeah," said the woman. "You can sure tell them that down at precinct office. I suppose you have all your papers in order." The aliens began a discussion between themselves. "Now take that tattoo down," she continued, taking advantage of this disagreement. The second man came up beside Lily, who still held on to the silent Paisley. "Listen, kid." The sergeant moved forward to stand just in front of Lily. "We can bring you nice, or we can bring you mean, but we're bringing you. Do you understand?"

Paisley lifted her free hand to touch Lily's where it held her, and disengaged it. "Ain't no use, min Ransome," she said. "But thank you, all the same." She pulled away from Lily.

"You've got no charges—"

"Shut it, kid." The woman motioned with her gun. "First, you give us your knife." Lily, after one quick glance around, handed it over to one of the men. "Now, we're going down to the office. Your friends here," and she favored the aliens with a contemptuous gaze, "can come if they want."

"This is ridiculous," said Lily. She turned away; the officer next to her caught her shoulder in a firm grasp.

"You own that 'bot?" asked the sergeant, looking up.

"Yes."

"Huh. Better tell it to come along, then." Black and gray shifted through the thickening crowd, more Security arriving. The aliens backed off. "Get that tattoo out of here," she finished, grimacing, "and let's go." They moved forward in a loose wedge.

"I demand to know what the charges are." Lily stood, refusing to move, but two more had joined the man next to her and they almost bodily lifted her, pushing her along. Paisley, unprotesting as a sleepwalker, disappeared into the crowd. "I demand—" Lily's voice, raising higher, was cut off by the sergeant.

"Public disturbance." Her voice had the bored inflection of an oft-repeated delivery. "You're under arrest under code twenty-three oh seventy-four."

7 Custody

✳✳✳✳✳✳

With an incredible act of will, Lily maintained her silence all
the way to the Security office, four sections down. Bach
floated along just out of arm's reach above her. As she
walked, she knew she recognized the station ident.

Three officers, along with the sergeant, brought her into
the precinct office and led her up to the booking desk.

"This is Remote, isn't it?" asked Lily, putting both palms
on the opaque counter.

"Where'd you think it was? Central?" said one of the men
as he went behind the desk and sat down at a terminal.
Several of the others laughed.

"Hush it." The sergeant motioned to Lily to step back.
"Where did you think you were?" she asked, favoring Lily
with a hard but not unsympathetic eye.

"Dairy," said Lily. "I can't understand—"

"Got a match," said the man at the terminal. "Bless my
stars—" He looked up at the assembled black-and-gray tunics before him, grinning. "We've caught us a Saress."

"Hoo."

"My, my."

"Let's have a closer look, then."

"I *said* hush it." They all fell silent. "Now." The sergeant
nodded to the seated man. "What's the record?"

He scratched at an eyelid. "Lilyaka Hae Ransome.
Twenty-five years of age. Ransome House, Apron District,

Unruli system. Booked in about ten years ago on this station on code seventeen oh fifty-eight."

The sergeant twisted to survey Lily. "Cut loose and run again, Saressa?"

"I prefer not to be addressed by that title," said Lily.

Beyond the booking desk and row of terminals a waist-high wall separated off a scatter of plastic desks. Here people had paused in their work to watch both Lily and the sphere floating above her. Beyond them a transparent wall sealed off the guard's enclave and a row of barred cells. Lily could see into three of the cells: two were unoccupied; one held a solitary rust-skinned sta who seemed to be asleep.

"What have you done with Paisley?"

"Paisley?"

"The girl who was with me."

"Oh—the tattoo." The sergeant leaned, half-sitting, on the counter, letting a boot dangle. "She's been put down where her kind belong."

"I would like to see her."

"With no claim on her, you've got no legal right."

Lily advanced two steps. "Claim? I don't need a claim. She's my friend." Her voice carried throughout the office.

One of the men hooted. The others snickered.

"Shut it." The sergeant frowned, standing again. "You've got enough problems, Ransome. We'll have to hold you until we can check your current status. You haven't reached your majority yet, and you have an outstanding charge on you. Now, let me see your papers on that 'bot."

"I don't have any papers," cried Lily, "but just try and make him work for you."

"She's got you, sir," said the man at the terminal. "I ain't never seen anything like it."

"Who has?" said a second man.

"Ransome." The sergeant walked over to Lily and took her chin in a firm grip. Lily felt the pressure of each individual finger on her neck. "Don't aggravate me. Sure, it's a novelty. But we've got techs who can take it apart."

"They can try," said Lily darkly. She jerked her head away from the woman's grasp.

"And we can blast it into very small fragments if you don't program it to cooperate with us. Do you understand?"

Lily shut her eyes, forcing herself to focus her breathing. Her hands had tightened to fists; she unfolded them joint by joint. "Very well," she said. "His cooperation, nothing else. And I demand access to the legal banks."

"Terminal in your cell along with the usual amenities. You've got a screen."

Lily whistled. Everyone in the office stared. When Bach began to sing, several stood up and came forward.

"Hoo."

"Did you hear that?"

"What is that thing?"

Bach, taking these interruptions in stride, finished gracefully, and Lily whistled a final, quick coda. Bach drifted down to rest on the booking desk. The men took several steps back.

"Take her in," said the sergeant. She surveyed the little robot. "Huh," she said, lifting her wrist com. They led Lily back past the transparent wall and put her into the cell next to the sleeping sta.

"Where'd you get that thing?" asked one man as he locked her in with a few keystrokes.

"My father's garage," replied Lily, her back to him as she went to sit on the single cot that graced the room. "Can I get something to eat, and a drink?"

"Hoo," said the man, leaving. "What a push."

A different guard, a young woman with the same slanted eyes as Lily but much darker skin, brought her a large carton of juice and a packaged dinner. Lily watched in silence as six people dressed in non-Security clothes came in and carried Bach out.

She sighed and pulled out the terminal, plugging in her screen. Numbers flashed on. She called up the legal banks first, but she gave up on it and called up a program on Remote system instead. Beyond the dark plastic bars of the cell she could hear the desultory conversation of the guards.

"Betting on the races?"

"Got one riding on *Jehane's Blessing.*"

"That old wreck?"

Remote came up on the screen, turning in the blank background. The unbroken yellow of sand flat traced vast patterns over most of its surface. Crews sank deep wells for its rich petroleum reserves, and cities grew, well-protected, in its hot sun. Lily tried to imagine a cloudless day on Unruli, but it only served to magnify her frustration.

"—and how they got it past the registrar with that name —it's cursed strange."

"Jehane's luck, they say."

"Keep your voice down."

A pause.

"Still." Lower now. "I heard Forsaken went over to him."

"Where'd you hear that?"

"Last mess. Just a rumor, though."

A short laugh, half-snort. "Not fancy likely to shout it about on the network if it's true, is they?"

Lily punched off the Remote program and stood up with a long expulsion of breath. The sound of her movement quieted the duty guards. She began to pace. Herede's words kept time with her: "Waiting takes the most discipline."

"Curse this," she said aloud. She halted in the middle of the cell and came to ready position. With a quick glance she gauged her space; she had already gauged her mood. "Half-moon," she said, bowing, and after the appropriate time began the kata. She did it five times before she felt satisfied enough to take stock of her surroundings again. The guards were both staring at her. Even the sta, having awoken at some undetermined time, watched with undisguised interest and, as she stood catching her breath, rose to its feet and walked over to the bars. Lily smiled, tentatively, but her smile faded as the sta leaned up against the bars. She had never had trouble before knowing which honorific, male or female, to use when addressing one of their kind. Now, suddenly, she was unsure; this sta was unlike any she had ever seen before.

"Saressa," the sta said; its sibilant growl had a pure pitch that unnerved her. "Have you any more of those dances that I might regard?"

"Certainly, essta—" She faltered.

The sta's expression assumed an alarmingly human mask of self-mockery. "Having been incarcerated here on charges of itinerancy and public drunkenness, saressa, I appreciate but do not require your politeness. Just the art, if you please."

One of the guards wandered up. "Humor—ah—him," he said. The other guard snickered. The sta seemed not to have heard.

"I appreciate your interest," Lily said. So she did kata along with several other techniques, punctuated by her brief answers to the sta's brief questions. After that, he—a designation Lily doubted, although "she" fit equally poorly—excused himself and went back to his own cot and lay down. Lily stretched, cooling down. The guards had gone back to their computer. In the washing cubicle she found a sonic cleaner for her clothes, a sonic shower, and a waste port. Afterward, on the couch, she levered the terminal out to face her. After all, to make progress one had to study the opponent's movements.

The legal banks told her nothing. She called up the docking banks and scrolled through them: "Berth Ir02, *Majesty Bell.* Ir07, *Franklin's Cairn.* Ge12, *Wisstargoss*—sta, here. Ge21, *Pester.*" The names blurred together. "Ac02, *Half-Barked.* Ac05 . . ." Then she saw it, three places down—berth Ac08, no name except Cha, just the ident number, and —for a moment she lost her breathing. "Tagged out. Approaching system out-window. Course logged for XYZ 74.01.050 jump point: Bleak House, Station-only system." Lily stared. They had gone. Had not even come in to pry her loose from Security.

Tiny numbers flashed. The screen scrolled on automatically and, after the proper time, scrolled again and again. Why should they have tried? She was a mere nuisance, a momentary pest. They had what they wanted and they had run with it, as they had, surely, meant to do all along. The screen scrolled on.

"Ransome."

Lily started around. The white-haired sergeant had returned, stood with a satisfied expression examining Lily.

"You'll be happy to hear a first-run boat came in from Unruli. Your parents have sent out a tracer on you. Good thing, *Saressa,* we happened to pick you up. You must have had quite a head start. Did you stow away?"

"What do you do with me now?"

"It has to go through channels. You'll be sent back like you were the last time. And I suppose the *Sar* will pay your fines."

Lily said nothing.

"Rich kid," said one of the guards to the other.

"My robot," said Lily.

"If Ransome House has papers, the 'bot'll go back with you. I don't mind adding, Ransome, that Tech is plenty interested in that 'bot. And they have questions for your parents—ah—I should say, the Sar and Saress."

"He's mine," said Lily, but her protest sounded feeble even to her own ears. She would lose everything. "And what about Paisley? She should go back with me."

"Paisley?" The sergeant shook her head. "Who is Paisley?"

"The Ridani girl."

"Oh, yes," the woman replied, enlightened. "Your—ah—friend." Her expression hardened. "Listen, Ransome, you seem to have a pretty cozy view of the Reft. An itinerant tattoo who is not only without a pass away from her legal system, but is found with a lethal firearm of unknown design under a code forty-two oh twelve, not to mention in a public disturbance, is not going to get a free trip back to whatever hole she sprang from. Do you understand?"

Now Lily stood. "I gave her that weapon," she said, advancing to the bars. "The blame is mine."

"Touching and noble. The tattoo will get the usual." She turned away, signaling to her aide, and left.

Lily grabbed the bars. "I demand to know—" The guards laughed and returned to their computer. "I want—" Her words emptied into uncaring silence, and she stopped, knowing that no one would reply.

"Saressa." The low, fluid voice of the sta startled her. "You claim a Ridani as a friend?"

"Is it a crime?" she asked bitterly, staring out the transparent wall into the precinct office beyond, where the sergeant spoke into a com-link.

"Unusual, certainly," replied the sta, unoffended. "Admirable, in its way."

"And damning, for Paisley. I don't even know what the 'usual' is." Her hands tightened on the bars.

"Indenture, I imagine."

Lily let go of the bars. "No." She looked at him. He stood almost next to her. Rust-colored did not quite describe his skin. Red-hued, perhaps. His mane hung lankly without the stiffness it should have had. "She's just a child. Fifteen at the most."

"Old enough. I believe it's five years to the State for itinerancy, for a Ridani. More with the weapons conviction."

"Esstavi, how do you know all this?"

That humanlike expression, so out of place on a sta's face, and yet not so at all on his, settled there again. "Having been brought in on similar charges, and being entirely unable to pay the fines levied on me given such charges, I find myself well versed on the penalties. Of course, being of slightly more respectable origins"—here his tone took on heavy irony—"I have received only two years indenture to work off. I believe in this District they send us to Harsh."

"But how can that be, esstavi? You have family—" At his expression, she paused. "But all sta have—everyone knows their clans never fail them."

For an answer he raised both hands. At first Lily saw nothing to remark in them, for they were much like her own, only with a hint of scales.

"Saressa," the sta said. "Perhaps your reticence does you credit." He turned a thin-maned back to her and returned to his cot, shutting his eyes. Eyes too human for a sta.

One of the guards snickered and, when Lily caught his eye, made an obscene gesture with his hands and looked pointedly over at the unmoving sta.

"You make me sick," said Lily. She went back to her cot

and stared at the still-scrolling screen. His hands. Four fingers and a thumb. Human hands. She stifled an urge to look across for confirmation.

After a bit she slept. When she woke, she found a meal, which she dutifully ate. In the next cell the sta seemed not to have moved. Two new guards sat, playing a game with counters on the table. She pretended to read Remote's information banks for a while, went through her entire repertoire of kata and after, having nothing else to do, went into the cubicle and cleaned up again. Came back out. Sat on the cot. Scrolled through the legal banks. Attempted not to think of Heredes, and his fate. Failed. Or of Bach. Or Paisley. Failed miserably. Did kata.

A sudden influx of uniforms into the outer office distracted her. A new Security officer arrived, with the white-haired woman, in civilian garb, in tow. Six red-uniformed government troops detached themselves from the larger party and came back to her cell as a Security officer opened it. Lily took one step back. Four entered, surrounding her, and propelled her forward.

"My screen is back there," said Lily. Two more fell in behind her; one placed a hand on her back. "That's my credit, my ID. How am I supposed to—"

"Come along." She cast a desperate glance back. The two Security officers watched with interest, but without sympathy. The sta, behind his—or was it her—bars, had risen and now stared after Lily with a sta-ish, and therefore unreadable, expression on her—or was it his—strangely unfinished and contradictory face.

"Where are you taking me? What is this for? Where is my robot?" Outside, a small vehicle waited under the awning, one solid door propped open. "This is illegal." She tried to sit down. They simply picked her up and shoved her into the back. The door shut.

Darkness shuttered her. She felt along the wall: two meters square, padded, one handhold. The handhold proved necessary when they negotiated locks. She did not bother to hammer on the walls. Eventually the vehicle halted. This time, prepared, she went with humility.

They led her through an empty warehouse into a small, bare room with one chair and left her there alone. white walls were on three sides, on the fourth, a surface black and smooth as obsidian. The lights of the room dimmed, and shapes took form behind the black wall: two women and a man seated on a higher level. Lily stood up immediately.

A chime sounded above. She heard the sputtering crackle of the intercom coming to life.

"Please sit." The disembodied voice came across as almost inhuman, but distinctly female.

"First of all," said Lily. "I intend to file a complaint as soon as I reach Unruli. Second, I will file a writ of action against Remote Station Security and their Technical division for the recovery of my personal property. Third, a protest to Central HOL protesting the treatment of a young Ridani who spent a brief time in my company. Do you understand?"

Behind the wall, the male figure leaned over to talk to one of the women. The intercom crackled.

"You are identified here as Lilyaka Hae Ransome, a female of twenty-five who has been reported missing from Unruli system. Let me inform you, first, that this report, along with all trace of your recent activities here on Remote Station, has been erased. Per the request of Intelligence. You no longer exist in government computers."

The static died away.

There was a long pause.

"What do you want me for?" said Lily in a very quiet voice.

"Second. You claim ownership of a robot of unspecified and, in our records, nonexistent make. Have you any explanation for this?"

Lily said nothing.

A new voice, male, came in. "The Remote Technical division has none."

One of the female shapes passed a com-screen to the man.

"I found it in the Ransome House garage." Her voice echoed, falling back on itself, in the close room. "And that's the truth, whether you choose to believe it or not."

They conferred.

"Third."

Lily halted, center again.

"The young Ridani."

"Paisley!"

"Did she speak to you of Jehane?"

"Jehane?" Lily opened her hands out in exasperation. "This is ridiculous. Jehane is some fairy tale, some story her people tell."

"She did mention Jehane?"

"She told me some old legend. I think that name was in it once or twice. Can I see her? I want to put on record that the weapon she was carrying was my property—that I gave her—" She faltered. Behind the wall, they leaned together. Static crackled then bled away.

". . . clear evidence," finished the male voice. All three straightened.

"Have you any reason to suspect that the young Ridani you call Paisley has been at any time or is currently linked with the Jehanish insurrection?"

"I have never heard of any Jehanish anything, but I'm beginning to think that—" She broke off, remembering, for once, prudence.

"Would you like to complete that statement?"

"No."

Static arced in a high, faint pattern above her. She circled the room four times before the intercom crackled back to life. The three questioners drew apart and rose.

"We have no further questions."

"But I have!" The wall already dulled and, as the lights came up, it reverted to its original obsidian sheen. "I have!" She slammed the side of her fist into the black surface. It hurt.

Behind her six guards filed in. She went without a word. She could not even imagine where she might be going now. But it was, of course, to a lock, and then into a ship—of course. Having presumably condemned Paisley, lost Heredes and Bach, and been, in the bargain, erased from existence at the order of Central Intelligence, she was to be sent

back to the truly empty House of her family. She went
meekly to her room or, better phrased, cell. They had left
food and drink. There was a washing cubicle. She ate and
drank and washed.

She was not aware of any ungrappling. When the first
window came, it took her entirely unaware.

> *Fire. A tracery half-broken. The wind fanned it. The*
> *building collapsed—roaring; weight. Trapped in dark-*
> *ness.*

And came out.

She was crying.

After a bit she recalled the futility of such occupation, so
she dried her tears and washed her face. She did kata,
basics, simply stood for long periods in her deepest stances.
In such a stance, kiba-dachi, centered physically at least, she
felt the ship go through.

> *Night. Utterly dark. The sightless must find a path.*
> *Wrists crossed. Long sweeps, half-moon, forge the*
> *ground. Light begins to rise.*

And came out.

She still held deep in the stance. And as her final test,
might as well stay in it as the ship came in to Unruli Station.
It gave her something to concentrate on while she waited.

Because of it, she was, while completely surprised, not
entirely unprepared when they went through again.

> *The angle of the left knee. Tendons. A slight shift.*
> *Vector. Each angle presupposes the next. Each prepares*
> *the other.*

And came out.

She was so amazed by her sudden understanding of how
to correct her straddle stance that she sat down. It was so
simple, so obvious.

It was two windows to Unruli. Where, by the Void, were

they going? It seemed suddenly absurd to Lily that after all that had happened to her, they—whoever they were, the government, presumably—would simply return her to Unruli and deposit her by Ransome House's outside lift. Her last ship had gotten to Remote on one impossible jump. She could be anywhere. She felt immensely heartened.

A bed stood platformed into one wall. She lay down on it and slept. It had been told to her on one occasion that no human could sleep through a window. On other occasions, she had been told one merely had strange dreams. It seemed to her, when she woke, that she had had strange dreams, but how many, and how strange, she could not remember. She stretched, did a few exercises, ate and drank and washed. This ship could be going anywhere—even as far as Central. And she thought of Bach's star map, and smiled.

The ship went through.

The guardian of the south: the spirit of power released. But to the west: the spirit of power in reserve.

And came out.

She was still smiling—of course, because it was an instant's vision, an instant's realization, an instant, going through. For the first time, she understood that here she would have to wait out events until she could see the pattern they were taking, and find her own part in it.

A subtle change in the floor and in the air signaled docking. In time, the door of her room slid open and six black-and-gray–uniformed officers escorted her out. They put her directly from the lock into a prison car. Her disorientation at locks told her they were, as she had expected, on a station. When the door swung open she emerged with as much dignity as she could muster. They walked sedately down a blank hallway. No one spoke. The corridor dead-ended in a double door that opened from inside. She had to step back to avoid its yawning. None of her guards followed her in.

She was alone in a small chamber. A hollow pop alerted her, and in the far wall a seam appeared, stripping away in a single layer to create an opening. She went obediently through it, and it closed behind her. In the next room, one chair of hard, molded plastine faced eight chairs padded with soft fabric. She allowed herself the barest of sighs and sat in the single hard one. A few minutes passed. The hollow pop sounded again, and a second door materialized. She rose, but before she could take her first step, four people walked into the room and the doorway vanished behind them.

She remained standing, out of astonishment. They wore the most outlandish clothing she had ever seen. There were three men and a woman, or at least one of the men she supposed was a man: he had a delicacy of face that was almost feminine, and she found the juxtaposition subtly attractive because it was so unusual; the oblong slant of his eyes resembled her own—although it might have been more cosmetics than biology—but his hair was blue.

They studied her with equal intentness as they disposed themselves in four of the comfortable chairs. However strange they looked, at least they were human, and not the mysterious alien Kapellans, whose motives she could not hope to fathom.

The blue-haired man lifted a hand to his mouth and coughed delicately behind it. It was, perhaps, a signal.

The woman spoke. "You call yourself Lilyaka Hae Ransome. You claim residence at System Mark fifty-three point twenty-four oh eight, called Unrule. This is correct?"

It was Standard, but strangely altered and heavily accented. "Both those statements are correct," Lily said slowly. "Am I to be allowed to ask questions?"

The woman looked at the blue-haired man. In her right ear four white stones stood out in bright contrast to her dusky complexion. She said words Lily could not understand, and turned back. "You may ask, in sequence, your questions." Her tone was neutral.

Lily folded her hands in her lap. "I would like to know where I am, first. And also, why I have been brought here, who you represent, what has been done with my companions, the robot and the Ridani girl, and when I will be allowed due legal process, which I do not need to remind you is my right as a citizen of the Reft."

"Some of these questions are not so difficult," said the woman. "You yourself already know most of the answers. For the first, it is not unreasonable that you know your location. We are currently at System Mark fifty-one point seventy-two oh thirty-six, also called—" One hand lifted, paused beside her face as if to frame it; a single red circle, like a drop of blood, dotted her forehead. "Nevermore Station. We have not heard of any Ridani child. Now, of course, you will answer our questions."

"Nevermore!" It lay off the main routes at the edge of navigable space, populated by pygmies and the usual Ridani enclave. Given its name, Lily had once heard, from the number of ships lost leaving it, trying, perhaps, to go out on Paisley's haunted way. "Why in the Void did you bring me to Nevermore?"

"Can't imagine," muttered the second man, the ruddy rose of his complexion deepening with impatience.

"As you must know, we want to know the extent of your involvement with Gwyn Himavant Simonides, also known as"—her voice took on the litany of the oft-repeated— "Elias Ram, Daniel Lance Fisher, Gwion, Blake Ne-Esthan Ash, Adam Trismegistus—" The blue-haired man chuckled. The woman, breaking off, frowned at him in annoyance. "You know well enough what we ask you," she finished.

"No, I don't," said Lily.

"You deny involvement with him?" asked the woman.

"I don't know *who* you're talking about."

"And of course you have no knowledge of his past activities or his current plans?" This from the ruddy man, face openly skeptical. "Have no connection with this business whatsoever."

"I don't know *what* you're talking about."

They exchanged glances. The blue-haired man yawned and rubbed with painted fingernails at some imagined blight on one bronzed cheek. His hand moved with a kind of alluring grace that suggested sensuality more than any other characteristic.

"And that, I suppose"—the woman's voice sharpened with irritation—"is why you have a model sixteen eighty-five composer?"

Lily blinked, shifting her attention quickly back to the woman. "A what?"

Conversation in the foreign language was exchanged between the woman and the blue-haired man. With a final comment, the woman dispatched the third man. The door appeared; he went through it, returned holding a hand-sized box. Behind him, in a metal harness, floated Bach.

Lily stood immediately, whistling his name.

Bach responded in full chorus. *Patroness, thou art unharmed?*

"That's enough." The ruddy man broke in on Lily's whistled reply. "It's proof enough for me," he said to the woman. She frowned and spoke in the incomprehensible tongue to the blue-haired man.

Can you understand? whistled Lily.

Certainly, patroness. The lady hath stated that their party should have brought a composer model expert with them. The gentleman respondeth that one is unlikely to expect working models of such design in an area— His song cut off abruptly, and he drifted down to settle with a slight roll on the floor.

"What have you done?" Lily started forward, but the man with the box stood in her way.

"The model is unharmed," said the woman in her neutral tone. "We were forced to switch off his melodic circuits. I'm sure you see the necessity." She nodded, and the man pressed a button; Bach lifted about a meter from the floor, and together they left the room. "You will," added the woman more forcefully, "receive the model back *after* you have cooperated with us."

The blue-haired man caught Lily's eye and, like a conspirator forced for the moment to play the opposite side, winked at her. His eyes, startlingly, were as blue as his hair.

"Has that convinced you," continued the woman, "that we have seen through your imposture?"

Lily returned to the single hard chair and sat down. "I

don't know what my imposture is supposed to be. I found the robot in my father's garage."

The ruddy man laughed, scornful now. "And fish can fly," he said. He reached for the com-screen he wore at his belt, coding into it, and stood up to hand it to Lily. "Next you'll tell us you don't recognize this man."

She took the screen. Stopped. Her hands congealed into immobility. It was Heredes. Obviously him, his picture on the screen. Looking, indeed, much the same as she knew him, but younger, with hair somewhat longer, and a single red crescent moon painted below one eye like a talisman. And there, on his chest, the medallion he had given her.

She stared, confused, a little frightened, but not totally surprised. She realized finally that they were all examining her. She uncurled her fingers from the frame, and gave the screen back to the ruddy man.

"You're not going to deny it?" Spots reddened on his cheeks.

Lily said nothing.

"This is a waste of time," said the blue-haired man suddenly in accented but perfectly understandable Standard. "These methods never work."

"You would know," said the woman, her tone taking once again an edge. Her dark eyes fixed on Lily, unwavering. "I don't care what methods I have to use to get the truth. That choice is yours. Do you understand?"

"My House has already sent out a tracer on me," replied Lily. Her voice stayed remarkably level. "They'll catch up with you eventually."

The woman sighed, long, deep, and exasperated. She stood. The two men stood. "I see you don't understand, or else you refuse to," she said. Her dress, one-shouldered, draped like a single bolt of rich green cloth around her, rustled as she moved. "You don't exist on your government's computers any more. You can't be traced."

She stepped forward with speed most startling for its abruptness and grasped the chain of Lily's necklace, flicking it out with a finely tuned twist of the wrist. The medallion settled damningly on the black cloth of Lily's tunic. "Don't attempt denial," said the woman. "We'll leave you to think about its consequences."

She left, the two men following her through the door. The blue-haired man, last through the door, paused to look back, his gaze considering and, perhaps, amused. Lily could not help but stare back at him, caught at that moment by a fascination with his exotic attractiveness that caused her to forget briefly their circumstances. He began to smile.

Then someone spoke beyond the door, impatient, and he too was gone.

Lily simply sat, frowning. A time like this was no time to be admiring one's enemies. Except that she could not imagine where these people had come from, or if they were truly a threat to her. She had felt an oddly undefinable character about them, as if her experience of life and theirs had no point of intersection. And Heredes—Hiro's bounty hunters seemed, in retrospect, a mere quibble.

Behind her there was movement. She twisted, quickly slipping the medallion back underneath her clothes. A door came into being, seeming to peel back from the wall. Through it an unintelligible voice and a series of tones and Bach appeared, unharnessed, coming through the door. Lily stood up, but the doorway was sealing back into place. Intercom traffic sounded beyond it: "Code red sector eleven Imp, all security assemble—" The door shut. Bach descended to one of the chairs.

Bach! Can you get us out of here?

Negative. Screens present. I regret my inability, but thou certainly understandest that against such devices attuned to my circuits, I cannot resist.

Who are these people? Are they from Central?

Information insufficient on Central. Harness activated by recent technician-originated point of origin. New construct. Therefore, I deduce similar origins for latest interrogators.

Do you mean that they came from the place you originally came from? She supported herself by gripping the back of a chair.

Affirmative.

The thick woven pattern of the chair's fabric suddenly

reminded her of the curtain in Heredes's study. "Then Heredes must be . . ." She trailed off, unable to complete the thought. Bach drifted closer to her, singing softly. *Why did they return you to me?*

His first response was more tone than answer. *Unclear. Disturbance on Station. Some debate over my disposal, followed by a call over communications and an unbuckling of harness and swift preparations for departure. That is all I witnessed.*

Lily let go of the chair. "But they implied—"

The lights went off. For three breaths, the room remained dark. They came back on with a flash of brilliance, but almost simultaneously, as if the two were connected, Lily felt surge in her stomach, a sharp lurch. She stumbled to one side, tripping over her own feet, grabbed for the chair back, missed; a second lurch yanked her back into the chair. Bach had rolled upside down. Surface lights blinking, he righted himself.

"Hoy," said Lily. She kept her hold on the chair's back. The lights went off again, stayed off longer, long enough for Bach to sing through *Brich an, o schönes Morgenlicht*— "Break through, oh lovely light of morn." They relit in slow stages, accompanied by a rhythmic pounding and a deep extended growl, like an engine heard through a tube.

A doorway peeled open. Lily threw herself into a half-crouch behind the chair. A man strolled in, gun held easily in one hand. Not just any man, but a tattoo. Purple and yellow and orange swirled in a joyous riot over his skin. He wore ordinary brown overalls. His arms were bare. Stopping, he saw her. His gun still pointed steadily, but not at her.

"Here you be," he said. He had an open, cheerful face.

"Who are you?" Lily asked, staying down.

"*I* be called Calico." He seemed to find this diverting, and smiled. "But I be here to release you."

Bach floated up behind her, attracting the man's astute eye. "I don't understand," Lily countered. "Why are you releasing me?"

His smile broadened. "But it be ya simple," he said. "Jehane hae come. I mun take you to him."

Now Lily stood up. "Who is Jehane?" she demanded.

A voice stuttered to life at his wrist. He lifted it to a colorful ear, listened, lowered it again. "Be you comin'?" he asked.

She glanced once at Bach. The robot winked at her with a single azure light. "I think I be," she said, half-resigned, and she followed Calico out of the room.

8   Jehane Arrives

※※※※※※※

He led her past the double doors. The blank hallway beyond receded into a shallow curve, the arc of the station. The featureless walls' subdued color, draining Calico's tattoos to shades of gray. On his bare feet, a glow from the floor revealed curlicues chasing themselves in orange and yellow around his toes.

"Where are we going?" she asked after they had gone about a kilometer.

"To safety." He flashed her a quick, bright smile.

"Where are we?"

He shook his head. A bit further, the curving expanse revealed a single doorway outlined on the wall. He went to it, laying a hand on the com-panel next to it, and it slid open soundlessly.

Inside, a worker's office and a living space combined into two small rooms: one with tools, the other a tiny cubicle just large enough for bed and terminal. The door shut behind them. Calico clipped off the gun and hid it under a plastic bucket. Waving Lily into the second room, he grandly offered her a seat on the bed.

"I be ya janitor here," he said as she disposed herself, Bach hovering above her. "So you be sure wondering why I be here instead o' with ya rest o' my people."

His mischievous look prompted her to smile. "I had wondered why you had the run of the place, after what I've seen of Security's treatment of Ridanis." Still bitter, she told him of Paisley.

He did not look surprised but he did grow somber. "Well enough it be for them," he commented when she had finished, "but a sore hard time I do see for ya lassie."

"And there's nothing I can do," she said, and grimaced, afraid that her anger was already turning into resignation.

"Perhaps. Perhaps." Around the eyes, through the wild design, she could now discern deep lines, aging hidden from the world by color. She glanced down at his hands; they showed wrinkles, lines under lines. "But ya new time be comin', min—" Here he paused.

"Ransome," Lily supplied. "Lily Ransome."

"Ah." He slid sideways past her and sat down before the terminal. "I did see them bring ya prisoner in, though I didna know it be you, min Ransome. Ya place here, do you see"—he waved his hand to encompass the hall and rooms she had just come from—"it be private to ya govinment, for ya special folk, as they feel true be ya dangerous."

Lily could not help but laugh. "Dangerous? What do they do with them?"

He turned in his seat to frown at her. "It be not for laughing, missy. Many bad things. Along ya hall, all along, be folk who never hae seen their homes for years and more, that were brought here ya long ago."

"But their families—" She broke off. She had been told twice that she no longer existed in government banks.

He turned back to the terminal. "And what better choice than ya old tattoo to clean and mend ya place. Poor enough, and with kin enough to keep, to hold ya mouth tight closed. But ya short time back, ya new folk come in, openlike, and they be made much welcome. They be looking for some thing or maybe some folk. Strange they be—dressed sore funny. One, by Dancer, e'en had blue hair." Calico swiveled in his chair and focused a pair of jewel blue eyes on Lily.

"They're the ones who talked to me. I didn't know what they wanted, except—" Except Heredes. "Do you know," she continued, pressing on past that particular point, "they don't come from here, from the Reft, I mean."

His gaze did not waver, but neither did it turn to incredulity. "I suspicioned much like," he said, and looked pointedly at Bach. "That one be sore strange, likewise."

"He's old," said Lily. "A long time ago, like our ancestors, he came from over ya way."

"Ah. You know ya story."

"A little bit of it. But those people, the ones who questioned me, they must have come over the way recently—just days or months ago. From—" She opened her hands. "I don't know where from."

"Jehane knows," said Calico.

The terminal beeped; he turned back to face it as information printed out on the screen. Lily stood up and looked down over his shoulder.

Nevermore Station. Condition: under attack. Status: indeterminate.

Usher Hub: Insurrection in progress; support from at least three cleared merchant vessels. Security forces in need of reinforcement.

Pendulum Hub: Clean, clear, no signs of incursion. Station citizens restless but still under control.

Raven Hub: Unauthorized docking: serious displacement of station axis—red red red—stabilization.

Core: Axis realignment stable. No threat to life systems.

Imp Hub: All communication cut off. Security personnel missing or dead.

"Ah," said Calico, smiling again. "That be ya Ridani sector."

"But this is a classified channel!" She leaned forward to stare at the screen. "What's going on?"

"Jehane hae come."

"He come, he come," murmured Lily, trying to recall Paisley's song. "To lead us far, to home, to home." She glanced down to see Calico's face, startled now, gazing up at her. "Is that right?"

"Ya lassie hae trusted you, or been in kinnas to you," he said.

"We were locked in a cell together."

"Indeed," said Calico. He punched more codes into the computer.

Lily stood silent, watching the old man's face: a kindly one, but much hemmed about by secrets and by knowledge endured from necessity, not choice. Then he smiled as a new message came up on the screen, a smile that, like an open lock, received all before it with impartial certitude of its function.

"We mun go," he said. "Ya way be clear. This sector be much deserted in any case, as it be sore off-limits but to ya highest level folk. So it were but little task to seal it off."

"But I still don't understand what's happening. Who's rebelling?"

"Jehane hae come," he repeated, still patient. "You hae been given ya story by ya lassie."

"But Jehane—" She raised a hand hopelessly and glanced up at Bach. She found it impossible to offend this old man by telling him that Jehane was merely a legend. After all the prejudice she had seen, she could not help but feel that someone, however shadowy, should champion their cause. "So people here have been waiting? Was it planned, this revolt?"

"Sure," he said. "All were held ready for when he chose ya time to arrive. And he hae asked special, to see ya prisoner that ya far folk hae had brought in. That be you, min Ransome. And ya time be now."

Lily followed him into the office, waited while he slipped out to check the corridor. She lifted the plastic bucket. The gun lay there. She picked it up and without further thought unloosened a trouser leg enough to slip it inside, where it hung against the cloth tucked back into her boot. Calico reappeared, beckoning.

Just around the next curve of the hall, Calico fingered a door panel and led her into a spacious office populated by desks and counters. They stood alone in the gloom. A lit terminal scrolled unreadable data past, oblivious to the vacant chair before it.

"Where is everyone?" she whispered.

"It be night cycle," he said, his normal voice resonating in the empty room. "But we did clear out all o' ya sector, except them as *he* were to see."

Through more offices, ending in a small room with a raised dais and four chairs—Lily stopped. The fourth wall, the one the chairs faced, was transparent. Beyond, in a chamber exactly like the one she had been interrogated in on Remote, sat three of the foreigners she had just spoken with: ruddy-skinned, blue-hair, and the hard-faced woman.

"Don't be scared," said Calico. "They canna see you."

"But I was—I could see—"

"Only if ya certain button be pushed. They see no but ya black wall—you might recollect that?"

"I do," said Lily, going up to the wall. "But if they're prisoners there, aren't I just as much a prisoner here?"

"Do but sit quiet. You shall learn enough, and be safe more than you been back in ya other place. True enough?"

"I can only take your word," Lily said. He regarded her gravely. "So I will."

With a hand leathery from age and work he touched her on the forehead, like a benediction, and left. The lock light winked red on the com-panel. As she stepped forward to test it, Bach began to sing.

Patroness, dost thou desire my translation of the conversation beyond?

Listening, Lily realized that she could hear the three people talking. They seemed completely unaware of her or Bach's presence. Their clothes were startling in the drab room: the sheen of gray on the ruddy-skinned man, the lustrous belt of green draped around the woman, and the heavy gold fabric, inlaid with some indistinguishable design, on the blue-haired one. He rose from the chair he was seated in, one pink-tipped finger lifting to brush at a cheek, and Lily realized that the bulk of fabric that had seemed to gather at his waist was in fact long sleeves, lengths of stiff cloth that hung to sweep with graceful elegance along the floor. Ruddy-skin was speaking.

"—but what else could we expect from a cyro colonization? Their computer systems—laughable! They've slipped badly from what they must have brought with them. And having to leave Rayonne on the ship because of their barbaric prejudices."

"That was not altogether unexpected," replied the woman.

Ruddy-skin rose. The material moved with his body, highlighting muscle and the length of his limbs. "Your sociologists have blessed us again. Unfortunately they did not predict this political disagreement, and the primitive methods being used to solve it."

The woman shrugged and looked away from him. "This is pointless quibbling, Anjahar," she said.

The blue-haired man was running one hand along the wall that separated him from Lily, as if he could feel her presence by touch alone; now he paused. When he spoke, his voice as smoothly featureless as the wall, he spoke in the other tongue.

He says, patroness, that this latest expedition was perhaps a fool's errand in whatsoever case, as the old man is now dead.

"Dead?" said Lily aloud. They could not mean Heredes.

Anjahar turned to glare at blue-hair. "That may be true enough, Kyosti, but dismantling his terrorist network is another matter, especially now that he is no longer around to protect them. And his sister still lives."

Kyosti waved a delicate hand in dismissal.

"She is negligable." The woman fixed her severe gaze on Anjahar. "But his saboteur's lattice must be eradicated once for all."

"Tell *him*, Maria," said Anjahar sourly.

A sister. Heredes was sending her to his sister's—by his own words. That he was involved in some dangerous mystery was clear now; perhaps had been all along had she cared to read the signs. That they thought her equally involved was, she had to admit, unsurprising at this stage. And what if Heredes was dead?

"I will not believe it," she said aloud.

What believest thou not, patroness? sang Bach.

Lily only shook her head.

In the other room, the com-panel beeped and the door

slid open. The woman stood. Both the men turned to face the opening. Six white-uniformed soldiers strode in. Two were tattoos, but they remained set apart from the others. The soldiers formed a column on either side of the doorway, raised left hands to right shoulders. A woman entered. Brisk, tight-lipped, she examined her three prisoners with uncompromising energy.

"Sit down," she ordered in ringing tones. Her gaze drifted, for an infinitesimal second, to the wall behind which Lily and Bach watched. None of the three sat down.

"By what authority have you detained us?" demanded the woman called Maria, moving forward to face the new arrival. "We are here on a safe-conduct from your government."

"Not *my* government," replied the woman. Thick hands, strong by their look, gave a swift tug to her plain white jacket. She looked immaculate. "Sit down."

Anjahar's complexion thickened to a blotchy red. "This is insufferable!"

"Anja." The bored tones of Kyosti cut across the ruddy man's anger. "We can't fight them all. Much as I'm sure," he added with a sardonic smile, "you would like to." He settled himself fussily in one of the chairs, attention partly on the soldier, partly on the wall.

The ostentation of the gesture served to distract the soldier from Anjahar's anger while Anjahar, breathing unevenly, his muscles tense under the gray fabric, sat down heavily in a chair. He cast a glance at Kyosti that could have been annoyance, or gratitude.

"By what authority?" repeated Maria.

"Sit, bitch," said the soldier. A slight movement of her hand, and the six guards fanned out into the room; four more entered behind them.

Maria did not move.

"I said sit." The dark woman gave a hard shove to Maria's shoulders.

Maria started back; as her knees came up against the chair she sat, ungainly, her beautifully draped dress slipping so that she had to grab at it. But she had, Lily saw, con-

trolled her anger, as if she had summed up the measure of
the soul within her captor.

Kyosti said something to Anjahar, who looked ready to
rise, and whatever he said caused Anjahar to settle back into
his seat with a slight grin.

*He assureth his companion that they be indeed amongst
the uncivilized,* translated Bach.

"Huh." The woman studied her three prisoners with disgust. "You may," she added with the greatest of generosity,
"address me as First Comrade." A stifled sound from Kyosti caused her to shift her gaze slowly from the hem of his
long gold tunic to the tips of his unruly blue hair. He smiled
serenely back at her. "Such as you," she finished, "unaware
of the distinction afforded me by the title, may also address
me as Kuan-yin."

As if he could not help himself, Kyosti began to laugh.

Kuan-yin drew her gun and pointed it at him.

"Oh dear." He stopped laughing, but Lily could not help
but admire the lack of concern with which he regarded the
gun. "You must tell me, what is your full name?"

"None of your business," she snapped, gun still raised.

"You have not yet told us by whose authority you hold us
here," interposed Maria in her most neutral voice.

Kuan-yin holstered the gun. The white uniform set off her
brown skin. She swept all three with a belligerent gaze. "By
Jehanish authority. The Jehanish rebellion is now in control
of Nevermore Station. We have ordered all ships to surrender to our authority or be blown up in their docks."

"I see," said Maria calmly. "What is this 'Jehanish' authority?"

A soft beep stirred the air behind Lily, followed by an
indrawn sigh. She whirled. The door slid open. She saw
Calico's face, but he retreated beyond her view, and a man
entered the room. Lily took one step back.

He had golden hair. Not just blond, not yellow by any
stretch of the imagination. Gilded by the ore itself, paling at
the ends. He moved with the grace of the wind, filling space
as though he were meant by the laws of the universe to be
there. Entering—becoming—the room, he saw Lily and of-

fered her an apologetic smile. It said, "Forgive me, for disturbing you, for causing you any inconvenience," at the same time, he beckoned to her to approach him, and she found that she simply walked over to him—and hated herself for doing so.

"Who are you?" she asked, unable not to ask; she felt as if her will had left her of its own volition, and gone to reside in this man.

He considered her first for a long moment, afterward turned his attention to Bach, clearly puzzled, half-amazed, but pleased. Then he walked to the window—he had that immediately definable posture that marked him as a master of whichever art he had chosen. His gaze as he studied the scene below was, if not benign, then effortlessly all-encompassing. Finally, having drunk his fill, he returned his gaze to Lily. She had not moved. His eyes were mild, a deep, rooted green, but piercing. His voice was, of course, mellifluous.

"I am Jehane," he said. "But you may call me Alexander."

9 Nevermore Hosts
     Alexander

✳✳✳✳✳✳✳

"Of course," said Lily without thinking. She blushed.

His expression did not change. "This, then," he said, drawing her gaze up to Bach, "is the peculiar or, shall we say, gifted, robot you"—his pause was a question—"own?"

"Not quite," said Lily.

A different smile curved his mouth. "Possess the loyalty of?" He seemed to be inviting her to embrace some amicable conspiracy.

"Yes."

"I see." He shifted to look down again into the other room, lifted a wrist communicator to his mouth. What he said Lily could not distinguish, but Kuan-yin gave the barest start and the expression on her face cleared to one of polite disinterest.

"You are under arrest," she said to her three prisoners, "under suspicion of collusion with the illegal government at Central. You will be allowed to clear yourself of suspicion."

Anjahar shifted impatiently in his chair. "If we answer the right questions?"

"There will be questions."

"And if we can't answer them, or if we refuse to cooperate?" Maria smoothed out her dress with a few unhurried strokes.

"Then you will deal with the consequences." Kuan-yin smiled.

Kyosti raised a languid hand and ran it through his hair. "Perhaps you have not yet realized," he said, his tone as amused as bored, "that a far more dangerous authority than your government at Central will retaliate for any harm done to us or to our ship." His gaze lingered as if he had not the energy to move it on Kuan-yin.

"Yes," breathed Jehane, leaning forward with more interest.

"That's the one you have to watch," said Lily, without meaning to.

Jehane's glance, like fire, shifted to her. "Why is that?" It was a question he already knew the answer to.

"He's not afraid." Lily looked down, as if the blue-haired man's attention might stop her from continuing to talk in this fashion to Jehane, but Maria was speaking to Kyosti in their second tongue. "It's as if this is a game to him," she added compulsively. "He simply doesn't care."

"Perceptive," said Jehane, a wealth of compliment in one word. His attention returned to the interrogation.

"My darling Maria," Kyosti replied in Standard. "We may as well toss our cards on the table, had we such implements."

"Which cards?" Anjahar's voice was sharp.

Kyosti shrugged. "As many as my feeble brain can recall."

Maria looked at Anjahar. The glance conveyed an order that Anjahar clearly did not want to obey, but he acquiesced with a frown that manifested itself as much in his posture as on his face. And by some imperceptible communication, Lily felt that he and Maria surrendered their wills to Kyosti, a gesture she recognized, having so recently done it herself. But their surrender was willing, and conscious, as if they accepted him as more capable of dealing with the kind of situation they now faced.

Beside Lily, Jehane stood silent, but his presence surrounded her.

"Go on," ordered Kuan-yin.

Kyosti remained silent for a space of five breaths. Everyone watched him. "Ah," he said suddenly, as if he had just recalled an important fact. "Jehane." He smiled. " 'It is customary for there to be modesty about him.' "

"What does that mean?" demanded Kuan-yin.

"We must inform you first of all that our ship is not hooked to this station but is in free orbit, and that by itself our ship has enough firepower to—shall we say—render this station inoperable and uninhabitable. Much as we must admire your military prowess in so swiftly and comprehensively taking control of—what do they call it?"—a chuckle —"Nevermore—really, how droll—you have no chance against superior weaponry."

"This may be true," said Kuan-yin, "but you would die as well."

"Ah, death." Kyosti examined the ceiling. "Sweet bedfellow. But we are simple pawns. And the shuttle docked here is a mere trifle. But after all"—he smiled warmly at the grim-faced Kuan-yin—"we are not enemies. We seek a handful of individuals who have committed a few violent crimes. When we have them all, we will go, quite quietly, I assure you."

"Where will you go?" asked Kuan-yin.

Into the silence made by Kyosti adjusting his sleeves, Lily lifted her head to find Jehane staring at her with intense interest. It was utterly unnerving, and overwhelming. "Back," she said, answering his unspoken question. "They'll go back, over the way."

"To the lost home worlds," he murmured. His eyes had the cold, enticing glitter of emeralds. "You are one of those they came to find."

"No," said Lily quickly. "I'm not. They just think I am. It was a mistake."

"No need to fear me." His voice was soft. "We can help each other."

But she did fear him, feared his power to usurp her volition. With great effort, she forced herself to turn away and look down again.

"Well," said Kuan-yin in the room below. "You've had enough time to think."

"My bane," replied Kyosti with an exaggerated sigh. "Too much time to think." Anjahar stifled a noise suspiciously like a laugh. The angry rush of red had subsided from his cheeks; he looked as if he were enjoying himself. Maria's face remained impassive. "But!" Kyosti raised one hand in a patrician's gesture. "Do not be hasty. You call your regions of space the Reft, I believe. We are from beyond it. We are"—he stood and made a gracefully florid bow to Kuan-yin—"your ancestors."

"As I thought," said Jehane in an astonishingly hard voice. He lifted his wrist band to his mouth, spoke into it.

Kuan-yin turned and walked to the door. "These men will escort you back to your cell," she said.

Kyosti blinked and turned to address the black wall. "Have I miscalculated?" he asked.

"Not entirely," said Jehane in a low voice, as if in answer. "But close enough." He watched as the entire party left the room.

"A handful of individuals for a few violent crimes." It rang in Lily's head, that phrase. Heredes, a criminal? Had they already killed him? Were they just cleaning up his associates? Herself among them? Bach drifted down and nudged gently at her back, like a reassurance. She laid a hand on his gleaming surface.

"Lilyaka Hae Ransome." Jehane's voice, not at all loud, permeated the atmosphere of the little room. He was regarding her with the same expression the Sar had when examining the first fruits of a new vein: Will this be worthwhile to mine? Will it prove valuable? "An interesting choice of name."

"How did you take Nevermore?" she asked abruptly.

"Never reveal your deepest secrets, my child," he said, "except to your heir when you are on your deathbed." He sat, a slow curling of his body. His uniform, for it was a close copy of the others she had seen below, was not white but a deep brown that set off his golden hair and green eyes, suggesting that agricultural world, that paradise, that a child like Paisley must ever yearn for. "But," he added, "with the entire Ridani population behind me, as well as the many, many discontent who have at last chosen to act, at an isolated station it proves easy enough to dismantle Central's authority and create a true people's government.

"What do the pygmies say about this?"

"They have their own business, and in any case live so very separate from us. As long as their tasks continue uninterrupted, they have no quarrel with me."

"And the sta?"

"The sta have reason to be in their own way displeased about the encroachments Central has made on their traditions and freedoms and territories. As Central has on all of ours. You must know this?"

"I don't know," said Lily, but she thought of Finch, and his surprising tirade against the new trade laws.

"But of course," Jehane rose. "What would you know of it?"

She saw that he had misunderstood her ignorance for that of a foreigner rather than the privileged. "What are you going to do," she asked quickly, to forestall his questions, "with your rebellion if you reach Central?"

He paused. "Institute the people's government," he said. "Return to the citizens of the Reft their freedom and their rights." He smiled. It was like the flash of a beacon light to one lost in Unruli's storms, inviting one to its shelter. "Of course."

She wanted simply to believe, but some instinct honed by the years of martial arts kept her sparring. "How can you possibly take Central?"

"There are already comrades working there for us. Workers of all persuasions, ready to act. A talented young writer, full of truth and passion, who even now prepares the ground with his sermons."

"If you win, you'll take the Ridanis back, over the way?"

He laughed, a charming sound. "You have heard *ya* story as well, I see. But of course the Ridani must be reintegrated as citizens, as equal citizens, of the Reft before such a course can be taken. But, Lilyaka Ransome, you yourself also know why, for that very reason, you can be of such great help to me." He took two steps toward her.

"Is it really your name—Jehane?"

"It is my essence." Another step. Lily retreated, pushing Bach with her. "You know what I need—referents, navigation charts, vectors. I must know that route." Two steps toward her.

She would have told him if she had known. Instead, she took two more steps back, maintaining the distance that separated them, as if his touch alone might put her completely under his control. "Ask your prisoners. They even have a ship. I can't help you. *I don't know.*"

His voice, his expression, held only pained bewilderment. "Why do you not wish to cooperate with me? *I* can assist you. They only hunt you. You will be safe with me." Two steps more.

No I won't, she thought desperately, even as she lifted a hand toward him, to accept his bounty. Bach stopped abruptly, come up against the wall. She was cornered. His benevolence terrified her. "I don't know anything!"

"Do not attempt to make me believe that. We did run you. You do not exist in government records. You control a completely foreign robot. This masquerade is useless."

"But I was wiped from the computers. *Your* people rescued me from prison."

He smiled slightly, clearly disbelieving her, and took another step toward her. "Will you cooperate?" Gracious, but the "or," although unspoken, was clearly said.

Lily bent, fumbling at her trouser leg, and came up with Calico's gun. "No closer, or I shoot." It was her last defense.

Jehane's smile broadened. "A challenge," he said lightly. "But will you?" With utter confidence he walked straight for her.

Lily shot him.

It was more a concussion in the air than a noise or a report, more instinct than volition. Jehane staggered backward, regained his balance and, slowly, lifted his right hand to his left shoulder. Blood filtered through the brown cloth, a damp, spreading patch.

"I'm sorry," said Lily in a much calmer voice, holding the gun steady. The act had somehow freed her of the overwhelming power of his will. "But I said I would."

Jehane tasted the blood on his right hand, as if considering its flavor. His left arm dangled uselessly at his side. "You keep your word," he said at last. "And I see that I underestimated you. But you will understand that this interview must continue at a later time, as you still possess information that I require. You will remain in custody until then." He smiled, as if to temper the effect of such a harsh judgment.

Lily said nothing.

He murmured into his wrist band. The door slid open with the gasp that Jehane had not uttered. Calico appeared.

"Missy!" he cried, much betrayed, when he saw the wound.

Kuan-yin rushed into the room, followed by guards.

"You little animal!" The soldier charged forward, disregarding completely Lily's gun, and shoved Lily into the wall. Lily's head struck the hard surface with a flash of blinding pain, and she dropped her gun. A white form picked it up. Kuan-yin gripped Lily's throat and squeezed.

"Gently, Joan." Jehane's voice came from the doorway. Kuan-yin released Lily as though she were infectious. Lily, gasping, could scarcely see, but she felt abruptly that Jehane had left the room. Her head ached.

Someone yelped.

"It bit me!"

Lily's vision focused enough to see Bach, a faint glow cloaking him like a nimbus, a guard rubbing her hand against her hip.

"March it up, female!" Kuan-yin's command cut into the air, daring Lily to resist.

But Lily merely whistled a short phrase to Bach and marched. Guards formed up around her. Calico's face peeped at her through the bodies, mournful.

"Missy," he said with a sigh, and he shook his head.

"I'm sorry, Calico," she said, hoping it reached him as they prodded her through the doorway.

They took her into the blank hallway. Kuan-yin's desire for revenge crowded like yet another presence beside her. But Lily, marched along, thrust through one of the seamless doorways, left alone in a cell, felt paralyzed. She could no more understand the power Jehane had had over her, or the instinct that had compelled her to shoot him in order to free herself than she understood with any concrete knowledge the whole course of events that had left her in this tiny cell. Bach, with that instinct he had for her, began to sing a soft chorale:

> *Ich will hier bei dir stehen,*
> *Verachte mich doch nicht!*
> *Von dir will ich nicht gehen,*
> *Wenn dir dein Herze bricht.*
> *Wann dein Herz wird erblassen*
> *Im letzten Todesstoss,*
> *Alsdenn will ich dich fassen*
> *Im meinem Arm und Schoss.*

> "I will stand here beside Thee,
>   do not then scorn me!
>   From Thee I will not depart
>   even if Thy heart is breaking.
>   When Thy heart shall grow pale
>   in the last pang of death,
>   then I will grasp Thee
>   in my arms and lap."

Lulled, she fell asleep on the floor.

She woke when a beep shattered the silence of the cell; a slot appeared above the floor and produced a tray of food and drink. She ate. To have such a tenuous understanding of herself was frightening; to be so quickly pushed into panic was embarrassing as well as dangerous. How often had Heredes told her, "Rashness will not save you, Lily. Only confidence and skill." But she smiled slightly as she found the washing cubicle and disposed of the tray down the recycle hatch. At least it had delayed the interview with Jehane. She laughed a little, thinking of his reaction to being shot: he had been more concerned with his miscalculation of her strength than with his wound. What plans might such a man have? How, indeed, could people resist him? Abruptly, she wondered how the blue-haired Kyosti would fare against him. Or Heredes? If he were still alive.

She began to pace, did what basic forms and kata she could in the restricted space. Pausing for breath, she happened to look up at Bach where he hovered high in one corner, out of her way. Some of his lights winked, and he began to sing.

Patroness, thou art concerned for the master Heredes, art thou not?

"Bach!" *Bach,* she whistled. *Do you know anything about him? Did the foreigners tell you anything?*

He sank toward her. *Negative, patroness. But I do not believe this group has him. They are human and doubtless from my ancient home, and if it is Heredes that they seek, they have not yet found him.*

As if he could have escaped from those others.

Pardon, patroness, but thou perhaps needest a reminder that we and the girl did indeed escape.

Around them, the light diffused out equally from all surfaces. Lily smiled. "That we did." She gave the robot a playful buffet at his equator.

She renewed her exercises with much more energy. Cleaned herself and her clothes when she had finished. There was no terminal in the room, so she sat with Bach and traded songs and games. After a time, the beep sounded again and another meal tray came through.

Only the juice, in its plastine cup, had any real flavor. She savored it. The cup itself had a few rough scrapes around its bottom edge. Her finger, tracing absently along them, began to form fanciful letters of them. *B* there, then an *E*. A smooth gap, more of the roughness, almost like little carvings: this could be an *R*, *E?*, surely an *A* next. An *O*. Well, perhaps a *D*. It was novel to one accustomed to seeing letters on a screen and to punching keys to create them to see how they might actually be formed manually. A double branch—a Y, of course.

She stopped. Drained the last of the juice in a single gulp and lifted the cup up to eye level. On the white surface the letters proved hard to see, but they clearly had been carved there. "BE READY." She turned the cup. "SOON." Turned it again. "JLH." That was all.

"He's alive." She breathed, holding the cup before her as if it were a holy relic.

She quickly took the tray and cup and shoved them into the recycle hatch, returned to kneel in the cell exactly opposite the door, hands open on her knees. Bach drifted down behind her.

When a low sequence of tones sounded from the air, she came instantly alert and to her feet. Bach sang a barely audible question. She put her hands out, flat, on either side of her: "stay back." A seam traced out a door, and with an inhalation it slid open.

He wore the familiar loose, white trousers and waist-belted tunic, and in one hand he carried a metal box. For an instant, she compared him to Jehane, who also had green eyes, but Heredes's hair and skin were much darker, and for all the mastery, of life and art and fighting, inherent in every motion he made, he carried himself unobtrusively.

Without a word, she ran to hug him. With that part of the mind that detaches under high emotion, she realized that he was only the fifth man she had ever hugged this closely: her favorite brother, her karate partner on reaching *shodan* together; that sleet miner from the Belts whose one season at Ransome House had included time in Lily's bed, and Finch, under rather different circumstances.

This was different. She loved him, a very pure, very simple emotion that had no expectations, no desires, no demands. It was new.

She broke off and stepped back from him. "I thought you were dead." Tears shone gloriously in her eyes.

Heredes laughed and came fully into the cell. The doorway seamed shut behind him. "Haven't I told you, Lily? It's terribly boring being dead. I stay that way for as short a time as possible." His eyes, examining her, seemed to come to some conclusion, and he relaxed.

"But how did you get away from those aliens? And how did you find me? You couldn't have known I was following you." As he walked past her, toward Bach, she turned with him as a plant turns, catching the sun.

He raised one hand in a dismissive gesture—one much like Kyosti's, she thought suddenly, but far more energetic. "As a species, Kapellans are careless. Their Darwinian flaw seems to be overconfidence. As for the other—" He walked a slow circle around Bach, studying the robot's entire circumference. "It was a process too complicated to explicate here, although I did return to Unruli briefly. But why did you think I was dead?"

"The aliens aren't the only ones after you."

"Ah," he said.

"There are also humans, like us, except they're not from the Reft."

He raised his eyebrows.

"They're trying to find you, I think to arrest you." Still he regarded her without surprise. "Maybe they're connected with those bounty hunters who tried to take you in at Apron Port."

"That could be."

"They had a picture of you. And all these names I'd never heard." He nodded. She frowned. "And one of them, later, I overheard him say, 'the old man is dead.' "

Whatever she had wanted, some reaction, she got it in full now.

"Dead!" His face changed utterly. He turned away from her, hiding his grief. Lily hung her head. There was a long silence. She heard him murmur, "May the Mother bless his spirit," and she looked up in time to see him trace in the air a series of movements, a final benediction. "He was a friend," he said quietly. "More than that. He was the one who laid our path."

"How can you know it's the same person—this 'old man' and your friend?"

"It's a very long story, Lily. We don't have time for it now. But I must ask you—" He walked back around Bach and up to her. The clean lines of his face gave not the least indication of a life that had endured long stories. "Where *did* you get a composer?"

"A what?"

Heredes began to whistle. Snatches of phrases, really, but the fifth bit was Bach's signature phrase, and Bach responded with a delighted full cadence. "Ah," said Heredes. "A sixteen eighty-five."

"He's a sixteen eighty-nine."

"The fourth of his line." Heredes sounded either impressed or skeptical. "The series number is sixteen eighty-five, and each individual unit was numbered from there."

"Can you communicate with him?" She felt to her embarrassment a swell of jealousy.

"Unfortunately, no, except with speech. I just know the basic codes in music. Where did it come from?"

"I found him in my father's warehouse about ten years ago. It was an accident, really, that I got him to work." She flushed. "He was the one who took the computer prelim test —that's why it was so high."

He chuckled. "I see."

"And when I went after you, it just seemed—I don't know—the right thing to do, to bring him."

"You've bonded him!" Startling him twice was much more than she had expected. He looked, perhaps, more astonished than proud. "That's quite remarkable, Lily."

"Thank you," she stammered.

"Remarkable," he echoed. "And lucky for our side. Tell me how you got here."

She told him, as briefly as she could. Bach added a few comments in Paisley's voice.

Heredes considered it all. "Realistically," he said at last, "I doubt there is anything we can do for the Ridani girl." He raised one hand to forestall her objection. "For now, at least. Consolidate our own rather precarious position first. Then we'll see. As for Jehane, well, I think we should release these three—ah—foreigners from him. I can't imagine that a man of his ambitions is pleased to know that a government far, far more powerful than Central exists, especially if it is out of his range, but he is not out of theirs." His gaze fixed for a space on something invisible to Lily, some thought or memory or speculation beyond what she knew. " 'It is customary,' " he began in a low voice, " 'for there to be modesty about him.' " He shook his head and looked at her. "Indeed. And if your name is erased from records, that leaves us a great advantage, doesn't it?"

Lily stared at him. "We're not going back, are we?" she said, half-unable to believe it. "We're not going back to Unruli."

"Going back?" He raised the box, fingered it. The seam appeared, exhaled as it opened. "I have some investigation to do. And you've come much too far to go back now, Lily-aka."

10 Queen of the Highroad

❈❈❈❈❈❈

They found the three foreigners just around the curve of the hall, in the second cell Heredes opened.

All three stood abruptly. Anjahar and Maria looked bewildered, in Anjahar's case succeeded by ill-masked fear.

But Kyosti, after the energetic rise, merely adjusted his sleeves with exaggerated fastidiousness. "You do take your time, Gwyn," he murmured. "These barbarians have failed to provide us with chairs."

"Hawk." Heredes gazed at the blue-haired man with admiration. "You look just the same."

Kyosti's expression changed swiftly, and one hand rose toward his hair. "But I've worked so hard—is it all for nothing?"

"This is ridiculous," snapped Maria. "What do you want with us?"

"In all honesty," said Heredes with a trace of asperity, "nothing. I thought I would release you."

"Into whose mercies?" Anjahar had backed into the farther corner. "Have you thrown in with this Jehane fellow? You're well acquainted with his sort of methods."

"Oh, dear," said Heredes. "You must know that my allegiance has never wavered. I had assumed you had some transport you could reach."

"I see," replied Maria. "You expect us to take you along. Or will you simply commandeer us?"

"I'm simply opening the door," said Heredes. "After all, we still retain a certain loyalty of a kind to one another, having fought for so long on the same side." He turned. "Come, Lily."

"Gwyn." Heredes turned back. Kyosti had stepped forward. "I have this sudden uncontrollable urge to tag along with you."

Heredes smiled. "Hawk, I don't need you at my back. I've got enough troubles."

Kyosti raised both hands, palms up and open. "No knife." He smiled winningly.

Heredes laughed.

"Kyosti, are you out of your mind!" Anjahar's face had the mottled flush of extreme agitation. "He's a known terrorist. We're here to arrest him."

"Anja." Kyosti's expression remained dispassionate, his voice languorous. Only his eyes glittered with suppressed vitality. "May I remind you that I am myself one of the same breed?"

"But you recanted." Maria glared still at Heredes, who to Lily's eye appeared the mildest of them all.

"Ah, well," said Kyosti. "One grows bored of rehabilitation."

Maria reached out to grip his arm. "You wouldn't consider it!" she cried.

"I fear I would." He disengaged her hand with deceptive gentleness. "And do."

"Lily," said Heredes. "May I introduce our new companion, Kyosti Bitterleaf Hakoni."

Lily gave a slight nod.

Kyosti swept her a flamboyant bow. "Charmed."

"Traitor," muttered Anjahar.

"Get out," snapped Maria. "You can be assured this will go out on report as soon as we reach the ship."

"Do convey my respects to Rayonne," Kyosti replied, unruffled. "Oh dear." He appeared to have misgivings. "My wardrobe."

"Hawk," said Heredes, motioning to Lily. "We're leaving."

"Sacrifices must be made—" Lily heard Kyosti continue as she edged out into the corridor, where Bach hovered, on guard. As Heredes came out beside her, she leaned toward him.

"Do you trust him?" she whispered.

"Of course not," said Heredes with all appearance of cheerfulness. "Now," he continued, brisker, but still soft, waving her forward. "We have to get past two sets of guards. Then I got us berths on a merchanter, a bit of a dogtag, I'm afraid, but it'll get us to Central."

"Central!"

"Then you'll go off to Wingtuck, and I've got some research to do."

"And I, Gwyn?" Kyosti came up beside them. The blank hall curved away behind, the cell doorway already lost around the unbroken bend of grey.

"You'll have much to do to refurbish your wardrobe, I expect," said Heredes, still soft.

"Dear, dear," murmured Kyosti, even softer. "And in such unpromising districts, as well." With an expert flick of the wrist he caught up the end of one of his sleeves. Watching his hands as he toyed with the cloth, Lily saw that their manicured delicacy disguised strength and agility. With an abrupt wrench, he tore the fabric and, insinuating one hand within the folds of the fabric, brought out a short circular rod of black metal, one end swelled into a little nodule. A second flick, and it telescoped out smoothly into a meter-long stick. "I grow old, I grow old," he sighed, positioning it now to act as a walking cane. "But sadly, trousers have gone out of fashion."

"First post," said Heredes. "We can slip by these."

He halted and lifted the metal box. A door wafted open as lights winked on its panel. Kyosti, Lily, and Bach followed Heredes through into a large office. The sound of voices drifted in and they all crouched. Heredes moved forward from desk to desk, concealing his approach to the doorway on the far side. Lily motioned Kyosti to precede her. His smile, barely discernable in the gloom, mocked her distrust, but he went, the cane path finding before him. The slight warm stir of air at her feet heralded Bach's sinking. As he came to rest on the floor, a small panel on his surface rolled back to reveal a miniature keyboard. Lily tapped a quick message to him before she crept forward after Kyosti. Behind her, air puffed noiselessly at her trouser legs as Bach followed her.

Halfway across she froze in the shadow of a desk. Bach slid in under it. Three of Jehane's guards entered the room through the door Heredes was headed for. After a cursory examination of the room, they went out a side doorway into a further complex of rooms. A shadow raised itself in front of the far door and, giving a sign with one hand, sank back into the shadows.

Lily got to the door just as Kyosti arrived from a different direction. Heredes was keying into the com-panel next to the door. The guards' voices neared, returning.

"Take them out, Lily," said Heredes in an undertone, not looking up from the panel.

She loped toward the side door, one hand a breadth away from the wall for balance. Bach and Kyosti followed her; she waved them back. As the three guards entered the office, she planted a kick into the temple of the first one. He collapsed. A desk obstructed her, shielding the other two. She vaulted over it, swung out from the edge, sweeping them both off balance, and pushed off into stance. One of the guards grabbed for his gun, the other for her radio—

Lily threw a spinning back kick, knocking the female back into the desk before she could reach her radio. Spun back around to tackle the one with the gun. She caught his arms and they both went down, Lily on top. The guard pushed against her. She twisted his wrist and with a gasp he released the gun, but his momentum rolled him up and over her. A sharp impact smacked into the body above her, and the guard went limp. She shoved him off her, got to her feet. Kyosti stood beside her, cane in one hand, holding the female at arm's length. With a quick snap, he struck the guard in the temple with the rod, then lowered her to the floor and removed the radio from her belt.

"So sorry to intrude," he murmured. "As you had them

well in hand." He glanced up. The far door had opened a crack; Heredes straightened from the panel. "But we are in a hurry."

"Thanks," said Lily. She vaulted herself back over the desk. Kyosti walked around it, following her back.

Heredes had eased the door open manually; he reconnoitered outside with a quick glance, motioned them through. They stood in an ordinary station corridor. The door slid shut behind them.

"Hawk," said Heredes suddenly, in the bright light getting an unadulterated view of his companion. "Haven't you got anything less obvious?"

Kyosti's blue hair was not as flagrant as his clothing: a brilliant gold cloth, embroidered with silver and red thread on raised patterns, cut in a floor-sweeping robe with trailing, scalloped sleeves and a high pointed collar. A gem-studded belt caught it in at the waist and a heavy gold chain hung around his neck.

"It is rather striking," said Lily, trying not to smile.

"You're a hard man, Gwyn," Kyosti muttered. But he unbuckled the belt and with surprising adroitness slipped the garment off over his head and, kneeling, dismantled and remantled it in rather the same manner as a person takes apart and puts together a puzzle. Lily could not help but examine him with interest.

He wore now only a light shirt with no sleeves, and shorts. He was slender, but very well formed. His arms and legs, entirely revealed, had not the hard musculature of a well-honed athlete like herself or Heredes but something smoother and equally sensuous. He glanced up, straight at her, and offered her a lazily suggestive smile.

The provocative intimacy of the gesture took her aback, at the same time as it captivated her. When she realized that she was returning his smile, and his interest, she blushed and looked away. To find Heredes watching her. She flushed deeper and fixed her attention on her boots until Kyosti stood up. He wore a dull gold tunic and trousers.

"My vanity weeps," he said, "but I persevere."

"Let's go," said Heredes with a touch of temper. "One more post, at the lock."

Heredes pulled them up just as the curve of the corridor brought the lock into view. Five white-uniformed soldiers, one a tattoo, who stood separate from the others, maintained the guard at the lock.

"Jehane must not be in this section now," said Lily under her breath.

Heredes shrugged a question.

"There'd be more guards."

He considered this. His face bore the same intent look as when he did kata: it must all be exact.

"We've got no cover for ambush," he said finally. "We need surprise. The composer will have to stay back, but come up fast." Bach winked agreement. "Lily. Can you give me a prostitute—a station-hopper?"

Lily made a horrible face. "Must I?"

"We'll let this be a lesson," he said gently, "that sex can always be used as a weapon against those without discipline." He looked at Kyosti. "And Hawk I have always imagined would do marvelously as a procurer. I'll come in when I can."

"You flatter me," said Kyosti, but his manner altered subtly. "Come, girl, a little more skin. What's under the tunic?"

Lily unbuckled her belt and took off the tunic, which Heredes appropriated. She wore only a thin undershirt; she was painfully aware of the swell of her breasts and the barest suggestion of nipples under the fabric, and most of all of Kyosti standing next to her.

"Very good," said Kyosti with much sincerity.

"Careful," said Heredes as they stepped forward, and Lily felt with sudden instinct that the command was not directed at her at all.

The guards noticed them immediately.

"A tad more sway to the hips," murmured Kyosti provocatively as they advanced. "That's better."

"This is humiliating," hissed Lily. For an instant the guards seemed a trivial consideration compared to his compelling, and unnerving, presence.

"You're stunning when you're angry," he breathed. "Let us hope that when we're out of this we can find a quiet room sans your watchful guardian. You seem very important to him."

"You're impossible," muttered Lily, flushing.

"Thank you," he said fervently, in a carrying voice. "Gentlemen!" He motioned Lily forward until she came to a halt a few paces from the nearest guard, who cautiously lowered his gun. "Thank you for entertaining such thoughts as you obviously are entertaining about my young protégée."

Five pair of eyes slid to examine Lily. Two more guns lowered.

"Hemmed in as we are by all this security," Kyosti waved a negligent hand toward them, "my young adept here has had little opportunity to improve her—ah—skills. And I'm sure you gentlemen know"—he favored each one with a penetrating gaze—"how important experience is to mastering a skill." Another gun lowered. Two of the soldiers smiled.

"How'd you get into this section?" asked the one with the unlowered gun.

"My dear boy." Kyosti's gaze was withering. "Surely you don't think the previous tenants were without their little pleasures?"

The gun wavered.

"He's got a point, Gar," said one of the smilers. "They must of got caught back here. And there's a room just off to the right here."

"Ah!" Kyosti moved forward, ignoring the raised gun, and clapped the speaker on the shoulder. "Such enterprise should not go unrewarded. Will you take the young lady aside?"

"How much?" said the lad.

"She'll arrange the transaction," Kyosti said generously. "It depends on your—ah—needs."

Lily grabbed the young fellow's wrist and tugged him behind her. "Come on," she said.

"Be a good girl, darling," said Kyosti to her stiff back.

"Hoo, ain't she eager," said one of the guards.

Gar's gun lowered slightly. Lily and the lad disappeared past a door. Kyosti began regaling the four left with an obscene story. Gar's gun lowered completely. Just as Kyosti finished, Lily reappeared alone.

"Sure," said the tattoo. "That were fast."

"Where is he?" demanded Gar.

"Putting his clothes on." Lily's voice had a clipped tone that might have been mistaken for breathlessness. "You want to be next." She headed for Gar.

Kyosti, quick to read the signs, took an unobtrusive step back into the midst of the guards. Even to a man of his experience, Lily betrayed not the slightest signal of the kick that took Gar in the groin. As Gar doubled over, Kyosti laid the meat of his cane with a crack along the back of the tattoo's neck. Lily was past him; she thrust an open palm out; the two soldiers focused on it, beginning to lift their weapons, and she whipped a crescent kick into the face of one, spun off it into a second to the other's ribs. They both staggered back. She dropped one with a punch.

But the tattoo had not gone down and was in fact struggling, gun still in one hand. Gar began to unbend. Lily was grabbed from behind by the fifth guard.

Heredes arrived. He dealt with Gar and the tattoo summarily, and he and Kyosti moved to find the last guard crumbling at Lily's feet, victim of a firmly planted elbow. Bach was coding into the lock panel; it blinked green and opened.

"I'm sorry, Lily," said Heredes as the door shut behind them. He handed over her tunic, which she quickly drew on and buckled. "But it seemed most expedient."

Kyosti laughed.

Lily felt a wave of anger rise in her, at his levity, but she quickly dissipated it by rebuckling her belt and ignoring him. "You were right," she said pointedly to Heredes, "about that lesson."

The lock opened.

"Walk quickly," said Heredes as they with one step

cleared the lock, Bach above them. "Berth Bossuet twelve eighteen."

"Bossuet." Kyosti chuckled, coughed, and chuckled again, but at a sharp glance from Heredes he subsided.

They split up, walking through several business sections, shops, a scattering of people who seemed, despite the insurrection and the occasional pair of Jehanist soldiers, to be going about their regular pursuits. Bach sank to Lily's waist level, where he was less conspicuous. A troop of white-uniformed soldiers rushed past, in the opposite direction.

At the next lock, two soldiers were questioning people. Bach sank to the floor and, as they came up to the crowd, rolled gently in among the mass of feet. Someone was arguing with the guards. Lily recognized him suddenly as Kyosti. He had found a hood somewhere to cover that hair. As she slid past into the lock, Bach a soft gleam at her feet, Kyosti shouted. The soldiers looked up and Kyosti slid in past the closing lock door.

The lock opened into a docking sector. Lasalle. Dupin. Another lock. Madeline sector. Lafourcade. Another, and at last, Bossuet.

The alarm sounded, a deep hooting. Another detachment of soldiers pounded past. People shrank to the sides of the corridor. Traffic slowed and stopped. Behind, shouts rang out at the lock. Lily strolled, quick, but not alone—a few other individuals had business more pressing than a general alert. She saw berth 1218, Heredes standing before it talking with a dark woman in mercenary's garb. Someone came up behind her, too close.

"A little haste, perhaps," Kyosti murmured in her ear.

Lily hurried forward just fast enough to put distance between them; as she arrived at the berth, the mercenary smiled at her with obvious sympathy. The berth lock was open; Lily went in without breaking stride, aware of the noise of confusion and shouting closing in behind them.

The hold clearly showed signs of age. An old ship, a trifle neglected, perhaps, but Heredes had said it was a bit of a dog-tag. Kyosti collided with her and she felt a hand press against her neck and hair, as familiar as a lover's. Against her back, his body was warm. Behind him, singing, floated Bach, followed by Heredes and the mercenary. The lock shut.

"Hawk!" Heredes's tone was as scandalized as a maiden aunt's.

Lily turned just as Kyosti removed his hand. He lifted the hand to his face in a gesture so alien, as if the contact between them could tell him something about her, that for an instant, like an hallucination, she wondered if he was human.

"We'll be going out fast," said the mercenary in a low voice, coming past them. "Especially if you caused that alarm. I'll show you to your—" She paused, taking in three where she had expected two, and she grinned at Lily, as if to say, Look what a mess these idiots have made. "*Your* cabin," she continued, directing a dark-eyed and knowing glance at Kyosti and Heredes. "You can share with me," she finished with a companionable nod to Lily. "By the way, my name is Jenny. Jenny Seria." Her grin broke out again, gently cynical. "And, from Captain Bolyai, as well as myself, a warm welcome to the *Easy Virtue,* queen of the highroad."

"This boat isn't really called that," said Kyosti.

"But of course it is." Jenny winked at Lily. "But frankly it's more a comment on our cargo than our crew." She led them into the ship, which was, judging by the spasm of conversation and command over the intercom, undocking even as they walked. "In here." She coded open a door into a tiny double-bunked cabin. Heredes shoved Kyosti inside. "How about the 'bot?" asked Jenny.

"He goes with me."

"My cabin is just down here." Jenny had a long-limbed stride that forced Lily to double-time. "I've never seen a 'bot like that before," the mercenary added. "Or a man with blue hair." She paused for the barest moment, as if testing the tension between them, then ventured, "Is the other one your brother?"

"My brother!" Lily, looking up, met Jenny's eye, a frankly speculative gaze, and smiled. "No." For some reason she thought of Kyosti's hand on her neck, and of Heredes's sharp reaction. "More like my father," she said slowly, much struck.

"That explains it," said Jenny. "Even my father got testy when I started bringing boyfriends home."

"Boyfriends!" exclaimed Lily, but Jenny had halted in front of a cabin door and now coded into the panel. Lily shrugged. "My name's Lily. Lily Hae Ransome."

Jenny gave her a little salute in acknowledgment as the door opened. "Come in," she said, "but watch out for small animals."

The high warning chime of final undocking rang out over the intercom.

"Get a seat, quick," said Jenny as Lily collided with a waist-high, golden-haired impediment. It yelped. The ship lurched, sending Lily tumbling past the impediment to land with a jar on the lower bunk. Another lurch slammed her against the bunk's side wall, but the third found her prepared, with a stiff grip on the edge of the bunk's pad. She rocked violently. A few rolling movements, like a restless beast at last settling down, shuddered through the ship. Lily let go of the bunk's edge.

Bach, upside down, winked eye to eye with a small boy of about five years whose light hair proclaimed him to be the impediment. The boy began to make distorted faces at himself in the gleam of Bach's surface.

"Gregori!" This admonition produced in the cabin as much effect as the quivering of a draft might in a closed room. The boy darted a glance in its direction and resumed his contortions. But Lily, more startled, found a young woman beside her on the bunk who was certainly younger than herself and who was drawn up into one corner like a frightened, but defensive, creature caught out in the wild.

"Excuse me," said Lily, rising. "I hope I didn't knock into you."

"Keep down," said Jenny quickly from the floor. "We're due another roll." The ship rolled, seating Lily with firm neatness. The young woman on the bunk smiled. "Milhaviru has some predictable habits," added Jenny.

"You may have guessed she didn't graduate top of her class at pilot's academy."

"But, Jenny." The other woman's voice was so soft it seemed barely to penetrate the air. "You said yourself we would be undocking without permission, so you can't fault Milhaviru for the roughness."

Jenny grinned. She pushed herself up with practiced ease and scooped the boy up into her arms. He wriggled in delight and grinned; seeing the likeness in that smile and in the strong set of his jaw, Lily knew whose child he was. "Always fair, that's my Lia," said Jenny. "But Lily, this is my son, Gregori, and next to you is Aliasing, my partner. I hope I read things right back there—that you'd a wish to be away from the two men, for now. Sometimes I let my instincts run before I have a chance to think."

Lily smiled back at her, finding her friendly and open manner balm to her confusion. Events had fallen with such chaos around her that she welcomed a moment to breathe. "Your training must have been good," she replied. "Because your instincts were right."

"You've had some training yourself," Jenny said, sizing Lily up. "We'll leave you alone as we can, in such space, but if you ever want a scrap, we've got a rec room on board that can be cleared out for a bit of sparring."

"You're on." Lily studied the other woman. Jenny was much taller than Lily, big-boned but lean, with that tight, high-shouldered look that comes with physical authority. By contrast Aliasing looked insubstantial.

"Want to play with the 'bot," said the boy emphatically. His mother let him down, glancing first at Lily.

"Of course." Lily sat cross-legged on the platform. "Did we really undock without authorization? Isn't that dangerous?"

Jenny shrugged. "No more than getting impounded by the Jehanists. Better to cut and run. They're spreading like fire out here on the fringe."

"But where did they come from? I grew up on Unruli, and I'd never heard of any rebellion until a few days ago."

"That's not surprising. Those of us on the road have come

across it—oh these past several years, growing—but nothing like it's growing now. Jehane, whoever she may be—if she or he really exists, that is—seems to have decided that the time, or her resources, are right."

"Oh, he exists," said Lily. "I met him."

"Did you?" Jenny pulled a hard plastine chair down from one wall and sat. Gregori, at her feet, was happily engaged in trading whistled phrases with Bach.

"What was he like?" breathed Aliasing. A curling tangle of black hair hung almost to her waist.

"He terrified me," said Lily.

Jenny chuckled. "You should see your face right now. But in any case, folk planetside really only hear what comes over the network, and you can be sure the government doesn't let any Jehanish news get down there. Too risky, by half."

"You mean they censor the news?"

"Where have you been, Lily Hae Ransome? Why do you think this old boat has the experience of cutting loose and running? Most of the cargoes she runs don't have permits. The captain doesn't even have a permit, for that matter. Most of our crew have some tattooed mark in their past that prevents them from getting work on authorized ships. Why else do you think we ship on a half-mended tub with a mediocre pilot whose vectors are slipshod and a captain who drinks too much ambergloss? Too many government regulations, that's why."

"I didn't really get a look at the ship," said Lily diplomatically.

"You will. Don't look too close. Not that I have much sympathy for the Jehanists either, especially their giving so much power to the tattoos—it'll only create a bloodbath. But I can't say I don't understand why so many are joining him. Central's been giving all the privileges to themselves, and not to the rest of us. I saw that well enough." The glance she exchanged with Aliasing was full of private meaning.

"I suppose I must confess," said Lily, uncomfortable, "that I'm the child of a Sar-house. So it's no wonder that I never noticed anything wrong."

Jenny regarded her with a level gaze: her eyes were dark, a suggestion of the void, pulled oblique at the corners. "I daresay we can learn to tolerate you, despite all that." She winked.

Aliasing laughed, and Lily realized that she was, for the time, at home here.

The next few days fell into a routine. Aliasing procured a second set of clothing for Lily. During the long hours of cruising to, or waiting for, windows, she sparred with Jenny and Heredes, sometimes even with Kyosti, accumulating a few bruises, met the disreputable crew of the *Easy Virtue*, and saw how life went on in a dog-tagging merchanter that smuggled for its living—she and Heredes and Kyosti being, evidently, their current cargo. Heredes refused to tell her the cost of their passage, although he did offer to man a bridge station on the odd shift; the captain, grateful for help, put him on communications.

Heredes, indeed, was taking on the attributes of her guardian. Whatever Lily's feelings about Kyosti, which could easily swing from annoyance to attraction to curiosity about his intriguing strangeness with the space of a few moments, she would at least have liked to get him to herself to question him about his and Heredes's past. Heredes, in response to those questions, deflected them so easily that she wondered where he had learned such methods of equivocation. To her outright demands he counseled patience. And when she asked if Joshua Li Heredes was his real name, he merely said, "As real as any name can be, defining so much with so little." Kyosti persisted in calling him Gwyn and in laughing at allusions whose source or meaning Lily could not guess at.

Five days into the trip, Lily returned to her cabin to find Aliasing helping Jenny outfit herself. Gregori had been banished to the top bunk.

"Trouble?" asked Lily as they both looked up at her entrance.

Jenny shrugged on a double-belted shoulder harness that sported a fascinating array of weapons. "Nothing that isn't routine for a smuggler," she said with a grimace. "The main routes into Central are so heavily policed and regulated that we've got to come in the back door. But the back door also means the back roads, and it's a little fey out there, the navigation points a little shiftier, if you take my meaning, and we've run into pirates more than once." She wore a skintight gray bodysuit; her hair, short anyway, was covered by a skullcap. She took out a forearm length metal rod and twirled it. "Heredes knows how to use one of these," she said. "We had a go at it today."

"Is that how he got that cut on his cheek?"

"Forgive me, but no!" Jenny contrived to look offended. "I've got better control than that. And anyway, your father is one mean old bastard and taught me a trick or two, much as I hate to admit it. No, your blue-hair had to try it. I don't mean to say he's useless, because he's really rather good, but he's not got the real knack, not like us. He lacks control."

"I wish I'd done more weapons." Lily took the stick when Jenny offered it to her and weighed it in her hands. "We did some, but I've always preferred empty-hand."

"That's because you're an artist." Jenny retrieved the stick and slid it into her belt. "I'm just trained to kill."

"Can I help?"

"You're not used to this kind of raiding. Stick to the cabin, for now."

Heredes had other plans. He persuaded the captain to let Lily sit next to him on the bridge for the next shift. Strapping himself in, he leaned to whisper to her.

"We're going to be running an irregular route here, Lily. This is possibly the best chance you'll ever get to see first-hand how they run the road virtually on manual."

Her reply was equally soft. "Isn't it a lot more dangerous?"

He smiled. He seemed placid, but beneath it—beneath it she suspected he thrived on chances like this. "Living is dangerous, Lilyaka," he said. He turned back to the com-console.

She watched the two harried sta navigators, doubling shifts to ensure accuracy; Milhaviru, the pilot, a sloppy, loudmouthed woman who sat still as sealed air now; Cap-

tain Bolyai, nervous at the sensors; the weapons man; and
the scanner operator. It was remarkably quiet:

"Homing at eleven ought two two three degrees. Forty-
seven bits." The sibilant tones of a sta.

"Check."

"Did you hear the one about the pirate's son who—"

"Shift—two point eight on vector."

"Vector shifted."

"Eleven ought three. Forty-eight."

"Closing imperative." Heredes's voice.

"Forty-eight. Forty-nine. Break."

They went through.

*The mind like water, formed to calm reflectivity. All is
mirrored.*

And came out.

The calculations began anew. A station, a solitary beacon
in a dark and isolate system, quavered a greeting and wished
them well.

They went through.

The mind like the moon. Light touching all equally.

And came out.

They drifted for an eight-hour rest shift on the edge of a
minor system. On a dog-tag such as this, with a necessarily
small crew, Lily saw how easy it would be to lose your ship
through a miscalculated window or on an incorrectly
vectored entrance just from fatigue. She wondered where
such ships ended up. And she saw how these folk might
easily come, like Jenny, to bear themselves with a cheerful
fatalism. Heredes woke her, and they returned to the bridge.

They went through.

*Infinity of stars. Place, in this dimension, a hand, so.
Bend, angle, shadow, each exact.*

And came out.

And were hailed. Heredes caught the channel and replied. Captain Bolyai stood anxiously beside him.

"This is the *Easy Virtue*. We are, I repeat, passing through."

"Throw down your colors, *Easy Virtue*, and prepare to be entered." The static across the channel lent a certain insouciance to this command.

Bolyai flipped on the alert. It echoed over the intercom.

"Captain!" The woman on scan gasped. "I've got them. Void help us. They're huge. Captain, look at those specs! Central's battle fleet has got nothing this big—Look at that hull!" Her voice trailed off in horrified awe.

"The *Easy Virtue* replies that she is not available to just anyone," said Heredes primly.

Static crackled. "We respect your finer feelings, *Easy Virtue*, but this is *La Belle Dame*, and she takes what she wills."

"Get me the closest window!" cried the captain, rushing to the scanners. The navigator began frantic calculations on the computer, but Lily saw Heredes's face freeze into stillness and thaw into anticipation.

"*La Belle Dame*," he called into the console. "Tell your mistress that my original country is the region of the summer stars."

Lily stared at him. Most of the bridge, catching the end of this, stared at him. Bolyai stepped back, about to speak.

"Stay on course, *Easy Virtue*. Don't attempt evasion." Static arced.

A second voice came on. "Hold your course. Please repeat your last statement." Heredes repeated it. A longer pause, scrambled with the faint hiss of static.

"*Easy Virtue*." A new voice. Female, yet something more than that. " 'Long and white are my fingers as the ninth wave of the sea.' " Even the sta, now, ceased at his calculations to gaze in astonishment at Heredes. "Are you coming over?"

"Of course," replied Heredes, and he unstrapped himself

and rose. "Captain, give me a shuttle and crew, and I can guarantee your safety, your cargo, and your ship."

"But who is that?" the captain asked, gazing at the scan numbers with bewilderment. "What is that? What pirate has a better than class seven fleet ship?"

"An entirely different breed of pirate," Heredes answered, not ungently. "And in any case, we have just met the queen."

"I thought we were on the queen," Lily said.

"That was a joke," Heredes said with perfect seriousness. *La Belle Dame* is the true and the only queen of the high-road. Shall we go?"

11   *La Belle Dame*

※※※※※※※

Kyosti came, and three of the crew, but the blue-haired man, after the jerky removal from the *Easy Virtue*, demanded and received the shuttle's controls. The massive hulk of *La Belle Dame* loomed outside the viewports. She was as large as the unmanned lowroad freighters Lily's father commissioned for transport of unprocessed ore, but she was also as sleek as an animal, a dark creature stalking the highroad.

"Do you know her, this ship?" Lily asked Heredes.

"This ship, no. She's new." He was tidying himself, straightening his clothes, combing his hair. "But I know her mistress. I know La Belle Dame." His voice had a husky quality, almost passionate. "These people are not from the Reft, Lily. Like Kyosti, they've come a long way to get here."

"Like you," she said, but he merely smiled.

Grappling hooks rang on the shuttle's hull as the big ship fastened onto them; the lock sealed on, and Heredes, Lily, and Kyosti passed into the ship.

Four armed men met them. One, to Lily's surprise, was a tattoo, standing with complete ease among her fellows. They wore striking clothes: large-sleeved shirts of silk, each a different color—scarlet, turquoise, emerald, and indigo—with collars and wrist bands of profuse white lace; tailored white trousers, wide belts, and ornately hilted cutlasses; high boots, rings, jeweled bracelets, necklaces of gold and silver and platinum. It was a uniform, but one individual to each man and woman. Kyosti sighed deeply, but forebore to comment on his own drab tunic.

The guards politely requested their presence on the bridge. Heredes politely agreed.

They followed corridors that seemed as numerous and as long as those of Ransome House. No grey walls here—from brilliant solid colors on the lowest deck the decoration progressed from simple geometric patterns, to murals, to, at the top deck, a complex interaction of color, pattern, raised relief, and texture that was evidently so fascinating to Kyosti that he lagged behind to examine it by touch. He had to hurry, finally, to catch them just as the lift doors began to shut.

The doors opened onto the bridge. The four guards hung back to let their three guests move out unescorted. Five plushly carpeted steps led down to a half-circle of silver floor. Chairs, individually crafted, sat before consoles inlaid with the material Heredes called wood. The crew, as brightly dressed as the guards, conversed in low tones to each other. Here, too, Lily saw Ridanis casually intermixed; it was this more than anything that convinced her that this ship, at least, came from outside the Reft.

Three huge screens filled the forward part of the half-dome above. One chair, on a low dais, sat with its back to them. Like a stilling hand, as the chair began to swivel in its foundation, its smooth, silent turn created a sudden immobility among the watching crew.

She was revealed as dawn is revealed: the slow, anticipatory unveiling that brings forth the sun. Her high brow was white as alabaster, her face framed by a close-cropped crown of blue-black hair that swept back and down to reappear over her shoulder in a single, sable braid reaching to her waist. She wore simple, black clothes—a shirt belted with gold clasps at the waist, a full skirt; her small white feet showed at the base. The high seat in which she sat seemed at once to dwarf her small stature and yet to be scant enough that it was a wonder it could hold her. Her eyes, even at this distance, pierced with the blue-white intensity of young twin stars. She rose, skirts rustling down as if a living creature clung to her.

"What have you brought me?" Her voice was as hushed as if cloth muffled it, but it filled, nevertheless, the bridge as air fills any space it enters. "Is this my eagle, is this my prisoner? Is this a ghost, or is it indeed the seventh age?"

Heredes walked forward, a solitary path across the silvering floor. He knelt at her feet on the dais.

With two fingers she raised his head until he looked up at her. "Is this truly my Taliesin?"

He lifted a hand to enfold hers, brought it to his lips, and kissed it with the reverence due a sacred object. "It is truly your Taliesin, Bella," he said, his voice so soft that the slightest movement in the room would have overwhelmed it. "Dead, mad, and a poet." He smiled as absently and thoroughly as a dreamer.

She studied him a time longer, then lifted her head to examine with unnerving steadiness Lily and Kyosti. "The hawk I recollect," she said in her quiet way. Lily felt Kyosti shift in apparent dis-ease beside her. "But who is this young woman?" Lily, meeting this gaze, felt the passage of respect between differences and familiarities, as judged as judging. This woman she could deal with, in the openhanded sense, although the formidable reserve behind that penetrating gaze might never allow for the intimacy of friendship. Caught up in her perusal, Lily was unaware that Heredes had turned his head to look at her.

A mere name could not satisfy the question the queen of the highroad had just asked—she dealt in relationships. And Joshua Li Heredes, by whatever name, was rarely at a loss for an answer. But he looked at Lily and could not define her.

First, she was his pupil: the lean athleticism, the posture of confidence that comes from mastery, the quick beam of her eye. Later, she had become something more than that, because she had excelled in a way no other he had taught had; there she stood with that controlled cast of face she had learned from him, worn away from the inside by the insatiate rabidity that drives an artist to seek further up the hidden path. And behind it all, the quality that had finally linked her to him completely: the core of restlessness that, like him with his master, she had never managed to still, could never still. It came very clearly to him the feeling when he had opened her cell, back at Nevermore, and she had, with rare spontaneity, come to him—and he knew with the swiftness of just-illuminated truth who she was.

"Bella," he said, as grave as he was surprised, standing now. "I would like you to meet my daughter, Lily."

Kyosti's astonishment was as much physical as his blurted, "Mother bless us." Lily felt him start, like a bolting animal glimpsing freedom; his hand touched her elbow, a delicate pressure, but one that seemed to claim something of her.

Bella looked not in the least disconcerted, merely thoughtful. Lily, once Kyosti's touch brought her back from her initial shock at Heredes's statement, realized that from her own conversation with Jenny, this could not be entirely unexpected.

"Then, my dear," said La Belle Dame finally, "I must offer you my welcome, and give you the hospitality of the ship while you wait."

"Are we waiting?" asked Lily.

"Of course, my child. Your father and I have some private business to discuss."

"But will our ship wait?" Lily asked it more of Heredes than La Belle, but he merely stood as meek as a servant beside her.

La Belle smiled, so ruthlessly cold a smile that Lily felt pity for those souls who found themselves opposed to her. "With our justly famous Sans Merci guns trained on them, I feel they will find that their patience extends indefinitely Adam." She beckoned with a single, imperious hand, and a man rose from one of the consoles and came to stand at the foot of the dais. He had La Belle's blue-black, straight hair but also, standing below Heredes, a dusky cast of skin and green eyes that reflected some trace of the older man. "Give your father your good wishes, and then offer your sister and the hawk some refreshment."

He bowed, salute enough on this ship, and stepped up to give a stiff shake of the hand and a few inaudible words to Heredes. He retreated as Heredes put his arm out to take La Belle's and the two of them walked as if on procession into the lift, the door sealing them off from the rest. The bridge crew turned with self-conscious busy-ness back to their tasks, leaving Adam alone to approach Lily and Kyosti. The four guards had vanished.

"Well, sister." Adam regarded her with a wary but not unfriendly gaze. "Shall we go?"

They said nothing more, except Kyosti's compliments to Adam on the ship's interior decoration as they walked along the top deck and into the dining hall and lounge. Plush couches, upholstered in patterns of spirals and chevrons, sat in intimate groupings across the carpeted floor. Wall hangings depicted unfamiliar scenes—a woman riding a horse with a swarm of birds surrounding her, a shoreline littered with a shipwreck's debris and a single body; a woman armed much as Jenny had armed herself, but with primitive weapons. Wooden tables and chairs were supported on legs carved into curving, sensuous shapes that begged one to stroke them. Adam sat Lily and Kyosti at one of the tables and left to fetch refreshments.

Kyosti, opposite her, leaned across the table and clasped her hands in his. "Lily!" he breathed in an undertone; farther away other people moved or sat in their own conversations within the hall. His blue eyes had a wild look to them, a curious mirror to the unruly mop of his blue hair. "Marry me!"

Lily blinked. "What?"

"Marry me," he repeated, his hands tightening on hers. He pulled her toward him, as if he meant to kiss her.

Lily drew back. "What does 'marry' mean?"

It was his turn to blink, to have to puzzle this out: seeing him at a loss was so unusual that Lily had to smile. Perhaps he took this for encouragement, because he bent closer to her. "You must have a word for it. Marry, mate, bond—"

"Bond!" Lily laughed. "Is that what you mean?"

"Yes. Yes, of course," he said, quickly shifting ground.

"But Kyosti, first of all, we don't even qualify."

"Qualify! Lily, when does love have to qualify?"

Lily felt that she would be in a better position to conduct this conversation were her hands not caught in his, but she did not attempt to free them. "What does love have to do with bonding?" she retorted. "My father certainly would have no interest in an economic bond with you, since it wouldn't bring him any trading benefits."

"Oh, wouldn't he," muttered Kyosti darkly.

"And since you're not a citizen, we couldn't enter into a child-sponsor pair-bond even if *I* wanted to."

"But Lily, surely two people in love have some bond they can share."

Lily regarded him with deep suspicion. "They can share whatever they want. I don't know what a legal bond has to do with it."

Kyosti released her hands abruptly and let his head rest on one hand, murmuring something to himself in a foreign language. His hair curled in blue waves around his bronzed fingers, pink tips revealed at intervals. He had a thin face, almost long-jawed, but too delicate and with too high a sweep of cheekbone to be so. His eyes, deep set, had the faintest trace of green, lending them depth and a certain unspoken mystery. They were currently fixed with apparent anguish on the tabletop. His lips, more apricot than pink, were set as much in petulance as in distress. They looked, Lily thought, touched by a sudden shy amusement, as if they wanted to be kissed, and so she stretched across the table and kissed them. His free hand trapped her there immediately, but whatever this threatened to develop into was cut short by Adam's return. He set his tray down with obvious intrusiveness and shot Lily a skeptical glance as she sat back and he settled in beside her.

"I don't think Father would approve," he said with a trace of sarcasm as he handed out drinks and pastries.

"Wouldn't he?" asked Lily with sincere interest.

Adam shrugged. "You know what a tyrant he is."

Lily laughed, unable to picture Heredes in any guise but that of her calm and intent sensei.

"You may laugh," said Kyosti. "I suppose as his daughter you've received special treatment." He and Adam exchanged glances, and some understanding passed between them, so that Lily felt that they were now in league against her.

"But I'm not—" She stopped. Better, perhaps, on this ship, to keep up the masquerade, to let them continue to think she was Heredes's physical daughter. And La Belle— La Belle surely would soon know that it was a spiritual designation, not blood, but to La Belle the distinction would probably be meaningless. She took a long, cooling drink from her glass. "I'm not sure—I don't understand why everyone seems afraid of him."

Kyosti simply gazed at her and shook his head. Adam's eyes, so close in color to his father's, bore within them seeds of bitterness, so that he looked, at this moment, nothing like Heredes at all.

"Any sane person is afraid of Taliesin, sister," he replied, that sardonic tone creeping in again. "He is the master of the art."

"Not the art you're thinking of, Lily," added Kyosti.

"Which art, then?"

"You don't know?" Adam was openly skeptical now.

"She doesn't," said Kyosti quickly. "I didn't believe it at first either, but—ah—Taliesin warned me off telling her the truth."

"He did *what?*" Her voice, rising in the air, shattered the quiet leisure of the hall. She rose.

"Lily." Adam's voice was low but insistent as he rose with her. "Let's go into one of the private rooms. We don't want to make a scene."

"Oh, by no means," she said scathingly.

But as she turned she saw faces shifting to regard the trio curiously. Kyosti stood up beside her, and there was a sudden scuff of chair and a man hurried out of the hall. He glanced back once, quickly, from the door. Lily had a brief glimpse of a brilliant red scar disfiguring his forehead, and then he was gone.

"So much for discretion," murmured Kyosti, smiling as the other people in the hall pointedly returned to their own business.

Adam gazed at the door, the skin around his eyes puckering up as he considered some thought that he kept to himself. He glanced at Kyosti, finally, shrugged, and turned to lead Lily and Kyosti into a room off the main hall. After he shut the door behind them, he locked it manually and motioned Lily to the couch. Kyosti sat in the single plush chair. Lily did not sit.

"Now what is this conspiracy of silence? Whatever the truth is, it can't be worse than what I can imagine. By the Void, Adam, if you are indeed my brother, I would think you would support me. I certainly can't expect that much from Kyosti."

"Now that isn't fair," said Kyosti immediately, as she had hoped he would. "But I do have my life to consider."

Lily turned on him. "I was under the impression you didn't care about your life. Do you really think he would kill you if you told me whatever the truth is?"

"Lily." He rose, his languid posture vanished. "What right do I have to tell you about his past if he doesn't choose to?"

"Lily has a point," said Adam. "It isn't necessarily in her best interest that Father keep her ignorant."

"That's right." Lily shot Adam a triumphant glance. "When I'm being chased all over the Reft by people I don't know but who think they know me, then it becomes self-preservation."

"After all," Adam pointed out, "when Deucalion betrayed him, he could have killed him afterward, but he didn't."

"Reassuring thought," muttered Kyosti.

"Who is Deucalion?" asked Lily.

"Your other brother," said Adam. "My twin. But he is no longer received in polite society, I fear."

"Hoy," said Lily. "What a family. But in any case, *I'll* protect you, if it comes to that."

"You'll protect us?" Adam flung himself into the chair Kyosti had vacated. "The family arrogance ain't a bad thing, sister, but it don't do to overdo it, if you take my meaning." His lips, less full than his father's, curled into a disdainful smile.

But Kyosti smiled, and he took this opportunity to dispose himself on the couch, elegantly languorous. "You haven't seen her fight."

"That's right," said Lily, looking Adam straight in the eye. "You haven't seen me fight. Do you want to?"

Adam smiled without humor.

"Do you know, Adam," continued Kyosti in his most lethargic voice, "perhaps we'd do best to let Lily question me alone for a bit. Then I'll take all the risks on myself."

Adam's expression had grown increasingly dubious, but he rose with alacrity. "Oh, I do agree. Especially if you create other reasons for him to protect you. I'll lock the door again as I go out." He paused. "You are the one called Hawk, aren't you."

Kyosti raised a torpid hand in acknowledgment.

"Is it true, or is it just another one of those popular legends, that story that you single-handedly held off an entire battalion of chameleon shock troops, in the retreat at the Betaos engagement?"

"Oh, dear." Kyosti sighed. "So tiring to remember. And my attire was quite ruined, you know." Adam gave a brief laugh, but he sketched Kyosti the trace of a respectful bow and left. The door shut behind him with a tangible click.

"Well, Lily," said Kyosti quietly, still draped becomingly on the couch. "Anything you want."

The first thing that came to mind, looking at him, and at him looking at her, filled her with a confusion compounded half of nerves and half of sheer, fluttering—but pleasant—agitation. To contain it, she began to pace, and to consider all the questions she had for him, because asking questions would prove easier than dealing with the sudden feelings he was arousing in her now that they were absolutely alone and unlikely to be disturbed.

"But I have so many questions," she began, flustered by the intensity of his stare. "I don't know where to start."

"You could start by sitting down. It's terribly wearying, watching you expend all that energy." He moved to leave room on the couch.

She sat, but she shifted restlessly back and forth in her space. He let one arm settle casually around her. The unfamiliar warmth, his proximity, his almost sweet scent when she turned her head to look at him, stilled her.

"You really are from back over the way, aren't you?" she said in a low voice, made the more taut by his closeness. "All of you, and him, too."

"Yes."

"Have they known all along we were out here? Did they just abandon us here?"

"I don't know. I'd never heard of the Reft. And it was a long trip out here. We had to calculate as we went."

"Just to get Heredes?" she asked, not quite a question. "Kyosti, how do you know him?"

"We worked together. In the war. I don't know how to explain it to you, Lily, because there's so much you don't know. Mother alone knows how many centuries of history you people out here have missed."

"We have our own history," she replied with a touch of asperity.

"Of course you do," he said, his apology made sweeter by the quickness with which he sought to conciliate her. "I'm just surprised that Gwyn let you identify with this place, rather than preparing you for your heritage."

"Which is?"

"The League. The home planets. The glorious revolution, from which he and I and others like us emerged both heroes and hunted."

"Like Wingtuck Honor Jones?"

"Mother help me." His gaze for an instant lost its focus on Lily and fixed elsewhere. "She's here, too?"

"I've heard her mentioned," replied Lily as dispassionately as she could, hiding her perturbation, she thought, at the sudden shift in his attention. "You said you worked together, you and Heredes."

"Ah, yes." He resettled himself on the couch; one side of his body touched hers, the slightest pressure, but it needed no more than that. "We worked as agents, sometimes on both sides to get what we needed, to break down the enemy's systems from within."

"You were saboteurs."

"Actually," he brushed at her cheek, his fingers a caress on her skin, "we were terrorists."

It took her a moment to reply because all her breath seemed to have become entangled with the quickened beating of her heart—and not because of what he was saying. She caught half a breath finally, and found words. "Who was this war against?"

"An alien power." He shrugged, shifting again; this time her hand slipped onto his thigh. She did not remove it. "You wouldn't know of them."

"The Kapellans." As she had with Heredes, she found it entertaining to surprise Kyosti and to watch his face as he strove to suppress that surprise. "I do have a model sixteen eighty-five composer, you know."

"So you do." With his free arm he pulled her halfway around to face him more clearly. "Lily," he began. Their legs tangled; she let one slide between his, and her hand crept up to rest on his chest. Under her hand the cloth had shape and texture, like raised reliefs, that she could trace with her fingers.

"Lily," he said again, but the tenor of his voice had changed.

Abruptly, staring up into his face, she felt like she was about to lose her footing, as if the ground was slipping away beneath her, an avalanche in Unruli's storms. "Is that all you've ever been, a terrorist?" she asked hurriedly, as if the question was her last stable anchor on unstable ground.

He laid a warm hand on the back of her neck. "By profession, I am a physician."

"Why did you come with us," she murmured, "back at Nevermore?"

"Because I fell in love with you."

She laughed, low and short, and, giving in at last to impulse, traced the curve of his lips with one finger. "That's not true."

"How do you know?" he said, the barest undertone. "How can you possibly know?" He pulled her closer to him, arms tightening to bring her into full contact with him. She was alive to the smallest movements of his body against hers, sensed almost like a touch the fresh, enticing scent of his skin.

"I'm not his real daughter," she whispered.

His eyes had lost utterly any lethargy they once held— they were brilliantly vital now. "Born or adopted. It doesn't matter."

"To you or to him?" Her hand rested in his hair; although it appeared coarse in its wild disarray, it was fine under her fingers. She drew them through it with sudden intensity, reveling in its texture.

He stopped breathing; at last let out his breath in a long exhalation. His eyes had narrowed, at the same time entirely focused on her and yet slightly removed, as if the strength of his emotion had forced him to a distance before he could completely encompass it.

"To anyone," he breathed. He shut his eyes and kissed her. Lily, with what vestiges of rational thought remained to her, could reflect that this final statement, at least, had been uttered with complete sincerity.

"Damn it," he said a timeless moment later, "how *do* you unfasten this?"

She laughed, because impatience was so unlike him. "I'll do it," she said, discovering that her own impatience made the task more difficult than it should have been.

Later, lying quietly together on the couch, she said as much to him.

"Ah, well," he murmured in her ear, one languid hand stroking her back, "patience is its own reward. Or is that virtue?"

Lily smiled, but she was too relaxed to make the effort of replying. Instead, she pressed herself closer against him, finding the angles where her body fit in along his, and promptly fell asleep.

He woke her sometime later with a gentle shake that dissolved into a long kiss.

"Much as I regret the necessity of suggesting this," he said finally, "I think we should put our clothes on." Five peremptory raps sounded on the door, and he quirked an eyebrow as if to say, You see what barbarians our hosts are.

Lily twitched a lock of blue hair away from his eyes and, disentangling herself from him, sat up and gathered up her clothing.

"Kyosti," she said as she pulled on her boots, "are you really a doctor?"

"Yes. My specialty is triage. Why do you ask?"

"Just curious." She ran her fingers through her hair to give it some semblance of neatness, and opened the door.

Adam entered. "Well," he said expansively, eyeing the even more unruly mess of Kyosti's hair. "I hope you got what you needed, sister."

"I got no better than I deserve," she replied, unable to keep a certain smug satisfaction out of her voice. "Though I have a few questions I wouldn't mind asking *you,* brother."

He grinned with the most outward display of friendliness she had seen from him. "I came to see if you wanted dinner."

"I'd love some," said Lily.

It was a lavish meal. A liquor Adam called cognac came with dessert.

"You eat well on this ship," Lily remarked.

Adam shrugged. "Mother, being a connoisseur, is kind enough to see that it rubs off on the rest of us. When the most famous chef in the League refused her offer of employment, she kidnapped him."

"Is he still here?"

Adam gave a speaking look at their empty plates and the single pastry remaining on the dessert tray. "Of course.

Much happier than he was before. But then, Mother has always had a way with men."

"I suppose," said Kyosti, not quite dismissive. "I grant La Belle has presence, but I've never felt any desire to become obsessed with her."

"No offense intended," Adam replied, "but you aren't an artist."

"No offense taken," answered Kyosti, "being, as I am, no better and no worse than I should be."

"Do you mean Heredes—that is, Taliesin—isn't the only one? Of her—ah—men?"

Adam burst into laughter. "No, really, sister, what notions you have. You are speaking of La Belle Dame, are you not?" He poured a second glass of cognac for her. "Of course not. But of course Father was the first. They were very young when they met, before she sent him out as her champion into the world. And he is the only one she ever bore children by. That means more than Mother, certainly, would ever admit to. But he's not her only one, by a far road."

Kyosti, with a single finger, turned Lily's head to face him. " 'She found me roots of relish sweet,' " he said in a low voice, as ardent as if he were making love to her again, " 'And honey wild, and manna dew, And sure in language strange she said' "—he leaned into her until his lips brushed her cheek—" 'I love thee true.' "

Lily could only gaze at Kyosti. Beneath that lazy confidence, beneath the apparent fearlessness, the act he played of apathy and tired cynicism, was a vehemence that both flattered and frightened her.

"You're very well read," said Adam, amused.

Kyosti flicked Lily's cheek with his finger, dismissively affectionately, and picked up his glass. "After all," he replied with a shrug, "I spent a long time in prison. But tell me, I thought only the League was investigating the navigation routes to this area."

"The League isn't the only one who has an interest here." Adam, when he was concealing information, definitely resembled his father. "We were on the trail of chameleons."

"Out here? By the Mother, Anjahar will have a fit."

"What are chameleons?" asked Lily.

"Your Kapellans, my love," said Kyosti. "And you don't want the trouble they'll bring."

"I'm still not convinced I want *any* of you and the trouble you've brought," retorted Lily.

Adam slapped her on the shoulder. "That's my spitfire," he said. "You'll fit right into the family."

"Thank you," said Lily demurely.

"But come along and meet the crew. The Mother alone knows how long it'll be until we see the parents again, and as your hosts we must keep you entertained. And of course, everyone wants to meet Taliesin's daughter." He rose, glass in one hand. "And the Hawk," he added, saluting Kyosti with his drink. "Is it true that you're the only person besides Mother to have saved Taliesin's life? That you carried him through five kilometers of the burning and decompressed space station you'd just blown up and then operated with only a laser pistol, a Swiss army knife, and a six-year-old Kapellan girl to assist you? Or is that just another one of those stories?"

"Kyosti." Lily touched his arm. "Is that true?"

"Did you say there was more of this cognac?" asked Kyosti. "It's very good."

How long they spent on the ship Lily was never quite sure. She met a great many people and drank too much; took on a wager to spar a great, hulking brute of a mercenary, laid him out in two passes, and drank more, mostly toasts to the victory; found herself alone in a cabin with Kyosti, who had acquired an entire new outfit that he insisted she remove from him piece by piece in order to examine it in more detail, which led to a long, pleasant, but ultimately muddled interlude after which, back in the hall again, she sat listening with one ear to some rather loud music and with the other to Adam regaling her with stories of his eventful childhood with an ungovernable twin brother —and slowly, she came to realize that she was wearing half her clothes and half Kyosti's. Another drink was urged on her.

"—which reminds me," continued Adam, "of the time Father had rigged the entire Boots Seven system's chain of vector charts to malfunction in ascending order when triggered by the exit signals of the Kapellan cruiser fleet, sending them to Mother knows where, or nowhere, so they'd never get to the Ringworm front, and Deucalion decided it was immoral to kill alien life-forms and sabotaged the sabotage, and Father had to run the entire malfunction manually while holding off enemy fire with only a Melep unit and that woman Motley to help him. And when he got hold of Deucalion afterward—"

Later, standing on one of the tables but adamently refusing to dance because she had a very clear feeling that Kyosti —who, lounging in a chair at her feet, appeared to be half-asleep—would think it undignified, she saw over the heads of her singing cohorts the door into the hall open and Heredes enter. She lost her equilibrium and fell to her knees. Kyosti started up to steady her. He saw she was staring past him, and he turned.

Heredes strolled up the hall, each footstep a damper on the volume until, as he stopped in front of Lily, the entire hall was quiet.

"Ah. Lily." He put his hands on her shoulders and bestowed on her cheek a fatherly kiss. She stared foolishly at him, terribly embarrassed, but unable to act to prevent it. "I'm glad to see you've been enjoying yourself." The look he shot Kyosti as he swung Lily down to the floor had the consistency of pure venom. When Lily collapsed against his side, unable to keep her footing, the ship tossed and turned so, he scooped her up into his arms. "But I fear we must go now. Captain Bolyai is doubtless eager to resume his trip. You may follow, Hawk," he finished with withering courtesy.

"I'm sorry, Daddy," said Lily in a very faint, very small voice, and she passed out.

12   The Mercenary's Tale

✳✳✳✳✳✳✳

Lily's first coherent thought when she woke was that it
would be a mistake to attempt to sit up. She did open her
eyes, but shut them immediately because the light was so
bright. She was on the top bunk in Heredes's cabin. Murmured words; she felt a hand on her shoulder.

"Drink this, Lily," Heredes said. She lay passive under
his ministrations. The cool rim of a cup pressed against her
lips and she drank. Finished, she attempted again to open
her eyes—this time seeing Heredes's face close to hers, his
expression tolerably amused. "Do you think you can sit
up?" he asked.

She straightened up, but the sight of the vast gulf between
her feet and the floor made her nauseous. Color shifted below, and Kyosti stood up beside Heredes.

"She shouldn't be up here," said Kyosti with awful disapproval and, closing his arms around her, he swung her with
deceptively gentle strength down to the lower bunk. She
shut her eyes again. He held her, her head cushioned in his
lap. "She should eat something," Kyosti added.

There was a long pause. Lily's head pounded.

"I will thank you," said Heredes finally, his voice taut,
"to take your hands off my daughter."

Kyosti did not stir, except to caress Lily's waist. "Your
true colors are beginning to show, Gwyn," he replied with

admirable calm. "But I feel it only fair to tell you that Lily and I mean to be married."

Because her head hurt her so, she thought perhaps she had not heard him correctly.

"Hawk, I will only say this once." Heredes's voice had the terrifying hauteur of a master challenged by a presumptuous clown. "First, you cannot marry a young woman who knows nothing of the worlds you would perforce be taking her to, who knows nothing of *your* antecedents."

"It isn't *I* who have kept her in ignorance," interposed Kyosti reasonably.

"You know very well what I refer to. Second, by the laws of the Reft, she is underage."

"At twenty-five?"

"Majority here is not reached until thirty, or for a woman, the birth of a child if that comes first. In this case, it hasn't."

Kyosti shifted beneath her. "And when have I said we would marry under the laws of *this* region?"

Despite her nausea, despite the drums beating noiseless patterns on the inside of her forehead, Lily could perceive through her skin the tension in the room.

"Third, and most important"—Heredes's voice was tight, under his breath, his anger utterly compelling—"*I* forbid it."

"How quaint of you," said Kyosti.

"Get away from her or I will—" He broke off.

"Kill me?" prompted Kyosti. "And after all we've been through together. My, my."

Heredes's voice dropped almost to a whisper. "Do you think this is a joke, Hakoni? It isn't."

Lily felt Kyosti's smile by the way his arms tightened around her. "Who to know better than me? You're too late, my dear Gwyn. Too late. Do you understand?"

The room held utter silence. At that moment Lily knew incontrovertibly that the only reason Heredes did not strike Kyosti was because she was lying between them. She opened her eyes.

"Get out," said Heredes. His eyes, fixed on Kyosti, were terrible. "Get out of here."

Kyosti did not move.

Lily broke away from his embrace, lunged to her feet, and staggered. "What's wrong with you two?" she cried, realizing abruptly that if she did not keep speaking, she would throw up. "I told you I wouldn't bond with you," she said to Kyosti. His surprise swept all trace of artificiality from his face. "You don't have any claim on me. You never have. And *you*"— shifting her gaze to Heredes caused her to trip over her own feet—"whatever other authority you may have over me, you have no legal authority, and *certainly* no right at all to dictate what love affairs I might choose, or not choose, to have." Her walk to the door was more stiff than the offended arrogance she might have wished for. She managed a final withering sweep with her gaze. "Is that clear?"

She left, to what she hoped was stunned silence. It was, therefore, disconcerting to hear Heredes start to laugh as the cabin door slid shut behind her.

She barely made it to Jenny's cabin before she threw up. Aliasing, with a minimum of fuss, cleaned her up and disposed her comfortably in the bottom bunk. Gregori sat by her feet while she ate bland crackers and drank three cups of juice, and Bach sang a slow, two-part canon. By the time Jenny came in, Lily felt much better.

"Had a wild night out, I see," said Jenny cheerfully, chasing Gregori off the bunk and sitting herself on the spot he had vacated. "What was *La Belle Dame* like?"

Lily shook her head. "I'm not even going to try that one. Indescribable."

"That's cruel, Lily." Jenny took a refill of juice from Aliasing and handed it to Lily. "They must have entertained you somehow, to leave you in such a condition."

"Well," Lily began tentatively, "while Master Heredes negotiated with their captain, we went to the mess hall, and got into an argument, and then—" She stopped, blushing at two very different recollections, one quite clear, the other confused by drink. "Twice," she said, as if appalled to have made this discovery. "He seduced me twice."

Jenny laughed. "I see you met and made quick work of one of them. Was he quite handsome?"

"He wasn't—" Lily faltered, suddenly irritated by her own confusion and by Jenny's laughter.

"He wasn't a pirate." Aliasing's soft voice quieted them. She was curled up on the floor, legs concealed as always in a swirl of skirt, her thin, brown arms propping her up. Even in the small cabin she appeared tiny but exotic against the drab walls, like some luxury item found unexpectedly in a poor household. But her gaze had a sympathy of expression that evaporated Lily's annoyance.

"Oh," said Jenny abruptly, understanding, and she reached out to pat Lily's hand. "It can't have been that much of a surprise, surely, the way he's been hanging after you."

"I just don't see," said Lily with sudden heat, "what gives them the right to squabble over me as if I were a piece of property."

"Well, Lily-hae, what do you expect from a couple of foreigners? And males, at that? But you're in good hands now." Jenny rose with efficient grace. "If we squabble, at least it won't be over you."

By the next cycle Lily felt completely recovered, although she avoided Heredes. Kyosti avoided everyone, and Lily did not seek him out because it was easier, just now, not to have to confront herself yet with the true scope of her feelings about him. Heredes, however, sought her out for a workout.

"I'm sorry I yelled at you," she said as they stretched out afterward.

"I'm sorry you got so drunk," said Heredes.

"Hoy. So am I," replied Lily with a smile.

"That isn't quite what I meant." He paused. "Lily." His hesitation made him appear almost vulnerable. "About Hawk—" She waited, uncomfortable and defensive now, but at last he only sighed. "Never mind. You're quite right that *I* have no right to dictate to you in such matters. But just remember, Lilyaka." His gaze was clear and direct. "You can come to me if you have any trouble, any problem."

"I know," she said, and they both smiled.

She spent a few more sessions on the bridge, and finally they were only a single window away from Central.

She and Jenny, having just sparred, put the rec room's furniture back up and sat down to enjoy carbonated water brought over from the mess.

"That's the other reason Central doesn't regulate this route," said Jenny, sipping at her water. "It's so damned slow. It cuts down your profit line quick enough to have to sit out here waiting for a clear window." She eased down into the plastine chair and lifted her bare feet up to rest on the tabletop. Her soles were paler than her skin, pinkish, leathery from the demands of a mercenary's training.

"How did you get to be a mercenary?" Lily asked.

Jenny grinned. "To get out of having children."

"I wondered"—Lily shrugged—"hired mercenaries don't usually get to bring their dependents along on their jobs."

"Easy Virtue isn't a usual ship. Too large for the kind of traffic she turns, but too poor to pay a decent crew."

"It must be a hard life for Lia and Gregori."

"Said most diplomatically, Lily-hae." Jenny gave her a mock salute. "What you mean is, how can they stand to be stuck in that tiny cabin all day. And how can I stand to leave them there."

Lily said nothing, merely took another drink, regarding the mercenary seriously.

Jenny sighed, more heartfelt, perhaps, than she realized, or perhaps Lily simply knew enough of her by now to read it so.

"I'm sorry," Lily said now. "I've never realized until the past few weeks how easy my life as the young Saressa was. What you're doing can't be easy for you."

"Given the alternatives? I don't know. Have you ever heard of Unity?"

"I've heard the name. Out beyond the Saladin route. Don't they export aris-cote?"

"Among other things, yes. Unity's a tidal planet, long, hot stretches of sand flat that just go on and on and on."

"It's a little hard for me to imagine," Lily said. "We never even see the sun on Unruli. But we do have lots of sand."

"The universal bane of machinery. Aris can only be har-
vested manually because of it. But Unity is so far off the
main routes that no one wants to immigrate there, and with
so many industries dependent on human hands, Unity has
just never had enough—hands, that is. They tried artificial
wombs—"

"I thought artificial wombs were illegal."

"So are contraceptives," said Jenny. Lily blushed. "Point
made, I think. They don't work anyway. A few are still bred
for the really noxious jobs, but Council settled on a different
way to solve the problem. They just trot us girls out at
sixteen and get us pregnant."

"You didn't have any choice?"

"None at all."

"Hoy," said Lily. The ventilation fans hummed in a drone
above them, a muffled pedal point to Jenny's story.

"I had a daughter at sixteen, a boy at eighteen. They were
put in crèches. The time came for my next go round—I was
sick at the thought of having to do it all over again. That's
when the Immortals came recruiting."

Suddenly that hard core resting beneath Jenny's cheerful
exterior became explicable to Lily. "Hoy," she said. "You
were an Immortal. No wonder you're so good. But I
thought Immortals couldn't retire."

"They can't," replied Jenny with a self-mocking smile.
"I'm not retired. I'm a fugitive."

"But we're going straight in to Central!"

Jenny took an unconcerned draught from her cup. "If
you haven't guessed by now, Jenny Seria is not the name I
was born with. And if I told you Aliasing's whole name
you'd recognize it."

"I don't understand."

"It's a long story. After graduating from the Academy, I
was stationed at Central, and I moved up as one does given
a little effort. It's actually rather an easy life, being an Immortal."

"Being celibate is easy?"

Jenny chuckled. "Our commanders believed in the con-
cept of self-control through lack of opportunity. We each

had individual rooms—cells, more like—that we were locked into during our sleep shifts. And a lot of us, at least at first, embraced the entire image of the Immortal. Including, you know, the idea that sexually frustrated men and women make better fighters.

"That's an interesting hypothesis," said Lily tactfully.

"Especially as we novices discovered that many of our colleagues were having affairs—well, for the women it had to be other women, because of the risk of pregnancy, but the men might go either way. It was also a cachet among the senatorial families and the other high-society folk in Central to have an Immortal to your bed, of whichever sex, despite the celibacy rule. I don't know, perhaps because of it. That's how I met Lia."

"Aliasing was an Immortal?"

Jenny threw back her head and laughed. Even in that movement, Lily could see the strict control she had over her muscles, almost scientific in its precision. "Lia is the only child of a Senator. Somehow she came out of it unspoiled—well, at least uncynical. Among her friends it was the fashion to lose their virginity—as if it were something simply to get rid of—to an Immortal. But Aliasing was honest in her infatuation and a little disillusioned with her life. She was only sixteen, but old enough—no doubt on Unity old enough—to see the great gap between all her rich friends using contraceptives, and all the young women who had no choice, or no chance, to use the same precautions. She's not without courage, is my Lia, as well as not without beauty. I never quite understood why she fell in love with me."

"You are one of the handsomest women I've ever met," said Lily.

Jenny smiled. "Thank you. Well, it was a little more obvious why she also fell in love with Mendi."

"Mendi?"

"Mendiya Leyhaennin Mun. Of the Tollgate and Halfway Muns. A very rich family, a bit independent of the government, or at least they pretend they are. But Mendi—well—the most beautiful man I've ever seen. Hair the color of the sun, skin like milk, his eyes—and his body. Well. How can you resist him?"

"Did you?"

"Of course not. Strangely enough, he was one of the Immortals who I'm sure was really entirely celibate by inclination. I still don't know to this day why he did what he did. Perhaps both Lia and I did attract him, but the truth is, I suspect he did it simply to get thrown out of the Immortals. Do you want something to eat?"

Lily laughed. "I want to find out what he did. But I hope I've learned enough patience to wait a few minutes."

"I guess we'll find out." Jenny rose and left the room, returning minutes later with ship's fare.

"You should have seen the meal I had on *La Belle Dame.*" Lily sighed, but she took her tray.

"Do you know, it first happened at a feast. I had just turned twenty-four. I'd been seeing Lia for about half a year, and she told me how attracted she was to Mendi. Even within the Immortals we called him the Untouchable. There are always those who are celibate because they're so unattractive in looks or personality or in devotion to duty that no one wants them. Mendi just plain wasn't available. I tried to cultivate him, as a friend. He was never at ease, but it wasn't lack of confidence, more that he was holding an explosive secret inside himself. He had that kind of inner power. Damn my eyes, but he was gorgeous." The memory softened her face, smoothing the cloak of implacability the mercenary seemed to wear underneath her usual face.

"You make me want to meet him."

"I'm not so sure." The soft look faded, replaced with a sardonic smile. "Faithless as a Senator's daughter, as we used to say, was our Mendi. Although that isn't fair to Lia. But anyway, Mendi and I were part of the guard decorating this one particular function, and I arranged with Lia to get him alone in a room upstairs with her. She can be as lovely as the dawn, that girl, when she puts her mind to it, and she was, for him. She's never told me what she did, but it worked. He became, as much as I suppose it was in him to be, obsessed by her. How it came about that he propositioned me, I don't know. But he did, one day, and I refused. I couldn't risk pregnancy. Lia had no contraceptives; she told me herself she was against it if only the rich could have them. So I could scarcely ask her to get me some from her friends so that I could tup her male lover, whom she worshipped. But it got me to thinking about the Immortals, and my time with them, and my future with them, and I finally just said, 'Tup them all,' and I slept with him." She pulled her chair in suddenly, leaning across the table, closing herself and Lily into an even tighter unit in the blank-walled room. Her voice dropped to a whisper. "Making love to him was like killing someone, totally engrossing but without joy. I think he hated it, not me, not women, but the act itself, or hated himself for wanting it." She gave a short laugh, almost derisive, and sat back. "But once you're blooded, you keep coming back for more."

"And you got pregnant."

"So I did. Not surprisingly, so did Lia. I was found out soon enough. Much to my astonishment, Mendi fessed up as soon as I was arrested, so they jailed both of us. Lia helped us escape, pretty much did the job herself. And damn my eyes if Mendi didn't squirrel off at his first opportunity and abandon us. That's when I began to think he'd done it to get thrown out. So there she and I were, fugitives on Central. We had a wild time; in the end, we had to leave the system."

"You went through a window pregnant?"

"More than one. Lia lost hers, of course; she almost died. I didn't even get sick. At the requisite time, Gregori was born. So here we are."

"Hoy," said Lily.

"That probably sums it up as well as anything." Jenny smiled. The intercom rang a pattern of chimes. "Time to go."

They stood, but Lily paused on her way to the door, turning back to face Jenny. "You know, Jenny," she began, a little tentative, "we haven't known each other very long, but I'll miss you." She put out a hand, and Jenny took it, a firm clasp.

"I'll take that as a compliment," said Jenny. "I wish I

could give you the *Virtue's* code, so you could put a stand-by on it when you get settled in and I could call you whenever we're back in here, but we can't risk the regular channels—they'd trace us and haul us in quick as a window."

"I know," said Lily.

The com came on again, reporting vectoring range. "Come on." Jenny sent Lily forward with a slap on the back. "Maybe I'll still have time to make love to that blue-haired doctor of yours before we go over."

Lily flushed, but very stiffly said nothing.

Jenny laughed. "I don't think you're ready to share him yet, Lily-hae, whether you know it or not."

"Sorry, Jenny," said Lily, looking shamefaced. "Maybe you're right."

"About old blue-hair?" Jenny put her arm around Lily and hugged her. "Sure I am. I'll miss you, too, Lily."

They separated, and Lily went on alone to Heredes's cabin. But stepping inside, she found no Heredes but only Kyosti, sitting the length of the cabin away from her, at the computer terminal. For an instant he had not yet registered her presence. His face, unguarded, held the stillness of one long-used to inaction, that quality of being past boredom, past fear, past happiness, but also, perhaps, in the tiniest corner of the mind, past sanity.

As if he sensed her, he looked up. His eyes widened, taking her in, and he stood.

They went through.

Blue hair with the ribbonlike fine texture of threads of cloth. Skin bronzed like the sheen of well-tempered metal, but soft, yielding, scented as all life is scented. Lips like the brush of air. Her name; said so, it defined her anew, from his lips: "You have risen to me out of the heart of light."

And came out.
She was in his arms, kissing him.

She jerked away from him and stumbled back against the door.

"Do you hate me so much?" he asked.

"How did you do that?" she said. *"How* did you do that?"

"Do what?"

She lifted a trembling hand. "You were there, over there, and then—"

He laughed, his face clearing, and came up to her and drew her against him. "I'm a ghost, Lily. I don't exist. What for you is an instant is for me an eternity." He lowered his head and kissed her, long and satisfying. "You don't hate me, do you?" he said at last.

"I never did," she replied, feeling lost in the intensity of his blue gaze, but her voice shook, and she looked past him. He *had* been standing by the terminal, and then he *had* been embracing her. There had been no time, nothing but the window, between those two actions. "You scared me."

"I never meant to do that, Lily." He bent to kiss her again.

The cabin door slid open and Heredes stopped in the entrance. For a timeless instant, like a window, none of them moved. Then Lily gently disengaged herself from Kyosti, with a final, brief kiss on his cheek, and turned to face Heredes.

"What's the plan?" she asked.

"*Easy Virtue* is docking at Northbynorthwest Station in two hours. Bolyai is sending us planetside by shuttle before that, and he wants us off quick and quiet. So get your things and meet us by the lock."

She gave him a mock salute, and left the cabin.

13   Wingtuck Takes Fright

※※※※※※

Through the viewports of the shuttle, Central appeared in blues and greens and browns and the white tracery of clouds.

"It's magnificent," Lily said, leaning toward Heredes so he could hear her above the tumult of the engines. "It's like a jewel. What's all the blue?"

He smiled. "Those are oceans, Lily."

"Hoy. That's all water?"

"Water and sweet air and the hot summer sun. It is, I believe, early summer where we're going."

"Summer. That's a season, isn't it? What's it like?"

Heredes considered this question for a long moment. He finally shrugged with a gentle grin. "To a young woman who comes from a planet which has two seasons, freezing hard winds with dangerous avalanches, and cold hard winds with catastrophic avalanches, I think only experience can answer that question." He looked past her out the port at the growing land mass beneath. "By the way, the planet is called Arcadia. Central is the government center in the north. It's different here, Lily, from what you're used to. Very different. Never hesitate to ask me any question."

By now she could pick out surface features, flat plains, winding tracks of blue, mountains thrusting up into the atmosphere. What would Unruli look like, divested of its clouds? A barren wilderness of rock. She turned away from the port. "I do have a question. When you go through a window, it's instantaneous, isn't it?"

Heredes blinked. "That's not quite the question I was expecting. And I can't really answer it." At the corners of his eyes as he thought she could discern the barest trace of lines in his dusky skin. "We perceive the window as instantaneous. However, there has been a great deal of debate about what the essence of a window in and of itself is. For instance, is it in fact no time at all? Or is it outside of time? And how do we account for the—the visions—that we have."

"But people, they always experience windows as an instant?"

"Most experts say it's physiologically impossible for humans to experience them as anything but an instant." He touched a finger to his lip, considering. "But I've also read that some adepts, in certain forms of meditation, certain frames of mind, perceive a window as time. Perhaps *time* isn't the right word. They perceive it as duration. I don't know if there's any way to measure it. I don't even know if it's true."

"I think it is true." At his surprised expression she leaned closer to him, her lips almost at his ear. "I think Kyosti is one of them."

He drew back. "By the Mother." His gaze flashed to the blue-haired man, who sat at the shuttle controls. "Lily, do you realize—" He stopped, frowning. "What if it's true?" he said to himself, still watching Kyosti. "Mother protect us. No wonder he's so altered."

"But I thought you would have known."

"No. It must have happened since I last saw him."

"When *did* you last see him?"

Heredes waved a careless hand. "Twenty-five, thirty years ago. I can't remember."

Lily said nothing, turned back to the port. Kyosti looked perhaps five years older than her. How old could he have been when he held off an entire battalion? When he saved Heredes's life? How old could Heredes himself be? Rejuv existed, expensive and not particularly effective; her own father indulged now and then. But the technology that had produced Bach and the sleek, massive bulk of *La Belle Dame* could surely produce miracles of life extension, couldn't it? Central's scientists still searched, and failed. What would they make of Heredes? What could *she* make of him?

She felt a hand on her shoulder, Heredes touching her, and she remembered what he had said to her long ago, at the Academy: "Trust me, Lily." She turned back to him and smiled. They spent the time until landing talking about seasons and surface agriculture and breathing air beneath a cloudless sky without needing artificial aids.

They landed, engines roaring, with a jar. As the shuttle slowed, Lily saw an airstrip, two buildings set on a golden carpet, and beyond that, the roll of hills.

"Those are trees!" she cried just as the engines cut down to idle, and Kyosti turned from his seat in front to grin at her. They unstrapped themselves, collected their packs and Bach, and disembarked down the shuttle's stair-step ladder.

"Look! Kyosti, the sky is the same color as your hair!" she called above the noise of the engines. Heredes took her arm, drawing her away from the shuttle as she stared. "Look! Are those flowers? They're the same color as your lips! There's no wind!"

The shuttle's engines swelled to a scream. It turned on the airstrip and flung itself into the sky. Lily stared at its arc into the infinity of blue, an arc fading into the golden, bright disk of the sun.

"Lily!" Heredes's sharp tone caused her to look at him. "Don't stare at the sun. You'll go blind."

"Oh." She reached down to brush tentatively at the grass with one hand. "It's sharp," she said, "but so light." Neither answered her; they walked across the clearing toward the two buildings. Beside her, Bach sang.

> *Bin ich gleich von dir gewichen*
> *Stell' ich mich doch weider ein;*
> *Hat uns doch dein Sohn verglichen*
> *Durch sein' Angst und Todespein.*

"Although I have strayed from Thee,
yet I have returned again;
for Thy Son has reconciled us
through his agony and mortal pain."

"Wait!" she called, running after them. They both halted,
Heredes in the lead. "Do you hear it?" she asked, stopping
beside Kyosti. "There is wind—I can just barely feel it on
my face, but can you hear it, in the trees? Like it's whispering, but something we can't understand."

Kyosti laughed and took her face, bright with discovery,
between his hands. " 'Shall I compare thee to a summer's
day?' "

"Is this a summer's day?" she asked, looking up into eyes
that were as blue as the sky. Kyosti laughed again and released her. Turning, she saw that Heredes was frowning, but
when he caught her eye he smiled. The wind moved in his
brown hair as a lover's fingers do, with a gentle caress. On
her face the sun felt like a warm hand, one entirely without
pressure or possessiveness. Nothing contained her; she felt
almost giddy. "It's glorious," she said.

"We'd better wait for Bach," said Heredes. The tone of
his voice mirrored the expression of animation, almost relief, she had seen in Kyosti's eyes. "He hasn't gotten used to
the elements yet." Lily turned.

Bach was rolling in a most peculiar fashion, as if the wind
kept upsetting his equilibrium. Lily walked back to him and
set a hand on the curve of his underside. Even in the sun his
metal-smooth surface was cool. The pressure of her hand
seemed to steady him; by the time they reached the men, the
robot had regained his stability. He sang a merry accompaniment as they walked across the clearing.

Both buildings were untenanted. Heredes rummaged
around, taking several blankets and filling his pack with
food and a canteen that he found in a dusty kitchen.

"Isn't that stealing?" Lily asked.

"Yes." He handed her the canteen. "Think of it as being
for the cause."

"Which cause?"

He considered her for a moment, but under his grave expression lay an obduracy that reminded her how little she really knew of him. "Our survival," he said. "Where is Hawk?"

"Outside, lying down."

"Getting a new tan already, I see," muttered Heredes under his breath. "Let's go." They went outside. Lily had to blink in the sun. Kyosti stood up, brushing grass from his clothing. Heredes tossed him the rolled-up blankets. "That's your share," he said. "We're lucky this post is abandoned. Now we hike."

Lily surveyed the deserted clearing. "I thought this planet was overcrowded."

"It is. But most of the population is in the north coast cities. All the agricultural zones are off-limits except for workers."

"Then won't we be arrested?"

"Lily. On any planet with as many regulations and restrictions as this one has, there is always a flourishing black market in goods and labor and unauthorized movement."

"Ah, Gwyn," said Kyosti as he tied the roll of blankets to his small pack with the long gold tippets left over from the dismantling of his robe. "Always so well informed."

"And you can stop calling me Gwyn. It isn't really my name."

"Mother bless us. What *is* your name?"

"Call me Joshua. That's as true a name as Kyosti or Hawk, I expect."

"I wouldn't know," said Kyosti, looking sly. "If Kyosti Bitterleaf Hakoni isn't my name, then I've forgotten the real one."

"Like Alexander Jehane," said Lily. "That can't be his real name. But I bet he'll never tell the one he was born with."

Kyosti began to laugh. *"Alexander* Jehane? Is that what he told you? What—was his mother fell upon by a thunderbolt?"

"Hawk." Heredes looked, for a moment, much like a disgusted parent. "Let's concentrate on business. Can you dye that hair?"

"But it's all the fashion." Kyosti touched his hair with a hand that seemed oddly pale, until Lily realized that he had stripped his nails of their garish pink color.

"Not on Arcadia, I think," said Heredes.

Kyosti sighed.

"I like it," said Lily, blushing, "but it is conspicuous."

"Very well." He managed a martyred expression. "We'll see if you still love me as a bleached blond."

"I don't even know what a bleached blond is," said Lily to Heredes.

It was cool under the trees. As they walked, Lily discerned a hundred noises blended into the expanse of air: the wind in its soft conversation with the trees; the snap of a branch breaking; the stuttering chitter of an unseen creature. The ground gave slightly beneath her feet, muffling the weight of their footsteps. Later a gurgling whisper approached them, growing louder as they walked. Neither of the men seemed alarmed. They came up to it at last: water, in a shallow, rock-strewn channel, rushing along as if it were the wind given substance. Kyosti stooped to drink from it, exclaiming as his fingers touched it. Lily knelt. It was bitterly cold. The water tugged against her skin. She could not bring herself to drink from it. They followed it down the slopes.

At dusk they came to the edge of the forest. Beyond them stretched low hills ribboned with fields and terraces. Above, the first stars winked into view. She stared up at them until Heredes called to her. They ate, and afterward he led her to the stream to wash.

"Wash in *water?*"

"Yes, Lily. It's how most people wash."

"Not in sonics?" She put a dubious hand in the cold rushing flow.

"Most planets don't have enough energy for that particular luxury."

"We certainly never had enough water on Unruli to waste it like this," she replied, but she washed her hands and face.

They went back together, and Lily got a blanket and lay down. Heredes went to sleep immediately. Lily gazed up at the interlace of shadowed foliage and stars in the black sky far above. If the earth were to let go of her, free her from its bonds of gravity, would she slowly rise, like Bach, into the infinity of that heaven? She fell asleep.

Woke. It was dark. The air smelled strange, overpowering. There was rustling behind her. She sat up. Past the line of trees, on the border of the low hills, a steady light rose. Security had found them. She was half up to her feet when Kyosti whispered her name, coming up behind her. He drew her back to trap her against him.

"What's wrong?" he whispered.

"There's a light—" She gestured.

He laughed under his breath. "It's the moon," he said. "Come with me."

"Where are we going?"

" 'Third seals,' " he answered, cryptic, and put a finger to her lips to still her question.

He led her to the edge of the trees. Wind sighed in the branches above them. There were two moons: one, tiny but definitely rounded, was already halfway up the sky; the other was just coming over the horizon. As they watched, it cleared the hills and began to rise in its muted splendor.

"It's the crescent." She turned to look up at Kyosti. In the moonlight, his hair shone as if gilded by silver. "That's the shape that he painted on his face, under his eye. In the picture that you—that that other man—showed to me, of Heredes."

"So it is," said Kyosti, not looking up at the moon at all.

"What does it mean?"

His eyes, too, had a silvery glint under starlight. He smiled. "It's one of *her* signs. La Belle's."

She gazed at the delicate curve of light hanging in the air, stars attendant like awed spectators. "It's beautiful."

"As are you, Lily." He moved into her line of vision so that she had to gaze up at him instead of the moon. " 'Now she shines among Lydian women as, into dark when the sun has set, the moon, pale-handed, at last appeareth, making dim all the rest of the stars, and light spreads afar on the deep, salt sea, spreading likewise across the flowering cornfields; and the dew rinses glittering from the sky; roses spread, and the delicate antherisk, and the lotus spreads her petals.' "

The night held them as if in her own hands; she was like a third presence, yet without personality of her own, an empty vessel to be filled with whatever emotion was projected most strongly upon her, investing her with a particular magic of some sorcerer's choosing. Lily gazed up at Kyosti's face, lit half in light, half in shadow. That he had power, perhaps only the power of experience, over her she felt; that he was far older than he looked she knew: his words themselves had the texture of an ancient time, beguiling her across an immense gulf of history.

"Who are the Lydian women?" she asked. Her voice faded into the air around them.

"Long since dead," he said, his voice delicate as the brush of wind. "It's rather a sad poem. But the words paint their own image of beauty."

"You're beautiful," she whispered.

"Ah, well." He eased her down with him onto the blanket he had had the foresight to spread out on the ground. "I've always looked my best under the kinnas wheel."

"What's the kinnas wheel?" They were tangled, weight half on each other, long lines of warmth pressed together. His breath stirred on her cheek. His lips touched hers.

"The wheel of the night." His voice was so low it seemed not to come from him at all. "They call it the honor that patterns you. But also," he kissed her throat, and she sighed and slipped her hand up to cradle the back of his neck, "the promise of love."

For the next two days they hiked across fields empty of human life, except the occasional shuttle high overhead and, once, bulky, slow-moving machines that appeared briefly, a choreographed line, on a distant ridge. Half-ripe crops waved in soft breezes, so alive, under the wind's hand, that she wondered at first that these were not animals. But some

of them Kyosti and Heredes could name for her, kilometers
of wheat, vast rustling patches of corn, convincing her of
their vegetability. And animals were everywhere: creatures
of the air, creatures burrowed down into the dirt or scurry-
ing away through the green. Part of the time she was fasci-
nated by this riot of free, uncontained life; other times, the
unsterility of it all revolted her. Kyosti rigged a hood for
her, to protect her face from the sun. His bronzed skin deep-
ened in color; in Heredes's dusky complexion she could see
no change at all.

On the third day they came to an irrigation pond. Reeds
choked the shore except for one bank that smoothed from
wild grass to pebbles lapped by water. Fields paled into the
horizon around them. Under the sun their backs had broken
into a sweat unrelieved by three day's march. Kyosti and
Heredes looked at the water, looked at each other and, with
whoops and cheers so foreign to their characters that Lily
stopped in her tracks to stare, they rushed down to the
bank. By the time she realized that this blue hollow whose
length and breadth each would hold fifty of her, end to end,
was all and entirely water, the two men had stripped and
plunged in. The sound of their bodies striking was like a
slap, startling her out of her amazement. Water drops
sprayed off from them as they laughed. Heredes, as if he
were walking on the hidden bottom, struck out for the far
shore, gliding like a gear through oil, arms working about
his head as if he were constantly pitching some object in
front of him.

"Lily." Kyosti stood several meters from the bank. Water
slipped off his chest and shoulders to dissolve back into itself
around him; it covered him just up to his hipbones, leaving
the hard line of his abdomen bare. He smiled and beckoned
her closer. She walked down to the bank. "Are you coming
in?" he asked. "The water's fine."

"You must be joking," said Lily. Heredes had vanished
around a curve in the pond. Behind her, Bach sank down to
rest half-hidden in the grass.

"At least take off your boots," Kyosti said persuasively.
"Feel how good it is on your toes."

She did. Her feet were hot. The water felt deliciously cool. "You must be terribly hot," he said.

She was. Fine sweat eased itself down the back of her neck, sloping on down her back. Her tunic and trousers were too heavy for this climate, but Heredes had insisted she keep them on to prevent sunburn—whatever that was. "I refuse," she said with dignity, "to get in that water. It must be filthy."

Kyosti laughed, but he inched closer to her. "My darling," he said. "I can run faster than you."

"I suppose," Lily conceded, admiring him as he waded another meter toward her. The water level fell noticeably; she forced herself to look away. He ran out of the water and grabbed her. Water speckled her clothing.

"Now, Lily." His eye was merciless. "Either you take those clothes off, or I'll throw you in with them still on."

She took them off, but before she had a chance to move he picked her up, charged into the water, and dropped her.

It was terrifying. The water closed around her, gave around her, like thick air, like nothing she had ever felt before. It splashed into her face, into her mouth and nose, but a strong arm pulled her up to stand. She gasped. Water lapped at her hips, yielding fingers. Before she got used to it, Kyosti propelled her further in. She gasped again at its touch on her belly, her breasts—he stopped and moved her around to face him.

"Well?" he asked.

She was speechless.

"If it's awful," he said, "you can get out."

She shook her head. "It isn't awful," she said, "it's . . . it's . . ." Words failed her.

He laughed. With a sudden twist and plunge he disappeared beneath the surface. The water rippled, and he erupted from it several body lengths away from her. "Come over to me."

She wanted to shake her head. Part of her was paralyzed with fright at this liquid that moved as if it were alive around her, some being whose intelligence she could not fathom—yet another part felt intensely the seduction of such smooth fluidity caressing her skin. In the end, her training got the better of her. "It is our limitations that train us," Heredes would say—she began to walk. The water tugged at her. Each step pulled against her chest as if G forces were being expended to halt her progress. But she kept going, a little grim faced, until Kyosti's arms caught her in a slippery embrace.

"That's my warrior," he said with admiration. He honored her with an intensive kiss made more fervent by the brush of water against their bodies and the quiet rustle of wind through the reeds.

"Hawk!" The shout from Heredes broke them apart. "Damn you to hell, Hawk!"

Lily sank lower until the water covered her to her shoulders, lapping at her neck.

"I've already been there," Kyosti replied cheerfully. "Anywhere else you'd like me to go?"

Heredes did not reply. Instead he swam past them, looking as if all his pleasure in this outing had been destroyed. Kyosti smiled.

"He doesn't want us to be lovers," Lily said. "Why not, Kyosti?"

He bent to kiss her. "Typical father. He's shocked by your sexuality, my love." She pushed away from him, but he only laughed. "We'd better get you out of the sun. You've gone quite pink."

That evening, they came on a work crew.

"Wait here." Heredes motioned them to lie just below a bluff that looked over the field on which the workers, perhaps one hundred spread far across its green-leafed and yellow-flowered expanse, were engaged in an arcane activity Lily could not decipher. He left.

"What's he going to do?" Lily whispered. Kyosti shrugged. "What are these people doing?"

"Picking strawberries?"

"*What* is a strawberry?"

"It's a long story."

"It could be aris." Lily rubbed her lower lip ruminatively.

"What is aris?"

"Got you at last. I don't think it could be, anyway. Not from what Jenny told me."

"Don't you know what it looks like?"

It was her turn to shrug. "I only see it processed."

Kyosti stiffened suddenly. "Your hood," he said. As she handed it to him, she heard voices. He tied the hood on, covering his hair, just as Heredes appeared with a dusky-skinned woman.

"Don't be alarmed," Heredes said. "I've found a Jehanist nest. This is Carmelita. They're going to help us get to the city."

She was middle-aged, with a weathered face and calloused, dirty hands. The look she turned on Lily was rapt. "You've met him?" she breathed. Lily nodded, but did not feel it politic to mention that she had also shot him. "It is an honor to help you, in your mission for Jehane."

"Ah, yes," muttered Kyosti under his breath. "Our mission."

Heredes had done his job well. For the next two days they worked out in the fields, getting a crash course from the workers on weeding supirina bushes, a delicate and time-consuming task whose fruits, in both senses of the word, would be received only by those well-to-do enough to afford the wine the supirina blossoms produced. At some point Kyosti managed to turn his hair color from blue to a faintly blue-tinged blond. He refused, despite Heredes's entreaties, to cut it.

On the third day the shift changed, and it was as easy as that. At Carmelita's suggestion, Lily had concealed Bach in a lean-to where old equipment rusted. With Heredes, she programmed the robot to wait for his return, when a method could be devised to get Bach into the city without attracting Security's attention. Then, surrounded by their quiet allies, they boarded the workers' rail and were raced across a blur of countryside into the city. Lily caught a glimpse of it—brown haze and a wall of buildings—before the rail went underground. It roared along, echoes dark around them. Kyosti seemed nervous. She put her arm around him, and he calmed. Heredes consulted with Carmelita over directions.

The workers dispersed at a large station. With a final exchange of words and a com-screen for Heredes, they left their benefactress and rode a series of trains into a labyrinth from which Lily doubted she could ever find her way out. Heredes eventually led them off a train and up, past turn gates, past incessantly chattering screens with news and weather and inexplicable dramas, past individuals lounging in all their dirt along the unscrubbed concrete tunnels, past uniformed Security, up escalators, into the sun again.

It was the same sun, but the view—so changed. There were buildings, a street clogged with traffic: pedestrians, bicycles, and motopeds, and a few trucks bearing cargo. Lily had thought Station on Unruli's moon was crowded; it was nothing compared to this crush of humanity. It stank here, too, but it had a more fetid flavor, torn now and then with a gust of freshening wind. The buildings, towering around her, had thousands upon thousands of windows that doubled the activity. Vehicles and people and unseen machinery roared about her ears. Security personnel patrolled in marked vehicles, on motorized two-wheelers, and on foot in pairs.

"Lily!" Heredes took her by the arm.

She looked at him. "I see now," she said. "And to think there's so much land out there."

"Where's Hawk?"

Kyosti stood three meters behind her. He seemed to be staring at an invisible figure directly in front of him. Lily pushed past a clump of people, grabbed his arm.

"Kyosti?" His eyes shifted to her and his hands clamped onto her arm. His mouth opened—no words. "Here," said Lily briskly. "Put your arm around me. That's right. Now let's go."

Heredes came up beside her, took Kyosti's other elbow. "This way," he said. "Turn here."

They turned off the main street. Kyosti's face lost some of

its blank-eyed stare, and he abruptly disengaged his elbow from Heredes's grasp.

"Well, Hawk," said Heredes, but he confined further comment to an exchange of glances with Lily. "Turn here again. And—ah, yes—Abagail Street. Twelve oh one. Twelve oh seven. Here we are." They went in. As the doors shut behind them, the noise from the street faded and cut off. Heredes examined the directory. Kyosti withdrew his arm from Lily.

"Floor twenty-one. We'll take the lift."

They came out on floor twenty-one into a small hallway flanked with two doors. One was blank. The other bore the letters Abagail Street Academy. Jones. Haji. Ramirez. In the anteroom a young man sat behind a counter typing into a terminal. He looked up. "May I help you?"

Heredes presented an amiable smile. "We're here to see sensei Jones. She *is* expecting us."

"Of course," said the young man uncertainly. "She should be in gym one."

"Thank you." Heredes led them into a hallway. "Gym Four. Three. Locker room. Locker room. Quite an establishment. Puts mine to shame." He winked at Lily. "Two. Here we are." He pushed open double doors, Lily and Kyosti following.

The floors were of wood. Lily noticed that first. Then the rank of mirrors along one wall. The other walls were a pale peach. Mats lay rolled up against the far wall. In the middle of the room sat a woman, cross-legged, meditating. Her head lifted at the sound of their entrance, turned. The woman's entire body tensed as she stared. She jumped to her feet.

"Joshua! What the devil are you doing here?"

"Wingtuck. My dearest—sister." He motioned Lily and Kyosti to halt, came forward with his arms open. "How kind of you to receive us."

She spun away from him and placed a smart kick directly into his abdomen. He gasped, hard, but he did not go down.

"Are you trying to get me killed?" she hissed. "Are you insane? I told you never to come back here." Her stance, her voice, as she faced Heredes, who was still struggling to regain his breathing, was implacable. "I'll give you one minute to explain. And one minute after that to get the hell out of here."

14 A Legal Bond

✳✳✳✳✳✳✳

For a moment there was silence torn only by Heredes's ragged breathing. Wingtuck Honor Jones looked suddenly past Heredes and caught sight of Kyosti.

"Jesus and Mary," she said. "Hawk?"

"Still Catholic, I see," he replied.

"One is always Catholic, Hawk," she snapped, but the fear on her face subsided as she examined him. "Good Lord, boy, you have changed. What happened to you?"

"That," said Heredes on an in-drawn breath, "is a long story. Is there somewhere more private we can talk?"

"Very well." She appeared, now, resigned to her fate. "My office. But who is this?"

"This is my daughter, Lily."

This explanation had, at least, the advantage of keeping Wingtuck in stunned silence through the entire walk to her office, just down the hall.

"Now," Wingtuck said as she settled into her chair. Her gaze kept straying to Kyosti as if she expected to see him sprout blue hair. "I directed you to a quiet place where you could lie low in return for you not bothering me. I don't want your trouble, Joshua."

"My trouble, as you so conveniently phrase it, having found me, is most certainly looking for you as well, Wingtuck."

"Most certainly," echoed Kyosti, with a sly look that Heredes, signing at him, banished.

"And the peace lasted much longer than I expected," added Heredes. "But all I am here for is to ask that you take Lily on as an instructor, to apprentice her, for the period we are here on Arcadia."

"Just like that?" said Wingtuck. "You walk in here, jeopardizing my cover and my Academy, and expect me to apprentice her? Is she qualified? Does she have ID? A visa? An extension for employment? Is she even a citizen of the Reft? Come now, Joshua. Let's be reasonable."

"My dear Wingtuck," said Heredes soothingly. "Getting an ID and a visa is the least of our problems—as you know perfectly well."

Wingtuck frowned. Lily watched her. She was a small-boned woman, tiny; Lily could give her a good fifteen centimeters in height and at least ten kilos in weight. But despite her size she had none of that suggestion of delicacy that Kyosti, by design or by accident, appeared at times to possess. She was hard as the metal-sheathed walls of Ransome House, impervious to the storms outside, utterly self-contained. "Why, Joshua?" she said at last. "Convince me."

Heredes smiled and settled with a pleased sigh into the deep padding of his chair. "Sweet Wing," he began. "We're in terrible trouble."

"Hawk, for one thing," said Wingtuck. "What else?"

"I beg your pardon," protested Kyosti.

"Yes," said Heredes. "Hawk for one thing." His smile disappeared as he examined Kyosti where he reclined in a sybaritic pose at Lily's feet. "Most important, my dear," his tone was grave now, "the Illustrious is dead."

Wingtuck's gamine face hosted a quick series of expressions: disbelief, sorrow, fear, resolving into determination. She crossed herself. "So they've come after us at last."

"Oh, yes," said Heredes. "Just about everyone, now that the Duke is no longer alive to—ah—cast his mantle of protection over us."

"I see." Wingtuck fixed a look of acute suspicion on Kyosti. "And what brings you here, Hawk? Where have you been all these years?"

"In prison," he replied in a most agreeable tone. "A foolish mistake, but it only takes one."

"And how, may I ask, did you get out of prison?"

He smiled with great sweetness. "I recanted. I was accounted a classic figure of rehabilitation and sent along with the expedition the League sent out here to round the last of us up, but, do you know, when my eyes fell on our Joshua, I realized how dreadfully bored I had become, so I absented myself with him and his beautiful daughter."

"Joshua! Have you lost your mind?" Wingtuck stood up. "Do you trust him?"

"Of course I don't trust him," said Heredes. Kyosti offered him a brief, if ironic, salute. "But what choice did I have? I couldn't leave him."

"Ah," interposed Kyosti, "but you wish you had."

"I certainly do," said Heredes. "I certainly do." He looked at Wingtuck. "He won't betray us."

"If he hasn't already?" She turned icy eyes on Kyosti. "How much did you tell them?"

Kyosti lifted a hand in careless dismissal. "You know how terribly weak my memory is," he drawled.

"I expect that it improves under drugs."

"My dear Wingtuck." Lily saw, by his face, that he was annoyed. "You know quite well that those kinds of drugs do not work on me."

"That's true," she muttered, unmollified. "But then why in Heaven's name did they bring you out here with them?"

He stood with abrupt swiftness. Anger emanated from him. "Because with all their fine philosophies of conflict resolution and nonviolence and rehabilitation for criminals" —a definite, heavy sarcastic emphasis here—"they'd rather not admit that they created us, you and me and *Master* Heredes and the rest of our kind, that they created terrorists, saboteurs whose creed had to be violence and murder and destruction. They'd rather not admit to the ways we won that war for them, calling us heroes and hating us and shunning us and fearing us at the same time." He spun away, so furious, and yet so contained, that Lily feared for his control, feared this hidden depth of rage in him. "Still, *still,* Wingtuck, they can't believe that our kind still exist among them, our kind, who choose violence first, not caring if we kill our enemies or ourselves, mouthing these sick, weak phrases of rehabilitation and then casting them off without a second's regret. They expected us to stop, as if all that training could be negated by a second's wish. Of course they brought me out here with them. They've forgotten that we can lie as easy as we can kill."

Wingtuck came out from behind her desk and walked up to Kyosti. He did not move, as if his words, sloughing his anger off him, had left him frozen without any further emotion to direct his actions. She laid her hand with surprising tenderness on his bronzed cheek.

"Sweet Jesus," she said in an undertone. "My poor boy. What did they do to you?"

He turned his face away from her hand and, with a movement more like collapse than rejection, sank to the floor beside Lily, resting his head against her leg. Lily blushed under Wingtuck's keen eye, but she put one hand, nevertheless, to rest lightly on Kyosti's pale hair. Against her, she felt his shallow, quick breaths slow and deepen.

Wingtuck went back to her chair. The plain white walls of the office framed her as she examined her three visitors. A large poster advertising the Abagail Street Academy hung by the door; behind the desk, a painting depicted a pair of round-hatted farmers knee-deep in a rice paddy.

"Vietnamese," said Wingtuck suddenly.

"I'm sorry?" asked Heredes.

"Your Lily. She must have Vietnamese blood in her."

Heredes turned his head to gaze at Lily, who, under such scrutiny, looked down at Kyosti.

"Don't look at me," disclaimed that man. "I'm not up on old Earth cultures."

"So she must," said Heredes. "It had never occurred to me."

"It wouldn't, round-eye," replied Wingtuck, almost insulting.

"What is Vietnamese?" asked Lily; as both Heredes and Wingtuck opened their mouths, she raised a hand. "No, don't tell me. It's a long story, right?"

Heredes only smiled.

"So the League rousted you out?" said Wingtuck to Heredes.

"No. The chameleons rousted me out."

"Good Lord!" She put her hands over her face, lowered them after a moment to lie clasped in front of her. "I thought I would never have to see another one of them. We *are* busy."

"Yes," said Heredes. "I let them capture me so I could get a look at what they had. Just one cruiser so far, I believe. Out for blood, of course. But they don't know that the League is out here, too. I didn't know the League was here until I tracked down Lily, who had come after me, believing that I had been kidnapped. But she, as well as Hawk and two colleagues, were in Jehanish custody at Nevermore."

"Jehanish?" The light, on Wingtuck's hair, had a way of catching on the darkest strands as she turned her head, as if swallowed up by their blackness. "Ah, yes. I know who they are. There's a well-known writer here, name of Pero, publishes underground, causes all sorts of agitation."

"Lily even met Jehane, lucky girl." Heredes shot Lily a dryly mocking smile. "We had to exit in some haste. Talking with Hawk on our way here, I discovered that the League is in contact with the government of the Reft."

"And what does Hawk know about this?" asked Wingtuck acidly.

"Nothing," said Hawk, not moving, his voice partially muffled against Lily's trousers. His eyes were shut. "They just brought me along for the ride."

"I'm satisfied that is true," said Heredes. "But we haven't gotten to the good part yet."

"Do tell." Wingtuck smiled caustically.

"Who should we meet but La Belle Dame, following the trail of the chameleons."

Wingtuck laughed. "Happy tidings for the Reft, for where La Belle leads the rest of the privateers shall soon follow.

But Joshua, all this being true, why didn't you just go with
La Belle? Why come here?"

"Because I want to know what the League is saying to the
government at Central and for how long they've been in
contact. We can't run forever, Wing, and damned if I'm
going to live the rest of my very long life cooped up on a
pirate's tub, no matter how luxurious."

"Groundhog," said Wingtuck. "All right." She leaned
back in her chair. "I accept that our interests demand we
link up for a bit. How do you plan to find out all this perti-
nent information?"

"I'll go into Central."

"Good luck. Security's tight as a bull's ass in fly time."

"Fetching phrase, Wing."

"Oh, I'm just a peasant at heart."

Heredes laughed. "No wonder you've survived so long.
But really, Wing, getting into Central is not what I'm worried about."

"No, you wouldn't be," replied Wingtuck, but her gaze
followed Heredes's—to Kyosti.

Kyosti's eyes were still closed. Lily ascertained that with
a quick glance and was astonished by the look exchanged by
Wingtuck and Heredes. It could have been spoken, it was so
blatant: "What, *he* won't be going in with you?" And
Heredes's look in reply, negative and sad.

"What are you planning to do, Kyosti?" Lily asked to
cover that revealing silence.

"I'd like to practice medicine again." He opened his eyes
and looked up at her. "But I don't have a license for this
region."

Wingtuck considered this. "I don't know, Hawk. You can
hardly hand them your Columbia diploma as verification.
And it would take years to go back through school."

"No school," said Kyosti.

She shook her head, pensive. "But they're desperate for
help in the community clinics—most poor people never see
anyone higher than a medical technologist anyway. If you
passed the med-tech exams, they might *offer* you a visa ex-

tension. Even with the massive unemployment here, they still can't fill those positions—"

"Long hours, bad conditions, poor patients." Kyosti smiled. "How much actual supervision by physicians is there? In the worst clinics?"

"I don't know. I don't imagine there's much. You'd probably have pretty free rein—and as close to conditions of battlefield medicine that you can get on a peaceful planet. But it doesn't pay well. Certainly not enough to dress as you were accustomed to, believe me."

"I sew," said Kyosti stiffly. "It's my one creative outlet." He lifted his head and surveyed, with his usual self-collected mockery, the surprised looks on Wingtuck's and Heredes's faces. "And in any case, any real occupation would be paradise for me."

"How long were you in prison, Hawk?" Heredes asked gently.

Kyosti's penetrating blue stare focused on the other man. "Sixteen years, seven months, three days. I can continue to the millisecond."

"I believe you," murmured Wingtuck, but her gaze was almost pitying. "What about Lily?"

"Haven't I convinced you?" said Heredes. "She can apprentice here."

"She can take her chances, like Hawk. There must be other work she can do."

"There isn't," said Lily. To Heredes: "Sorry."

"Just consider, Joshua," continued Wingtuck. "To give her instructional duties, to pay her any credit at all, she has to go on the employment rolls. To get on those, she has to have an extended worker's visa. Legalities, you see. She'd never get a visa extension for this work—I have to hire from legal Arcadian citizens. You don't understand the magnitude of the problem on this planet. Why do you think Jehane is so popular here?"

"If we don't help each other, Wingtuck, then we're all lost."

Wingtuck said nothing.

"Wing," said Heredes slowly. "Is there no other way to make Lily legal?"

Wingtuck gave a short, hard laugh. "Bond her to a permanent resident."

"Of course!" Heredes stood up. "I should have thought of that."

"No!" cried Kyosti, and he also stood up, and Wingtuck, perceiving trouble, rose as well.

"Kyosti." Lily's voice sounded quite reasonable. "Sit down." All three regarded her with astonishment. Kyosti sat. "Obviously," Lily continued, "a long-term economic bond is out of the question. But a child-directed pair-bond—after one year, when I hadn't yet conceived, it would automatically be dissolved." She looked at Heredes. "Is one year enough time for what you need to do?"

"Yes," he said meekly.

Lily turned her gaze to Wingtuck, but, seeing a smile caught just below the older woman's expression, she favored her with a quick wink. "So where can I find a partner?"

"That depends on how many credits you have to spend, or what political beliefs you're willing to—ah—embrace."

"Hoy," said Lily. "I had no idea it was so easy. But the only other person I've heard of on this planet is that writer, Pero." She grinned. "And if he's a Jehanist, he's hardly likely to want to bond the woman who shot his leader."

But Heredes merely looked thoughtful. "An agitator," he said, as if to himself. "That might be just the thing." He cut off Lily's question with a wave of one hand. "So, sensei Jones, you'll take her?"

"You make my life difficult, Joshua," said Wingtuck with an exasperated sigh. "I'll see her through her paces first."

"Where would you like me to warm up?" said Lily.

"Gym Three." Wingtuck turned and removed two garments from a cabinet. "Here's a gi."

"Thank you," said Lily. "Are you coming with me, Kyosti?" He followed her without a word out of the room.

"Well," said Wingtuck expansively. "She does you credit."

Heredes smiled. "You haven't seen her do her forms yet. She's much better than I deserve. But thank you."

"Taliesin." She sat on the edge of her desk, one leg dangling, and regarded him seriously. "How many of us are left?"

"I don't know. Fewer than you imagine, I fear." He sighed, pacing a slow circuit around the small office. "La Belle had some information. They say Sibaia, Haggerty, Annet, and Hovas are still at large."

"Robin?"

He shook his head. "Dead. And Collobrieres as well."

"May the Lord bless and keep them," she murmured, crossing herself. "Senegambia?"

"I don't know."

"Katajarenta?"

This surprised a laugh from him. "Mother's Breasts, Wing, they'll never catch her."

"Foucart?"

Heredes halted, turning to face her. "Now there's an interesting case. According to Bella, both he and Korrigan have turned bounty hunter, and are existing on the edge of the law, but legally."

"Huh," said Wingtuck. "I'd hate to have one of them contracted out on me. Insharish? Keng? Buru? Hyacinth?"

He shook his head. "Dead, captured, or broken. It's been a sad toll. And I only know what I heard from Bella."

"The bastards. Hawk was right about their gratitude. Good Lord, how *did* he get out of prison?"

"He recanted. Evidently they believed him."

"Hawk could charm his way out of a snake pit. Jesus—" She gave her hard, unhumorous laugh again. "He did, more than once, Taliesin." She rose and went to him, putting a hand on his shoulder. They stood close and easy together. Physically, they appeared to have little in common except perhaps a similarity in their shade of skin. But their eyes, in expression, the set of their faces, their posture, the musculature of their lean bodies, revealed some bond, some long, difficult road of shared experience that bound them as tightly as any blood tie. "Why isn't Hawk going into Central with you? What did they do to him in that prison?"

"I wish I knew, Lotus," he said, soft as the room ventilators. "All I know is that according to Bella's sources, he was in prison for twenty years, give or take a month."

"And?" He waited for her to consider. "But Hawk said sixteen years. Hawk is never wrong." She removed her hand from his shoulder, troubled.

"Yes," said Heredes. "What were those axioms we had? Loud as Agina. Drunk as Korey. Ugly as Periwinkle."

"Irritable as Wing." They both laughed, but Wingtuck sobered first. "Sharp as Hawk's mind. If they had him in solitary, he might have lost track."

"Our Hawk? Who feels the rhythms of the universe in his body? The pulse of the stars in his blood? 'Body is soul, spirit is flesh, and all thus combined touches the universe, no separation.' We could put him down on any planet, in any system, and he could tell us the hour and the day and the season. No. When he says he was imprisoned—most of it in solitary, he admits that—for sixteen years, seven months, and three days, he means sixteen years, seven months, and three days. Lotus, he has lost three and one half years of his life. They no longer exist in his mind."

"I don't understand."

"He told me that he suspects that all the clocks and calendars were set forward, on his release, in order to confuse him into revealing information."

"Very amusing."

"He was completely serious." He moved to seat himself on the edge of the desk, watching her now as she paced. "So you see why he's not going in with me."

"My God," she said.

"Oh." He raised an admonitory finger. "And I almost forgot. Lily thinks he doesn't perceive windows."

"That's ridiculous. I was on the Gesie run with him. He hated windows—instants he couldn't measure as time. He used to get ill from it."

"Not any more. Lily says he moved three meters inside a window."

"Sweet Jesus, Taliesin." She turned her back to him, staring up at the Academy poster, a woman forever frozen with the ridge of her high side kick touching the recoiling chin of a man falling in graceful lines to a white floor. "What has he become?"

He smiled, a rather forlorn thing, watching the straight, proud lines of her back. "Something more like his mother, I think, and little enough we know about her kind."

"Enough to know that her kind never lie."

"I expect that particular habit we can credit to his human half."

"Taliesin." The flat calmness of her tone caught him midway to standing, an immobilized gesture. "Can we really trust him? My God, when I think of the things—what if he really did murder Hannibal? His best friend! We never had any proof."

"Only Maisry's insistence that he was innocent, and we all knew what her word was worth. I can still remember the smile she had on her face when she said it. But Lotus, by the Mother's Heart, we can't abandon him. I can't abandon him." He rose completely. "And anyway, he won't betray us."

"Let me rephrase that, in the time-honored fashion. Do you trust him with your own daughter?"

"Too late, I fear." His voice had the barest trace of self-mockery. "He's already slept with her."

She whirled. "Jesus and Mary, don't joke—dear God." This last in a whisper. "Why didn't you stop him?"

He met her eyes. "I am ashamed, Lotus. I never expected it. Not until it was too late."

He moved to stand behind a chair, running one hand along its smooth back. Wingtuck waited. "You have no idea how quickly he acted. How could I have expected that? You know how he was—he took three *years,* courting Maisry, before *she* finally persuaded him to her bed."

"And took fifty-two seconds," added Wingtuck with caustic precision, "holding her dead body in his arms at Betaos, to go berserk. You were there."

"Yes, and so were you, and Paula, and Collobrieres, and an entire chameleon battalion."

" 'But that was in another country,' " said Wingtuck. "Don't change the subject."

"By the time I realized—how in the Mother's Name could I have stopped him? What can you threaten him with?"

"You could have killed him—no, I don't suppose you could have. You could have warned her."

Silence. His hand stilled. "Yes. I could have warned her, with the half-truths we know and the rumors we can only guess might be true. But I could have. If, Lotus, *if* I had expected him to be interested."

"He'd been in prison for twenty years, for God's sake. Don't think the rest of us have your low sex drive, Joshua."

Heredes laughed unexpectedly. "But Wing, he'd been out of prison three or four years already—if that was his only impulse, he would have acted on it long before he met Lily and we wouldn't be discussing this entire subject."

She paused, taking in her next breath for another volley of words, and sighed instead. "And his sexuality is only half-human anyway. Oh, you're right, you couldn't have expected it. But why did he want her? Appearance couldn't be enough to sway him, not when he knows what the consequences are—if not to her, then to him. You said it yourself: body is soul, spirit is flesh, there is no separation." Silence sifted into the office until Heredes, moving, shattered it.

"Why does Hawk want anything? I don't know. I only hope the choice wasn't entirely mercenary on his part."

"To get your protection? Maybe that was his motive, to begin with. It will have gone far past that by now. And Lily, she's so young. How could she have resisted him, when he turned the full force of that half-alien charm on her?"

"How, indeed. I didn't know you were attracted to him, Lotus."

She laughed in her unamused fashion. "My dear friend, I wouldn't touch him with the proverbial ten-foot pole. What are you going to tell her?"

"About Hawk? I don't know the truth about Hawk. He has to take that responsibility."

She came to stand beside him, laid a hand on his unlined face. "Do you ever feel old, Taliesin?"

He smiled. "But I know the secret of immortality, my Lotus Blossom."

"And your Lily is a beautiful child." She smiled. It transformed her face as a bud, opening into flower, is transformed. "No wonder that Hawk could not resist her, being, as she is, Taliesin's daughter."

"Flatterer," said Heredes.

She kissed him on the cheek. "Let's go see her, this prodigy of yours."

In Gym Three, the prodigy limbered up while Kyosti paced. Mercifully there were no mirrors to reflect the unfortunate mixture of anguish and hostility on his face.

"You can't do it!" he exclaimed.

Stretching on the floor, she sank into horizontal splits, bent at the hips to touch her chest and face to the polished wood planks. "Why not?"

He stopped, spun to face her. She pushed herself up to look at him. "Because I love you!" He crouched beside her, reaching for her as if to pull her to him.

With an impatient gesture she waved him away. "What other alternatives do you suggest, then?" He said nothing, turned half-away. She was struck yet again by the high sweep of his bone structure, the suggestion of delicacy that she could not reconcile with his strength. "Kyosti," she began, attempting now a reasonable tone, "a one-year bond is such a temporary thing. It won't mean anything anyway, it's just to get me a visa extension."

He gazed with melancholy fascination at the opposite wall. "I'll probably kill him," he said as if he were talking to himself.

"Kyosti!" She leaned on her elbows, frowning at him. The lack of self-pity in his despondency disturbed her. "I probably won't even sleep with the man."

Like a drowning man who has seen a life raft, his face brightened. "Promise me, Lily. Promise me you won't."

"Hoy." She rolled up to her feet. Against her bare soles the floor felt eager for her to work along it. "I'm probably whistling down the wind the handsomest man I'll ever meet," she said to the ceiling, thought of Jehane, and reconsidered. "The second handsomest." She threw a set of back thrust kicks, added a hook, a crescent, and came to rest beside Kyosti. He rose. "All right. I promise." She put out a hand for him to shake. With a trace of confusion, he did so. "Now will you stop acting stupid?"

"You don't love me," he said, but it was not an accusation, merely a bald statement.

"Oh, Kyosti." She flung away from him, executed a quick series of strikes, the last of which, a spinning back knuckle, came to rest just at the tip of his nose. "I haven't even known you a month."

"Is it one of the other two that you love?"

She dropped her hand. "I beg your pardon?"

"One of the other two men you slept with before you met me."

She had to look around the empty room, so clearly did she feel he must be talking to someone else. "I never told you," she said slowly, "that I'd slept with two other men."

He smiled, more like himself now, that languid confidence. "You didn't need to."

"Heredes couldn't have told you. He didn't even know one of them." She stared at him. "What—you can read my mind?"

He shrugged, at a loss. "But it's there—it's—"

"Yes?" she said sweetly.

"I can't explain it, Lily," he said in some distress. "It's like a—I don't know—" He shook his head, his wild mop of hair like a symbol of his confusion. "I can just tell," he finished with complete finality.

"Well," said Lily comprehensively. "That's rolled up my flanks, as Heredes is used to say. Any other revelations?"

"Actually." He lowered his eyes to examine the grains in

the wood beneath, raised them finally, unwinking blue with a hidden depth of green, to gaze at her. "There are."

The door opened, and Wingtuck and Heredes came in. A look suspiciously like relief fled across Kyosti's face. With a brief, apologetic smile, he retreated.

"All right, Lily," said Wingtuck. "Let's see what you can do. Kata first."

Lily bowed. But after the second kata, Wingtuck waved at her to stop. Heredes was failing in his attempt not to smile. Kyosti watched Lily with possessive interest.

"Oh, all right, Joshua!" said Wingtuck in her most irritable tone. "For God's sake, you needn't smirk at me."

"But—" Lily faltered. "I'm sorry, I—"

"My dear girl," Wingtuck interrupted impatiently. "If you don't know how good you are, you'll soon find out. Joshua, you offend me." She observed that Heredes was coughing into his hand. "You may cease laughing."

"You're taking me?" Lily asked, a little shaken.

"Yes."

"Thank you!" Lily came forward impetuously, halted, managed a reserved bow to sensei Jones, which that woman returned with awesome formality.

"This appointment is contingent upon your obtaining a visa and a bond with an as yet unspecified male citizen of Arcadia. You will be issued three gis, and forwarded enough credit for a week's food and lodging—there is a good hostel on Bettina Street where you may be able to reserve a double." A disapproving glance for Kyosti here. "You will begin as an assistant. Progress thereafter depends on your enthusiasm and your ability. This Academy has a reputation to uphold. You will report at oh eight hundred hours tomorrow. Is that clear?"

Lily bowed.

"What name will you be using?"

"Ah—Lily?" she ventured.

"First names are unacceptable," snapped Wingtuck.

Lily considered, serious at first, but her eyes met Heredes's and her lips quirked up slightly. She bowed. "Heredes, if you please, sensei Jones."

Wingtuck laughed. "You're as incorrigible as Joshua. So be it, sensei Heredes." She saluted her with a slap on the back. "Go on. I'll see you tomorrow. Though I won't, I hope, see either of you gentlemen here again."

Kyosti offered her an elaborate bow; Heredes smiled.

They found with comparative ease the hostel on Bettina Street and installed Lily and Kyosti there in a "double," which consisted of a bed not much more than a meter wide, a metal clothes cabinet, a terminal with folding chair, and a tiny water-based washing cubicle.

"Hoy," said Lily, but Kyosti was so cheerfully stowing their possessions in the cabinet that she felt she could not complain about their surroundings. "What are *you* going to do?" she asked Heredes.

He sat on the bed watching Kyosti. If he had any misgivings about this arrangement, he showed no sign of it. "First I've got to get you ID."

Kyosti coughed, turning from his work, and surveyed Heredes with cold civility. "I think I can manage for myself and Lily," he said.

Heredes considered him a long moment, that slender frame leaning against the cabinet, and he saw with sudden clarity the three features that really marked Kyosti as half-alien, for him at least: the delicacy of his face; that distant green tangent hidden in his blue eyes; but most of all, and most subtle until you knew what to look for, the slight elongation of his body which covered thirteen pair of ribs. "Very well, Hawk," he said. "You can of course do it for yourself, but we're not arguing over Lily."

Kyosti frowned, but he said nothing.

"Then," continued Heredes, "I shall fetch Bach. After that I believe I will hunt down Mr. Pero."

"Why Pero?" asked Lily. "It seems to me that he'd be hard to find, and terribly suspicious. And I'm not sure I want to ally myself with Jehane in any fashion. He's"—she shook her head—"not my type. I like to think for myself."

"Don't think of it as allying with Jehane," answered Heredes. "Think of it as expedience. Pero will serve very well precisely because I believe I possess the means to convince him to agree."

The days fell into a pattern. She rose and went to the academy, worked out, observed, began to be allowed to instruct. Returned to the hostel to eat in the common room with Kyosti. Then they would retire to the privacy of their room. Lily began to feel, inexplicably, that his need to touch her was more physiological than emotional, as if she were the one drug he could become addicted to. Still, she felt disinclined to complain.

On the fifth day she returned home to find Bach, but no Kyosti. She and Bach, nevertheless, enjoyed a musical evening together. When Kyosti appeared, very late, he showed her their new com-screens—hers credited to Lily Ash Heredes, his to Kyosti Maisrei Accipiter. He had also, he informed her the next morning, applied to take the technologist's certification exam. The next night he insisted she put Bach in the washing cubicle while they made love.

They slept late, woke, only to lay together in lazy, sensuous amiability. Bach serenaded them with a muffled aria from behind the cubicle door:

Bereite dich, Zion, mit zärtlichen Trieben,
Den Schönsten, den Liebsten bald bei dir zu sehn!
Deine Wangen
Müssen heut viel schöner prangen,
Eile, den Bräutigam sehnlichst zu lieben!

Prepare thyself, Zion, with tender desire
the Fairest and Dearest to behold with thee soon!
Thy cheeks
today must shine the lovelier,
hasten most ardently the Bridegroom to love!

Kyosti delighted in kissing her; "I'm marking you out as mine," he would say, as if it were a private joke only he and she could share. When the intercom buzzed, Bach answered it in Paisley's voice. If this disconcerted Heredes at all, it could not be discerned by his voice.

"I'll be up in ten minutes, Lily," he said over the crackle of in-house static. "I have a visitor with me."

They were dressed in five. The door lock chimed and Heredes entered.

"Well, Lily," he said, kissing her on the cheek. "I've brought Mr. Pero." He turned and beckoned.

Quite the darkest man Lily had ever seen came into the room. Bach retreated into the washing cubicle. Pero was neither handsome nor plain; he had a face she would have called good-humored except for the intensity that, scoring it, gave it an added dimension. He smiled, very warm and very encompassing, and put out his hand to shake hers.

"Lily Heredes?" He had a deep, musical voice. "Your guardian mentioned an arrangement that might be beneficial to both of us."

Lily blushed.

"Actually, my name is Robert Malcolm," continued Pero, "but you must call me Robbie. All my friends do. Pero is not my real name, just my pen name, after all."

"Pero," said Kyosti acidly from his reclining position on the bed, where he was examining Pero in minute and unimpressed detail. "How original."

"In fact," replied Robert Malcolm with cheerful sincerity, "it's not original at all. I stole it from an obscure history tape. But I'm afraid—" He paused, glancing at Lily.

"This is Kyosti Maisrei Accipiter," she said hastily. "He's a medical technologist."

"Indeed!" Pero put out his hand. "And where do you work?"

Kyosti rose with bored cordiality and shook the proferred hand with extreme reserve. "I hope," he said in his most languorous tones, "to be working soon in one of the Ridani districts."

"That's marvelous!" Pero seemed, remarkably, to be entirely free from artifice. "And I should add, min Accipiter," he continued, with a shrewd look at Kyosti's aloof expression, "that since my sister has recently vacated the second bedroom in my apartment out in the Zanta District, it would be convenient for all of us, if Lily and I do indeed reach an agreement, that you and Lily might then share that room. Now, Lily," and he quickly turned his attention to her, "shall the four of us go walk in Teapot Park and discuss this business further?"

Lily of course agreed with alacrity. Kyosti was too astonished to refuse.

15 Robert Malcolm

✳✳✳✳✳✳✳

"Hoy," said Lily, handing a wet plate to Robbie to dry, "if you're going to call a general strike, I'd better assign myself as your bodyguard."

Pero laughed. He had an easy laugh, quiet and good-natured, and was more likely to laugh at himself than at others. "Sometimes I think you think I can't take care of myself," he said.

"After living with you for almost six months, Robbie, I *know* you can't take care of yourself." But she smiled, taking any sting from the words. "I can't decide whether you live on luck or on good intentions."

"I live on Jehane's cause," he said, serious now. "And as long as I am needed for his work, I shall live."

Lily, returning his open gaze, wondered for the hundredth time what it was he had seen in Jehane, in the same Jehane who had terrified her, to make him cast his devotion, his energy, his life so absolutely at Jehane's feet. At first she had assumed that Jehane had merely hypnotized Robbie into his service as he had, in some sense, attempted to hypnotize her, but she had long since given up that theory as too simplistic. She shrugged and washed another plate. "It amazes me Central hasn't arrested you yet," she said finally, "especially after all those protests you engineered last autumn because of the tax increase. Not to mention the riots in the Ridani districts.

"I am not responsible for riot, Lily."

"Not yet, and not on purpose. Central did bring that one on themselves, considering they canceled the entire range of pregnancy credits for Ridani women. What could they expect? Poor Kyosti, stuck at the clinic for sixteen days, what with all the injuries and the curfew."

"Certainly I blame Central." Even in private conversation he declaimed, as if some secret audience only he knew about were always watching, or as if Bach, humming now at his usual place plugged into the apartment terminal, were recording him. "For inaugurating pregnancy credits in the first place two hundred and fifty years ago. Without any provision for ending them once the population rose high enough, of course we would reach a point of dangerous overcrowding, having institutionalized the very reward system that brought us to this pass." He finished with that flourish of righteous dismay that she had come to recognize in his delivery.

"But, Robbie, there had to be some way for the colonists to push the population up—there were so few of them."

"My dear Lya." He pronounced this *Lie-ah*. It was a liberty she would have let no other person take. "Nature long since provided a way to increase the population. You enjoy it with your physician." He paused. "And yet remain childless."

Lily threw up her hands, spraying water drops across the counter. "You win! You win! I should know better than to argue politics with you. How do you know Kyosti's really a physician, anyway? He's been at such pains to present himself as a mere technologist."

"I'm afraid he only told me as a sop to his pride. I hope I don't offend you, Lya."

She considered. "No, I don't think you do, actually. I don't understand Kyosti at all, not really."

"I wonder if he is difficult to understand, or whether he doesn't want to be understood," he replied, and regarded her expectantly.

Lily thrust her hands back into the cooling water. "Let's not talk about Kyosti right now. I've been mad at him all evening." Robbie's expectant gaze did not waver, except for one eyebrow that quirked up. Lily smiled, a little one-sided. "I guess I asked for that. Maybe I'll feel less guilty if I tell you. We went out for a drink after classes, at the Academy —me and four of the other instructors. Did you ever meet—? Anyway, one of them is good-looking, uncompli- cated, about my age, and we've been flirting on and off ever since I started there, and—" Now she paused. Robbie smiled. Lily blushed. "It didn't go that far," she said, "a little kissing, I mean—and I don't see what business Kyosti has dictating what I do with my own body. It's not like we're bonded."

Robbie began to laugh.

"You're laughing at me!"

"You are feeling guilty, aren't you?" he said.

"And so I'm all hot and bothered and then he isn't even here when I get home!"

"Thoughtless of him."

Lily laughed. "Especially considering the long hours he works. You know, Robbie, I think you're the most nonjudg- mental person I've ever met."

"I judge injustice," said Robbie, "not humanity."

"Finished." Lily put the last plate on the counter. "What else can I do before the neatest person I've ever met arrives and yells at us for being so messy?"

But it was a mistake to ask Robbie lighthearted questions when his mind was on revolution. "I have two courier runs you could do for me," he said. "One needs to be in Byssina by tomorrow evening. It's a diskette, and they're setting up a new underground net to broadcast. It's got the codes they need."

"Is this to replace the one the Immortals destroyed last month?"

Robbie looked stern. "Murdered three citizens. This kind of thing cannot, will not, be allowed to continue." For a moment he stared into the distance of a vision Lily could not see.

"And the other one?" Lily asked, reminding him that she was still here.

"Yes. The other one. I need someone to meet with the district organizer from Roanoak. This is a bit more difficult, since you need to pass documents both ways."

"From Roanoak? That's the district Kyosti works in. Is he a Ridani?"

"Yes, and that makes it doubly difficult. But the rendez-vous has been set at a three-di bar, where one might be expected to find a few Ridanis outside of their own districts."

"Gambling? Oh, well, I used to watch the three-di tournaments on the nets, so I may as well see them in person. I see the strangest places working for you."

"Not for me." Robbie looked almost embarrassed, as at an honor he felt he was not worthy of. "For Jehane."

"I don't do this for Jehane," she said. "Don't ever make that mistake, Robbie. I do it for you."

"You only say that because you haven't met him."

Lily hesitated. She had avoided the topic of Jehane whenever it had come up previously, but now—she had, after all, known Pero for almost half a year now. "I have met him."

"Then there can be no question. You found him inspiring."

"I don't think that's the word I would use. I found him—" Words failed her. Pero's face, so free from guile, bore its usual intent, expectant expression as he watched her. *Bach,* she whistled suddenly. *How did I find Jehane?*

Across the room, she saw lights stir on Bach's gleaming surface. He retracted a plug from the computer terminal and rotated to face Lily and Robbie. Pero's desk, a couch, and three chairs separated them. "Patroness," he said in Paisley's voice, "it is my belief that thou foundest him forgiving."

"Therefore," stated Robbie. He dried the last dish with a final flourish.

But Lily was chuckling quietly to herself. "I'll help you, Robbie. If for no other reason than the favor you did me by agreeing to the bond."

"It was hardly a favor, Lily," he said.

"What do you mean, it was—" She stopped. Walked to

the couch and sat down. And experienced so sudden a rush
of illumination that she wondered how she could have gone
so many months without realizing. Because of the initial
exhaustion of her work at Wingtuck's Academy? Because of
Kyosti, who drew her more and more into his strange sense
of expectation that she and he had the bond, and not she
and Pero? Because of Pero himself, whose unfailing affabil-
ity might mislead one to think he was also completely altru-
istic? Bach floated up next to her, blinked lights. "Hoy. He
traded me for something. And I don't mean credit. He made
a deal with you, didn't he? Robbie!" She stood up. "Do you
know where he is?"

"In Central."

"I know that. I mean, are you in contact with him? Can I
talk to him? Robbie! He just disappeared one week after we
got here, told me to stay quiet and wait patiently, and just
disappeared. He didn't even tell me what he was going to
do."

The door brushed aside and Kyosti entered.

"Kyosti!" said Lily. "Where is Heredes?"

He halted. " 'To darkness are they doomed who devote
themselves only to life in the world.' Frankly, Lily, I neither
know nor care where Joshua is."

"You're impossible."

"Ah," he said. "Kiss me before you make such a pro-
nouncement."

"I don't know how you can work for twelve hours in that
clinic and come home in such a good mood," she said in
disgust, but she went to him.

For an instant he returned her kiss with his usual enthusiasm. Then he caught himself, as if from a blow, and recoiled
violently away from her.

A sense of anticipatory stillness fell suddenly over the
room. Pero took one step back. Lily froze.

Kyosti grabbed the back of the nearest chair, lifted it in a
single swing up over his head, and brought it down full force
to the floor. The sound shuddered through the apartment.

"Don't do this to me!" he cried. And he went for the
computer.

Bach, in a brilliance of lights, placed himself in front of the terminal. Lily leapt forward and pinned Kyosti's arms to his side. He began to twist from side to side, trying to throw her off as if he was entirely unaware of who she was, and she felt her hold slipping.

Then Robbie was there. They pushed him toward the couch, but their hold was tenuous. Kyosti struggled against them, wild, as if rage were his only sentience. He was very strong.

Bach sang out suddenly and bumped up against Pero where he fought to press Kyosti into the couch. An appendage snaked out from Bach's surface.

"Let go of him," said Lily abruptly, and jumped back. Robbie did so just in time to miss the flash of light.

Kyosti slumped down onto the floor, still conscious but stunned.

"Into the bedroom," ordered Lily, and she and Robbie half-carried, half-shoved Kyosti into the room and shut and coded the door locked.

For a moment, they simply stared at each other, panting. Bach hummed in possessive agitation before the terminal. Finally Robbie walked over to the chair. The force of the blow had scored scars into the floor, and the plastine supports had fractured. One had shattered.

"Good thing he didn't get to the terminal." He had to use two hands to right the chair. "I had no idea he was that strong." He picked up the shattered remains of the support and stared at it pensively.

From the bedroom door came a slight sound. Bach stopped humming.

"Lily." It was so subdued they barely heard it. "Lily. Forgive me."

She went to the door, laid a hand on it. Bach sang a question; she shook her head.

"Lily. You can't touch other men, Lily, not in that way. You have to understand that. Please, Lily."

She touched the first half of the unlocking code into the panel.

Robbie set the plastine support onto the shattered chair. "Are you sure it's safe?"

"No. But better to find out now than when I'm not prepared." She opened the door.

But Kyosti merely pulled her into his arms and began to kiss her as if he meant to imprint himself indelibly on her, to the exclusion of all others. After a few moments of this, Lily felt it prudent to shut the door behind them.

Pero regarded Bach with a look remarkably like a conspirator's. "Can you get a message to Heredes?" he asked.

Bach winked, speaking again in Paisley's voice. "Affirmative. It is my experience, however, that the timespan necessary to achieve contact without exposing the master's masquerade, if one is desireth of interfacing with him directly rather than through the masking channels he and I have devised for exchange of our usual flow of information, will be of a rather longer duration than you are perhaps hoping for." Two more lights blinked. "Given the circumstances."

"Let him know," said Pero. "But don't jeopardize his cover. The information he's sending us is too valuable."

"Affirmative. It is my belief, if I may be allowed to express one, that my patroness will prove herself perfectly able to defuse the current situation."

"It isn't the current one I'm worried about." Pero went to his desk and picked up the notes he had been scrawling before dinner. "It's the future ones."

Bach sang something incomprehensible, halted abruptly.

"But," said Pero, "I have a speech to write. Can you take it?"

Bach settled into a chair with a melodic phrase that sounded remarkably like pleased anticipation. "Affirmative," he said.

Pero stood silent for a long moment, glancing once through his notes.

"Workers of Arcadia. Our rights as citizens have been disregarded too often. Central has imposed taxes on us that are not in force in Central itself. Central has cut power to our homes. Central has drafted our young men and women into their own military expansion—against what enemy, I ask you, but the very workers who feed them? Central has spilled our blood when we have protested legally against the measures they enact to prevent us from exercising our right to vote. It is time we act directly against these measures, and all the others like them. We are two billion souls, citizens. We are strong. We are righteous—"

"—we will not let the threat of Central's troops, let the threat of the Immortals, deter us. We will work without violence to bring Jehane's revolution to Arcadia. To bring his reforms, his hope, to the Reft. Jehane will come. He will bring justice. But, comrades, it is up to us to prepare the ground on which he will stand. Join me, on the first day of spring. Join me, in sending a message to the Senators, to the Immortals, to the government in Central. Join me. Strike."

Pero's voice echoed out from the terminal, deep and passionate, touched by the barest of accents, a suggestion of a musical lilt.

Kyosti, reclined on the couch, smiled with a slight mocking glint in his eye. "That's very good, Robbie," he said. "Although I always preferred mine with fire and brimstone."

"Fear is only used against your enemies, not your comrades," said Robbie. "I will not make a mockery of the workers who risk their lives in this cause."

"Is that coming out of the underground link at Byssina?" Lily asked quickly. "The one I ran the codes to two weeks ago?"

"It is," said Robbie. "You did a difficult job well, Lily. I know that Security had been watching for that transfer, but you avoided them."

"She must take after Joshua." Kyosti turned his head to regard her. His ashen hair, cut shorter since the riots, drifted along her shoulder. "Frightening thought."

"It could be worse, I could take after you," retorted Lily. Kyosti smiled. "What time do we have to leave, Robbie?" she asked.

"You don't have to come with me," he said, for perhaps the fifth time.

"I want to."

"I dislike seeing you miss so much time at the Academy, Lya."

"It's true sensei Jones has been lenient." Lily shrugged. "Frankly, as much as I'm learning in my work there, there's something missing, some element—I'm not sure. I *like* helping you, Robbie."

"Of course you like it," said Kyosti in a quiet voice. "You're Joshua's daughter."

Pero frowned.

"And furthermore, Robbie," continued Lily briskly, "you don't make a public speech very often. Security's got to be out looking for you. Even if they do think you're a committee of ten writing all those broadcasts and news sheets, they still must want someone they can hang as 'Pero.' You *need* a bodyguard."

"Very well," he acceded. "Let me change." He went into his bedroom.

" 'It is a sacred duty for all of us, soldiers of the revolution, democrats of all continents, to unite our forces, to come to an understanding and to organize.' "

"That's very good, Kyosti. Are you helping Robbie write his speeches?"

Kyosti smiled slightly, as if he would have laughed but did not have the energy for it. He gazed obliquely at Lily, caught in thoughts she could not guess at.

"It's funny," she continued. "Robbie devotes his life to Jehane's cause, but Jehane's never been on Arcadia. He's never spoken in front of angry crowds, with Security ready to come in at the slightest provocation, or risked getting arrested for setting up yet another underground news network. To the people on Arcadia, Pero is Jehanism. But I'd bet you that if Jehane ever succeeds, Robbie won't get a bit of the glory. He won't even ask for it."

Kyosti shrugged. "A megalomaniac like Jehane succeeds on the strength of his followers' sincerity," he said.

"Is that another quote?" she asked.

"Maybe I'll come with you," he said suddenly. "Bach can guard the home front, can't you, old boy?"

A single light winked on Bach's surface, but the robot did not deign to turn away from the terminal or otherwise acknowledge Kyosti's statement.

"He's addicted to that machine," said Lily with disgust. "He's on it constantly. I can't understand why our electric bill isn't higher, except I'm afraid Bach fixes it."

"We all have to be addicted to something." Kyosti regarded her again with that unreadable look.

"Not me," said Lily, standing up as Robbie came out of his room. "Let's go."

16 Pero Speaks

※※※※※※

Outside, a cold wind hit them, and Kyosti went back to ge[t]
a heavier jacket. Lily and Robbie strolled into the commu[-]
nity park that fronted their apartment block to wait for hi[m.]

"How many do you expect to join the strike, Robbie?[ ]
she asked. "It's hard to believe that tomorrow will be th[e]
first day of spring." She bent to brush the grass with an ope[n]
hand. That cold air alone might wither the green plants t[o]
brown she had never conceived of, nor the slow budding t[o]
life as the weather grew warmer. It was as if the air itsel[f]
carried some virus, growing and dying.

"What I expect and what I hope—it's hard to separat[e]
the two, Lya. But first of all I need transport workers t[o]
strike, because then there will be inconvenience to Centra[l]
and the Senators will take notice of us."

"Haven't they already?"

He smiled. Against his dark skin, his teeth seemed ver[y]
white. "As a nuisance, perhaps. But Security has not ye[t]
moved against Pero—the mythical Pero, who is no one ma[n]
or woman, but all men and women. That is why Pero ca[n]
never die."

Lily looked away, out over the pond. The wind had die[d]
away; the water lay like frosted glass in an unbroken su[r-]
face, catching the distant reflection of treetops and apar[t-]
ment windows in its even surface. "I hope not," she sai[d,]
"Robbie. What deal did Heredes make with you?"

"I thought it was all understood, Lily. I really did."

"I believe you. Of all people, I believe you, Robbie. But why am I always the last person to whom it's all understood?"

"I assume that is a rhetorical question. I thought Heredes told you."

"I know he got false ID, and that he wanted to work in Central to get information. And that to work in Central, and especially to gain employment in the kind of classified position he must need to get what he wants, that you also have to live in Central, and that your movements are closely watched. That's what I know. I thought he just dropped me off at Wingtuck's Academy until he was finished, and that you, in your vast kind-heartedness, took me in. But that's not the case, is it?"

Robbie moved onto the pebbled scree that bordered the park's shallow pond and leaned against the waist-high fence built there, he had said, to keep people out of the water. Why anyone might want to go into it, filthy as it was, Lily could not imagine, nor how such a low fence could restrict access. "But you and your robot form a vital link, Lily. I thought—" He shrugged.

"Bach and I?"

"For several years," he began again, as if a random thought had struck him, "I have attempted not only to break into Central's computer system, which is difficult but not impossible, but also to get the information I obtained *out* of Central. That had proved impossible, so far. But I was assured that your guardian is a master of such techniques. He promised to feed information on Jehane and his movements, movements tracked on Central's classified strategy computers, out through your robot and into my hands. And he has. This information gives me an incomparable advantage in working for Jehane's cause here on Arcadia. For instance, the last transfer included a bulletin from Unruli, where Central evidently uncovered a large Jehanist nest and carted the entire group off to the nearest prison planet."

"Harsh. I already know someone there, the Ridani girl I

met. And lost. But an entire group from Unruli! Hoy. I wonder if I knew them."

She subsided into silence. From a distance they must have seemed parting lovers, she with her hands crammed in her coat pockets against the cold, head bent under the seriousness of his mien, but eyes lifted to catch his words; he, still leaning against the fence, but almost as if it alone supported him, dark hands resting lightly on his blue-trousered thighs.

"I hope you're not disappointed in me, Lily," said Robbie at last.

"In you?" She smiled, rueful. "No. Maybe a little bit in Heredes. You'd think he'd trust me with more knowledge."

"In this line of work, Lya, knowledge can be dangerous."

"So can ignorance. Ignorance can kill." Across the park, she watched as the door to their block opened and Kyosti emerged. "For instance," she said.

"This is none of my business," said Robbie suddenly, hurriedly, "and I say it only out of concern for your well-being —" He faltered. Uncertainty was so unlikely an expression on his open face that Lily could only stare. "Do you love him?"

"Love him?" Kyosti advanced toward them, the increasing wind tugging at his pale hair; his hands were hidden in his pockets. "I don't know. How can you love someone who has never told you the truth?"

"You love Heredes."

She smiled. "And it seems to you he has as many secrets as Kyosti?"

"Doesn't he?"

"But Heredes has always told me the truth—not much of it, granted." She brought her hands up to her face and blew on them. "I trust him, Robbie. I always have."

"Then is trust a necessary corollary for love?"

"It must be."

He shook his head. "You're speaking with your head. That's your flaw—if I may presume enough to say so—"

"You will anyway," she said with a grin.

"You don't act enough from your heart."

"Don't I? Maybe you act too much from yours."

"Perhaps. It wouldn't be the first time I've been charged with that particular failing."

"Which failing is that?" asked Kyosti as he came up to them. He removed a hand from his pocket and closed it around Lily's hands, drawing them down.

"Perfection," said Lily.

Kyosti smiled, as genuine as it was possible for him to be. "I'm sorry, Robbie," he said. "But I'm afraid that the only cure for perfection is death."

Robbie laughed. "Isn't that the only cure there is? Shall we go?"

The meeting was held in Elfin District. A stage had been constructed in a warehouse. From her vantage point at the back and to one side of the makeshift construction, Lily could look out over the crowd. Robbie sat next to her, his eyes closed, in perfect stillness. On her other side, Kyosti sat elbows on knees, examining the crowd.

"I don't like this," he whispered. "It smells like a setup to me. Did Robbie arrange this, from the ground up? Or was he asked to speak here?"

"I don't know." Lily glanced at Robbie, but did not want to disturb his meditation.

"Did you see the light switches as we came in?"

"The ones just behind us?"

"Yes." Beyond, the crowd stirred restlessly, perhaps two thousand souls, as a dark woman spoke to them from the stage. Several other speakers, finished or yet to go on, loitered backstage or sat near Lily and Kyosti and Robbie. "We'll split up," continued Kyosti. He spoke in an undertone, so quiet that even Robbie, were he listening, might not have heard. "One to the lights, the other as close to the microphone as possible. If anything happens, we'll have to act fast."

Lily leaned into him, lips brushing his ear as if she were nuzzling him affectionately. "You think Central Intelligence set this up? To bring one of Pero's voices to light?"

"I don't think anything," said Kyosti. He let a hand slide up her waist, caressing her. "But I know this line of work. Haven't you heard the Boy Scout motto, 'Be prepared'?"

Lily giggled. "What's a Boy Scout?"

Kyosti pushed her away. Robbie had risen, gave them each an intent nod, and, to the accompaniment of fevered and in-unison applause, walked out onto the stage.

"Comrades," the woman proclaimed, her words merged with the crowd's roar of approval, "I give you, the man who speaks for all of us. Pero."

"I'll get the lights," said Lily, her voice almost drowned by the cheers. Kyosti nodded and rose as well.

"—Comrades! I am not Pero. All of us are Pero. All of us speak out against injustice, against—"

Lily found the lights, stood by them, listening. "—we will show Central, we will show our Senators, we will show the Reft, our disapproval. They will attempt to make us fight. This is a peaceful strike. With peace, we will win. Do not fight. Do not resist. But do not retreat!"

Over the thunderous applause and cheering that greeted this remark, the shot ricocheted like an echo of the crowd's intensity. Robbie faltered, staggered, and fell. Lily started, shocked out of action, and only by reflex did she cut the lights.

Darkness shuttered the hall, but triggered her thoughts. In the instant while the rest were still frozen, she was already running toward the stage. She elbowed past a group whose high voices revealed panic. A scream shattered the sudden muteness of the crowd.

"Lily!" Kyosti's voice, close by.

"I've got you." She shoved a person aside and came up next to him.

"Lead." Kyosti spoke in a low voice, but already shouts and cries filled the warehouse, covering his words. "I've got him. Let's go."

Lily created a ruthless path through the crowd that was converging on the stage. "Where is he?" voices cried. Others swore. "Damn Central!!!!" yelled others. "They ordered this!" "Kill Senator Isaiah—Senator Feng—Senator—" the names went on. Lily shut the door behind them just as the lights went back on. On the street, browned-out lamps lit dim circles of light across the sidewalks. Two trucks sat along the curb.

"Gun in my pocket," gasped Kyosti. Robbie lay in his arms. Blood spread through the cloth of his shirt, spreading a red stain over his abdomen. He was unconscious. "Hijack a truck."

But Lily was already at the door to the first truck. It opened, and the surprised driver was thrown unceremoniously from his seat onto the ground. "Get in," she called to Kyosti, and she helped him pull Robbie onto the seat between them. She got the truck started just as the door from the warehouse opened and the first stream of people poured out. The vehicle jerked forward, and she floored the gas. She took the first corner at forty, the second at sixty, but deemed it prudent to slow down after that.

"Hold on, Robbie. Damn you, hold on," Kyosti was muttering next to her.

"Where are we going?" she asked.

"Roanoak. I can use the clinic."

"I don't know how to get there."

"Don't you read maps, Lily?" Suddenly he sounded amused. "Mother help us. I always study my ground."

"I don't expect people to get assassinated. Damn it, where do I turn?"

He laughed. "Ah, the good old days. Left here. Five blocks, then the Glacier Expressway for twenty miles."

"Will he live that long?" she cried. She could not take her eyes from the road to look.

"I don't lose patients," said Kyosti in a hard voice. Cloth ripped, and a bloody rag fell at her feet. "Primitive," he said. "Not even a laser. A damned slug. I'll have to get it out. Yes, this right, my love."

Traffic on the expressway was light. After all, only transport and cargo vehicles used it, and the occasional private vehicle of a Senatorial family. "I hope every single transport worker on Arcadia strikes," muttered Lily. "Bring the whole damn planet to a stop." Signs she had never seen before flashed past her. She slowed to five kilometers over the speed limit, tried to drive between the white lines and raised dots. Kyosti worked in silence beside her. She heard Robbie's breathing, as ragged as the bloody cloth draped over her shoes.

"This exit," said Kyosti suddenly. "And here. And—" They passed the white neon identifying Roanoak station.

"I know from here," interrupted Lily. Within minutes they pulled up before Roanoak clinic.

It was dark. Kyosti followed her, Robbie in his arms, as she went up the steps. Lily had been here once before, had seen the Ridanis Kyosti cared for treat him with a trust astonishing for tattoos used to nothing but scorn and hatred from their unmarked brethren. Had heard it in their embarrassed thanks, seen it in the shy lift of their eyes to meet his.

Their footsteps echoed along the empty corridor. Not even a janitor here to question them or to greet them. Malnutrition, eye and respiratory diseases, together with gynecological problems in the women—Kyosti had told her once that was what he treated, mostly. She thought of that, because she did not want to look at Robbie. She was afraid to look at Robbie. At all that blood, draining out of him. And she remembered what Kyosti had said, as they were leaving Zanta: "The only cure for perfection is death."

"Damn it," she said, feeling sick with it, heavy with fear, "don't die. Don't die."

"Open that door for me." Kyosti's voice was perfectly level. "We'll go into the back room."

They walked through the common room, where Kyosti examined most of his patients, through to the back, where he treated the delicate cases. He laid Robbie gently down on the examination table, began rummaging in a cabinet.

"I need—" He paused. Robbie's eyes fluttered, opened. One hand twitched limply. Lily grabbed it, squeezed.

"Maitreyi," Robbie whispered, like a gasp, or a prayer. His face was clear of pain, but his eyes were distant.

"Keep him talking," said Kyosti. "He's in shock. I don't want him going out again until I've got that bullet out." He drew on gloves, pulled one onto Lily's free hand, picked up instruments, lifted aside the makeshift bandage he had wrapped around Robbie's abdomen.

Lily gagged, forced herself to focus on Robbie's face.

"Hand me these when I ask for them, Lily." Kyosti transferred several instruments into her gloved hand. He gave Robbie a shot, waited a few moments, and then began to ease tissue aside.

"What's Maitreyi?" asked Lily, bending down closer to Robbie's face. The scent of blood sifted into the air, overpowering.

Robbie sighed, caught his breath as if at Kyosti's careful cutting. "Maitreyi," he murmured.

" 'Then what need have I of wealth?' " said Kyosti, almost wistful. " 'Please, my lord, tell me what you know about the way to immortality.' " And he laughed.

Lily glared at him, tightened her hand around Robbie's. "Who is Maitreyi?" she asked again.

"As fair as the dawn." Robbie's voice seemed to come from a great distance. "My beloved."

"Give me the blue one," demanded Kyosti, and she handed him an instrument. The one he set down was red, trailing red onto the plastic sheet that covered the table.

"I didn't know you have a beloved, Robbie," Lily said. "Where did you meet her?"

Robbie's eyes seemed to gain focus. "Veritas," he breathed. "Where I grew up. The Finegal Revolt."

"Oh, yes," said Lily. "You lost your whole family—" She faltered, cursed herself for bringing up death.

"All but my sister Mathilda," said Robbie. He gasped again, but the sound was stronger. "I would have died, too. Fallen-in, burning building. But she came. She pulled me out."

"Give me the—ah—the one with the yellow tag on it," said Kyosti. "Ah, better and better. Almost there."

"Was Maitreyi one of the revolutionaries?" Lily asked.

Robbie's mouth twisted up into a smile both sweet and detached. "Troop," he said. "Government trooper." His eyes faded out of focus; Lily pressed his hand until he came back, a little way. "She came to the hospital, later—curious, I suppose, to see the burnt rebel she had saved. I loved her."

"Did she love you" Lily asked softly.

"Who can tell?" He gasped, hard and pained. "I felt that."

"Good," said Kyosti. "Keep talking."

He spoke between gasps. "We made plans—two comrades and—and I. To escape. It was a prison hospital, you know. She—she found out about it. Turned us in."

"But that's terrible!" said Lily, forgetting her fear for him in righteous anger.

"Is it? Each day the sun betrays us, going down to night. But do we blame it? She did her duty."

"Got it!" said Kyosti. "Nasty beast. Give me the—thank you. Don't move, I'm sewing."

"But the night has stars," said Lily, still caught in Robbie's betrayel. "The night has its own beauty."

"Just so," said Pero.

"How poetic of you, my love," said Kyosti.

"But Robbie, what happened then?"

"Life separated us." Pero's eyes, filling with pain now as he rose out of shock, focused clear and strong on Lily, and he smiled, out of hurt and out of a curious equanimity. "We have no weapons against that."

"I'm sorry, Robbie," she said, her throat tight with sadness.

"Sorry? Never be sorry for love, Lily. That is what sustains us."

"My dear Robert," said Kyosti, "if you can philosophize, then you are certainly going to live."

Lily turned away from both of them, disengaged her hand, and stood with her face pressed up against the wall.

Kyosti examined Robbie's eyes, his pulse, gave him a shot, watched him relax. Lily still had not moved. "Lily," Kyosti said, soft.

"I'm all right," she said into the wall. "I'm just not used to having someone I care about almost die on me."

Only Robbie saw Kyosti's face, bitterness compounded with an agony that was quickly suppressed. "I hope you never get used to it," he replied. "Believe me. Let's clean up here, love, and then we'll move Robbie into one of the wards.

in the next building. He'll be safe there until he's well enough to move."

There was a pause. Lily turned. Her face was as pale as if she were the one brushed by death. "All right." Her voice gained strength as she talked. "Where do I start?"

He handed her a sponge. "Scrub. By the way, I didn't know you'd driven on Arcadia before."

She gave a hiccuping laugh. "I hadn't. I've never driven on a road, or in traffic. But I know how to switch gears and steer well enough to avoid avalanches."

"Mother bless us," said Kyosti with some feeling. "I'm amazed we made it here alive."

"So am I," said Lily.

Robbie smiled weakly at both of them.

17 Throwback

❋❋❋❋❋❋

"Half of the transport workers walked off the job the first day. By yesterday half of those left behind had joined them. All sorts of people stood in the picket lines at the stations, not just the transport workers. Sensei Jones called me and told me she is closing the Academy temporarily until the strike is over. Central issued their ultimatum after five days: end the strike or they'd call out the troops. And yesterday they called out the troops."

Robbie regarded her over a spoonful of soup. "And?"

"Poor Robbie," Lily answered. "Stuck in that ward seeing Kyosti once a day for five minutes, painted red and orange so you'd blend in, and never hearing a bit of news until they got you home today. You missed your triumph. I watched down at Zanta Station. Every single picketer had to be dragged away, but none of them resisted. No arrests. No injuries, except one man got his hand stepped on in Ruana, and a woman trooper got her cheek scratched. I can't remember where that was. The whole coast, all the strikers, it was the same thing. They stood their ground until Central called out their guns, and then they didn't fight, but they didn't retreat."

Robbie sighed. "The Ridanis were unnaturally quiet, I thought."

"They were hiding you."

"They know," he said. "I fear they are in for hard times,

Lily. They know that eventually there will be violence, and that the worst will hit them."

She frowned. "There's one thing I've always wondered about the Ridanis. If they just didn't tattoo their children, they could break the cycle of prejudice, couldn't they? So why do they keep tattooing?"

Robbie laughed, surprised. "Have you ever asked a Ridani that question?"

"No," Lily admitted. "I'd be too embarrassed."

"As well you should be. The patterns they wear on their bodies—proudly, despite everything—are at the very heart and soul of their religion, their culture—the culture they brought with them when they came to the Reft with the rest of humanity. It would be like asking you to . . ." He hesitated.

"To repudiate martial arts and Master Heredes? Of course I wouldn't, and I'd cling to it more fiercely, and with more pride, the more I was pressured to give it up. I know that well enough." She paused, thinking of how she had left Ransome House, and they sat a moment in companionable silence.

"What are you going to do now?" she asked finally.

"Call a second strike for the first day of next month," he said. "In commemoration of the first. Speak again on the eve of it, in public. Central must get the message we are not simply a nuisance. That we mean to change our lives."

"Hoy," she said. "You're making my life difficult. Only this time let Kyosti and me organize the speech. Please?"

Robbie smiled. "I'll trade with you. Three courier runs, and it's in your hands."

"Throw in how I can get ahold of Heredes, and it's a deal," countered Lily.

With a quick phrase, Bach rose from his place in front of the computer. *Patroness,* he sang. *I beg of thee, do not jeopardize thy master's masquerade. When he beeth free of encumbrance, he will with certainty summon thee.*

"Bach! How can I bargain when you're working against me?"

Forgive me, patroness. There is, perhaps, other currency in which thou mayest deal.

She whistled her approval, and Bach sank happily back to the terminal. "Very well, Pero," she said. "We organize the speech, you don't go out without me as your bodyguard, and you tell me where all the information you're getting from Heredes is going. I haven't seen anything to account for all the hours Bach sits at that damn machine."

Robbie laughed and drank the rest of his soup straight from the bowl. "Done. You don't see anything because it doesn't come in here," he said. "I don't quite understand it, but Bach and Heredes send out the information in a spiral, so it comes in at differing locations on a random cycle. Then I collect it and send it back out in bits to various repositories, where it can be transferred, by courier run or otherwise, either to cells on Arcadia or out onto the road where merchanters pass it along to those folk who otherwise wouldn't hear any news of Jehane at all."

"Like Unruli," said Lily. "We'd never heard of him. That's why it struck me so when you said Central had arrested a bunch of Jehanists there. Although, Paisley . . ." She trailed off, remembering how quickly her interrogators on Remote had accused Paisley of that particular sin. "Meanwhile, you've collected information about how Central works. How long until you can sabotage it from within? Or is that what Heredes is planning?"

Robbie shook his head. "You're ahead of me, Lily. I don't know what else Heredes is planning. But I don't work that way. I work with people, I educate them, I tell them the truth. They join me because Jehane's cause is just. A coup will just give us a new Central to replace the old one."

"What will Jehane give us?" she asked, but she took his bowl and spoon and carried it to the sink before he could answer.

Pero dictated the second strike from his couch, although the millions who heard and heeded his voice did not know that. Lily ran courier runs for him, more than three, once had to knock out two Security officers when the secrecy of a cell was breached. She missed more days at the Academy.

Kyosti organized the speech, which took place in a warehouse in Wara District; this time Pero spoke and no shot interrupted him. Ten thousand heard him in person, uncounted others heard the broadcast. On the first day of the second month of spring, the entire north coast metropolis came to a halt.

"How did you get home?" Lily asked Kyosti when he walked in very late that night.

He merely smiled and went straight to Robbie. "How's my patient?" he asked, sitting on the end of the couch.

"Walking very well," said Robbie. "Wanting to get out again."

"You have your wish," said Kyosti. "I'm giving you to the Ridanis."

"What!" cried Lily.

"Call up the underground nets," said Kyosti. "You won't see anything but those same damn Senators preaching to their constituents on the official channels. Isaiah, Feng, and Metoessa. You'd think they'd get tired of talking."

"I never get tired of talking," interposed Robbie. "Let's be fair."

"I don't believe in being fair," said Kyosti. "I know how these people think."

"Hoy." Lily was peering over Bach's shoulder. "I saw troops out this afternoon, but—" A screen scrolled past. "Void help us," she exclaimed. "Three hundred arrested in Ruana. More than five hundred arrests in Elfin and Byssina. They estimate more than ten thousand arrests over the coast. It says here a striker was beaten to death at the Wara District detention center. And—" She straightened suddenly, turned, speechless.

"Ah, yes," said Kyosti. "Now you see why I am giving our estimable Pero to the Ridanis."

"Oh," said Robbie. "That."

"Yes, that," replied Kyosti.

"A new warrant for your arrest," murmured Lily as if she were unsure whether or not she was dreaming. "They're offering a reward of one hundred thousand credits for information leading to your arrest. That would make most people, especially these days, rich."

"Central will never find you in the ghettos," continued Kyosti. "Not even the Immortals will find you. Maybe Joshua could. Don't argue with me, Robbie. I hate righteous people, because they're hypocrites. But you, by the Mother, you aren't. So you'll do as I say."

Most of Lily's courier transactions took place now in three-di bars, because of the mix of its clientele, and because gambling could never be stopped—even with doubled Security patrols and a strictly enforced curfew. Especially when military pilots were among the most celebrated participants in the three-di tournaments.

"But it's been quiet all month, Kyosti," protested Lily. "If I make this run tonight it will cut the backlog of classified information that Bach's been sitting on; it'll complete the entire sixth level of coverage. One more level, and we'll—"

"You love this business, don't you," said Kyosti. Watching him, Lily thought how much he had changed since she had first seen him. Most of those blatant affectations had vanished, although the seeds of them still lingered in his habitual postures and the slight drawl in his voice. At the moment, he looked—she would have said annoyed, but it was more than that.

"My hours at the Academy have been cut back because of the curfew, Heredes long since disappeared, and now Robbie has been gone a month. What am I supposed to do? And yes, I do like it. It's the most exciting sparring I've ever done."

Kyosti continued to stare at her. It unnerved her, as if he, the predator, having caught his prey, was now no longer sure he wanted to consume it. *"Abai'is-ssa,"* he breathed. The word was so alien that for a horrifying instant she thought she was not looking at Kyosti at all, but at some other creature. "Spare me her, at least."

"Hawk?"

"Lily, sit here," he demanded. He was Kyosti again, but with too much energy.

She sat down on the couch, leaving a meter between them. She checked the placement of the chairs—out of his immediate reach. Bach, at the terminal, had changed his hummed tune midphrase: *Monitoring, monitoring,* he sang now, one azure light winking in her direction.

"I had three patients in six hours, Lily. There wasn't a soul on the street when I walked from the clinic to the station. Not even transients. Just Security and government troops, waiting for the third strike. Robbie's sweet peace is going to shatter tomorrow, and you're not going out to-night."

"All right," she said in her most neutral tone. "I can do it later."

"Get out of it now, Lily, before it destroys you."

"Kyosti—" she began.

He sat up abruptly, like an animal startled out of hiding, and grasped her wrists in his hands. With an effort, she did not pull away from him. "I should never have slept with you!" he cried. "I know it, I knew it, but I couldn't help myself. You'll hate me when you find out the truth."

He fell silent. She said nothing, afraid to disturb this mood.

"You'll hate me," he repeated, almost relishing the sound of it.

"Kyosti. What is the truth?"

He looked away. "I can't tell you."

"You don't trust me."

"That's not true!" He jerked his gaze back to her. "It's not you I can't trust. It's myself."

When she did not respond, he began to examine the room, his gaze drifting over its contents piece by piece, measuring them, or his place between them: the desk, empty without Pero; the terminal scrolling out official news headlines, half-hidden by Bach; the tiny kitchen counter; the high window that looked out over the park. "They caught me," he said, as if to the room.

"Who caught you?"

"The League. I was the prodigy. I thought I was invulnerable. I didn't believe they would arrest me." Still he did not look at her.

"How old are you?" she asked.

"I used to think I was sixty-four."

"Void help us," she gasped, losing her careful balance of equilibrium. "How old is Heredes?"

"Do you know how long I was in prison?" he asked, as if he hadn't heard her. "Sixteen years, seven months, three days. Eleven hours and thirty-two minutes." This close, she could see clearly the blueish strain in his hair, and she began to wonder if blue was, in fact, its natural color. "But you know, when I got out, they told me it had been twenty years, two months, seventeen days. Eleven hours and thirty-two minutes." A mocking smile curved his lips. "A clever trick to play on me. Did they think they could deceive me? Scare me into betraying my comrades?"

"Then what were you doing on that ship?"

Now his gaze focused on her, an acid stare. "Getting as far from prison as possible," he snapped. "They were fools. Didn't they know—my sense of time is absolute. Absolute."

For some reason, this display of arrogance restored her shaken composure. "I see," she said.

His hands still held her wrists. "But afterward. I used to get sick in windows, before. They so offended my sense of time. Physically sick."

"You don't anymore," she replied, on surer ground here. "Kyosti, you moved." It was an accusation.

"But they don't exist," he said. He looked at her helplessly. "They don't really exist. Windows. They last forever —not forever—Lily. Do you know what is inside a window?"

"No one does."

"Hell," he whispered, as if it were the greatest secret he knew. "Or heaven. Take your pick."

"I don't understand."

"Of course you don't." His voice was bitter and he released her wrists. "Have you ever been put in sensory deprivation? Do you even know what it is?"

She left her hands on her lap. His bitterness was easier to deal with than his abstraction. Behind her, Bach broke from his "monitoring" hum into a single phrase: *Wir durfen niemand töten*— "It is not lawful for us, to put any man to death."

"I was in solitary, but it didn't work. They couldn't break me. So they put me in sensory." He stared toward the window. "You can't see, you can't hear, you can't smell—" His voice faltered. "There's nothing to touch." His eyes, almost sly, almost wary, slid back to her. "Finally they took me out." This time he took her hands gently, pulling her against him as if the memory of that time drew forth from him a need to have all these sensations in full. "Lily, my love," he murmured. "What if I was in that prison for twenty years and two months and seventeen days? What happened to those three years, seven months, fifteen days? Where did they go? Is that what exists inside the windows—lost time?" He laughed, short and hard. " 'Sharp as Hawk's mind,' " he said with scorn. "Mother help me, Lily. I don't know."

There was a long silence. His pale head rested on her shoulder, the touch of his lips on the bare skin of her neck. He kissed her neck, the hollow of her throat, the line of her jaw, her cheeks, her mouth. Sensation began to rise in her— but he drew back suddenly, releasing her, and stood up.

"So, Lily," he said, the assumed weariness back in his voice, "we don't go out tonight. We don't go out tomorrow —" As if the entire conversation had not taken place. "The Mother knows I've created enough violence in my time to see it coming now. Poor Robbie. I'd hate to be an idealist." He smiled.

It was his familiar smile, but behind it, like a half-voiced suggestion, that indefinable sense that it was different, that something about him was just removed from her experience —but she could not complete the thread to find where it attached. He turned his candid blue eyes on her, eyes concealing, like some buried treasure, the truth that lay deep beneath. She was suddenly reminded of the sta who had been incarcerated in the cell next to her on Remote, but she did not know why.

"Why did you recant?" she asked.

He laughed. "What amuses me," he answered, "is that no one ever suspects the real reason. Well, certainly, I did it to get out of prison. They wanted to believe me, poor souls. They wanted to believe all of us, us throwbacks, that we would repent our wicked ways. But it wasn't the solitary. I was solitary enough as a boy. It wasn't even the sensory, even though they thought it was. No." He wandered to stand by the window, staring down at the budding park, the slow unfurling of green. "They gave up. They put me back in the main wards. I couldn't stand all the people. So I recanted, and they let me out." He measured her across the distance. "Eventually I got used to having people around me again. But I can never go back."

"To where?"

"You misunderstand. To *what* I was before."

"I don't know what you were," she said.

He did not reply. The light, coming through the window, highlighted part of his face, but mostly he was shadowed.

"Or what you are now," she added.

"Ah, Lily, didn't you know? I'm a shaman."

"All these words!" she snapped, all at once resentful. She stood up. "I don't understand most of them. And you don't mean me to. Why should I bother to ask anymore?"

Silence gathered like water pooling in a sink of ground.

"Now I see," he said in a low voice. "You don't trust me."

"What reason have you given me to trust you?"

"I gave you myself."

"You gave me your body. I don't know what that has to do with your self."

He changed. She felt his anger, even at such a distance, felt with frightening instinct that same moment of anticipation before he struck, shattering the chair. Felt that he was only controlling himself by such a massive force of will that if she were to move even a finger, twitch even a lip, he would lose every vestige of rationality. Green gleamed in the depths of his eyes. His very stillness was a threat.

"How can you say that to me?" he uttered, hoarse, and he

walked into their bedroom and shut and locked the door behind him.

She waited, straining, for noise; surely he would break something, hit something. Silence, but for the distant buzz of transport vehicles and the faint click and hum of the computer, conversation lost beneath layers and layers of muffling cloth.

"I'm sorry," she said, but the words dissolved as mist does under the sun.

A cool touch—she jumped, stifled a yelp, and whirled. Bach nudged up against her. On a sigh, she sank down onto the couch. Bach settled beside her, and sang, a soft chorale. After a bit, because she recognized it, and recognized that it was, in a strange fashion, appropriate for Kyosti, she joined in.

> *O Haupt voll Blut und Wunden*
> *Voll Schmerz und voller Hohn!*
> *O Haupt zu Spott gebunden*
> *Mit einer Dornenkron'!*
> *O Haupt, sonst schön gezieret*
> *Mit höchster Ehr' und Zier,*
> *Jetzt aber hoch schimpfieret:*
> *Gegrüsset seist du mir . . .*

"O head, full of blood and wounds,
   full of sorrow and full of scoffing!
O head, wreathed for mockery
  with a crown of thorns!
O head, once beautifully adorned
  with highest honor and renown,
  but now highly abused:
Let me hail Thee!"

That night she slept in Robbie's bedroom.

In the morning, Kyosti brought breakfast to her bed as if it were an offering. She accepted it. That afternoon he suggested they walk in the park—helped her on with her jacket, wondered aloud how Robbie was getting on, put his arm around her as they strolled across the green. It seemed, under the warm spring sun, easier to accept this truce than to probe any further into the sources of their disagreement or, indeed, to attempt even to define her feelings about them. On the shore of the pond, under a flowering tree, he stopped her. Kissed her in a way he had never kissed her before, with a tenderness that made her feel afraid for no reason she could describe.

The shots splintered their reconciliation. Two heads snapped toward the direction of the sound.

"That's coming from Zanta Station!" gasped Lily. Another volley of shots, the scattering sound of automatic weapons ricocheting through the high-rise of apartment blocks. "They're firing on the strikers!" She broke away from Kyosti, started to run toward the sound.

He caught her, pulled her so tightly against him that she could not even struggle. "Don't bother," he said. "There's nothing you can do for them."

"Damn them!" cried Lily as a third round of shooting shattered the quiet of the park, like a distant celebration. Now, a faint counterpoint, they heard the first cries, screams and yelling nearing them.

"They're panicking," said Kyosti. "Let's go home."

"Kyosti! If people are hurt, you've got to help them."

"What? In the middle of the park, using their own clothes for bandages?"

"Why not?"

"For one good reason." He turned her, stared straight into her face. "Learn this now, Lily. We know Pero. We know the Ridanis have him. We have Bach, and the link to Heredes, and we're passing that knowledge out to the rest of the universe. If they take us in for questioning, if they decide we know something—we can't take that risk. People get hurt, Lily. That's what happens in rebellions. People die. Get used to it."

"Damn you, Kyosti," she said, but now she was merely bitter. "Why are you helping Pero? Why are you helping Jehane, anyway?"

"Because I can't get out of the habit," he said.

18   Alley Cat

******

Bach had four screens up on the terminal, monitoring the range of news. On three of the screens, crop statistics scrolled past. The fourth was blank. By evening, all official channels were broadcasting either a looping message for all citizens to return to their homes or a long speech by Senator Isaiah.

". . . due to the unprovoked acts of violence against government personnel, we are forced to impose a state of emergency," he declared in his familiar sermonizing voice. "Stay in your homes. In three days we will allow limited movement for the delivery of food. Brownouts will be instituted immediately in four-hour rotations throughout the metropolis . . ."

"Except in Central, I bet," said Lily, turning him down as he began to moralize. As if in harmony, their lights dimmed.

In the morning, Bach found an underground net broadcasting on a new channel. Fifty dead in Esau. Full-scale riot in Byssina—no casualty count available. No contact with the Ridani districts. At least twenty dead at Peko Station.

There was no news of Pero. The underground nets that had gotten on-line broadcast his old speeches. Central raised its bounty to 200,000 credits.

On the fourth day, an old Ridani man arrived, bleeding from deep gashes all along the left side of his body, at their door. As Kyosti tended him, he told his story.

"Ya terrible trouble. Roanoak done burst—riot; worst I ever seen. Ya six troopers be dead, min, first day. Central sent in ya squad o' Immortals." His sigh held great tragedy. "One o' their fellows fell behind, like. Ya crowd fell on him, hundreds. Ah. Ah." It could have been gasps of pain at Kyosti's probing, or at the memory. "Beat him to blood and innards. Couldna even tell if he be tattooed or not, but for ya white uniform. Ah. Terrible, terrible. They come back, ya Immortals. They didna even spare ya children. It be all blood, min. All blood, running down ya streets. You be sore needed."

Kyosti looked at Lily.

"You have to go," she said.

He held her for a long time before he left, as if he could thereby take the essence of her with him, and then she was alone with Bach.

At first, because she could not go to the Academy, she moved the furniture in the main room and worked out. But the enthusiasm with which she had begun all this, that rush after Heredes, faded as her isolation grew. The unseen but deeply felt center of existence seemed to recede from her. She practiced less. Began to devise, with Bach, circles within circles of disseminating information. Together they built a stand on wheels for him, which he could propel by a clever redirection of his flight mechanism. This harness allowed him to accompany her on the increasing numbers of courier transfers she now ran; having no direction to follow but her own, she spent most of her time on Pero's work.

Kyosti called her when he could, but there was little he could say over the screen. Once, touchingly, he said he missed her. He looked exhausted. The underground nets reported that hundreds had died in the Ridani districts, that they were still occupied by government troops. But even on the underground nets, they had little sympathy to spare for the tattoos.

Spring unfolded toward summer, a process that amazed her, having never seen it before: slim trees, branched with light-leafed twigs like veins and capillaries against the white and blue sky, swayed slightly at their tops, brushed by the wind, wetted now and then with an obscuring screen of rain. Farther lay the sheeted silver-grey of the pool, moved in scalloped ripples by the breeze.

She heard Robbie speak for the first time since the final strike one night in a three-di bar. Bach had been sent into a back room by the proprietor; he plugged into a terminal and coded information back and forth. Lily waited at the bar. The tavern itself had its overhead lights dimmed to brown-out dinginess, but above each billiards table, like twenty-four minor suns, hung a white globe of bright light that illuminated the depths of the table and the faces and fore-arms of the two players. At the hexagonal corner tables a handful of stas played humans at the sta mathematical game of *bissterlas*.

"Comrades, citizens of the Reft. You know I speak for you. You know that only together, only by struggle, only by perseverance, can we win."

It startled her, Pero's voice crackling out over the speakers behind the bar; it was a new speech. She could detect no weariness in his voice, only a touch of sadness. She wondered where he was.

Listening, still watchful, she noticed the young man playing three-di at the table nearest her. First because he was a Ridani, and that was unusual enough, but second because he had a certain lightness of gesture, a mercurial mobility, that reminded her of Paisley. He glanced a final shot into Corner C and took the game from an old, grizzled woman with pilot's bars on her cap. A younger man, smartly dressed, stepped up and took challenger's corner.

". . . let Central divide us and we shall surely fail. We all suffer from their oppression. But we must bear our griev-ances to Central. We cannot blame our relatives. We cannot blame our neighbors. We cannot blame the Ridanis. No one but Central is to blame for this assault against our rights. Save your anger for Central. Save your hatred, if you must have hatred, for Central. Save your energy for the strug-gle . . ."

"Yeah," said a man in trooper's fatigues to his compan-ion. They had paused to watch as the young Ridani made short work of his latest challenger. "So they kill an Immortal, we supposed to throw them a party? Pero makes a bit of sense now and then, I can say 'cause we're private, but them damned tattoos—" They moved out of Lily's hearing.

A new man, middle-aged, a respected merchanter's pilot patch on the sleeves of his gray tunic, came forward to match the Ridani player. Bets passed through the crowd that was growing around the table.

Most people who traveled out over the highroad got their first lesson in the vector drive by watching the three-di tournaments. It was true that the navigation teams, supported by computers, found the correct velocity vector for each individual window within each individual system's current alignment, but the pilot sent the ship through. And it was while watching pilots engaged in billiards, on those huge transparent boxes filled with heavy air and shifting physical windows that led the player like a maze of angles through the game, that the average citizen felt most reassured about the reliability of this form of transportation. After all, the point of the game was to go from point A to point C *or* from point B to point D by the safest, quickest route.

The merchanter lost. As another challenger came forward, Lily nodded to the proprietor, who had just ducked away to check on Bach. "Is the transfer going?" she asked.

A quick nod. "Smooth."

A man, military pilot's stripes on his sleeve, came up for a drink. "Smooth?" He took his drink and followed their gaze. "That tattoo? I seen him over at Charson's. No one's managed to figure out how he's cheating."

"Maybe he's a pilot," said Lily.

This only brought a laugh. "A damned tattoo? Hoo. But we got a treat in store for him tonight. Tseh-Lee's here; she'll split him good. You'll see."

He left.

"How much longer?" Lily asked.

"You tell me," said the proprietor. "Hour, maybe."

In an hour the Ridani beat three more challengers. Bach emerged from the back room, looking ungainly but relatively normal in his four-legged stocks and complaining about his unwieldy disguise in an almost inaudible melody, just as a well-groomed, dark woman in military uniform— obviously the fabled Tseh-Lee—stepped up to the table.

"Hoy," said Lily and whistled as if to herself, *Just this game, Bach. I want to watch.*

Patroness, I feel it my duty to remind thee that any delay jeopardizes our—

Bach. He lapsed back into his quiet complaint.

The customary tiny beaded braids of the Ridani clustered around the young man's head, but his hair was shorter than Ridanis usually wore it; Paisley's had hung halfway to her waist. A stark geometric pattern covered his face and arms. His hands had a certain delicacy that reminded her of Kyosti. But most striking of all, he had that grace that is peculiar to those people who never consciously think about the impression their body and movements make on observers— the spontaneous coordination that is five parts effortless stillness and five parts impulsive momentum. Watching him, she wondered what indenture was like on Harsh, what kind of work a child such as Paisley would be given. He beat the military pilot by a ratio of seven to four.

The pilot challenged him to best of three, and in the second game defeated him six to five. But despite the win, Lily felt the tension grow. Bets increased to ridiculous proportions. The Ridani must have made a huge sum already— troopers crowded as close to the table as was allowed. On their faces as they stared at the Ridani she saw the hatred Pero had spoken of.

He's going to get beaten up, she thought. No one will bother to stop it—just like with Paisley getting arrested. Just like with Paisley.

Hush shuttered the table. The military pilot began, and the only sound was the slip of her hand on the cue and the hard sigh of the ball through the box. The vector speeds and settings were at the highest level the program could deliver, a difficulty unlikely to be met in real space. She got through six of the ten windows before a "fail," and the troopers relaxed.

"Can't no one beat that lead," someone muttered, and was waved to silence as the Ridani bent to the start.

He went through all ten windows to finish with an ease that seemed arrogant and, perhaps, deliberately insulting.

"Damn," Lily murmured as the Ridani collected his winnings and escaped out a side door. Three troopers followed him. "I don't care what Kyosti says. It isn't fair. Bach, come on."

Stepping outside, a warm drizzle met them, a soothing, light hush on the alleyway that they entered. Out to the left a dimmed streetlamp illuminated a damp patch of street. To the right, in the shadowed end of the alley, hidden except for the nebulous suggestion of sharp, jerking movements and the low exchange of muffled noise, three soldiers beat up a huddled body. They did not hear as she and Bach came up behind them.

"For pity's sake," said a low voice, indrawn from pain, breaking through in a sudden lull in the blows, "you can have all the credits."

"Hoo." A spiteful, hostile voice. "But ain't he a generous one. Well, it ain't credit we want, you mangy cheater, but satisfaction for insult given." There was a simultaneous crack, a gasp of pain.

One of the soldier's behinds loomed squarely in front of Bach. Bach winked an emerald light at Lily. She shrugged. He snaked out an appendage.

When the light flashed, she took the second soldier in the face with a jab, followed with an elbow up through the chin. Shifted her weight and back knuckled the third, swept him down.

"Can you run?" she hissed to the figure on the ground.

He moved, pushing up, gasped in anguish. "My arm— broken. I don't know."

Bach whistled a warning. Lily spun, blocking by instinct, caught a punch on her forearm, punched twice, kicked for the groin. A second flash of light, dimmer, followed by a slight gasp; all three soldiers lay still.

"Come on," Lily said. Grabbing an arm, she yanked him up.

He yelped, a suppressed scream, and she transferred him
to her other side and pulled him forward with her toward
the street.

"Can you go faster?"

His breaths came in labored gasps. "Mother of All," he
swore in a soft, choking voice. "It hurts." He said something
else under his breath, a curse, and stumbled. "I'm afraid the
left ankle is broken as well. And I can't see out of my right
eye, either."

"And you're obviously not even the damned tattoo," muttered Lily, but she continued to support him.

"I beg your pardon?" Now the voice came much stronger,
laced with anger.

They came into the reaches of the streetlight and Lily
turned her head to look at him. Stopped—for the space of a
moment stared at him. It *was* the Ridani man. He suddenly
laughed, a sound bitter with an anguish that went beyond
physical pain.

"Sure," he said. "I bain't be speaking ya tattoo speech."
His voice was heavy with sarcasm.

"Move it," she snapped. Leaning heavily on her, he let
her lead him down the gloom of the far side of the street.
His breathing, punctuated by wordless exclamations,
marked his distress; otherwise he was silent. Bach motored
quietly along behind them, a dim light winking in each direction.

Detouring through a back street, she helped the man sit
on a dirty step that led to a boarded-up storefront. Bach
labored up to them.

Patroness, he sang in a soft voice that the Ridani, panting
heavily in exhaustion and pain, could not hear. *My wheels
are sticking! This device beest the most shameful use of my
locomotive abilities I have ever in mine entire existence been
made to endure. Indeed, I could be*—She did not have the
breath to tell him to stop. Bach, perceiving this, halted. *Dost
thou require my assistance?* he sang, a solicitous tone.

"Just a rest," she said. Rain stilled the shift of her feet on
the pavement. At the Ridani's left hand, where it rested
half-off the step, a small green shoot had broken through the

concrete, splitting it as it drove upward into the air. The street was entirely deserted, eerily quiet.

"Sure," said the young man suddenly in his soft voice. "You must be wanting sommut o' me. Or else ya confusion hae taked you." Even in the shadow she could see the discoloration of blood on the right side of his face. His left arm was swollen. "And being as you saved my kinnas, min, I do be in ya complete service tae you. So be it." He bobbed his head in a sarcastically menial manner, gasped at the pain.

"Serves you right," replied Lily. She undid her belt and rigged it to hold up his broken arm. "Now, can you go on?"

"Light o' glory," he said, a mockery of Paisley's innocent accents, "ya blessed be green grass angel."

"Oh, shut up," Lily snapped. She felt, somehow, that this satisfied him, because thereafter he went along very meekly. By the time she got him up the back stairs and onto Pero's bed, he was content to collapse there without a word and, even, to lie still under her tentative ministrations. His left arm, swollen and red, was nevertheless straight, but there was a large lump on the bone, hard and extremely painful to him.

"If it's broken, at least it hasn't shifted," she said as she wrapped the arm immobile in gauze. "I don't think they broke anything else." The glazed, withdrawn cast had retreated from his eyes, and he followed her with his gaze as she moved about him. "You're going to have some ugly bruises, and they'll hurt like the Void. I'm going to wash—this will sting."

"What's your name?" he said suddenly.

"Ransome," she said without thinking. "Well," she added more slowly. "People here call me Lily Heredes. What's your name?"

"I be called Pinto." He still regarded her steadily, as if she and the bowl of water formed some fascinating composition of form and angle. In the other room, Bach hummed at the terminal. "Why did you do it?" he asked.

"You wouldn't believe me," said Lily.

"It can't be worse than what I'm thinking," he said, mocking her.

"You know, you sound much better when you're not faking the accent," she said, hoping to distract him. "I watched you play. You must be a good pilot."

"Sure and glory," he answered in his broadest accent. "Is that what you be wanting? Or be you thinking to get the credits, like the others do." He laughed, a harsh sound that made her wonder how long it had been since he had laughed for the pure joy of laughing, or because he was happy. "Or mayhap just a wee tattooed tumble i' ya bed?"

"You won't give up, will you?" She stood up. "Hoy, you're stubborn. I knew a Ridani girl once. You reminded me of her. That's why. Now go to sleep." She left without waiting for his response, shut the door behind her.

In the morning she was making breakfast when the door into Pero's bedroom opened. It was apparent immediately when Pinto stepped blinking into the burgeoning light of midmorning that he shared another trait with Paisley besides that quick fluidity of movement and grace: he had the beauty that only people who are entirely innocent of their own handsomeness can have, untouched in a curiously immediate way. Even with the cut, puffy lip and swollen eye, his face and the stark patterns illuminating it caught her gaze.

He had strapped his broken arm against his chest. He wore a tunic and trousers of blue that Kyosti had sewn for Pero some months ago. On the Ridani the garments hung loose, and the trouser legs, rolled up, revealed both one swollen ankle and the geometric pattern marking his feet and toes.

"I found these clothes," he said. "Don't worry, I'll clean them. Mine aren't fit to be worn right now."

"The owner's not coming back any time soon."

An uneasy silence settled.

"You said I would ache like the Mother's own wounds," he said at last. "I do."

"Then sit down."

"It's not fitting."

She turned from the counter. "What's not fitting?"

The stark, three-toned pattern on his face seemed to delineate the obstinacy of his expression. "By kinnas, I owe you my service. You cannot then serve me instead. It is dishonorable."

"Hoy." Lily brought a tray of food and juice to the table. "To you or to me?" When his expression did not change, she laughed, a certain echo of his mockery last evening. "I thought as much. Would you sit down? I don't know what you mean by kinnas, so how can it affect me?"

"Of course you don't know what it means, ya *jaidin torkyo*—"

"Sit down," she repeated.

There was a pause. He limped over to the couch and sank down beside her with obvious relief.

"Have some juice?"

He accepted it, grudgingly.

"Tell me what kinnas is."

He ate all his food first. She let him eat all hers, without letting him guess it was hers, because he was obviously starving.

"You won't understand," he said finally. "Kinnas is honor. Acceptance of duty. The pattern you're marked with —fate. It's knowing self-control. It's integrity, humility. It's defiance. Do you get the idea?"

"The kinnas wheel," Lily said reflectively, caught in trying to remember Kyosti's words. She did not notice the surprise on Pinto's face. "The wheel of the night. The . . . the honor that—" Her gaze fixed on the window, seeing past the tops of the park trees to a more distant scene of trees and moonlight. "The honor that patterns you. But also, the promise of love." Her gaze dropped suddenly. A blush crept up her skin to feed rose across her cheeks.

Amazingly, Pinto laughed. Not derisive, not mocking, just softly amused. "I've used that line myself," he said in a companionable voice. "It always works. But that doesn't mean"—he added hastily, facing the sudden hostility of Lily's gaze and the hot flush of anger on her pale complexion—"that doesn't mean it isn't true." He smiled, a smile of astounding sweetness that transformed his face. "Because it is true."

"Who is that man," Kyosti said before anything else, "the one I talked to yesterday while you were out?" His face was marked by lines of exhaustion, more pronounced than usual, and the apricot blush of his lips had a hard set that the faint static of the terminal's picture could not conceal.

"What—Pinto?" She glanced back over her shoulder. Pinto, reading on her com-screen as he lay on the couch, looked up at the sound of his name. "A refugee," she finished. "You look tired, Kyosti."

"Do you suppose I got any sleep at all last night?"

Lily stared at the screen. Behind her, a slight cough signaled Pinto's rise from the couch, his slow limp into Pero's bedroom that stretched into an infinity of unspoken words. "You are tired," Lily said at last as the bedroom door shut with a soft but final sound.

"Has the beauty left in a tactful manner?" Although Kyosti's expression had not changed, she felt an undercurrent rising in his tone like the telltale sparking harshness in an overheating mineshaft engine.

"Oh yes," replied Lily. "He's back in the bedroom with the other ten men I've invited to move in with me since you've been gone. Don't be ridiculous. Have you heard anything of Robbie? I hear his speeches, but he's disappeared as thoroughly as Joshua."

It could just have been the inconstancy of the terminal's picture; the blue of Kyosti's eyes seemed only a veil masking sparks of green deep in his wide irises. She realized he was not listening to her. "I'm coming home."

"Don't bother. Not if that's your only reason."

"Don't threaten me, Lily."

"Threaten you? Do you think I'm going to change the locks?"

"You're mine, Lily. Don't you understand that yet?"

A shrill whine shattered her anger. Behind Pero's desk Bach switched appendages and now welded new supports onto the carriage that supported him when he went out with Lily. The whine faded, replaced by a soft spitting growl.

"Kyosti," said Lily in a quieter voice. "Listen to me. I

think you'd better come home so you can rest. You must be exhausted.

For a moment she thought he would acquiesce. "He'll be gone, won't he?" he asked.

"I told you he was a refugee, and a hypersensitive bastard, too. But I saved him from being beaten up, Kyosti. I can't just throw him back on the street, not the way things are now. Not with people blaming Ridanis for the state of emergency. You of all people should know that."

"If you've touched him, I'll have to kill him, you know," he replied in a perfectly calm voice.

"Hoy. Why don't you just kill me and then all our problems will be solved."

Bach's welding sputtered and gave out and he sang a brief question.

On the screen, Kyosti's expression changed. Now he looked horrified. "Don't be offensive!" That undercurrent had risen entirely to the surface—shaken and hoarse and wild. "Never say that to me again!"

"Never tell me how to conduct my life."

"You don't understand."

"If I don't, whose fault is that?"

He said nothing, only stared, at his screen, of the image he must have of her: tight-mouthed, flushed with anger, hurt. "I'm sorry, Lily," he said, a certain incoherency still intense in his voice. "Don't hate me."

"Kyosti, you are becoming irrational."

"No, I'm not. That's the frightening part."

"I can't stand this! Are you going to come home or not?"

There was a long silence. Bach winked at her from Pero's desk, but she ignored him.

"Kyosti?" she asked, suddenly afraid, because his expression had changed yet again. The wildness had drained from his face, but the bleak resignation that had replaced it was somehow more ominous.

"No," he said. "Forgive me, Lily. I should never have slept with you. You have no idea—" He flinched, as if at some terrible decision. "It will be better for you if I never see you again. Believe me, Lily. I'm sorry."

"Kyosti—"

But the picture snapped into obliteration, and Lily was left with static. She stared at the blank terminal, turned it off. The silence expanded toward infinity.

Eventually a door clicked and opened.

"Be it he don't care for ya tattooed company," said Pinto from the doorway.

Lily stood up so quickly her chair tipped over, clattering onto the floor. "Do you think the whole planet revolves around whether or not you're tattooed? Don't you have anything better to do than feel sorry for yourself?"

"You didn't have to bring me here."

"You don't have to stay."

For a long moment he did not move. Finally he limped to the couch and, sitting, raised a tattooed arm to cover his eyes as if from a bright light. "I've got no where else to go," he said at last in a soft voice.

"Void help us," breathed Lily. Outside she could see the clouds lowering grey over the park, and rain began, chasing a pair of Security officers under the incomplete shelter of a tree. The fine mist veiled the scenery beyond. She ached. Like Pinto's bruises, that after two days still violated the patterns of his face and body, but her hurt was fresh and did not mark her physically. She sighed, willed herself not to remember her last glimpse of Kyosti's face, and flicked on the terminal again. Its noise would at least obliterate her thoughts.

Senators Isaiah, Feng, and Metoessa flickered into view on the screen.

"Damn this," said Lily as the camera focused in on Senator Isaiah's high-boned, thin face. She reached to switch the channel.

"Turn it up!" said Pinto urgently. He had lowered his arm.

"Hoy," muttered Lily. But she glared at the screen, very willing to have another victim to vent her frustration on.

"—doctrines such as those Pero preaches lead to every sort of crime and encourage every sort of criminal to embrace such sentiments in order to indulge in an orgy of felonious villainy. Shall we let murderers and thieves and whores rule us? Shall we hand the controls of our ship to illiterates, to common tattoos, to wreckers and rioters? Where then shall our cargo, our people, our children, end up? Lost in a window? This is what agitators such as Pero wish for you, citizens. This is—"

"Must we listen to this idiot?" Lily cried, punching off the volume.

Pinto did not seem to be listening. His lips had a grim, set look to them, and his gaze, although focused on the Senator's face, seemed, instead, to be fixed on a scene beyond the screen. He looked up when she switched to a weather channel. "Don't tell me that offends you," he said. " 'Shall we hand the controls of our ship to *common* tattoos?' What eloquence!" For an instant he looked about to cry, but the expression passed into a sneer.

"Where were you educated?" asked Lily suddenly. "Pilot and all?"

"Not downtrodden and ignorant enough for you?" he asked sarcastically. "And here I was thinking you must be a Jehanist sympathizer. That irresistable desire to help the oppressed. So noble."

Lily was too astonished at his sustained belligerence and too drained by her argument with Kyosti to respond with anger. At first she just stared at him, and he shifted his good arm as if to protect himself.

"Hoy," she said finally.

"Sorry," he muttered.

Bach's sudden sung phrase caused them both to start. Lily turned quickly.

"What's he saying?" asked Pinto.

With one hand resting on Bach's surface, Lily leaned forward to examine the writing that now scrolled up on the terminal. It was in code; she could not decipher it.

Who is this from, Bach? she asked.

Classified message. Request meeting. Information transfer. Highest secrecy. Location: Tachtau Overrun, paternity. Imperative: twenty hundred hours.

"But who is it from? When?"

There beeth no signing, patroness, but the code beeth identical to that used by Pero's transmissions. It requesteth, I surmise, a rendezvous for tonight since no date is given. All contained herein supposeth the greatest need for action.

"But where the Void is Tachtau Overrun? What is it?"

She realized abruptly that Pinto stood at her shoulder, careful not to touch her, but peering around her to read the screen. She began to shift, to hide it from him.

"Don't tell me you're a Jehanist," he said. "I know where Tachtau Overrun is."

"Can I get there by twenty hundred hours?"

"You'd have to leave within the hour to get there by twenty hundred hours. It'll take at least eight hours to get there, more with the rail delays."

"Can you show me how to get there?" she asked, no longer bothering to conceal the screen.

"You *are* a Jehanist, aren't you," he said suddenly. "I'll take you. I know shortcuts that I couldn't explain to you.

"Why? How can I trust you? Why do you want to help me?"

"Tables turned, aren't they?" he said, suddenly gleeful. "You'd never believe me. Just remember, you hold my kinnas. I can't break that. 'Whither thou goest, I shall go.' Something like that."

"Do you mean I'll always hold your kinnas? Forever?"

"No. Only until it's returned. And if I'm lucky tonight, I'll save your life, or your dearest one's life, and be free of you."

Lily knelt, let her cheek lie against Bach's cool curve, feeling the smoothing vibration of his soft singing hum. "Are you lucky, Pinto?" she asked.

"I'm tired. And I hurt."

They left within the hour, leaving Bach to monitor.

Pinto knew shortcuts. Lily wondered where he had learned them, because several of them involved sections of rail reserved for government use. They arrived at Tachtau Overrun at twenty oh five hours.

It was simply an interchange of rail lines. Despite the state of emergency it was crowded, travelers changing trains to a myriad of destinations: Muir, Esau, Abba Gate; Security manned the entrances to the trains to Tchelik-in-Central, Khafaje Center, Subadar.

"Hoy." Lily paused along a wall to survey that shifting mass of color and movement.

"Who are you meeting?" asked Pinto. "What does she look like?"

"Paternity," said Lily. "Is there a destination called Paternity?"

Pinto blinked. "Is that what it said? Nothing I've ever—wait." He grinned slightly, almost engaging. "What about Abba Gate? It used to be a big joke with us—" He broke off suddenly, looking upset about some memory. " 'Abba' means father in some ancient language."

"Might as well try it," said Lily. "Otherwise we'll never find him. He's very dark," she continued as they walked. "Good-natured face." Shook her head. "You just watch out for Security. I'll look for him."

"Goodness," said Pinto mockingly. "In deep company, I be. There it is."

The crowds sifted past them, a constant flow that ebbed and lulled in spurts. Busy, intent on their own purposes, these were people linked to Central, she thought, and happy enough with the current government—she glanced at Pinto beside her, at two women in construction worker's coveralls, and at a single tattooed man sweeping the floor—not all.

The stream of people swept past her. In the gaps between them she saw a trickle of arrivals coming through the turnstile one by one, as if presenting themselves to her, and then blending into the crowd.

All but one.

She stopped so suddenly that Pinto ran into her and they both staggered forward two steps before she pulled up.

"Hoy," she breathed. "*Abba* Gate."

The man had halted just beyond the turnstile, put a hand in his jacket pockets as any traveler might fumbling for some remembered item. But his eyes swept the crowd twice unobtrusively. She noticed it because on the first circuit they met hers. He smiled.

She walked forward as if she were blind, wove her way through the press of traffic by instinct and was standing in front of him before she realized that she might be attracting attention.

But he still smiled. "Well, Lily," Heredes said. "I was hoping you would be the one to meet me here."

19 Heir

✳✳✳✳✳✳✳

"Yes, my work is finished," said Heredes. "There is just one last appointment I must keep, the one I'm going to now." The *clack-clack* of the wheels serenaded his words. "I know what I need to know, and I have something to give to you, Lily—a final gem of information for our friend." He glanced at Pinto, sitting stiff and reserved beside Lily.

Lily also looked at Pinto.

"I can get off at the next stop," said Pinto.

Heredes smiled and said something in a language Lily did not recognize. Pinto looked surprised, then suspicious. But his reply, in the same language, was brief.

"Ah," said Heredes. "If she has your kinnas then I see we can trust you." Pinto spoke again, a rush of words this time, but Heredes waved him to stop with a laugh. "I don't know the language that well, and in a much different dialect."

"But you do know it," said Pinto. "You must possess the kinnas of one of my people."

"A long time ago, and she is, I'm afraid, dead now."

Pinto merely nodded his head, a gesture so respectful and meek that Lily could only stare first at him, then at Heredes. "Is it all settled?" she asked, leaning closer to Heredes. The noise of the train as it rattled along the track masked her words. "How do you know we can trust him?"

"Kinnas is a strong force, Lily. Do not underestimate it. And in any case, never let pass an ally, if you have a moment to gather one. You never know when you may need one."

She sighed. "Why didn't you tell me that you traded me for the information? To Robbie?"

Much to her surprise, he laughed. "I never realized what I made you into," he said, quite at variance, "not until you came running to my rescue. 'He wore a lily on his brow—' Well." His nondescript gray tunic and trousers blended into the grey metal of the train bench they sat on. "And now I'm certain."

"Certain of what? You talk in circles alot, Master Heredes. You're very good at concealing information."

"Master Heredes? This will not do, my child. You had better call me Taliesin."

"That's what La Belle called you," said Lily. "Don't tell me that's your real name?"

"The one I was born with." The admission slipped so easily from him that at first she thought she had heard incorrectly. The train pulled into a stop. The doors slipped open and a blast of fresh air entered along with the new passengers. "Taliesin ap Branwen a Jawaharlal," he continued. His voice took on a rolling, lilting quality that mirrored the roll of the train as it started forward again. "Or so I was baptized in the church of the Blessed Mother, in Gwynedd District, planet Terra, in the year of the New Age 209. Taliesin, son of Branwen and Jawaharlal. They were devout believers, or at least my mother was, and she rather held sway, in terms of cultural transmission at any rate, as you can see from my name." A pause, during which Lily simply regarded him with astonishment and the train descended into a tunnel. "On the other hand," he continued in his normal voice and without much regard to her surprise, "I suppose you can't, having no knowledge of Cymru." A wordless shake of her head confirmed that statement. "Perhaps I did neglect your education," he murmured, more to himself than to her. "Well, Lily, regrets never lead you forward. Remember that."

"Of course," she said in a breath, as if she feared too loud an expression would cause him to disperse into the air from which he almost seemed to have come back to her. If Heredes was born N.A. 209, if the Reft's calendar was still in line with that of their ancestors', then Heredes was more than 120 years old. "Hoy," she said. His eyes, green as the burgeoning spring, watched her intently. "Are you really that old?" she whispered.

He smiled.

She realized abruptly that this was not a subject she wanted to discuss in such surroundings. "What was it like, where you were born?" she asked instead.

"Green and low and rich." That lilting, musical strain informed his voice again. "Not rich in credits or great vast fields of grain or outward things, rather poor in outward things, in truth, but rich in the heart, in the mountains worn down by the ages of life lived about them, and the small jewels of lakes, and the small fields of corn, and the sea, brushing the shore. And song, of course. I think I sang before I talked. Air to breathe, rain, the soft winds; the kind of beauty that never leaves you, even when you've left it far behind you. We moved to the city when I was fourteen."

"Didn't you ever go back? Even to visit?"

"I meant to, once. There's a lesson there—one of the secrets of a saboteur's life, Lily, of that life you have to lead if this life, the one you're living now, is what you're living for." His smile bore equal parts bittersweet memory and that distant gleam of anticipation. "Never hesitate, once you've decided on a course of action. I hesitated, and I may have lost the chance to return to the place where I was born. But—" With an encompassing gesture of one hand, he dismissed the past.

"But regrets never lead you forward," said Lily.

"You're very wise, Lilyaka. You must have been well taught."

"Certainly not," she replied indignantly. "I was lucky to survive my training."

He laughed. "You see how like me you are. By the time I was twenty years old I was in jail—I robbed and rioted and fought and hated until the law grew sick of me. But sensei came. She worked with delinquents, succeeded rather better

with me than anyone expected. I got out early on good behavior and studied at her Academy for ten years, like you,
although you of course avoided prison."

"I did run away once," she pointed out.

"Isn't that why the Sar sent you to me in the first place?
You were a sullen child, Lily."

"Was I?"

"Yes, but full of energy." His hands lay unmoving on his
lap, like the symbol of his inner composure. "After ten
years, my sensei told me she had taught me everything she
could. She told me I was good, but that I would never be a
true master of the art."

"But—"

Heredes raised a hand, interrupting her, and smiled. "She
said I was too precipitous. That's a quality you can't un-
learn. I competed for a few years after that, in martial arts
tournaments; it's a very popular sport in the League, like
three-di or *bissterlas* is here. Then I became an actor." He
chuckled at her expression. "No, not one of your network
actors. I studied acting for six years, then joined a repertory
company on Sirra—that's one of the League planets—and
after that was offered a gem of a position in the Bharentous
Repertory Company. It was while I was with them that I
met the old man, the Duke, and he recruited me for the
rebellion, for the band of all work. That's what I did for the
next forty years, until, of course, we won."

"You were rebelling against the Kapellans, weren't you?"

"Has Hawk been talking to you? What history do you
know?

Lily considered. Beside her, Pinto dozed. Across the aisle,
a man read, a woman slept, a child holding her hand. "Humans came from a few neighboring systems, explored, and
found the pygmies. But the population grew too fast so they
shipped out whole populations on the lowroad ships—that's
how we got here. But the coordinates back to the home
worlds were lost—something. Even when the highroad fleet
showed up no one could get back. A couple ships, those that
Central didn't impound, tried to. Maybe they did. But usu-

ally it's said that they got lost on the way and just drifted forever."

"The highroad fleet." The train rattled on through the tunnel, black walls like starless space. *"Custer's Luck* was the flagship of that fleet."

"You know about it?"

"Of course. It was legendary. The hard-luck fleet, they called it. Twenty-eight of the finest ships ever built, sent out to explore and to search for the earlier colonizations—like Reft space—three of those ships returned. The vector drive was new. I suppose they just hadn't got the hang of it yet. Obviously some of those ships got out here, but none ever returned with news of the Reft that I know of. And the League had more pressing problems. But it's the names I remember—they struck me so: *Custer's Luck, Swan of Tuonela, Pope Joan, Pyrrhus, Enfants Perdue, Chernobyl, Forlorn Hope—*"

"The *Forlorn Hope!*" Lily exclaimed. "That's the name of the ship that old spacers say haunts the route back. Out beyond Nevermore and Jeremiad."

"What, like the *Flying Dutchman?* No, I don't suppose you've heard that story. Well, it makes one wonder."

"What problems did the League have?"

"The Kapellans."

"That's right," said Lily suddenly. "You and Kyosti and Sensei Jones were terrorists."

For a moment, when he frowned, she understood why Kyosti and Adam might refer to him as a tyrant. "Hawk *has* been talking. But not, I dare say, about the right things."

"He isn't *that* forthcoming," she retorted. The look she directed at Heredes, one eyebrow quirked slightly up, her mouth's line bent with a softly sardonic pull, caused him to chuckle.

"Like me? I'm afraid that is an accusation that is quite true. But it's just as bad to tell too much. That's a lesson one learns as a saboteur: Always stay one step ahead of the pursuit. Especially if that pursuit is Kapellan in origin. We ran into the Kapellans in the course of our explorations, or they into us—who knows. For a decade or two they treated us like younger siblings. Offered us their vector drive. Of course, they were merely sizing us up, and just about the same year the hard-luck fleet went out—our twenty-eight best ships—they decided it was time for the League to join their Empire. We had no choice. We were their subjects for over two hundred years. But in the last forty of those years we built the revolt. We broke down their systems from within, and when the call came for the League to take up conventional arms, the Kapellans were partly crippled. And we succeeded.

"What did you do—besides blow up space stations and run an entire Kapellan fleet into their vectors wrong?"

"Hawk didn't know about—has *Adam* been talking to you?"

Perceiving that *Adam* would hear about it someday, in no uncertain terms, Lily merely shrugged. "I don't remember. There are so many stories, after all."

"Touché," he acknowledged. "Which means, 'your point.' We did everything. Blew things up, yes. Killed people when we had to. Rerouted information so it never got where it was meant to go. Sent false information in its place. Sabotaged entire computer systems, mechanical systems, so they shut down when we wanted them to. It was very effective. Now the League and the Empire live with a very jittery truce, abetted on our side by a huge privateer fleet that works the neutral territories that divide us from them, and by the Kapellans' natural aversion to violence."

"But if you helped bring about the League's freedom, why is the League hunting you?"

"Because we know too much. Because they don't trust us —'our kind,' as Hawk would say. Why should they? We dealt double-sided decks for so long that we could as easily pass our loyalty to yet another side. The Duke protected as many of us as he could while he still lived, but most of us chose to go underground. That's how I ended up on Unruli. I never expected to find the Reft—I had no real idea that it even existed, just old records of a colonization seeded this way."

"How did you get here, then?"

"I knew someone who shall remain nameless, who knew someone else, who *was* nameless as far as I was concerned, who was willing to ferry me around until, much to my surprise, I found Arcadia and Wingtuck. How she got here she has never told me. She directed me toward Unruli."

There was another stop and dozers started awake, then settled back. Through the windows of the train, Lily saw the station sign, the ubiqitous Security in doubled numbers, and a pair of tattoos emptying trash. With three coughing lunges, the train lurched forward and smoothed into its clacking glide.

"Did you like it?" she asked.

"Like what?"

"Being a terrorist."

"Did I *like* it?"

"Enjoy it, I mean. You did it for forty years."

"I suppose I enjoyed it, as anyone enjoys work at which they excel. But I did it because it needed to be done. It was more in Hawk's line to enjoy it."

With an abrupt shift, she pulled her weight back so that she was no longer leaning toward him. "What do you mean by that?"

"Lily." Now he was stern. "That's not meant as criticism. Your Kyosti didn't join the ranks out of a feeling of duty."

"And you did?"

"Part of me desired the adventure, I admit that. But the Duke himself chose me. I was one of the first, and in my own way I helped develop our methods of working. But you're right—I have no grounds on which to criticize Hawk. And I don't really think he joined because he loved wreaking havoc. That was more in Maisry or Korey's nature. But Lily—" His hesitation was so totally unlike him that Lily's irritation dissolved. "Please never agree to marry Hawk by the customs he would urge on you." He raised hand to forestall her comment. "I know I have no right to say that. I'm not saying you shouldn't keep him as your lover. You have less choice about that than either of us imagines, I think." He paused. "Lily. What's wrong?"

She put her face against his sleeve, hiding against him

Shook her head first because her throat was too tight to allow words. Gripped his arm. "He said—he said—"

He had to lower his head to hear her. "Poor child," he murmured.

"He had to go to the clinic. I haven't seen him for weeks. Then he called and said—he said he should never have slept with me. He said it would be better for me if I never saw him again."

"Did he now? Mother bless us." He looked up to see that Pinto was watching them.

"It was my fault," said Pinto suddenly, his voice low. He glanced around the compartment as if afraid he might be overheard. "I answered the terminal when Lily was out. I don't think he liked me. Maybe I was a little rude."

But Lily, at these words, lifted her head. "That's not true, Pinto. It was nothing to do with you, not really."

"Mother bless us," repeated Heredes. "What are you going to do, Lily?"

"When we get back, I'm going down there," she said, a bit defiantly. "I'll make him come back."

"My dear child." Heredes embraced her suddenly, held her, tilted her back so he could look at her face. "You're very brave."

"Brave!" She pulled away, regarding him with so affronted an expression that he laughed. "You still haven't told me—"

"Why Robert Malcolm?" he finished for her. "Because I had to be sure, Lily, that you could take the burden. And what did you do?

"What did I do? With Robbie? I helped him—I—" She began to laugh. "It was a test, wasn't it? Did I pass?"

"Of course you passed," he said, as much with sorrow as with joy. "You helped him."

"You don't believe in Jehane anymore than I do, do you?"

"Jehane? Who knows what he'll turn out to be. But I like Robbie. He's clean; he's genuine; he's honest. 'Of one growth.' That's the root of the word 'sincere.' And I needed someone to bond you. But I have to admit it was impossible to resist assisting a saint."

"Being so far from one yourself?" she said, chuckling. "It's funny, that's the same reason I helped him, at first. Later I got to like it."

"Lily, my dear child, my spirit choose wisely."

"What do you mean?"

He made a gesture with his arm, small, in the constricted space, so as not to draw undue attention, but very expressive. " 'Yet all aesthetic contemplation affords only a short-lived respite from the vigilance of an ever wakeful consciousness, and true liberation can only be achieved by the saint, the moral hero, the great ascetic, whose "will to live" has vanished, who has seen through the illusion of the senses, and who practices resignation.' " He finished with a flourish fit for an audience. Pinto regarded them curiously. The man across from them looked up from his com-screen.

"That's all very well," said Lily in a low voice, "for a Byssinist like my mother, who is very devout, but I don't see what it has to do with me." The man shrugged and returned to his reading.

"You and I, Lilyaka Heredes, are not the stuff from which moral heroes are made. That in the end is how I recognized you as my daughter: that complete inability to practice resignation." He smiled.

"You know, I often wonder. The Ridanis say something like—that the pattern on their body reflects the pattern of the universe"—she paused to glance at Pinto, but his eyes were closed again—"and that gives them purpose. And Byssinists strive for annihilation, or dissolution in the Void, or, well, the illusion of the sense vanishing. But what about people like us? If we can't be moral heroes, then what meaning is there for us in life?"

"That's the real secret, isn't it?" He stared out at the rushing mat of tunnel wall as if he could read something there that was only a blank to her. "What meaning is there for us in life?" His gaze, returning to Lily, had nothing unsure or bewildered in it, only a steady certainty. "Only what we bring to it, Lily. For our kind, that's enough. That's one of the reasons we're so dangerous."

"Are we? Did passing the test include me in 'our kind'? You haven't told me what my burden is yet."

"Haven't I? You are my daughter, Lily, the daughter of my spirit, my only true child. You are Taliesin's heir. I declared you on the bridge of *La Belle Dame,* which makes it bound and legal, and, as any legal document, available to the public without constraint."

"But you have other children. Adam and his twin."

"Heir. From the Latin *hered-, heres,* akin to Greek *cheros,* bereaved. You are Taliesin's heir, Lilyaka. You alone. That makes you dangerous, it makes you feared, but most of all, it makes you very valuable. Don't ever forget that."

The train slowed, clacking half-time, quarter-time, stopping.

"We get out here," said Heredes.

Pinto started up, looked at the station signs. "But we should stay on another six stops," he began. "This isn't the interchange for Zanta."

"I'm not going to Zanta," said Heredes.

Lily shook her head when Pinto began to speak again, and the Ridani had no choice but to follow her as she followed Heredes off. The station was crowded, but even so, Heredes walked very close to Lily, Pinto trailing behind. She felt a hand slip into her jacket pocket.

Heredes was leaning on her almost as if she were supporting him. "You now have a diskette," he whispered. "Jehane's latest movements. He's taken Harsh. I have finally calculated the pattern of his movements. He's good, is Jehane. He's encircling, slow, and in a few years he'll cut Arcadia off. This will help Robbie no end. Don't let anyone else see it."

"But—you think he's going to win?"

He shrugged, drawing slightly back from her now. "Times come when change is necessary. It's a natural process."

"Things are born, grow, and die," said Lily, thinking of the animate disorder of the park. "And make way for new things. Is that what you mean?"

He stopped her, in the midst of that crowd. Pinto halted

as well. "Words can mean anything, Lilyaka. It is the gesture that will tell you the truth."

He embraced her, and she felt his warmth envelop her as completely as the sun embraces the day in cloudless summer weather. But when he thrust her back, she saw tears glistening in his eyes. "I love you, Lily," he said. "Never forget that."

"You're leaving me again," she whispered. A terrible sadness ripped through her, and she was afraid. She tightened her grip on his arms.

As she watched, his face lost its emotion, lost its tenderness, and he made her release him.

"No matter what happens," he said. "You do not know me. That's a command, Lilyaka." An instant more he studied her. With a brief smile he slipped away into the crowd.

She stared after him.

"Who is he?" asked Pinto, moving closer to her.

"Damn it," she said. "No." And she followed, trailing Heredes, Pinto at her heels.

"Ah, Lily," he said, "he did say—" She ignored him.

They were halfway across the station, Heredes a good hundred meters in front of them, when the white uniforms burst through the crowd in a tight phalanx.

"Citizens! Stand where you are." The announcement crackled out over loudspeakers. "Do not move. All entrances have been sealed by order of Central Security. You are in no danger if you stay where you are."

Movement came to a halt so quickly that Lily and Pinto, still going forward, barely avoided running into several people before Pinto grasped Lily's arm and dragged her to a stop.

"Don't be an idiot," he hissed in her ear. "Those are the Immortals."

White scattered out into the crowd, precise lines expanding in a spiral. The Immortals. White uniforms, faces as clean of emotion as their uniforms were of color. Deathly efficient in their search.

A sudden flash of movement caught at her eye, a flurry of

running. White spun and rolled inward, pressing civilians back, broadening an empty space in the center of the station.

"Encircle!" The command cracked out above the shocked silence of the crowd.

Against the people shifting back, Lily pulled forward until she came to the edge of crowd. The Immortals had cornered him—not cornered, but exposed him by driving him out into the opening they had created. One woman in a white uniform staggered backward, clutching her abdomen. Heredes stood in fighting stance. The Immortals fell back slightly, but their circle filled in until only the spaces the crowd might look through onto the scene were left.

Heredes faced them, twenty of them at least, but he was so utterly alert, so poised for attack that no one moved toward him, none spoke.

"Comrades!" he called into the unnatural silence. His voice filled the air, a ringing call that caught at the attention more like a spell than like simple volume. " 'I see this system,' " he cried, " 'and on the surface it has long been familiar to me, but not in its inner meaning! Some, a few, sit up above and many down below and the ones on top shout down: "come on up, then we'll all be on top," but if you look closely you'll see something hidden between the ones on top and the ones below that looks like a path but is not a path—' " His voice held them, commanded them to listen, even the Immortals. He had grown like a trick or an illusion until he held the entire station silent to listen to him, as if he was an actor quoting from some long-forgotten play. " 'It's a plank and now you can see it quite clearly, it is a seesaw, this whole system is a seesaw, with two ends that depend on one another, and those on top sit up there only because the others sit below, and only as long as they sit below; they'd no longer be on top if the others came up, leaving their place, so that of course they want the others to sit down there for all eternity and never come up—' "

A black-and gray-uniform shouldered through, appeared on the edge of the circle. "Surrender to our custody and you will not be hurt!" the officer shouted.

"Surrender?" cried Heredes. But his eyes now swept beyond the Immortals, beyond the man commanding them, to rake the crowd. "You are my hope," he shouted, and his words, his gaze, seemed to pinpoint, to touch, each face, each individual—touched Lily. " 'Whatever happens, do not break ranks! Only if you stand together can you help each other—' "

The Immortals surged forward. He may have taken a couple out first; it was hard to tell. Pinto kept tugging her back; she kept pulling forward.

"He said—he said—" cried Pinto above the crowd's sudden noise, and she fell back against him, remembering what Heredes had said. More uniforms, black-and-gray Security now, pushed forward. She did not see them take Heredes out, did not see him at all after the Immortals converged on him. She did see four Immortals being supported or carried toward the exits.

"Citizens!" The crackle of the loudspeaker sounded again, hushing the crowd into a frightened silence. "This station is now under Security's jurisdiction. To those who are innocent of any treason against Central, we apologize in advance for the inconvenience." A few groans greeted this statement. "You will all be conducted for questioning to Security precinct office. There will be no exceptions. Remain orderly, and our task will run smoothly. Do not, I repeat, do not attempt to evade this sweep. All exits are secured."

"Bless the Void," said a woman next to Lily. "Was that the agitator Pero?"

Her simple comment was taken up and spread like fire through the crowd until it ranged out of Lily's hearing.

Pinto pulled Lily around to face him. "Was that Pero?" he asked, urgent now as the black-and-gray uniforms of Security filtered through the crowd and began to line up the masses of stranded travelers.

Lily stared at him. His bruises still showed under the pattern of his face, showed along his arms. For an instant she marveled at how handsome he was. "It doesn't matter." She shook her head, aware now how true that was. Heredes had known it was coming. Had he even set it up himself, to assist his saint, to give Robbie time to move again, to mount the next campaign? But she could not imagine why he should do so.

A woman in black-and-gray shouldered past a pair of clear-skinned men to come up to Lily and Pinto. "What's a damned tattoo doing wandering loose in this district?" She beckoned to a comrade.

"He's my servant," said Lily quickly, but at the same moment felt Pinto squeeze her arm slightly, a warning.

"Take this," he said with an assurance that surprised Lily and pulled a small diskette from his pocket and handed it to the Security officer.

The officer began to reply, a scornful comment, but her companion suddenly silenced her. "Look at the damn seal," he said. She did. She whistled. "Yeah," said the man. "We better get the captain." He looked at Pinto. "All right. You and the woman can come with us."

They turned and began to weave back through the crowd toward the entrance.

"Don't worry." Pinto motioned Lily forward when she hesitated. The people around them stared at them.

"What do you think you're—" She faltered as she realized that the Security officers were not guarding them but rather leading them, expecting to be followed. "What are you doing?" she whispered. "You know I've got—" She stopped. He didn't know Heredes had given her the diskette. "I can't be questioned!" she hissed, leaning against him.

"Don't worry," repeated Pinto.

"What, you know a damn Senator?"

He smiled, caustic and bitter. "How do you think a damned tattoo got to be a pilot?" he asked.

20 Pinto's Luck

✳✳✳✳✳✳✳

Lily gazed, incredulous, numb, out of the spotless windows of the opulently appointed railcar onto an early morning landscape that seemed as much of a dream as Heredes's arrest. No noise, no crowding, no dirt. No house that ever exceeded two stories. No house within a hundred meters of the next. Flowers bordered the rail tracks, manicured and delicate. Lawns spread into the distance. Trees, entire groves of trees, demarked estate bounderies. Whole apartment blocks, along with the tiny parks alloted them, could fit into some of these estates. Had Robbie seen this place with his own eyes or had he simply the sure instinct of righteousness, the unutterable faith, that knew that such wealth and selfish privilege existed and that it must come, at last, to an end?

At last, pulling into a station, Pinto nudged her and she rose with him. "Sure, and here we be," he said, drawling out the accent for the benefit of the two Security officers who escorted them. Or guarded them.

They came out of the station, a tiny building of some organic substance carved into an intricacy of overlapping shapes, curls, and elaborate forms that caused her eye to linger disquieted on the patterns of Pinto's tattoos. Was there a similarity, or was that just her fancy?

An avenue, bordered by neat lines of low trees, stretched to a white house of columns and porticos and a glinting, golden roof. Ransome House and all its mines might have fit under this place, she thought as they walked. The sun illuminated flowering bushes and tracts of brilliant flowers; lawn, clipped to plush uniformity, spread in all directions. A fine spray of water shed its soft hiss over the green. Once, in the distance, she caught a glimpse of a charming cottage, white-walled, streaked with green vines. A walkway of cunningly fitted stone branched off the avenue; they followed it, curving into the shadow of a grove of slender trees, out onto a smaller lawn surrounded by a hedge. This lawn was tenanted.

A woman, old by her stooped back, rose from the two young children who sat on a blanket at her feet and turned. Her face, lined by the sun and by some old sorrow, bore a frown as she blinked into the light, but as sudden as a cloud clears the sun, the frown vanished into radiance.

"Jonathan!" she cried. She rushed forward, halted an arm's length from the young man to survey the two officers with disdain. "I will sign the manifest," she said.

"Do you duly swear you recognize the citizens in question. . . ." The Security officer droned his questions, got her palm print, and they left, bored with the entire detail.

"Who has hurt you?" cried the elderly woman, indignation breaking through the joy in her bearing. She enfolded Pinto in a tender but encompassing hug that carefully avoided pressure on his bound left arm. "My dearest child," she murmured. "How I have missed you."

"Nanna," he said, and Lily was shocked by the affection in his voice.

She thrust him back from her, studied him with a long-practiced eye. "How have you been, my darling boy? How have you lived these past years?"

He looked away from her. "Here and there. I got work from companies and captains desperate enough to employ me for as long as they had to. Between those times, I play three-di."

"And is that how *this* came about?" She was scolding him, but her hand touched his bruised face with such gentle solicitude that Lily felt impelled to look away so that she would not think too painfully of Heredes.

"Nanna! Nanna!" The older of the two children, a girl of about Jenny's child Gregori's age, ran up and hung with spoiled impatience at the woman's skirts. Pinto stared down at the girl, an ethereal, blond wisp of a child, with an expression on his patterned face that Lily could not read. "Nanna, we don't want no tattoos here."

"Mind your tongue, Arabinthia!" The frown eased back onto the woman's face. "Oh, Jonathan, you shouldn't be here. When I got the call, I had to say yes, but *he* told you never to come back."

Pinto lifted his gaze with an effort from the pale little girl, glanced at Lily. "We have to see him."

Nanna also glanced at Lily, briefly measuring. "That's impossible. You're free from that trouble now. Can't you go?"

"Please. Nanna. You must help me."

That Nanna was not proof against such a plea Lily could see immediately. She disentangled the girl's hands from her skirt; she frowned; she prepared an argument, gave it up. She could not deny him. "I'll take you in the back way. Go to his study. He's always there at eight."

"I know." Pinto's eyes strayed to the exquisite blond child.

"Arabinthia." Nanna's voice was commanding now. "Can you sit with your brother for ten minutes without moving?"

"No," stated the child, staring with fixed hostility at Pinto.

"I didn't think so," said Nanna.

"Can so," the girl reneged.

"Oh, I daresay not."

"Can." The girl ran back to the blanket and threw herself on it with stubborn determination. A blond boy, barely able to walk, was holding onto a large animal-shaped toy and gazing at Pinto with great interest. "Sit!" proclaimed the girl to her new charge. The boy sat.

"Come with me," said Nanna.

Lily tried not to watch them as she trailed behind them through the garden. She was jealous, she knew it, at their intimacy, at the affection this woman gave to Pinto, that he, unlikely as it seemed, returned to her. They came to the house at last and Nanna relinquished her darling boy with such genuine reluctance that Lily felt ashamed of her envy.

With a delicate key the old woman opened a door of wrought glass into an airy, comfortable room that held a large desk, a terminal, two plush chairs, and a wall of shelves displaying a myriad of exquisite curios. Lily sat down in one of the chairs. It was astoundingly comfortable.

"Well?" she asked, contemplating Pinto as he prowled the room like a creature reassuring itself of its territory. "You got me out of that station pretty neatly, I'll admit. But we don't have much time. Now what?"

The other door, the one that led into the interior of the house, opened. With her eyes raised to watch Pinto and her back to that door, she had only the young man's expression to measure this new arrival.

His face opened, a look of such heartbreaking sweetness, such loving vulnerability, that, an instant later, seeing that expression close into wariness, into a guarded tightness, as though he were bracing to receive a blow, she wondered if she had dreamed what she first saw. Under the vivid swirl of tattoos his bruised eye and lip seemed just part of the pattern. Lily stood and turned to face the newcomer as he shut the door with a stiff, deliberate shove that was not welcoming. Of course she recognized him. She could hardly fail to. It was Senator Isaiah.

"Hello, Father," said Pinto.

"I told you never to come near this house again. It would have been better if you had left Arcadia completely."

Pinto smiled, caustic. "Certainly, sir, although you neglected to bribe a company to hire a common tattoo to pilot their ships."

"Don't come wallowing to me." Senator Isaiah walked between Lily and Pinto and crossed to stand behind his desk. "You chose the profession. I bought you into Central's finest Academy." In person, the sharpness of his thin face was emphasized by a pallor in his skin that had not been

evident on the screen. His pale eyes surveyed Lily, snapped
back to Pinto. "Who is this woman?"

"My kinnas, Father. *If* you remember what that means."

"Spare me that superstitious nonsense. Do you owe her
credit, is that it? Am I to clear your debt? How much?"

"Just my life. However little that may be worth to you."

For the first time Senator Isaiah seemed to take in Pinto's
battered face, the bandaged, immobile arm. Pink flushed his
high-boned cheeks. "Who did this?" he demanded.

"Some of your military men, who were beating me up for
being too proficient at three-di."

"Is that how you make your living now?"

"I don't have much choice."

The Senator pivoted abruptly and strode to the glass
door, his gaze locked on some sight out in the garden. "You
ask a great deal of me, Jonathan. How can I possibly dis-
charge such a debt?"

On the other side of the desk Lily looked at Pinto and
found that he was regarding her steadily. She took one step
forward. "Release the man you arrested last night," she
said.

In the silence that followed this remark, she noticed how
truly quiet it was here; not the damped-down hum of suppressed activity, as at Zanta, not the filter-laden muffling
that permeated Ransome House, but a stillness that could
only grow in a place where a handful of people lived in a
space so enormous that it could absorb effortlessly the tiny
noises of their existence.

Senator Isaiah turned back to face her. "Pero?" he asked.

"He isn't Pero," said Lily. "You've caught the wrong
man."

Those pale eyes scrutinized her as if she were alien. "If he
isn't Pero," he said in that reasonable tone she recognized
from his broadcasts, "then who is he?"

"He's my father."

"I see." The Senator settled himself carefully in his desk
chair, propped his elbows on the dark surface of the desk,
his chin on his clasped hands, and regarded Lily thoughtfully. With the fingers of his left hand he drummed a slow,

soft, almost mesmerizing pattern on the back of his right hand. "That is a blatant lie. He is far too young."

"He's older than he looks."

"I am older than I look." The drumming stopped. "I can afford the maximum dose of rejuv. Do you suppose I neglect to take it? I could give that man thirty years. How could he have a daughter your age?"

She was so used to thinking of Heredes as older that it was only as she now looked at Isaiah that she realized the truth of his words. The Senator was probably in his sixties. Rejuv might have kept his hair from graying, might have smoothed the wrinkles on his face, but the lines at his eyes had a deep-set quality to them, and his shoulders bore the burden of aging: that growing, inexorable awareness of death. Void help us, she thought, he's Kyosti's age; Heredes must be at least twice as old as him. She remembered how much Jehane had wanted her, thinking her a fugitive from the League. How much would this man want her if he thought she knew such secrets?

"He isn't Pero," she repeated.

"That may be true," replied Senator Isaiah. "That I cannot deny. But our evidence is incontrovertible. Sabotage. Our classified computer banks have been violated; secret information has been passed through an unknown conduit into the hands of whatever Jehanist sects fester on this planet. Do you think we would continue to tolerate this situation?"

"You can't try him and sentence him as Pero if he isn't Pero."

He lowered his clasped hands to lie, reflected in the smooth sheen, on the desktop. "How do you know he isn't Pero?"

"Because—" She halted.

The Senator smiled, an endearment hard as stone. "If he isn't Pero, then who is? It's worth five hundred thousand credits to you."

Lily looked at Pinto. She could see no resemblance between this hard man and the young Ridani. Pinto's tattoos

disguised his features too well. Perhaps their only likeness
was pride.

"Get me Pero," said the Senator, "and you can have your
man and the credits. That is the only offer I will consider."

Did they even know what Robbie looked like? Did they
still think Pero was a committee, rather than an individual?
But even as she thought it she knew she could never do it.
Not really even for Robbie's sake, or for her own con-
science, but because she knew with painful clarity, with a
knowledge that she suddenly wished she did not have, that
Heredes would never forgive her for saving him with such a
betrayal. *That is a command, Lilyaka.*

"I'm sorry, Senator," she replied in a voice that surprised
her with its calmness. "If I could find Pero for you I would,
but I can't."

"Very well spoken," he applauded, and he rose. The interview was over.

"Father!" Pinto walked forward and grasped the Senator's arm. "I know you can free him. Help me. Please, Father. You raised me as your own child, in this house. You
educated me. You loved me once."

She saw the resemblance. It was that surprising sweetness
of visage that could soften Pinto's face for an instant. She
saw it now, but not in Pinto, rather in the hard lines of
Senator Isaiah's face, subdued now by another emotion as
he lifted a hand to touch with infinite tenderness Pinto's
unbruised cheek.

"My child," he said.

The door into the interior of the house clicked and, accompanied by a light trill of laughter, opened.

"And you must see my husband's study. He won't mind
being disturbed."

A vision entered, ethereal as gauze, exquisite as a rare
curio. Halted, wide eyes taking in first Lily and, wider now,
Pinto, with every evidence of astonishment. The door, flung
wide as well, housed two curious and extremely well-dressed
females. The vision herself was young, not more than Lily's
age, and her frail blondness proclaimed her to be the tiny
Arabinthia's mother.

"I'm sure you know Eugenie Feng and Ducera Mughal Demoivre, Samuel. But who are these"—the barest pause as her gaze examined Pinto—"people."

Senator Isaiah lowered his hand and with an impatient gesture shook off Pinto's hand from his arm. "Nothing to worry about, my dear. I was just calling the guards." With a firm finger he pressed the desk intercom and spoke a concise command into the air. "They will be escorted off the estate."

"You relieve me." Her eyes did not leave Pinto. Pinto's eyes remained locked on Senator Isaiah. Into this gap pierced the bright, knowing voice of the darker of the two women at the door.

"Senator! Never say this is the same little tattooed boy who used to run tame about your house. Before you bonded with dearest Binthia, of course. You weren't in company yet, Ducy, but I used to come over quite a bit with my sister when she was on senatorial business. It was such a lark. But Senator, I really wouldn't have recognized him."

"One wouldn't expect you to, Madame Feng." Senator Isaiah drew back farther from Pinto, slipping around his desk chair so it stood between him and the young man. "It's so very hard to tell them apart, after all."

Ducy tittered. The vision smiled.

"I must say it was a delightful prank while it lasted." Eugenie Feng blinked innocently into the glare of her audience. "But of course, while it could pass in a bachelor establishment, it wouldn't suit at all for a family man."

"Not at all," murmured the Senator. "There you are." This last addressed to six blue-clad guards who waited respectfully in the hall until the three women moved far enough into the room that they could pass through to stand, three each, by Lily and Pinto.

Pinto still stared at Senator Isaiah, a horrified fascination. "I thought you would help me." His voice had the hoarse roughness of a broken whisper. "I thought you would help me."

At first, in the silence, the Senator did not meet the young man's gaze. But like some kind of hand-by-hand reconstruction, Lily watched as a cold determination informed Isaiah's face, setting it back into a hard mask. He lifted his eyes to meet Pinto's, dispassion facing a desperate plea.

"If not for my sake, sir—" Pinto's voice broke, then stabilized. "If not for my sake, then at least for my mother's. For her."

"Remove them," said the Senator.

Pinto jerked away from the hands that closed on his good arm, started forward. The desk chair blocked him from the Senator. "You loved her!" he cried. "Don't think I don't remember that. You bought her beautiful dresses. You called her your beauty. You bought her jewels, you bought her anything she asked for. You built her the cottage on these grounds that I was born in! Can you deny that?"

Pale eyes inspected the clear vulnerability of Pinto's face. The Senator sighed, a grandiose gesture. "Like the rest of her kind," he said in the tone usually reserved for teachers imparting the obvious truth to their slowest pupil, "your mother was a common whore. One pays a whore, boy."

Pinto gazed as if blind at the Senator, and when the two blue-clad guards stepped up beside him, laying their hands on his jacket, he seemed not even to notice them. Beyond him, the vision's smile appeared to be fixed into place on her face.

"You disgust me," said Lily. The Senator's gaze jumped to her, his mask of dispassion slipping for a moment to reveal something much uglier underneath it. "You disgust me," she repeated, and she used the surprise her comment created to edge forward toward him. "You and the rest of your kind make me sick."

"Young woman." The mask solidified into a skin impervious to emotion. "There will be no scandal in this house. Remember that I could easily have both of you executed."

"He's your son!" She leaned on the desk, bracing her hands. The guards moved up beside her.

"No female tattoo can possibly claim any *one* man for paternity."

"You wouldn't kill your own son!" Hands touched her arms.

The Senator shifted his gaze from Lily's outrage to Pinto.

The young man's eyes still had not moved from the Senator's face, but he stood limp as a sleepwalker, and expression had fled his face utterly. With a slow, thorough examination that summed up the worth of a soul in its scrutiny, the Senator surveyed Pinto and then, with a light shrug, turned away from him to face the vision and the other two women. "One piece of trash more or less is worth nothing to me," he said. "Get them out of Central, by JooAnn Gate."

Lily launched herself over the desk, grabbed the Senator. If she could only—but the Senator struggled against her, and she had no hands free. Five guards converged on her. Someone screamed, light and ineffectual. Lily kicked, taking one guard down, a second, lost her grip on the Senator, but her left arm was caught, held, vised behind her back, her right arm—when they shoved a gun up against her temple she stopped fighting. They weren't very gentle.

"If I could have taken you hostage, you damned—" she yelled as they propelled her out of the room. They shoved her down a hall, down another hall, down steps, outside, and threw her into a truck. The doors swung to with a hollow crash, followed by the scrape of a bolt sliding into place.

21   JooAnn Gate

✳✳✳✳✳✳✳

She slammed her fists into the closed door. "I killed him!" she cried. The metal did not yield at all under her fist. The truck jerked forward, drove. She hit the door again.

Behind her, a noise. She did not recognize it. She spun in time to see Pinto collapse. That sound again, not a cough, not a laugh, but as final as either of them. He was crying—not even crying, but sobbing.

She knelt beside him.

His entire body, slender as he was, shook with the force of his weeping, the wrenching sobs of the hopeless lost. He had already gone past the point where he could stop himself, gone far past rational sorrow.

"I'm sorry," she whispered, and she put her arms around him. He did not resist. Perhaps he was past resisting. He wept against her, face pressed into her shoulder. In her arms, he seemed fragile. Damp from his tears seeped through the cloth of her tunic. She gazed at the far wall.

She had not had a choice back there: by not betraying Robbie as Pero, she had not betrayed Taliesin. Still—still, there must be something she could do. There would be a trial. It could drag on for months. There must be another way to free Heredes. Pinto shuddered against her and she tightened her arms around him.

Later he lapsed into silence, exhausted. She lowered him gently to lie on the floor.

A narrow grill cut through the side of the vehicle above the cab. Standing, she could see the white, sloping roof of the cab and beyond that a slice of the landscape. She watched until the rumbling sway tired out her legs.

"How long will it take to get to JooAnn Gate?" she asked, settling down beside Pinto, who sat in a forward corner, arms wrapped around bent knees, eyes fixed on the dull floor.

"Four hours." He did not move. "Far enough that no suspicion will devolve on *him.*"

She stood again to look out the grill. "I just hope we're going toward Zanta and not away from it."

"We are." He laughed. It was not a happy sound. "Ya luck be running high, ain't it?"

Lily gazed out the grill. Park and building blurred past. The constant vibration of the truck made her feel nauseous. She pressed one cheek against the hard metal patterning, letting the rush of air gust against her face. Her hair brushed the ceiling of their cell. She shut her eyes.

Joshua Li Heredes. Taliesin. She could reconstruct his face very clearly in her mind. It was his smile that she remembered best. Even at his gravest, the sensei instructing his class, a whispered jest, a stifled laugh at some mistaken command, would bring that smile to his lips, to his eyes, touching like a brief traveler before it fell back into gravity. As long as she had known him he had always been quick to see humor, to respond to the absurdity in any situation.

Maybe that was the quality that lent him patience. And patience, more than anything, she would need now, to win him free. She sighed; patience, Robbie, Bach, and Kyosti.

The wind coursed along her skin, knotting the strands of her hair, slipping between her lips to dry out her mouth. Kyosti. How could any one person be at once so impossible, with that strange obsessiveness and those disturbing lapses into instability, and yet so very appealing? This time when she sighed, breath touched by a low sound from the back of her throat, she stroked her cheek briefly with the back of her fingers. But that soft pressure only made her aware of the edge of steel cutting into her other cheek, and she pulled her face away from the grill and the gusting air. The grill had embedded its pattern into her skin, an impermanent tattoo marking one side of her face.

"Pinto, look," she said, displaying herself.

"I prefer not to," he said into his knees. "The less I see of Central the better." But some quality in her silence caused him to look up, and for a moment he stared at her. His lips quirked up. "You aren't going to get into pilot's academy looking like that."

"It's a good thing I don't want to get into pilot's academy, then."

His smile lasted a brief space longer before he turned his face back down to rest on his knees. Lily sank down in the other forward corner and allowed the motion of the vehicle and the hissing blow of the wind to lull her to sleep. She dreamed, vividly, of Kyosti.

"Lily," he said, and his bronzed hands touched her. She sighed and pressed into those hands.

"Lily." She started awake. Pinto pulled back from her. "We've stopped."

The back hatch yawned opened. The guards pulled them out at gunpoint, handcuffed Lily's hands behind her back. High walls surrounded them. In the far distance Lily heard a constant noise, like Unruli's storms, a tumult that ebbed and swelled but never ceased.

The guards halted them at the end of the alley next to a metal door. A beep sounded; one of the guards lifted his wrist band up to an ear, listened, murmured back into it.

"No use even trying to use the gate," he said to his fellows. "They got a broadcast running in a couple minutes about that Pero guy. We'll have to hike it down to Auxiliary Gate Five."

They conferred in undertones.

". . . might have expected . . ."

". . . not just the troops . . ."

". . . we could go see . . ."

Deciding, they motioned Lily and Pinto in through the door. The corridor they marched down seemed almost like a mine shaft. Smaller halls, like shoots into smaller veins,

thrust off at intervals. They turned into one of these. It grew
a little dim, and they rounded a corner and came into an
observatory that looked out, through plastic windows, over
the great square that fronted JooAnn Gate. A square that
lay outside of Central. The gate, a massive front of metal,
rose at least fifty feet above the square. Narrow terraces
pushed out from the wall to hang over empty air. Figures
populated the terraces, uniforms and big, stationary guns.

"Here," said one of the guards. "Let's see what that
broadcast is." He flicked a switch on his com-unit and Central Center snapped on.

"—the arrest of the agitator Pero yesterday provided con-
clusive evidence that this man only wishes to terrorize and
disrupt the peaceful lives of the citizens of Arcadia. There is
no so-called social liberation involved in this man's
agenda—"

Below, as turbulent as if it were the first flush of a storm
touching the plaza, a crowd of people had gathered, so
many that Lily could not even begin to estimate their number—ten thousand, fifty thousand, one hundred thousand?

"All the gates," said one of the guards, listening on a
different frequency. "Every one's got a mob like this."

The speaker continued, and as she spoke, the crowd
swayed, responding to her words, but not in sympathy. "—
and after interrogation, Pero has admitted the truth of these
allegations. Listen to me, citizens!"

A railing graced the transparent wall. Pinto gripped it
and stared down onto the plaza. From their vantage point
they looked on at an angle—the seething crowd, noiseless
behind the window, the grim, closed front of JooAnn Gate,
the motionless troops stationed on terraces above. Afternoon shadows stretched out across portions of the crowd. A
broad expanse of stairs led up to the great entrance.

"—he has admitted, *admitted* that this revolution is
purely for gain, for what credits he can steal from the riches
we have all worked for. And if you don't believe me, if you
don't believe that I, elected head of your Senate, am telling
you the truth, then simply wait a moment, citizens."

On the far edges of the square more bodies pressed toward the front, spilling out of the side avenues that led from three angles into the six-sided plaza.

"Yes! Pero himself will tell you *now* the truth. He has recanted, citizens. He has repented—he admits he has lied to you, exploited you for his own ends. Hear him, citizens!"

The crowd pressed forward, pushing up the steps toward the gate.

Lily looked at Pinto. He looked at her. The guards fell silent. Voices mumbled in the background over the channel, someone being led forward.

"Comrades." Heredes's voice. Quiet, so that they saw the crowd still as it strained to listen. " 'If you stay together they will cut you to pieces.' " Silence. A strange, popping noise, a shattering crash that echoed across the channel. " 'We advise you to stay together!' " he cried, and his voice drowned out the yells coming from the background. " 'If you fight their tanks will grind you to a pulp. We advise you to fight!' "

The crowd shifted violently, like liquid building to a boil.

"Stop him—" A voice crackling through in static. "Pull the—"

" 'This battle will be lost.' " His voice. " 'And maybe the next will also be lost, but you are learning to fight, and realizing—' "

A flurry of yelling overwhelmed him, but a second crash sounded, and his voice resounded out again, a cry that mesmerized them all. " 'Realize that it will only work out by force and only if you do it yourselves—' "

A shot, no echoing ricochet because it came over the channel. Two more shots in quick succession.

Utter silence.

A murmured voice. A fourth shot, hard and final.

She didn't think. She went for the door. Two guards grabbed her. She fought. She had to get to him, to get to him. More hands. She kicked, she twisted, but her hands were cuffed; she felt them propel her backward. She fought forward. They flung her. She hit the plastiglass so hard that it stunned her.

Was half-aware of Pinto clasping her, saying something

urgent to her, but she couldn't hear, could scarcely see. The plastiglass pressed up against her face. At first she thought the smoke coiling up in spreading screens throughout the crowd was her vision clearing. She could not make sense of the whole, but there, a woman pushing away from a reaching finger of smoke; a man covering his face with his hands; a body, convulsed, carried by two men. Everyone was moving so slowly.

"—the traitor Pero—"

"—execution by—"

"—return to your homes or—"

Snippets of words caught at her, but made no sense. An officer, up on a terrace, winced and staggered and fell. Below, a woman holding a gun, firing up. A man cowering, shielding two children. Another officer, on a farther terrace, recoiled and fell to her knees.

"I've got to get to him," said Lily.

Her movement came up against Pinto. "It's no use," he hissed, trying to contain her. "He's dead, Lily." He pushed her back up against the wall.

She dropped abruptly to her knees. She could not speak. It was as if all her expression had fled her, as if out there on the plaza she spoke, she cried, she reacted to those four shots.

The great guns shifted, yawed down and to one side, aiming into the midst of the crowd. Five men shoved through the crowd, running for the side streets.

The guns shuddered to life, bursts, like muffled coughing, like sobs, shaking the plastic wall so slightly. But this time, they did not fire smoke.

The square erupted into turmoil. She stared, as at herself.

"Murderers," Pinto breathed. "Mother bless us, they're trampling each other."

"Come on," growled one of the guards. "Do we got to stand and watch this? Let's get rid of these two and go home."

"He's right," said another. "It ain't even a fair fight."

Chaos, that was what she saw. Smoke ringed the plaza. The sobbing of the guns echoed as if far distant from her.

People fled every direction. At the three avenues it was as if the crowd were recoiling back into itself, but into a space that no longer had room. All across the square bodies lay in tangled wrecks, stained with the force of their deaths: shot or trampled, who could tell the difference now? She heard nothing; it was a horrific pantomime played out to her, except for the muffled reports from the great guns above.

They had to drag her out of the room. Once in the hall she could walk. Pinto limped beside her; she noticed that first, then the six guards, then the walls around her, the walls of Central which were, she now knew, no better than a fortress.

And Pero still lived. She still lived.

"That was your mistake," she said. No one heard her. She would avenge him, that became clear to her. No matter what she had to do: wait fifty years, or join Jehane, or blow Central into oblivion. "So be it," she said.

Auxiliary Gate Five was barred and triple locked. She was aware of things like that by then. The guards, pushing them through the first set of bars, did not even escort them to the outer gate itself, merely opened a series of barriers by remote control. But the final set of bars slid away to reveal a deserted, minuscule plaza shaded by trees and by the lowering of evening. Far away, more a suggestion than a definite sound, the frantic noise from distant JooAnn Gate rose and fell in waves.

A sudden report cut through the lull, splitting off into a ricocheting echo around them.

"Run for the street," shouted Pinto.

They ran, but heard no further shots. Pausing in the lee of a row of lush trees, she saw that Pinto was laboring. She draped his good arm across her shoulders so he could get weight off his bad ankle. His hard, gasping breaths came at least as much from pain as from being winded.

"Where did that come from?" she asked. "The wall?"

"I don't know. It might have been, but maybe from one of the houses out here. Let's get out of here."

"I hope you know where we are." She surveyed the narrow avenue that stretched out before them, four-story buildings suspiciously silent and empty bordering it. Even with the growing dusk the windows stayed unlit. "Because I don't."

"This should be Shiang. If we can find a delivery depot, if the cargoes are still running, we're only about four hours from Zanta."

"If," echoed Lily.

Pinto's smile, shaded by the overhang of trees, was mocking and bitter. "Didn't I tell you about my luck? It extends just as far as my literal survival. Sometimes I make the mistake of expecting too much of it."

She stared at him. Stared at him so long that he removed his arm from her shoulders and drew back from her. Then she realized what he was referring to. "I'm sorry about your father, Pinto," she said in a soft voice.

"Mother's wounds," he muttered. "Lily—" He faltered. "Was he really—was he really—your father?"

"Yes."

"I'm sorry." His voice shook. "I'm sorry." He began to limp away from her.

"Are you all right?" she asked as she came up beside him. He shrugged. "My ankle hurts."

"Isn't pain the price of life?" she asked with deep bitterness.

Pinto cast her a sharp, doubting glance that dissolved abruptly, surprisingly, into a smile. He lifted a hand, tattoos swirling in a maze about his palm and fingers, a maze that seemed to extend into infinity. "The price of a soul," he answered.

Pinto's luck held true. They found Shiang Depot just as twilight passed into night. The cargoes, controlled by some untroubled computer system, were still running on their blind, predetermined paths.

They switched lines once, had to wait an hour because a unit of government troops had stopped to rest on the platform dividing the depot. Cargoes roared past at intervals, shaking Lily and Pinto where they huddled in the dense shadow of old construction. Finally the troopers moved on. The new line took them to Zanta C Depot, five kilometers from the apartment. Clouds covered the wheel of the night. It began to rain.

The dull misting hid them as they trudged along the edge of streets. Even the streetlights were unlit here, except at the intersections where the bulbs cast perhaps a third of their normal illumination. It was eerily silent. Pinto's uneven footsteps and her smooth ones blended into the hush. Her hair soon stuck to her face and neck in scattered, lanky strips. Light caught now and again on the bright surface of beads woven into Pinto's braids, but it was just a momentary glamour.

They came, at last, to the park. Around them the darkness eased away, as if dissolving into the steady mist of fine rain. Lines of vegetation, treetops etched against the lightening sky, hedges bulking with opaque thickness lower down, came into being by slow degrees around them as they crossed the park, following the path that circled the pond. The water lay like a sheet of void beyond them. Farther, where the path curved, a solitary form leaned against the railing that divided path from shore. Lily put a staying hand on Pinto's chest. He halted.

But something about that form, about the way it leaned, the angle of its arms along its side, was familiar to her. It shifted, head turned, and she knew he had seen them.

"Come up behind me," she whispered to Pinto. As they neared the form, he neither stood nor tensed. Slender, short-haired, about Pinto's height. Ten paces away he spoke.

"Is that you, Maud?"

"Robbie!" It all came out in an undertone. Lily closed the gap between them with accelerating speed, obliterated in a hug. He thrust her away almost at once.

"Is Maud with you?" He glanced behind her, measured and dismissed Pinto's form.

"Maud?"

"My sister Mathilda. I sent her up, to the apartment, to bring you down. I couldn't chance the apartment being under surveillance."

"But you're dead, Robbie," she said, suddenly and bitterly angry with him. "No one's hunting you anymore."

"Robbie?" A new voice, soft, uncertain.

"Ah, Maud." He turned, and a young woman, his height but heavyset, came up beside him. Her gaze took in Lily and Pinto. She shrank away, but Robbie's grasp pulled her back. "You remember Lily," he said.

"But she wasn't up there. No one answered, but the terminal must of been left on, because I heard singing."

"Good," said Robbie and Lily at the same time.

"Who are they?" hissed Pinto, rain damping his voice so it only reached Lily.

"It's Pero, of course," said Lily. "The real Pero." Her voice shook. "The living Pero."

"Let's get inside," said Robbie. "I need your help, Lya." He began to walk at a quick pace toward the block. Lily came up beside him, Mathilda and Pinto behind. Dawn crept, a slow seeping of color, into their surroundings.

"Where am I going now?" Lily asked.

"Off Arcadia," he replied, as if such a course were so self-evident that her question was superfluous. "To Jehane."

22 To Jehane

✳✳✳✳✳✳

They dried and changed their clothes first, careful with power because their block was suffering a brownout. Bach, ecstatic at Lily's return, sang a hymn of thanksgiving and afterward plugged himself back into the terminal and began to search the banks for out-going ships.

"Why do I have to leave Arcadia?" Lily asked. She sat on Pero's desk, legs dangling, while Robbie rummaged in its drawers.

"Because they'll be looking for you." He did not look up from his task. "Not *you* in particular, but Pero's wife, Pero's family, Pero's roommates. They'll want to tie up all the loose ends. I don't doubt your capacity to protect yourself, Lya, but your skills are more valuable elsewhere. I'd send Maud too, but she won't go."

"Damn right I won't," said Maud from the other room. "Now you *really* need someone to look after you."

"Do you know where we were?" Lily asked. "We were in Central, talking to Senator Isaiah." Still he did not pause. "Robbie. I could have turned you in. I could have saved Heredes's life by giving you to them in exchange."

His hands paused, half in a drawer, and his face, that face of complete conviction to its purpose, lifted up to gaze at her. "I know."

She thrust herself off the desk, spun, took short steps around to him, shorter steps back around the desk to come up behind him.

"How could you let him die?" she cried.

"I never suspected he meant to do what he did," he said.
"But Lya," and that deep musicality informed his voice as
he straightened, head and shoulders lifting, to gaze with
rapt intensity at Lily. "He died the glorious death. He has
allowed the movement to grow. His death gives new meaning to Pero, who will be born again. We didn't win this
battle. We won't win the next one. But this is the long struggle. Some of us will be privileged to offer our lives as the
stepping-stones on which it builds. And as we are killed, so
the people will come to understand the necessity of the
revolution. So the government will divide, will disagree on
the methods used to humble us. Even now there is dissent
on Pero's murder. Already we force them into crisis. They
have declared martial law, no gatherings over three souls in
a private dwelling, no movement at all without escort in
public. You could be shot in the street, without cause, just
for exercising your right to stroll with your children on a
fine summer's day. And as each crisis casts Central into
disorder, as each crisis disrupts the corruption of their bu-
reaucracy further, so we prepare the ground for Jehane. Until the day he can come and sweep all before him. This is just
the first step."

Maud stood in a bedroom door, gazing at her brother.
Pinto had ceased working in the kitchen to turn and stare.
But Lily smiled, sad, touched with irony, perhaps with bitterness still, and shook her head at the futility of being angry with him.

"I've got something for you," she said instead of everything else she might have said. "Heredes's last gift." She put
the diskette on the desk.

Robbie regarded it and her for a moment, nodded, and
returned to his task, sorting through the accumulation—
little enough—of items in his desk. At the terminal, Bach
sang out.

"What have you found?" She crossed to stand by him.
Pinto and Maud went into the bedrooms to pack.

Schedules scrolled up on the screen:

*outbound ships, canceled, canceled, security clearance
only, canceled.*

Protests had been logged by captains and company managers.

"There's got to be underground traffic," said Lily. "Or
better yet, see if you can find some dog-tagger that's desperate for a pilot. Robbie, what's the name of that port that
borders Roanoak district? It's that really old one, rundown."

"Isn't it Kippers? Why do you ask?"

"Because we're picking up Kyosti on the way. Look at
what's routing through Kippers, Bach-o."

Bach found her seven notices on an unranked channel.
Shunting him to one side, she sat in the chair. The first three
did not even respond to her call. On the fourth she got voice
clearance only. A thick male voice greeted her, so obviously
filled to the ears on ambergloss that she cut the connection.
The fifth, hailing her call with a spirited, *"Panda's Box,* I've
got your frequency," was cautious but interested. But when,
after a period of circumspect negotiation, it transpired that
the *Panda's Box* shuttle was not at Kippers at all but at the
farthest west port on the coast, more than thirty hours
away, Lily excused herself. Six did not respond. Seven
quickly established it wanted no tattoo near its controls.

She went back to the first: no response. Second.

"Frequency acknowledged," said a soft, high voice, almost drowned in static. "Voice clearance only. We are looking for a pilot."

"Voice clearance only," Lily acknowledged. "I have a pilot in exchange for transportation out of system. My name is
Ransome. What ship is this?"

Static arced and spit behind the blank screen. For a long
moment Lily feared the connection had been cut.

"Lily Hae Ransome?" The voice almost faded into nothing.

"I'm coming on visual," said Lily suddenly, and punched
in the codes. An instant later the screen blossomed into life.
"Aliasing!"

"Oh, Lily!" The delicate face was drawn into the thinness of exhaustion and fear. "Do you really have a pilot? We're desperate. We came into system on a run almost a month ago and Milhaviru went on a binge and almost killed us going out, so Captain Bolyai threw her off, but we couldn't risk looking for a pilot through official channels so Jenny and I came down on the shuttle—days and days ago but we still haven't found—" She broke off. Even in her rush of words, her voice never lifted above a whisper. "Do you really have a pilot?"

"Yes. Are you at Kippers?"

"It's a terrible place." Her eyes glanced to either side as if she feared observation. "But Jenny said they'd never search here. But I'm afraid. There's riots all over down here—it's all tattoo districts." Her voice faltered and gave out.

"Why did Jenny bring you down? Aren't you safer up on the ship?"

Frail lips trembled. "We thought—I thought—maybe one of my old friends—but I called, just one, and now"—emotions filled and fled her face in a dizzying shift of expression—"now I'm afraid they're looking for us. We have to get out fast."

"Where is Jenny?"

"Out looking. How can we reach you? I don't know how to tell you to get here. She'll call you."

Lily soothed her, gave her a code, and signed off. At his desk Pero had finally decided on what to keep and what to dispose of.

"Maud," he called. His sister appeared with two duffel bags. "We have to wipe off every surface that might take prints, and incinerate any leftover items." She set down the bags and went into the washing cubicle.

"Robbie," said Lily. "I've got us a ship. Now how do we get to Kippers?"

"That's settled." She watched as he copied the diskette into Bach's memory, followed him after to the washroom where he collected several damp, soapy cloths from his sister and, handing one to Lily, returned to wipe his desk.

"Three streets from here there's a Security vehicle with four troopers whose allegiance is to Jehane."

"Can we really trust them not to turn us over to Central?"

His dark eyes lifted and a brief smile marked his face. "I have an instinct for Jehanists. They will deliver you to your ship."

"I wonder why I trust you so much," she replied. He merely looked at her, but he did not answer. "They'll catch you eventually. Someday the government is going to kill you."

"Of course," said Pero, and he went back to his washing.

They ate, finished their cursory cleaning, waited until a sudden signal brought Lily to the terminal. Gray dissolved into the face of Jenny Seria.

"Lily-hae!" Grimness underlay that assured nonchalance. "Are you coming aboard?"

"If you'll take us."

"How many?"

"Three and the 'bot."

"One's a pilot?"

"Yes, he is."

A grin cracked Jenny's face. "So what's wrong with him?"

"Nothing. Of course, he's Ridani."

"A damned tattoo!"

"Jenny. He'll do the job."

The grin, banished by surprise, returned. "Beggars can't choose. He's on. What about you, Lily-hae?"

"I'm a fugitive now—but it's a long story."

"Come aboard, by all means. Fugitives are welcome on the *Easy Virtue*. But get here fast."

"Just tell me where you are."

They said good-bye to Pero in the apartment. Maud wept a little; Pinto shook his hand; Bach wished him well in his own voice.

"How will you live?" Lily asked him.

"I will live on the goodwill of the people," said Pero. "I will live on the work of those who have already sacrificed themselves or their loved ones. I will live on the promise of Jehane."

He led them to the Security vehicle. They climbed into the back of the truck, and the doors cut them off from him.

A young trooper, nervous but exhilarated, talked incessantly about the growing, but still-secret, support for Jehane within the Security forces, especially after the execution and subsequent rioting. He regaled them at some length with examples of conversion. Finally, he lapsed into silence. They passed through several checkpoints: the truck stopped; voices conversed; the truck went on. At one point the truck came to an abrupt halt. A hail of shooting sounded around them. A sudden blow shuddered the entire vehicle. Lily flung herself half-across Pinto to prevent him from falling. The trooper fingered his gun and directed it at the back doors. From the cab, a voice called back.

"Coming into Kippers. It's wild as pitch out here." The truck lurched forward—shouts were exchanged. Some barrier seemed to be passed and they drove on smoothly. Lily pushed away from Pinto and went forward to call into the cab.

"Fifty-seven seventy-eight," she directed.

An interminable fifteen minutes passed. But at last the truck slowed and stopped and the engine cut off with a last cough.

"Cursed whore-mother tattoos," snapped the driver. "They're just asking to be shot."

The trooper undid the doors, swung them open. Lily scrambled out—to see Jenny in full mercenary's rig coming out of the shuttle's hatch. Lily ran forward. Jenny lowered her gun.

"Lily!" Her eyes cast back to the truck. Dents puckered the red stripe along one door that identified it as a Security vehicle. "I thought you were a fugitive."

"They're Jehanists."

"So they say. Let's board and get clear. Where's your pilot—" Her face froze in astonishment. "Damn my eyes. It's Isaiah's tame monkey. Grown up."

Pinto halted. "Go fly your own tupping ship—"

Lily grabbed his arm and squeezed, hard. "Jenny, this is Pinto."

"I know you," said Pinto suddenly, still staring at Jenny. "You were—the Mughal banquet—the blond—"

"A friend of yours is on that shuttle." Jenny's voice sliced through his indecision. "So move it up."

Recognition flooded Pinto's face. "Aliasing," he said in a breath. "She disappeared." He pulled away from Lily and jogged toward the shuttle. Bach followed him.

Lily turned back toward the truck.

"Lily." Jenny's voice cut hard and urgent through the air. "Move it up, woman."

"There's just one thing, Jenny. I have to find Kyosti. He works in Roanoak."

"What—old blue-hair?"

"I'm sorry. If you have to leave me, do it. But I can't go without him."

Jenny sighed, and her mouth turned down. "All right, Ransome. I'll give you two hours. But these pretty soldiers stay with me until you get back."

"But—"

Jenny cut off the driver's protest with one motion of her gun. "You'll stay with me. Round up your boys and give me your guns. How do you expect to find him?"

Lily, divesting the four troopers of their guns, turned to the driver. "Where's Roanoak E Depot from here?"

"Less than half a kilometer. Straight down Mash Avenue."

"Then I can find him. Two hours, Jenny. I'll return this then," she added to the driver, slipping a hand-size stunner into her boot. She set out in the proferred direction at a lope.

Most of the loading berths sat empty. A Security truck roared by and she dodged just in time under the confines of a raised platform. And, looking up, realized it was a rail shoot that connected with the cargo tracks. She followed it. Branched to the right where it met the main tracks and jogged down them. A warehouse loomed on her left. The tracks rose, arcing up into a bridge. She crouched at the rise.

Off to the left she saw a gate, crowded with troops inside
and a fluid mass of people outside. Surely that must be Mash
Avenue. She dropped off the height of rail and ran along the
side of the decrepit warehouse toward the gate. Broken concrete, cracked and jagged, polluted with shoots of green
erupting up through it, caught at her feet, but she neither
lost her balance nor broke her stride.

Old warehouses, long deserted by their shattered windows
and half-slung doors, covered her approach to within
twenty-five yards of the gate. The crowd sounded a steady
undercurrent to the louder noise of an altercation at the
gate. A woman's voice screamed words at the phalanx of
troopers stationed behind the broad entry gates. A low vehicle pushed forward, nosing the metal mesh until a single
shot shattered through the sound of the engine, and the
vehicle backed up abruptly. People yelled and shouted and
dashed out of its retreating path.

But there was an exit gate, a smaller, one-way set of bars
and barriers. About six troopers watched it, but their attention was mostly focused on the entrance. An incredible
shouting broke out away down the avenue.

Honking and shouts accompanied the slow advance of a
Security vehicle. The crowd threw itself on it, battering at
the metal sides, shattering windows. Troopers opened the
gates, charging through to aid the vehicle. Any number of
civilians pressed into the port. Lily strolled across the me-
dian strip, up to the exit gate.

"Excuse me," she said to the trooper who stood blocking
the first section of the gate. "But I need to get out."

The trooper stared at her, started at the sudden commands from the entry gate, where civilians were pouring
around the Security vehicle and through the gate. Lily was
out through the gate before she got any reply.

She had to shove through the crowd, but no one hindered
her because she was moving in the opposite direction. At
last she cleared the worst congestion and found the avenue.
The traffic was definitely against her, but all on foot. At the
gate she had seen untattooed people. Now, as she walked

down the broad avenue as quickly as she could without running, she saw fewer and fewer unmarked faces.

These people were headed away from the direction she was going in. Some at a run. A volley of shots, faint and snapping, echoed out along the avenue until the swelling noise of human agitation covered them. A cluster of youths smashed a shop window with rocks. One at their fringe grabbed at Lily. She brushed him aside, went on. Glanced back once, but they had scattered into the shop, looting.

The press of crowd increased against her, pulling her one way, pushing her another, but she fought forward, shoulders hunched, as if against the winds of Unruli. Came out into the plaza fronting Roanoak E Depot. And saw what the crowds were fleeing.

Tumult. Turmoil. Perhaps it had once been a riot. The debris of the protest—clubs, torn clothing, bodies—lay still beneath the agitation swirling over it. Someone hit her, full collision, and she was knocked off her feet. Rolled, came up crouched, but no one had stopped. Another body brushed roughly past. Screams, shouts, uproar. The crack of command. Five precise shots.

A gap opened, and she could see the depot. Emerging out of it, in an exact line, the stark white uniforms of the Immortals. They advanced step by commanded step. The crowd roiled away from them, recoiled back. Shots peppered into the swarm. Those who reached the line of the Immortals were dispatched with ease by a flash of slim, metal clubs that seemed choreographed in its ruthless efficiency. The crowd broke under their advance despite the amazing disparity in numbers.

Lily swore under her breath, retreating with the crowd until she could separate off and, pushing along the edge of the plaza, duck into a side street. It would be hard enough to retrace her way to the clinic—and with this . . .

Distant commands: "Break line and pursue in order." Lily ran, took a side street, and another, and came out on the edge of a tiny, withering park, hardly larger than her apartment. She paused to catch her breath and her bearings.

A sudden rush of running and yelling, followed by a

flurry of shots. She threw herself behind a bench. A group of Ridanis ran past. One staggered, blood seeping at her abdomen, and fell. Six of the others stopped, grabbed her, pulled. But four Immortals, practically sprinting in step, surrounded them and with a supreme economy of effort beat them until there was no motion left. And turned to face the bench. Lily stood up.

Two men. Two women. They studied Lily with eyes of inexorable dispassion. Lily had a vivid vision of Jenny in such a uniform. She grinned. Hopped the bench casually, raised one hand and with the other tipped the gun out of her boot and onto the ground. Then she sat on the high back of the bench, feet on the seat itself, and folded her arms in front of her.

"Even though you aren't a tattoo," said the woman with the bars of highest rank, "why shouldn't we shoot you?"

"Because," replied Lily, "I'm going to meet my lover."

Two of them laughed.

"Say it's true," said the officer. "Why should we let you meet this lover, tattooed or not?"

Lily stood up and jumped lightly to the ground. "Because I challenge any one of you, no weapons, to single combat. If I win, you'll let me go."

Two laughed.

"If you lose?" asked the officer.

"Your choice."

"All right." The officer nodded at one of the men. "Make it quick."

He divested himself of weapons, put them in the keeping of his comrades. They backed up to give him room. Lily came forward. More dirt than grass under her feet. She tested it under her boots, getting a feel for her traction.

He lunged. She sidestepped, caught him with a clip to the back of the head before he could pull up and turn, caught the back of one of his knees with a kick. But as his balance broke backward, he fell into it, rolled and pushed up onto his hands, booted feet thrust into her abdomen.

She doubled over, gasping, but kept the force of his roll tumbling backward and flipped him over her. They both spun up to their feet and away. A dull ache spread out along the muscles of her belly. He rubbed his head, and smiled.

Now he began to circle in. He was lithe, strong and straight from his training. He shifted closer, whirled, and attacked. Her dodge cleared all but her shoulder—his fist slammed into that, but she spun with the blow, closing in with an elbow to his face. He slugged her, straight onto a breast. Staggering back, she barely caught his next blow on her forearm, deflecting a kick with a sweep of one leg. His hand, ringed with something metal, skimmed her cheek and tore the skin.

She dropped, but only into her deepest stance, and took his open belly with a clean reverse punch. He fell like a stone into a heap on the ground. She leapt backward, found the bench, and cleared it so the high back stood between her and the Immortals. Pain throbbed through her abdomen, her chest, her leg; stung like the whip of cold wind on her cheek. Liquid swelled and trailed down her face.

"We keep our word," said the officer. "You have until he can walk again."

Lily took ten steps back, turned, and sprinted. No shots followed her. Her leg ached with each pounding step. Blood trickled down her neck. Each pulse shot through her chest. She ran all the way to the clinic. Not even tattoos bothered her, and she saw no more Immortals.

At the steps leading up into the clinic, she had to stop. Not just because she was gasping for air and fighting the spreading pulse of pain, the cramping in her injured leg. There were others wounded. Her first glance, halted, rising as her wind came back, fixed on a child, chest ripped open as if by a rending knife. She heard weeping. A man moaned, clutching an arm to his body; he shifted, and bone showed, sticking through his flesh. Lily stumbled up the steps, trying to avoid all the bodies cast there like so much debris. A tattooed woman in a medical jacket walked among them, clipping tags about their necks. As Lily reached the clinic door, two clinic workers emerged and designated the next patients to go in.

"Be you have to wait your turn," said one, laying a restraining hand on her bruised arm.

She winced. "I'm not here for injuries. I'm here to see min Accipiter."

A look passed between the two workers. One nodded. "He be in ward B."

She knew where it was. It was the same common room where she had gone—so long ago—when Pero had been shot. Inside the clinic, hush prevailed, a low murmur of talk. Injured Ridanis crowded the seats, sat with the patience she had seen in Paisley—not expecting anything more—in orderly lines in the halls. A worker helped a man limp out of ward B, and Lily slipped inside, the broad door sighing shut behind her.

Seats, benches, floor: all were crowded with bleeding, torn, wounded Ridanis, a sea of patterns that had, like a common thread running between them, the red markings of blood.

Kyosti was bent over a boy, hands probing with insistent gentleness at one leg. The boy cried out, and Kyosti, with a skill she could only marvel at, soothed his crying while ripping off the trouser to see the wound better. His hair stood in wild, pale disarray about his head. Blood stained one cheek, dried there as if from hours ago. His medical jacket had once been white; now red mottled it. Strain pulled at the delicate lines of his face. He looked on the edge of breaking down from exhaustion. She thought she had never seen him as handsome as he was now.

Ridani eyes rose to scrutinize her. Silence unfurled along the room until at last the boy, sensing some emotion outside his pain, shifted his head to look at her. Kyosti looked up at the boy's face. And, with a slow turn of his head, followed the boy's gaze.

For an instant as long as a window they stared at each other, his blue eyes fixed on her dark ones.

He rose.

"Lily," he said. "Help me carry this young fellow into the back room. I have to stitch up his leg."

She complied. She watched in silence as he worked, efficient as the Immortals. The boy cried, but he could limp out of the room, clean and sewn-up, when Kyosti was finished.

"Kyosti," Lily began. He washed his hands.

"Why are you here?" he said over the rush of water. "That was incredibly stupid of you, Lily." With a hard wrench he shut off the taps and turned to glare at her.

"We have to leave Arcadia."

"What? Right now? Do you suggest I simply abandon my patients in all their blood?"

"Kyosti!" She took a step toward him. He backed away. "Kyosti, Heredes is dead." His expression did not change. He seemed not to have heard her. "Central murdered him. They said he was Pero."

Kyosti glanced down at his bloody jacket. "I heard Pero was dead. I thought it was Robert."

"Don't you care?" she cried. "It was Taliesin!"

He laughed. "I'll believe he's dead when I put these hands on his cold corpse. Maybe not even then."

"How dare you!" she screamed. "How dare you say that!" She flung herself at him, furious with grief, but he dodged her, avoided her blow.

"Why don't you go away—I have work to do." His hands gripped the examining table as if he would fall if it was not there.

"I'm leaving, Kyosti." Her voice fell, lost its brief touch of hysteria. "Don't you understand that? I may never come back."

"You're better off without me, Lily. I've only brought you trouble, and I'll only bring you more."

"Kyosti." The barest whisper. "Don't make me leave without you."

He laughed, short and hard, and let go of the table. "What difference would it make whether I go with you or not?" But his eyes asked something else.

She bowed her head. She could not meet his gaze. The floor, not very clean, lay in all its neutral glory beneath her. "I left Ransome House," she said to it. "I left Wingtuck's Academy. Robbie's in hiding. And Heredes—" She stopped, voice catching on his name.

He turned his back to her, picked up his examining kit, fastened his stethoscope about his neck. "And I'm all that's left." He made it sound like an insult.

"Kyosti. That's not how I meant it." She moved around the table. "Come with me." Came up to him, put out her hands.

"Don't touch me," he said.

While she was still staring, he walked carefully around her and left the private room.

She could not move. The examining table, thin paper sheet covering its cold surface, metal-smoothed corners, transfixed her vision. There he had gripped with such force. With one hand, tentative fingers, she touched that place. It was cool. He had left nothing of himself there. She swallowed. There was moisture on her cheek, but when she raised a hand to touch it, it was just blood. Here and there her body ached, but it was like an old sorrow, dulling into oblivion.

After all, she had to get back to the shuttle. Her feet moved as if someone else were willing them to. The door swung back. It took an eternity to get from the private room to the door of ward B. All the Ridanis stared at her deliberate progress. She arrived at the door at last. Best just to leave. But she had to look a last time.

She turned. Kyosti had knelt before an elderly woman. She had deep gashes all along one side of her body. He examined them, graceful in his competence, painstaking, absorbed.

Paisley's story came unbidden to her mind—perhaps some people never could find their true home, like the Ridanis, lost far down the way. Or never recognized it for what it was until they had lost it. To lose Heredes was a thousand times harder than leaving, and losing, Ransome House. But although she had lost Heredes to irrevocable death, she had at least known what he was to her. This time the recognition had indeed come too late.

In front of all those eyes, tears welled up as she looked at him, and she began to cry. Noiseless at first, until a sob caught in her bruised chest.

His head turned. He stared at her, as if at revelation. Unfastening his stethoscope, he laid it on the lap of the elderly woman and stood up.

"Forgive me," he said to the room at large as he unbuttoned his medical jacket. "But I love her." The jacket slipped to a crumpled heap on the floor.

The elderly woman stood up. The rest, those that could, one by one, stood, and when they were all standing they bowed to him, a brief, respectful salute, and averted their eyes.

He came up beside her and put his hands on either side of her face. "Lily," he breathed, lifting her so that she looked up at him.

"I love you," she said, wondering, because she had just this instant realized it was true.

He smiled, that brilliant, languorous, suggestive smile she had seen the first time he had smiled at her. "Of course you do," he murmured, and his lips touched hers, the briefest brush. "Mother's Breasts, Lily," he said in an undertone of suppressed hysteria, "let's get out of here before I have to haul you into the back room." He let go of her as if she were scorching him.

He led her out a back way, pausing long enough in an empty storeroom to take two clean medical jackets from a shelf. He handed one to her, put the other on himself, and they left the clinic.

Roanoak was deserted—silent, empty, seemingly uninhabited. No one walked the streets. Once, in the distance, they heard a shouted command, but that was all: the Immortals, with terrible efficiency, had obliterated the riot.

Side streets led them to the plaza that fronted E Depot. It was so utterly changed a scene from the one she had just fought through that she could not help but feel that she had somehow been dislocated in time, as if she had just gone through, or was still in, a window.

Thin streams of plastine fiber fluttered over the ground. The litter of violence lay strewn across the plaza: clothing, signs, abandoned weapons. There were no bodies. The quiet that lay over them was ominous in its intensity.

"Have they killed everyone?" Lily whispered. "Hoy, they worked fast."

Kyosti's head lifted, as if he had caught a scent and was trying to trace it to its source. He moved forward abruptly, and Lily half-tripped over a ruined motoped in her haste to follow him. He halted beside a pile of debris, knelt, and uncovered the body of a Ridani woman. Shutting his eyes, he laid a hand on the side of her face. Lily stopped behind him. The woman had been shot at least four times, once in the neck, the rest in the chest. A slow bubble of blood rose out of her partly open mouth.

At last Kyosti removed his hand and, rising, stepped over the body and began to walk on.

"She's still alive," said Lily quietly.

He paused. "She'll be dead within the hour, Lily." She still hesitated. "And she can't feel anything."

Lily lifted her gaze from the body to look first at Kyosti and then at the deserted square. "We're going to be seeing alot of this, aren't we?"

"Ah, Lily," he murmured. "You're no longer what you were when I first met you."

"No, I don't suppose I am. Let's go."

At the gate into Kippers the mob had vanished and the troops stood vigilant but relaxed. To get them inside, Kyosti used the simple expedient of presenting his technologist's identification and informing the guard on the other side of the gate that there were wounded troopers he and his assistant had been called to attend. Once inside, Lily guided them to berth 5778.

"Damn my eyes." Jenny swung out of the cab where she had efficiently trussed and tied the troopers. "You found him. What happened to your hair, Hawk?"

"A minor cosmetic change," said Kyosti. "I'll let the color grow back."

In the shuttle, the engines were already going. Pinto strapped in front counting down the check of his instruments. Aliasing had a hand on his shoulder; when she saw Lily, she stepped back and strapped herself in beside Pinto, at comm. Bach sang a relieved greeting, but the chair restraints prevented him from going to Lily. Behind, Jenny closed the hatch. The comm, tuned in to some underground frequency, sounded suddenly in the quiet left by the dampening of engine noise.

"Pero is not one man, not one woman." It was Robbie's voice. Lily strapped herself in next to Kyosti. The shuttle shuddered and coasted forward, taxiing to the strip. "Pero is the voice of the people. Pero cannot be murdered by the oppressors." Jenny strapped in across from Lily. Out of the window, buildings and berths cleared into the length of runway. "Pero will never die. Pero will always be resurrected. Such is *our* power."

Pinto reached out across Aliasing and flipped off the comm channel.

Into its absence, Lia said, "What are you going to do?"

Silence first, but for the muffled rumble of engine through the hull.

"I don't see we have any choice," said Lily finally. "We'll join Jehane."

"Oh," said Lia. "After all," she finished as Pinto responded to the go-ahead over comm and the engines arced in volume, "if Central is hunting you, he's one person who will welcome you, and protect you." She glanced briefly at Jenny as she said it, but Jenny was busy glaring at the screen on her lap and did not notice the comment.

Beside Lily, Kyosti had fallen asleep, head tucked against her shoulder, one long-fingered hand resting on her thigh. Lily kissed his hair softly. "His heir will take his place," she murmured. "It was inevitable."

The engines screamed and shoved and she was pressed back into her seat by the thrust of takeoff. The shuttle banked sharply to the left, lifted, leveled, and began the long ascent toward space. Lily, gazing out the window, watched Arcadia dissolve from detail into the indistinct clarity of distance. All that blue, all water—the kind of beauty that never leaves you.

"Good-bye, Master Heredes," she said. Bach sang,

Ruht wohl, ihr heiligen Gebeine,

die ich nun weiter nicht beweine;
Ruht wohl, und bringt auch mich zur Ruh'.
Das Grab, so euch bestimmet ist
und ferner keine Not umschliesst,
Macht mir den Himmel auf
und schliesst die Hölle zu.

"Rest well, you holy remains,
   which I shall no longer mourn;
   Rest well, and bring me also to rest.
   The grave, that is destined for you,
   and holds no further suffering,
   opens Heaven to me
   and closes the gates of Hell."

The shuttle continued to climb, a steady curve lengthening into the infinite expanse of sky.

About the Author

Alis A. Rasmussen was born in Iowa and grew up in Oregon. She graduated from Mills College, in California, having spent her junior year abroad studying at the University of Wales. She is currently living in San Jose, California, with her husband, three children, and two newts. She has a brown belt in Shotokan karate and occasionally practices broadsword fighting in the Society for Creative Anachronism. In addition to the *Highroad* trilogy, she is the author of a fantasy novel, *The Labyrinth Gate,* and is at present at work on a new novel.

Here is a preview from

REVOLUTION'S SHORE
by Alis Rasmussen,
Volume II in "The Highroad
Trilogy":

REVOLUTION'S SHORE chronicles Lily Ransome's rise to ship's pilot under the command of Comrade Jehane, spearhead of the desperate uprising against the corrupt government of Reft space. Lily must decide for herself whether the revolution's ends justify its means, and more than once her loyalties are called into question. She must also cope, both as a woman and as a superior officer, with her growing love for the mysterious Kyosti—and her ship is the first to face a new and possibly deadly threat. A starship of unknown intent, far superior to any constructed with Reft technology, has arrived on the highroad . . . the road to lost Earth.

Jehane's wrist com beeped, and a woman's breathless voice came through.

"Comrade Jehane! Please return to the bridge!"

He lifted his wrist. "Is there some trouble? I thought at last tally that all was in hand."

"We have a new ship, comrade. It came in at oct quadrant, where there isn't even a charted window. And she's—Void bless us, comrade—" Even over the thin speaker, the tremor in her voice was obvious. "She's huge. I've never seen a hull that size. She doesn't answer to comm, and so far cautious fire has made no penetration whatsoever."

"Has the cavalry arrived at last?" Kyosti murmured obscurely.

"What the Void is cavalry?" Lily demanded, shaken by the sudden instinct that she knew who had just arrived.

Jehane lowered his wrist and raked them with his glance. "Come with me," he ordered. Lily followed him silently, Kyosti at her heels.

The atmosphere on *Boukephalos'* bridge was taut with uncertainty. As they entered, the man on scan looked up.

"Comrade." His face was creased with worry. "I've had tac running through all our records. Central's battle fleet has nothing this big listed in our files."

"Status?" asked Jehane as he sat down in the captain's chair, slipping on his headset and levering out the console and screen to display over his lap.

"The ship has halted at the following coordinates." Scan reeled off a list of numbers. "She's currently making no movement whatsoever, hostile or friendly."

"No response to our overtures on any channel," said the woman at comm.

"We're scattershotting fire from three ships, close enough to warn but not to hit. There has been no reply or action of any kind," added the officer at weapons.

"I don't think," said scan abruptly, "that ship cares one bit about us. We could just as well be flak on entry: something just to fly through."

Jehane's face was a study in disapproval crossed by the intense interest with which he studied the specs unfolding on the screen before him.

Beside Lily, Kyosti sighed and shifted his weight.

Jehane glanced up. "Do you know anything about this?" he asked.

"Is there some reason I ought to?" Kyosti retorted lazily.

Jehane sighed, as ostentatious a gesture as any Kyosti ever used, but toned down into an expression of long-suffering patience. "I won't bother to insult your intelligence by replying directly to that question, comrade. I somehow doubt that you are unaware that we met, albeit not personally, at Nevermore Station some time ago. I haven't time to fence, as I'm in the middle of a rather large and important engagement."

As if on cue, comm spoke up. "*Aberwyn* reports that the cruiser *Singh* has taken a disabling hit and officially withdrawn from the action. *Suffrage* reports that the cutters *Manticore* and *Gryphon* are in retreat, heading for a quince quadrant window, and *Forlorn Hope* reports the cruiser *Lion's Share* dead in space and its attendant *Zima Station* in full pursuit of an unidentified cutter class ship. *Nova Roma* reports it has sustained irreparable damage to its weapons systems, and *Bitter Tidings* reports it is evacuating the merchanter *Disenchantment,* whose hull has blown." She paused. "Shall I go on?"

"No. Let comrade Kuan-yin coordinate the data for now." He returned his attention to Kyosti. "Now, do you?"

Scan swore, a long, obscene oath. "Another ship just appeared in sept quadrant. It'll take time to analyze its spec, but we've got no immediate match on our long-range—"

"Comrade!" Comm broke in. "I have comm traffic on a narrow beam between the incoming and the resting vessel. Transmitting both ways."

"Can you break in?"

She shook her head. "It's too tight a channel, and we're too far away in any case. I've got—I'll put *Nova Roma* on it; they're closest."

Lily took a step forward. "Comrade Jehane. Let me try. I think I can get a reply from the first ship."

Jehane cocked his head to one side to examine her. The careful line of his mouth lent his stare a preciseness that seemed piercing. "Ah." One side of his mouth quirked up. "You've finished observing our little sparring match and have decided to act, I see. Thank you."

"Lily," said Kyosti in an undertone that spoke volumes.

"Someone has to tell her about Heredes," replied Lily. "I intend to do it—in person, if comrade Jehane will let me."

Jehane smiled and waved her towards comm; his eyes sparked with interest as she walked across to the station and, after waiting for the woman to set her channel, leaned closer to the mike and spoke.

"I am calling from the . . . the—" She hesitated, trying to recall Heredes' words on the tiny bridge of the *Easy Virtue,* caught in an isolated backwater of space facing an imposing ship which they could not possibly outrun. "The region of the summer stars. I am calling for La Belle Dame."

For a long moment only the hiss of the channel answered her.

Then, *her* voice.

"Who is this?"

Jehane's eyes narrowed as he took in the brevity and unselfconscious authority of the question.

Lily glanced at Jehane, returned to the mike. "This is Taliesin's daughter. I have a personal message for you, if I have your permission to come aboard."

"Wait," commanded Jehane. "I want to know

who you are speaking to, and what intentions they have here."

"*Who I am does not concern you, Alexander Jehane,*" said the woman, as if Jehane had spoken directly to her and not to Lily. "*And my intentions have nothing to do with your revolution. You need not fear that I intend to interfere in any way. I am merely here looking for someone.*"

Lily felt with sudden numbing certitude that she knew who La Belle was looking for: Heredes.

"That is all very well," said Jehane conversationally, "but what assurances can you give me that it is true?"

La Belle laughed, shattering the crackle of static. "*I don't give assurances. But neither do I expect my word to be questioned.*"

If Lily had not been glancing that way at that moment, she would not have seen the look of absolute, utter fury that transformed Jehane's face for an instant. Then she blinked, and it was gone, obliterated into his usual bright, controlled intensity.

"Go, then," he said calmly. "Give her what information she seeks, and return. Your robot will remain safely with me, here, while you go."

"I don't think—" began Lily, and then thought better of protesting. Signing off comm, she gave Bach brief instructions to remain behind, and with a salute to Jehane, left the bridge. Kyosti followed her.

"What are you doing?" she asked as she waited for the elevator.

"Going with you."

"Did Jehane give you permission?"

"I wasn't aware I had to ask for it," he said languidly. "Ought I to?"

"Well, he didn't stop you," she muttered, "so he must know what he's doing."

Kyosti laughed. It was not a complimentary sound. "Jehane is seething with rage in there, my heart. If he hates me because I am nothing he can control, then what do you suppose he feels about La Belle, who could blast his revolution out of the sky with her single ship?"

"But La Belle isn't interested in the revolution."

"Very true," he agreed. "But La Belle is a link back to the League, and if the League rediscovers Reft space officially, and arrives here in all of its advanced technological glory to welcome the Reft back into the community of humankind, then where is Jehane?"

"Exactly where he wants to be." Lily frowned at Kyosti as they stepped inside the elevator and she keyed in the sequence for the shuttle bay. "*If* the government of the League is as representative and equal as you claim it is."

"Oh, yes," said Kyosti with a tone much like sarcasm in his voice. "Oh, it is. That's why they hunted down people like me and Heredes and Wingtuck. They dislike being reminded of what humanity once was, before the golden age: 'Villains, vipers, damn'd without redemption. Dogs, easily won to fawn on any man.'"

Adam met them at the docking bay. He welcomed them graciously, even gave Lily a brotherly hug, but a suggestion of a frown tightened the lines at his eyes and mouth, and he seemed preoccupied.

"Just in time," he said obliquely, glancing at Kyosti, as he led them to an elevator that took them somehow straight to the bridge. Lily remembered how far they had had to walk the first time, and she wondered if La Belle's business was in fact not what she had expected it to be: not news of Heredes, but someone else—and this hurried shortcut to the bridge an indication of a preoccupation that extended beyond Adam to the entire ship.

As the doors sighed open onto the bridge, Kyosti took a step out after Adam, stopped, and took an audible breath in, as if he were scenting the air. "Just in time for *what*?" he asked sharply.

To their right, a second elevator door opened and a man tumbled out and rushed forward to fling himself at the foot of La Belle's dais.

"I've worked for you—good service!—for seven years!" he cried. "It's your sworn duty to protect me!"

The man's stark fear permeated the bridge like a rank smell as La Belle's chair swiveled slowly around, revealing her: face set as in stone, black hair braided tight and lapping in its fall her knees. She regarded the man at her feet in awful silence.

"What did he do?" whispered Lily.

Adam shrugged, answering her in a low voice. "It's the typical story: asteroid miner comes in to some station on leave, runs across a sweet adolescent je'jiri girl in full raging heat who'd slipped her clan for a night on the prowl. And of course all intelligent people are avoiding her like the plague, and trying to get calls through to whatever ship has hired out her clan. But people like him usually figure that as long as the je'jiri isn't already mated, they're safe. Brainless idiot. And then of course once he realized he was marked, he ran—and tried to cover his trail by pretending it had never happened."

At last La Belle spoke. "You lied to me." Her anger was bone-deep, and implacable.

"Oh god, oh god," the man wept. "What else could I do? I had to leave. They were on my trail already."

"You knew the law." Her voice hardened with each word she spoke. " 'No human will mate or have intercourse in any sexual or sensual fashion with je'jiri.' Code Ex-eleven-oh-four of the Codified Law of League Space. Which even a privateer acknowledges."

He stammered something incoherent, lifted a hand to his hair. His forehead bore a brilliant red scar, like a brand, puckered across his dark skin.

" 'In dreams you hunt your prey,' " murmured Kyosti in an expressionless voice, " 'Baying like hounds whose thought will never rest.' "

But Lily, glancing at him, saw that he was strung so tight that the merest touch might shatter him. The usual bronze of his skin had washed out to a ghostly pallor, accentuated by the unearthly color of his hair.

"But she was still an adolescent—and she consented—" The man gasped. His gaze darted to the elevator doors, halted for a frozen heartbeat on Kyosti's still, taut form, and skipped back to La Belle.

"Then you are either uncontrollably libidinous or simply stupid. The je'jiri *are not human*, man, and their ways are not our ways."

"They're savages," muttered Adam under his breath. "Little better than animals."

"You have violated every tenet, the very foundation, of their culture, as admittedly alien and atavistic as it may seem to us. Yi took the hunt on. *I* cannot stop it."

He lay in crumpled anguish at her feet, weeping with noisy and awful terror. The bridge crew stood utterly silent, watching him without compassion. "But you are La Belle Dame," he sobbed. "*You* could stop them."

She stood up. "I am La Belle Dame Sans Merci," she said with the bite of diamond, "and I do not suffer fools gladly."

And to Lily's left, the third set of elevator doors opened.

In that first instant, she could have believed that Kyosti had somehow moved from her side to the elevator without her knowing, and emerged again onto the bridge; a kind of vivid double entrance made possible by some quirk in his character.

The—other—took two steps out of the elevator and stopped. He had the same tall, slender form crowned by startlingly blue hair. Then he turned, and she saw his face.

The shock of the absolute inhumanity of the man's—the alien's—features shook her: first, the strange, unearthly pallor of his skin matched against brilliant green eyes pierced by an acute and vital intelligence. The features of his face had a delicacy that lent it an almost angelic cast, a beauty that might be said to surpass human beauty, but for—

But for its contrast with the alien's behavior. He froze, like any hunting thing, and cast his head about, eyes half-shuttered, as if he were smelling out the room, scenting and placing each individual. The movement repelled her: it seemed grossly primitive, as violent as Unruli's unpredictable storms, tied by tide and wind and gravity and the unbreakable bond of the gross senses to the cycles of earth, to the unforgiving grip of the deepest, oldest part of the brain.

The man on the steps of the dais had ceased weeping and now groped up to a crouch, gathering himself in like an animal driven to its last, desperate fight.

More of them emerged from the elevator—two, four, seven in all. Each scented the room. The male who had first come in had locked his gaze on his prey, and he trembled, as if the wait was unbearable. He lifted his hands, and Lily saw that each finger was tipped with a pale, sharp claw.

A strong, bitter smell permeated the bridge: *their* scent.

Except for the trembling male, the rest, having finished their scenting, stood stock still. One stepped forward—Lily thought it was a female, although it was hard to tell.

When she spoke, she spoke directly to La Belle in a voice deeply accented with alien sounds. Her teeth were a carnivore's teeth: pointed and deadly.

"Do you contest the kill?"

La Belle did not move. "No," she replied.

A sigh rippled through the je'jiri, and the male lunged forward.

Beside Lily, Kyosti gasped, a strangled sound, and collapsed to his knees.

The man fought, at first—some instinct for survival that humans had never lost—but ranged against this inhuman lust for the kill it did not avail him long.

The je'jiri male set claws into his face and chest and ripped open the man's throat with his teeth.

Blood pooled out and dripped in streams down the steps of the dais. The last rattling sigh of the dying man echoed across the bridge.

Adam swore under his breath.

Lily felt her knees sag as bile rose in her own, intact, throat, and she put a hand out to grip Kyosti's shoulder, to steady herself, but he was shaking, trembling, and he had thrown a hand up over his eyes as if it could protect him from what they had just seen. Someone in the far reaches of the bridge was vomiting.

The je'jiri male waited a count of ten, and then sniffed, scenting for a smell now eradicated from the universe. He set his hand, palm down, in a sticky puddle of blood, and brought it up to his face, marking each cheek and his forehead, and last his lips, with red.

Then he rose and retreated, clothes stained with brilliant, wet scarlet. And the others came forward, one by one, and repeated the gesture: hand, palm down, in blood, and the precise, ritualistic marking of their faces.

The female went last, and as she rose, all of them turned and looked at Kyosti until because of their scrutiny the attention of all the people left on the bridge was on him.

The female spoke directly to him; alien words, but her meaning was clear: it is also your obligation to mark the kill.

Kyosti shuddered, a tremor that passed through his entire body. He shook away Lily's hand on his shoulder and stood up.

THE HIGHROAD TRILOGY is a story of love in the face of death, duty in the face of fear. Alis Rasmussen sets up a web of conflicting loyalties against a background of shifting societal structures, and Volumes II and III of the Highroad series will prove that she is definitely a talent to watch. Watch for REVOLUTION'S SHORE, on sale in June 1990 from Bantam Spectra Books.

"Dan Simmons is a breathtaking writer."
— Harlan Ellison

Hyperion
by Dan Simmons

On the eve of invasion by intersteller barbarians, seven citizens of the Human Hegemony have come to Hyperion on a pilgrimage toward almost certain doom. They travel to the Time Tombs within the realm of the Shrike, whose powers transcend the boundaries of space and time, sharing their incredible stories in the hopes of unraveling the mysteries of the Time Tombs, of the Shrike and of Hyperion itself.

"Dan Simmons' **Hyperion** is some sort of extraordinary book. It's been quite a while since I've come across a novel that is at once so involving, so conceptually complex, and written with such style."
— *Isaac Asimov's Science Fiction Magazine*

And don't miss the stunning sequel to **Hyperion**
The Fall of Hyperion
by Dan Simmons
A Doubleday Foundation Trade Paperback
on sale now, wherever Doubleday Foundation books are sold

Buy **Hyperion** on sale now wherever Bantam Spectra Books are sold.

"MacAvoy is truly a writer of talent."
— *The Washington Post Book World*

The Third Eagle
R.A. MacAvoy

"MacAvoy is clearly a writer with immense gifts
and not improbably one of the future giants
of the sf/fantasy field." — *Booklist*

Wanbli was a warrior, and it was right for a bright young
warrior to find new worlds, to sail out into the galaxy and
away from the backwater planet his ancestors settled genera-
tions ago.

He'd thought he was leaving his home forever. But when his
adventures sweep him into the lives and struggles of the crews
of the scavenger ship *Condor* and the colony ship *Commit-
ment*, Wanbli finds his adventure turned into a vital mission,
carrying with it the weight of the survival of both ships and
possibly the very future of his world.

Buy **The Third Eagle** on sale now wherever Bantam Spectra
Books are sold.